The Children Left Behind

Eliza Morton was born in Liverpool and worked as an actress. She is known for playing Madeline Bassett in *Jeeves and Wooster* and Lucinda in the Liverpool sitcom *Watching*. As well as TV, she has also worked in theatre and film. She trained at Guildhall School of Drama and with the Royal Court Young Writers' Group. She is an award-winning short story writer and has also written drama for TV, film and theatre. In her formative years at convent school, she spent her weekends playing the piano accordion in northern working men's clubs. She lives with her husband – the actor Peter Davison – in Middlesex and is the author of *Angel of Liverpool*, *The Girl from Liverpool* and *The Orphans from Liverpool Lane*.

ALSO BY ELIZA MORTON

A Liverpool Girl
A Last Dance in Liverpool
Angel of Liverpool
The Girl from Liverpool
The Orphans from Liverpool Lane

Eliza Morton

The Children Left Behind

PAN BOOKS

First published 2024 by Pan Books
an imprint of Pan Macmillan
The Smithson, 6 Briset Street, London EC1M 5NR
EU representative: Macmillan Publishers Ireland Ltd, 1st Floor,
The Liffey Trust Centre, 117–126 Sheriff Street Upper,
Dublin 1, D01 YC43
Associated companies throughout the world
www.panmacmillan.com

ISBN 978-1-0350-1528-3

1 3 5 7 9 8 6 4 2

A CIP catalogue record for this book is available from the British Library.

Typeset in Sabon by Palimpsest Book Production Limited, Falkirk, Stirlingshire
Printed and bound by CPI Group (UK) Ltd, Croydon, CR0 4YY

Visit **www.panmacmillan.com** to read more about all our books
and to buy them. You will also find features, author interviews and
news of any author events, and you can sign up for e-newsletters
so that you're always first to hear about our new releases.

For Alice

Prologue

'Bob! Matty! They're coming, look – Jerry!' gasped Alice Lacey, her eyes round with fear.

Crouched behind a low wall on the high, windy ridge of Everton Hill, the three children had a perfect view of the Luftwaffe swooping over the River Mersey. Two sharp cracks were followed quickly by flashes that splintered the dark and lit up the sky a vivid orange. Tipping her head, Alice heard the whistle followed by the soft thud of a bomb falling, and then another. And another. The air-raid sirens wailed as an unpleasant sulphurous smell wafted across the river, making their throats and nostrils itch. The Liver Birds on top of the Liver Building, with their outstretched wings, looked like Greek gods. Along the water, the squat silhouettes of the warehouses made them seem indestructible – and yet, the bright moon surely meant Liverpool was a sitting duck tonight.

Alice turned to the boys sitting either side of her, white-knuckled, their mouths gaping open. 'Told you it'd be like nothing you've ever seen or heard,' she said. 'Me hairs are standing up on the back of me neck like knives. Are yours?'

1

'Bloody Nora!' said Bob, as another explosion came. The sky lit up again. He winced and instinctively ducked. Alice felt his hand find hers, their fingers threading together as the air around them hissed. There was a jolt, something that shot through her like electricity. And there it was again – the crack, the split in the sky. Was it getting closer? Were they coming right overhead, here to Everton Hill?

Matty had clamped his hands over his ears. 'We should go to the shelter now,' he said. He looked around him, chewing his lip. There was another small group of people standing a little way away, transfixed by the Heinkel planes, the night flares and a fallen power line that was jerking and spitting fire like a dragon.

Bob, with his scruffy shorts and a baggy jumper so scrappy it looked as if the cuffs and hem were edged with lace, leapt to his feet, excitement fizzing through him. 'No, let's stay. It's the craic, isn't it?'

The surface of the Mersey, in a sudden blaze of light, looked like it was covered in silver ruffles. Alice felt a fear like she had never felt before. Different from the fear she'd felt when her ma had scarlet fever and nearly died, or when Bob had almost drowned when he had fallen into an Emergency Water Supply oil drum. Worse? No. But different. What they were witnessing now was more deadly – an evil, unnatural force.

Matty leapt to his feet, picked up a stone and chucked it randomly. Alice continued to gaze, wide-eyed, across the Mersey.

'Alice? Shall we go to the shelter?' said Matty. But

she just pushed her wild brown hair off her face, still transfixed by the sight of the planes that had looped back and were flying low again, roaring over the water.

'Alice, answer me. If you want me to read your mind, give me something to work with. I can't stand here waiting to get bombed. We've seen it now. Your great idea, but we could flippin' die. You as well, Bobby. You daft or summat? Let's go.'

Bob twisted his head. 'I'm excited,' he said, fidgeting and hopping about. They could feel the throb of the aircraft reverberating in the quivering earth beneath their feet. 'The sky's on fire. You can see every field out in Wales. Our Tommy's there. Evacuated. He rides on a pig and eats Welsh cakes with treacle.'

'I'm glad I'm not in Wales,' said Alice.

'Aye. Our mams don't care enough about us to send us to a safe place, don't care if we have bombs dropping on our heads. That were a loud one!' Bob added, at the sound of another ear-splitting explosion.

Alice grinned. 'Me cousins have gone with me auntie to Parbold, but Ma needs me to help with the house and the flaming coal scuttle. It would be too much for her if she was on her own. Da's down at the docks all the time. She's terrified it'll be him and his pals who cop it next.'

'I just want this war to go on long enough so that I'll be old enough to join up. *Pow-pow*,' Bob said, shooting his imaginary gun. 'I wanna fly a Spitfire,' he added, raking a hand through his mop of blond hair.

'You're only nine. You saying you want this war to go on for seven more years?'

'The last one nearly did.'

'That'll never happen. It'll be over by Christmas, me auntie reckons,' said Matty.

'No one knows anything,' said Alice. She paused. 'Look, there's more coming! Horrible mechanical birds . . .' she murmured.

'Your da, Alice? Port Authority reservist, isn't he? It's the docks they'll be going for again tonight. You worried?' said Bob. There was another loud explosion, and the small fires dotted about on the hillside on the opposite side of the river began to lick into life.

'Let's go,' said Matty seriously. 'Your ma will flip her wig, Alice. She'll be running from shelter to shelter looking for you.'

'You chicken, Matty?' asked Bob, hands jiggling the marbles in his pocket.

'No. But if anyone knew we were here outside . . . They'll be over our heads soon. Alice, come on.'

'Don't you worry about me, Matty. I can look after myself.'

But then she gasped. A figure was coming over the top of the hill, hurrying towards them. 'Ma!' Alice cried, leaping off the wall and losing her footing.

'Alice, what the blazes are you doing out here with those two eejits?' Ida Lacey cried. She was breathless, hair flying from under her paisley turban, with an expression on her face as though she was in actual physical pain. The sky flashed, red this time, full of fire and dust and ash. More whistling, followed by a terrifying roar.

'But doesn't it look beautiful, Ma? The sky. The colours. We came out to look.'

'Beautiful? What the heck are you on about? That's

people's lives being destroyed. Head in the clouds, Alice! I could wallop you, I could. You need a dose of this war to wake you up to the real world.'

'How did you know I was here?'

'Bob shouting his mouth off to Mrs Bannock down the grocer's that he was going fire-watching. And these days, Alice, you don't have to be a genius to work it out. Where Bob goes, you go. You two stick together like glue, more's the pity. I would have thought better of you, though, Matthew.'

'Ta very much, Mrs Lacey,' said Bob.

'He dared me,' said Matty. 'I didn't want to come.'

'Matty's a chicken,' retorted Bob, and started making clucking noises and flapping his arms.

'Jesus, Mary and Joseph, if you were one of my own, I'd crown you. Go home, boys.'

'Where's Da? The docks? Them planes are heading for the docks,' said Alice.

There was another *whump-whump* and the screeching of a plane. 'Never mind Da. Come on!' said her mother.

Alice hurried along, the boys following: Bob sturdy and strong, Matty so skinny he looked as if he might fall over if you were to blow on him. She could feel her heart pounding, thumping in her chest. They were halfway down Scottie Road, but there would be no trams running tonight.

'Missus, you lot should be indoors,' cried an ARP warden. An arc of water spilled out from the stirrup pump he was holding, and he looked down and frowned as though he were puzzled to see that his shoes were wet, even though he could surely feel water

5

seeping across the soles of his feet. 'You can't go down there. Road's blocked off.'

Ida stopped. 'But how will we get back home?'

'Where d'you live?'

'Dryburgh Terrace. Far end of Liverpool Lane. By the overhead railway.'

'You won't make it. Come with me.'

He led them around the corner to a co-op store and banged on the door. When it was opened by a young woman, the smell hit them first – damp, musty and overpowering. Alice pinched the sides of her nostrils together. There was the sound of a hacking cough. A small oil lamp lit the cramped, low-ceilinged room. In the gloom she could see a couple playing cards, bodies hunched sitting on the edge of the beds, some lying under blankets trying to sleep, a young woman and a man dancing.

'Any room?' said the warden. 'The shelter at the top of Scottie Road's chocka.'

The girl sitting at the desk took their names and let them in. Bob and Matty went down the stairs to the basement first, followed by Ida and Alice, taking care not to trip over a few people sitting on the bottom steps.

Peering further into the darkness, Alice could see two figures on a small camp bed wedged into an alcove. They seemed to be doing something unspeakable under a blanket.

'Filthy beasts,' said Ida, shocked. 'Come on, Alice, don't look.' She grasped her daughter's hand as they began making their way through the rows of beds.

*

'Stand back!' cried the ARP man when Ida and Alice got back to Dryburgh Terrace the next morning, exhausted. They had left early after the sound of the all-clear.

Nothing could have prepared them for the scene waiting for them. Opposite their house, where number eight used to be, there was now nothing but a gaping hole. Dwindling fires and plumes of smoke were everywhere. Windows were blown out and shattered. An ambulance was parked in the middle of the road. Their neighbour Miss Quick, clutching a photograph in a silver frame and a Bible to her chest, was picking her way through the rubble, stopping now and then to sort through the debris or pull a single shoe from under a lump of cement.

Two men stood nearby. One, heavy-featured and stiff-looking in an ill-fitting grey suit, was making notes with a clipboard. The other, in brown with a bowler hat, counted to himself as he walked from one heap of rubble to the next. 'Three houses lost in Sidney Place. St Mary's orphanage almost hit. Missed by a hair's breadth. The outhouse damaged, though,' he said.

The other man nodded seriously.

Alice tugged on her mother's sleeve. 'Ma, Miss Quick's bloomers,' she murmured. 'Snagged on that washing line . . .' Poor Miss Quick. How embarrassing, thought Alice as she clambered over a pile of bricks, reached out and unhooked the bloomers from the jagged post. It seemed like the final indignity. She rolled them up into a tight ball and slipped them into her pocket.

Ida was staring in disbelief at the devastation all around them. 'This is just the beginning, isn't it?' she asked the man with the clipboard.

He nodded, looking pained. 'Yes. A lot worse to come, I'd say.'

And yet, how could he know – how could anyone know – the extent of the trauma these terraces would experience over the coming year? That the washhouse would be hit by a bomb and the grocer's shop would become a heap of rubble? Or that the SS *Malakand* would burn for two days down at the docks, the flames so fierce you could read a newspaper by their light all night long? And Alice's father would be nicknamed 'Lucky Lacey' after crawling out half-dead from the wreckage, having sheltered under a wet tarpaulin? Who could know that an incendiary would whizz through Mrs Bannock's front room while she was peeling a turnip, killing her instantly? Or that shrapnel would smash every window of every house in the terrace, and yet another bomb would mangle the overhead railway into twisted metal?

The man in grey frowned. 'God willing, that fellow with the toothbrush moustache will come to his senses soon. We live in hope. And whatever happens, we'll rebuild. We'll rise from the ashes and we'll be better for it. This city is resilient. And the people with it.'

'Hard to imagine how, looking at the way their lives have been destroyed . . . their homes lost . . . Where are all these families going to live now?' murmured the man in the bowler hat, poking the tip of his umbrella into the rubble.

'We should see this as an opportunity to improve things for these people. This is what we've dreamed of. Slum clearance. The chance to bulldoze this whole street, as well as all the dreadful slums and tenements around here.'

'What Hitler makes a good fist of, we might finish off properly, you mean?'

'I suppose I do. Yes, I suppose I do . . . But that's an awkward way to put it. Don't let anyone around here catch you saying that. Hey, you, sir . . .' he called out to a young man approaching one of the houses. 'You can't go in there.'

'But I live here,' the young man said, bewildered.

'Sorry. It's dangerous.'

'Who are you to say we can't go into our house?' said a woman lurching along behind the young man.

'We're from the Corporation. Here to inspect the damage – and I've done just that, and it's not fit for purpose. The beams. They're shot to pieces.'

'But we need to get our things . . .'

'Stay back,' he replied.

Ida's neighbour, Miss Quick, looking thin and harried, approached them. 'Sir, I need to find my cat . . . Pennywise . . .' Her lip trembled.

'I'm sorry, but next door has completely gone. Which means, without a buttress, these houses could collapse at any minute. The cat, I'm afraid—'

'There she is, Miss Quick!' Alice cried. Miss Quick turned with a gasp to where Alice was looking, then hurried over and scrambled under a rope barrier to scoop up the cat. It mewed faintly.

The man sighed. 'Take the cat and wait over there.

We'll find you all somewhere else for tonight. Somewhere better, safer, warmer.'

'But I want to stay here. My house. My home. Shove off,' said the cantankerous first woman, jabbing a finger at him.

Alice winced as the wind blew hard and another pane of glass shattered. She saw another man running up the street towards them.

'Excuse me,' he said as he reached them, slightly out of breath. He was wearing oddly shaped spectacles and a jacket buttoned up with the buttons in the wrong buttonholes. Ida turned to face him. 'Do you live here?' he asked.

'Yes – across the road and a few doors down.'

'I'm looking for a boy. Brown hair? Heavy fringe? Nine years old.'

'Ma!' Ida turned to see Alice standing on a small heap of bricks, waving at someone far off. Everywhere around her was destruction. 'Matty! Bob!' she called, cupping her hands around her mouth, then shoving two fingers between her lips and whistling at them to get their attention. 'We found Pennywise!'

Miss Quick was beaming, cradling her cat.

'This lad a relative of yours?' Ida asked the man, distractedly.

'Relative? Well, he's . . .'

'*Matty!*' yelled Alice.

The man didn't finish the sentence, just turned and followed Alice's gaze. 'Ah . . . I think that's the boy. That's Matthew. That's the lad.' For a moment he just stared, watching Matty step gingerly from brick to brick. Then, in a sudden, surprising gesture, he

10

scooped a chain out from under his shirt collar, unclasped it and took it off, pressing it into Ida's hand. 'Will you give the lad this?' he said. 'It's a St Christopher medal. Some call it superstition, I know.'

If Ida hadn't been agog at the wobbling chimney stack she had just noticed on top of the end house, she would have asked him why he wanted the boy to have it. It seemed odd that he didn't want to give it to the lad himself. *What's he to you?* she would have asked.

But before she had time to think about it, the man was moving away, picking his way through the rubble. He disappeared over the mound of bricks just as a fireman arrived and began to unravel a hose, shouting for everyone to move back as water began to splutter and gush from the end of it.

Ida said, 'Tell Matty to come here. Fella in a fancy suit gave me this for him.'

'Pretty,' said Alice, taking it from her mother, threading the chain through her fingers and turning over the gold medal. It was engraved with a stooped figure carrying a lamb on his back. 'Can I have it?'

'You certainly cannot,' said Ida. 'Matty! Come over here before Alice gets her thieving hands on your necklace!'

And then in that same moment, there was a loud crash as the end house teetered and the smouldering roof gave way under the pressure of the fireman's hose, collapsing in on itself.

'What was that?' said Alice, wide-eyed.

Ida sighed. 'That was the sound of another person's life going down the Swanee. But you know what they

11

say – we survived yesterday, we'll get through today, and we'll do it all again tomorrow. Come on, let's go and find your da, and then we can all have a nice cuppa.'

Chapter 1

Ida Lacey stood with her sewing basket staring up at St Mary of the Blessed Angels orphanage, with its red-brick walls and Gothic windows. An alabaster statue of the Virgin Mary smiled down at her serenely from an alcove above the arched front door.

There wasn't much life at this end of Liverpool Lane nowadays. A section of the road had been bombed and then cleared away by the bulldozers. The flower-sellers had gone, and the grocer's shop with them. But St Mary's, with its discreet entrance through a side door, was still standing; God was protecting us, the nuns said. They had stood resolute against Hitler during the war, and now they would do the same against crumbling joists and the Corporation's bulldozers. Nothing would change at St Mary's. The same statue of Saint Theresa of Lisieux. The same grotto watched over by Saint Bernadette. The same purple-and-white winter crocuses that pushed through the hard frost every year.

Ida had passed the orphanage many times on her way to Paddy's Market, but today the building

13

seemed to lean right over her and sigh. Could a building do that?

'Come with me to my office,' Sister Cyril said.

Ida hesitated as Sister Cyril, with her round eyes and smooth cheeks that pillowed out from her white coif, led her down an echoing corridor into a small room. She had expected the ecclesiastical furniture, and the crucifixes and statues on the shelves, but she was surprised to see that there was also a stuffed owl and a badger in a glass dome, as well as a few African artefacts: a small drum, colourful woven raffia bowls, a carved wooden statue of two women at a well. Two musky-smelling candles burned at the feet of a statue of Our Lady on the windowsill.

'Our work stretches to each corner of the world,' Sister Cyril said, when she saw Ida looking at the shelves. 'Sit down. Thank you for coming.' She settled herself behind a large mahogany desk, watching as Ida took the uncomfortable chair facing her.

The nun pursed her lips.

'I expect you're wondering why I asked you here?'

Ida had an idea the nun was going to ask her to arrange the flowers in the chapel.

'I've heard you are good with a needle and thread. Sister Bernadette tells me you are part of her Make Do and Mend group at the church, yes? And the Stitch for Soldiers, during the war?'

Ida nodded.

'I have some girls I'd like you to teach sewing skills. All of them orphans of the living.'

Ida frowned. 'Orphans of the living?'

'Here because the parents won't have them. Or aren't capable of looking after them. Whatever the reason, some of the orphan girls here – no surprise – are wild, unruly. But there's something else you should know. I must warn you. This handful of errant young ladies are all in the family way. Shocking, I know, but we try to keep them separate from the other children as much as we can. Some are here because their parents are too ashamed to have them under their roof. The war hasn't been kind to families. And others – well, how it happened that they fell pregnant while under our care is anybody's guess. Only the Lord knows. I'm not even sure I want to know. We can't keep them under lock and key every hour of the day, can we? Especially when they're possessed by a kind of madness that tells them they can do what they want, when they want.'

'No, Sister,' mumbled Ida.

'But it's important that these girls put themselves to some use in the few months while they wait, until we send them to the mother and baby home to have their wee ones. God knows they've made enough of a mess of their lives already. The sewing – the doing something with their hands – it encourages these girls to be productive,' the nun said, ploughing on. 'Besides, we have heaps of the children's darning and hemming to do. It's difficult for the sisters to keep on top of when they're trying to teach the small ones, feed them, and get them to bed and Mass. So, it's all to the good. If you . . . well . . . agree to teach them sewing for us, then the girls can do it instead of the sisters. We have a shortage of seamstresses here. The older girls who turn up here are mostly hopeless at even the basics – you'd be surprised how many can't even knit, let alone darn. We would pay you, Mrs Lacey.'

Ida sat twisting the gloves in her lap. There was a long silence. It felt unsettling. The nun tapped her fountain pen on the edge of the desk a few times. 'Any questions?'

'Only . . .' Ida hesitated. 'The girls. You say they're here because . . . ?'

'We are an orphanage,' Sister Cyril said, in a clipped voice. 'We take the babies from the mother and baby home who haven't been adopted. We had a good few war babies after the war. Children of GIs, many of them. Girls were forever having their heads turned by a man whispering nonsense in their ears at the dance halls. And then we have the orphans of the living. Those children whose parents can't cope. Especially the ones whose families have lost their homes after the Blitz and somehow haven't been able to get back on their feet. Hitler has split whole families apart in Liverpool. It's a tragedy. The Corporation sends them to us and we do our best. Some of the children that we look after go to school. Others, the unruly ones, we teach here. Our aim is to find good homes for all of them, of course. We pride ourselves on that. We take the utmost care.' She finished her speech and placed her hands in her lap.

'And the girls . . . in the family way . . . the ones I'll be teaching. After they have their babies, then what?'

'What d'you mean?'

'Where will they go?'

'Nowhere. They'll have their babies, who will be adopted and go to good homes, and the girls will come back and carry on here just as they were, until they are eighteen. Or twenty-one, if they want to stay and work here. Hopefully cross-stitching and darning like demons. Their parents won't have them back, that's for sure. These girls are unwanted, you do understand? Everyone here at St Mary's is the same: the children, the babies, these girls. No one wants them. They are unwanted and unloved, Ida. Except by us. And God, of course. Of course, God.'

Chapter 2

The hot sun was beating down on Dryburgh Terrace, and the dust from the city on a day like today caused seventeen-year-old Alice Lacey's eyes to itch and her palms to go dry. The sun was fierce.

She had come upstairs to wash her face and hands in the bowl but was now standing at the bedroom door, watching her father tying the corners of an old tarpaulin to two of the bedposts. He pulled up the double bed and jammed it against the open window. After shoving the bulk of the tarpaulin outside the window, he went downstairs and out through the kitchen door, then took the other two corners and tied them onto the rusty angle irons screwed into the wall in the back yard. It created a sagging hammock.

Alice had crossed to the window to watch, her fingertips resting gently on the windowsill. She smiled as he waved up at her and gave her the thumbs up.

They had survived it. The war. Her father had been left with one useless arm and a vivid red burn mark on his face that looked like a map of the British Empire; her mother's nerves were shot; but they were all here, all alive, the house still standing. Alice thought back to the celebrations at the end of the war and how hopeful they had all felt. Two babies that had come along after the Blitz finally ended: the twins, who always made people smile. The tables down the middle of the street, dancing until the small hours, a band that had marched all the way from the top of Liverpool Lane playing 'God Save the King' and then, when they got to the docks, 'All the Nice Girls Love a Sailor'.

But here they were, five years later – and although VE day had felt like the start of a new era, a chance to rebuild, not much had changed in the city. Still surrounded by rubble and bulldozers, still the rationing, still the struggle to put food on the table and send the kids to school wearing shoes that weren't stuffed with cardboard. The new baby, Gabriel, two years old now, who had arrived as a blessing and another fresh start, had gone some way to cheer them all up – but it was still another mouth to feed.

She watched as her father leaned in towards the kitchen tap, to which he had already attached a hose-pipe that snaked out the window. He switched the tap on and then, a moment later, aimed a great arc of water onto the tarpaulin.

Droplets glittered like diamonds, pattering and bouncing on the surface. The sound of children's voices could be heard down the street. The twins, Brian and Gwenda, with their mops of wild brown hair – whom her father affectionately called Biscuit and Gravy – had already run across to the hollas and told everyone what was happening. Kids scrambled off the tyres that they had hung on ropes from lamp posts and others appeared, blinking in the sunlight, from inside an abandoned car. A few others dropped the sticks they had been bashing against bin lids and raced towards the ginnel that ran along the back of the terrace. A makeshift ladder had been placed against the back wall of the Laceys' house. Brian was the first to clamber up it in his vest and underpants and catapult himself off the top of the wall, bouncing into the pool of water gathering in the tarpaulin with a great yell, while his father continued to spray water and laugh. Bodies appeared as if from nowhere.

'One at a time, Biscuit!' Albert Lacey yelled. 'This tarpaulin won't hold!' The warning only encouraged them. A wiry boy grabbed his friend's hand and they launched themselves head first off the back wall, landing in a tangle on top of Gwenda, who hadn't moved quickly enough.

'Oww! Gerroff!' she yelled.

'You all right, Gravy?' shouted Albert. Gwenda poked her head out, grinning, and crawled out. 'Me drawers are soggy. But I'm goin' again, Da!' There were cheers and laughter.

'Bloody tykes! Shurrup!' cried Mrs Hallett, sticking her head out of her bedroom window next door; but when she saw the scene below, she softened and smiled. Everyone liked the Laceys. How could you not be charmed by their wild Irish good looks – their dark brown hair, bewitching hazel eyes and pale skin? They might be as poor as church mice, but God had made it up to them in startling beauty.

It was a risky business – the tarpaulin was ancient and straining at the seams – but no one cared. Sopping wet kids in their vests and pants launched themselves off the top of the wall, splashed into the water, and scrambled out over the side before running back out of the gate to join the queue again.

Ida appeared at the door with Gabe on her hip. She had a small shopping bag looped over her shoulder. 'Albert! If that tarp breaks, we've had it! We said it was too dangerous last year! And your arm won't hold up. Careful of your arm!'

'Ma's home!' he shouted to the kids.

'I mean it, Al. Enough!' she said, marching inside and yanking the hose off the tap.

'Good things always end,' he sighed, looking at the water as it dribbled to nothing. 'Go on, scarper. Fun's over, yer scallywags.'

The kids moaned. 'Hey, missus, please, switch it back on,' said a boy with a mucky face.

'No, love. Go home, all of you.' She put Gabe on the kitchen floor and started taking cans of corned beef and baked beans out of the shopping bag.

'Please,' said Gwenda.

'Five more minutes, Da,' implored Brian. 'Just one more squirt?'

'All right, one more,' and then, with a devilish grin, he reached in through the kitchen window while Ida's back was turned, re-secured the hose and turned the water back on, spinning around and spraying the hose up in the air so the droplets fell like a summer shower. There was more screaming and laughter as the children leapt about, giggling and yelping.

'Right, that's it. Off you go, kids.' He turned to his wife. 'Don't want to be in the doghouse again, do I, Ida?'

'State of this place. Water all over the back yard,' she said. 'You lot'll be the death of me, I swear.'

'It were grand to see their faces though, eh, love?' said Albert half an hour later as he sat smoking in the back yard, face raised to the sun. 'And at least we don't have to bath the kids this week.'

'I suppose,' she sighed. But then she paused. 'What's the matter? Why are you squeezing your arm like that? Is it hurting again? That fire . . .'

'Nothing. Nothing to worry about. Don't be reminding me of that, either.' His eyes darkened.

Ida knew he still had nightmares, waking up with terror in his eyes, sometimes shaking and even screaming. She regretted bringing it up.

'Where's Alice?' she said suddenly.

No one had noticed, in the commotion, that Alice had slipped out. She was waiting under the overhead railway, standing in the shade, trying to find relief from the blistering heat. Bobby McGurk, nineteen now, two years older than Alice, grinned as he approached, waving his hat. He planted a sweet kiss on her lips and then they took the first train to Sandhills, sitting in a small carriage with balding tufts on the seat. She could feel his thigh up against hers as the train rocked on its tracks. The man sitting opposite, a little drunk, smiled. Alice smiled back.

'This city, eh,' the man said, gazing out of the window, and shook his head when he looked back at them. Alice wasn't sure what, specifically, he was talking about. Maybe the great gaping wounds in the landscape left by the bombing. Or the tinnies and boarded-up houses; or maybe the talk of how the overhead railway wasn't worth rebuilding. 'Still, I'm leaving my job at the GPO. Need a change, need to travel. I've had it with telegraph poles. I'm joining the merchant navy. That's the way to see the world.'

'Hey, me too. That's what I want to do,' said Bob. 'I missed the war. I were too young. You were lucky.'

Alice bristled. She rearranged her skirts and flicked back a piece of her hair. The reassuring squeeze of her hand from Bob didn't help. He had been going on about leaving his job at the docks and joining the merchant navy for weeks now.

'When you've been up one pole you've been up 'em all. I can't get excited about these new ones with the footholds. I've tried my best.' The man continued to talk about the merits of various telegraph poles, and Alice wondered idly if he was put on trains to try to persuade boys like Bob to join the merchant navy – an inebriated undercover recruitment officer. But he was friendly enough, asking them where they were going and did they want the window opening.

'I thought he'd never stop,' said Bob when they got off the train and began making their way towards the Throstle's Nest. 'Blimey, who would've thought someone would have so much to say about telegraph poles?'

'Never mind the telegraph poles. The merchant navy. Are you serious about that?' she said, frowning.

'Shush. I love you,' he said, waving her question away.

'Bob, answer me. Don't be annoying.'

'Annoying? Me? Don't you like it? I'm planning to annoy you for the rest of my life. Give us a kiss . . .'

'*Bob* . . .'

'If I do decide on the merchant navy, I'll have experience when I come back. I'll get a better job. Dock work isn't for me. Neither is National Service. Just square-bashing. I get out of it if I'm in the merchant navy.'

She traced a finger over the back of his hand. 'If I thought you were being truthful, I'd agree with you. But you just want a bit of excitement. What's wrong with dock work?'

'Nothing, unless you've heard what the fellas are saying about how little we're paid, how badly they treat us. I'll have a better wage at sea. Dockers are desperate.'

'You talking about me da?'

He paused. 'Now you mention it. Aye.'

He turned and kissed her gently on the bridge of her nose. 'I'll have leave when we're back in port and we'll make up for it, Alice. I'll have money in my pocket and I'll treat you like a queen. Blackpool Tower. Sour martinis at the Adelphi. Buy you a new dress. Them tortoiseshell hairclips you like. Eh, and silk scanties from George Henry Lee's . . .' he said with a grin. 'Come on, let's get a drink. Matty will be waiting.'

They went into the snug and Bob ordered two pints of stout, a shandy and a pickled egg. Matty arrived five minutes later and joined them, squeezing in next to them both, with Bob in the middle. Alice thought Matty looked serious, but then he often did in his chauffeur's getup. You could hardly call it a uniform.

He wore a black peaked cap, a mismatched high-necked jacket with silver buttons down the front, and a pair of solid shoes.

Bob took a sip of his stout and then clapped his arms around their shoulders. 'Me two favourite people,' he announced, tightening his grip. Alice suspected he was about to do his party trick, where he popped the whole pickled egg into his mouth and then smiled stupidly, and sure enough that's exactly what he did. A few people even gave him a round of applause when he stood on a chair, to encourage him – though he hardly deserved it, she thought. Matty started to laugh.

'Matty, you've seen him do this a million times before and yet still it makes you laugh like a drain. If you were a good friend, you'd tell him to flamin' well stop.'

Bob grinned his eggy white grin, then tried to swallow it down. His eyes were popping and he began thumping his chest with his fist. He got off the chair and started staggering around the bar, pointing desperately at his throat. The woman at the piano stopped playing and got up, a horrified look on her face, and the barman shouted, 'You dying, lad, or what?'

Bob doubled over, holding his position for long enough to raise the tension in the bar . . . before straightening up with a broad grin on his face, twirling around and bowing over his arm, cap in hand.

'Got yer! That was tasty. I'm getting another one,' he said, brushing himself down.

On his way over to the bar, he stopped next to the

woman at the piano, sat down beside her and started banging along on the keys.

'He doesn't know how to play. Not even "Chopsticks". Will he ever stop showing off?'

'Never. How are you, Alice?' said Matty.

'I'm all right. Has he told you he might go away? He wants to join the merchant navy. Says he has to go where there's work. But it's not decent work. Still the same old backbreaking grind. Why can't he be a chauffeur, like you?'

'He can't drive. I think that's high on the list of requirements.'

Alice punched him lightly on the shoulder. 'At least he can swallow pickled eggs in one go and make a fool of himself. Must qualify him for something.' They looked over at Bob, now chatting energetically with the barman.

'I was lucky, there's not many of us can drive. And a licence costs money. If my boss hadn't paid for mine, I wouldn't be driving either.'

'Why is Bob wanting to join the merchant navy, though? I hate the Meccano factory, sitting on the line doing the same thing day in, day out, and I have to put up with it – not for much longer, by the way. I've got plans. But going off to sea? That's running away and coming back to where you started every time, whatever he says. Can't he find something better here?'

'That's what lads do. Not much for them in Liverpool. And he feels cheated because he never got to fight in the war. But about that. Mr Morley, my boss – you know who I mean?'

'Course I know. Morley and Worboys? The architects?'

'Aye. He says he'll meet you. I've told him you have a head for figures. And you'd be punctual. I said you're a good girl. If you're interested.'

Alice felt her heart racing.

'What's the matter with you?' said Bob, carrying a tray of glasses.

'Matty's Mr Morley wants to meet me for a job,' she said, her eyes shining.

'Does he?' His face lit up.

'I can't believe it!' said Alice. 'What's he like, Matty?'

'Right lah-di-dah,' answered Bob. 'He says *barf* instead of *baff* and *grarse* like *arse*. I met him at your Chauffeur Club, didn't I, Matty? He wears those funny little round glasses on a string that posh fellas wear.'

'Pince-nez,' said Matty.

'Yer what?' said Bob.

'It's French,' said Matty. 'For pinching the nozzle. He's a good fella. But he is posh, like. His name is Hedley Clement. Hedley Clement Morley.'

'And you say he paid for your licence, Matty?' asked Alice.

'Aye,' answered Matty.

'Awful generous of him, Matt. What's he getting in return?' said Bob, and he laughed and ruffled Matty's hair. 'You pretty boys always attract those types of fellas who dance up the other end of the ballroom. What'd you do to get the job? Hey, Alice, Mr Morley's right keen on Matty, I heard.'

27

Matty squirmed away. 'Leave off. What are you saying? He's not like that. My aunt knew him. Knew he was looking for a driver.'

Bob laughed again.

'Mr Morley's married. And he's a good man and he's been good to me,' said Matty seriously. 'He'll not give you any trouble, Alice. Not in that way. Not like some bosses do with lasses who work for them. Think they have a right to . . . you know . . . just . . .'

Bob's eyes widened. 'Better bloody not do. Anyone who comes near my Alice, I'll punch their flaming lights out.'

'Shurrup, both of you. I've got a tongue in my head and I can handle myself with any fella. Thanks, Matty. You think I might actually have half a chance to get out of the factory? I dream about that every night. Them Meccano nuts and bolts come to me in nightmares. They become little people, dancing in my head. Wait until I tell me da.'

'More than half a chance. Just be yourself when you meet him. You'll charm him, I bet.'

'Aye. Hedley Clement Morley will be lucky to have you, Alice. Just you remember that,' said Bob.

They walked out into the cool rush of air. 'Kiddie's minding the Rover,' said Matty. A small boy appeared from a doorway and ran up to him. Matty put a few pennies in his hand.

'Aren't you gonna say thanks, mister? You still got all your wheels. I didn't take none of 'em,' he said.

'Thanks for nothing, you cheeky beggar. Scram,' Matty said. He turned to Alice and Bob, raised his eyes and opened the car door as if he was on duty.

Alice slid into the back. The car smelled of leather and polish. She ran her finger over the chrome handles. She could feel the cool hide under her thighs.

'This is so exciting. I feel like Princess Elizabeth,' she said, leaning forward as Matty started up the engine and they drove off into the night. They passed the docks, the lights swinging away into the distance, and were soon driving down Scotland Road with the engine roaring; then on towards the cluster of roads at the end of Liverpool Lane, to Dryburgh Terrace.

Matty stopped the car outside Alice's house in the small terrace in the shadow of the docks. Dryburgh Terrace had seen better days, but it had survived, at least – most of it was still standing after the war, which was more than some in this city. Alice got out.

'Come back here,' said Bob, winding down the window.

She smiled and leaned in. He pulled her towards him and kissed her hard on the lips. Matty watched out of the corner of his eye.

Alice skipped off, her dark hair flying behind her. 'Thanks for driving, Matty. Ta-ta,' she called over her shoulder.

Bob wound the window back up as they set off to the other end of Liverpool Lane, the grander, more elegant part of the city. 'I appreciate you looking after Alice. You'll keep an eye on her, then?' he said.

'Yes, but it wasn't easy, what you asked. I'm only his chauffeur, Bob, and I'm sitting there asking Morley to give your girlfriend a job because you want me to keep tabs on her while you're halfway across the world? Anyway, it's only an interview, there's nothing sorted. You'd better hope she doesn't make a mess of it.'

'She won't. If I'm away, I want to make sure she's in safe hands.' Bob looked out of the window at a group of women gathering outside the Locarno dance hall. 'You make sure she's a good girl for me. Look at that bunch. Cheap frocks and silver heels, hoping to bag some poor fella. I swear you'd suffocate on hairspray and Woolies perfume in that queue. I don't want my Alice behaving like one of them loose Judys while I'm at sea.'

They made their way slowly down Scottie Road. Matty shifted uncomfortably in his seat. 'Bob, you've got to tell her you've already signed up for the merchant navy.'

'Aye, I know, I know.'

'You're scared, aren't you? What she'll say. Especially when you might be away for months.'

'Don't be daft.'

'Then why haven't you told her?'

'I thought I'd ask her to marry me first.'

'What?'

'Ask her to marry me.'

Matty was silent for a moment. 'That's between you and Alice. But she'll see through that, pal. She's sharp as a tack.'

'I love her, Matty. Nothing to see through. Wouldn't you do the same?'

Chapter 3

Ida took a deep breath, standing in the porch of St Mary's. Today was her 'Tuesday afternoon'. She had been doing this job for several weeks now and still couldn't call it anything but her 'Tuesday afternoon', and not even Alice was quite sure what she was going to do when she trotted off with her sewing basket and patches of material.

She found Sister Cyril sitting in the refectory, banging a spoon against a tin dish. A line of small children trooped in. Despite the smell of cabbage, so heavy that it seemed to suck all the air out of the room, so many of these little ones managed to seem so joyful. Playing tick around a table, rolling a marble between them, laughing as they shared a secret or a joke. A room full of lively, squirming, wriggling, giggling children.

'Come with me to my office. So, Ida, we need twenty dresses. We have visitors next week. Important people. The Monsignor, and a couple who want a baby boy. You can get the girls to help with smocking. June still can't seem to get to grips with the stitching. I gave her a nightshirt to darn, and she made such a mess of it. Wilful. We can't shake her out of this mood, we've tried everything.'

'Oh dear. I'll talk to her. She's a spirited thing underneath all that sadness.'

'Tsk,' Sister Cyril said, sticking her tongue against the roof of her mouth. 'Please don't tell me you're blaming Hitler for these jezebels finding themselves pregnant.'

Ida went back out into the corridor, which smelled strongly of polish – if it wasn't the cabbage, it was always the smell of polish and candle wax getting up your nose in this place – with the basket of half-finished dresses under her arm. Making her way into a little room next to the chapel, she pulled several chairs into a semicircle and when the girls trailed in, she patted the air to shush them all.

'Settle down, girls. Settle down.'

'Miss – June here, she keeps crying.'

June, her face half hidden by long, limp curtains of hair, sniffed.

'If it's too much, dear . . .' Ida began.

June's face collapsed into tears.

'Miss, she got another letter from her ma saying she wants nothing more to do with her. Said she'd cross the street if she ever set eyes on you again, didn't she, June?'

June's lip trembled.

'Don't know what's worse, love. Me ma said she loved me with all her heart, bun in the oven or no bun in the oven – said she only sent me here because she couldn't afford me,' said Doreen. 'She was lying. She signed me over to the nuns when I got me cravings and started to eat all her precious pickled onions. Said I was eating her out of house and home. Enough was enough.'

'That's mean,' said Mildred.

'To be fair, Milly, we only had one room and the shared bathroom, and a cooker on the landing for five families. You couldn't swing a cat. Me da tried once and nearly killed the poor thing. So, with a baby coming, and me ma's snoring and her bad feet, and Da turning up when he liked for a bit of you-know-what and a pan of scouse . . . It were no good.'

'Chin up, love,' said Mildred, patting June's knee. 'You've got to see the funny side if you want to get through this. There's plenty who go under, but you're not the first here whose mam and dad won't have anything to do with you now you're up the duff.'

'There's always hope, Junie. Look at Ange here. Her ma's had a change of heart and said she'll have her back after she's had her babby, lucky sod.'

'You haven't met my mother,' said Angela darkly.

'Don't waste this hour crying, June, love. It's the only time we have away from the nuns. You're pretty enough. When you get out of here you'll find a husband. And then, you never know – you could take your baby back.'

Ida smiled; or at least, the corners of her mouth lifted.

'What we doing this afternoon, Mrs Lacey?'

'I thought we could do smocking and quilting today.'

There was the sound of a loud belch from the back row, followed by giggles and snorts of laughter.

'Burping when you're pregnant means you're having a hairy baby, Milly.'

33

'Then I'm about to give birth to a chimpanzee,' she said, thumping her chest. The girl next to her laughed and they all giggled.

'Quiet, girls.'

'Mrs Lacey, the indigestion. It's fierce. Did you have that when you had your babbies?'

'Yes. It's just the baby pressing on your stomach.'

'Better out than in,' said the girl.

June started to cry.

'Don't say "baby". It sets her off. Doesn't it, love?'

Ida paused, pressing her fingers against her temples. 'Today, girls, like I said, I'm going to teach you smocking. If you can learn to smock, you'll find it's a godsend.'

'Maybe if I could have smocked, my Harry wouldn't have done a runner and I wouldn't be in this mess.'

Two of the girls laughed.

'Maybe if I could've known how to darn socks, my Bill wouldn't have taken me up the ginnel.'

'You're so foul-mouthed, Doreen,' said Mildred with a grin.

'You're a fine one to talk. No different to the rest of us. We're all just good girls who like doing bad things, aren't we, Miss?'

Ida blushed. The nuns wouldn't have let these girls get away with this kind of talk, but if these sessions allowed them to let off steam, she didn't mind.

'I've also brought you a bag of little squares of material so we can do some quilting. And some I've already done at home, to show you how they end up.

Three layers to make up one square, and the number of squares depends on how big you want your finished quilt. Has anyone quilted before?'

'Never quilted in my life,' said Doreen. No one put their hands up.

'In that case, you had better pay close attention.'

Angela yelped loudly and everyone turned to look at her.

'Miss, I'm in agony. I think it's the babby coming.'

'Are you sure?' Ida was suspicious of the timing, but she was taking no chances. 'Go, dear. Go and find Sister Cyril.'

'Sid won't do anything unless her waters are splashing all over her polished floors. Twinge won't hack it. She's still got three months to go. She doesn't go to the mother and baby home until three weeks' time.'

'Sid?'

'Sister Cyril, she means,' piped up Doreen.

'Go and find one of the sisters and say I sent you. The rest of you, sort through the squares and find three of each roughly the same size.'

'I think I should go with her, Miss,' said Doreen.

'I'll go too,' said Mildred.

'No, that's not necessary. Sit down, please.'

'I'm coming as well. Hold up, Junie. Move.'

'And me,' said Angela.

The exodus continued, with a clatter of chairs as girls bustled through the door, with Ida pleading for them to come back.

'So, June,' sighed Ida. 'Seems it's just you and me.'

June looked at her soulfully, lips trembling, and burst into tears yet again.

'Don't cry, love,' said Ida. 'Everything will be all right. I'm sure it will,' she added, feeling her cheeks go hot at what she knew to be a lie.

Chapter 4

On Friday, Alice woke early and did what she always did on a weekday morning. She rose at five thirty, went downstairs and emptied the ashes from the ash-pan under the range. This was the time of day she enjoyed the most. With the half-light sloping in under gaps beneath doors and between the threadbare curtains, she moved around the small house quietly as a thief, picking up discarded socks, putting her sisters' and brothers' shoes neatly in pairs in front of the range, carefully folding tea towels.

The war had ended five years ago, and she still couldn't quite get used to the silence that peace had brought. No air-raid sirens, no screeching of ambulances and fire-bells, no *whump* of bombing or throbbing of planes' engines, no ack-ack fire. No Ida yelling to them all to put saucepans on their heads and hide under the table.

Her father had fallen asleep in the armchair in the parlour, with the old alarm clock balanced on a large biscuit tin on the table beside him. Someone had unscrewed the bells and lost them, so he had stuck a piece of Meccano across the top and balanced a pile of coins on either side of the ring hammer. In the kitchen she made herself a pot of tea, contemplating the day ahead. She looked at the wall clock and listened to the gentle, calming ticking. At a quarter to six she put her fingers in her ears. In the parlour the hammer on the alarm clock juddered from side to side, knocking over the piles of pennies, which clattered down onto the biscuit tin and scattered over the dining table. The noise made her father sit bolt upright in his chair and rub his eyes.

'You can just ask me to wake you, Da,' said Alice, coming into the room.

'I fell asleep in the chair again. I need to be startled. It's the only way to get me up.'

Alice picked up the coins that had spilled over the floor, pocketed a few that had rolled towards the skirting boards, put the kettle on again and went upstairs to dress. She had more than two hours before she had to leave for her appointment at Morley and Worboys. Afterwards she would go to the Meccano factory and clock in late with an excuse about having to do the messages, which would cost her a morning's work and more grief from the foreman – but it would be worth it. She had chosen to wear the cotton print Magic-Grow dress her mother had bought her three years earlier. Since then, a flounce had been added at the hem twice, so it was living up to its name. It had a wide belt and detailed pockets, and it was respectable enough for an office job.

'Gwenda! Brian!' she heard her mother call up the stairs. 'If I've said it once, I've said it a thousand times! Don't make me drag you out of bed again!'

She sounded exhausted, her voice raspy and hoarse. Alice's mind turned to Bob, who lately, she sensed, was beginning to grow impatient. If being married and having kids meant this daily struggle, would she ever be ready? she wondered.

Her mother appeared, with a rag over one shoulder and holding Gabe to her chest, shifting her weight from one foot to another in a slow rhythmic dance, rubbing the child's back with her flat hand as his eyelids became heavy. 'Alice, why are you still here? And what on earth are you wearing? You look like you're going to a dance, not to work.'

'No, I don't. I'm seeing someone. A fella. Posh fella. About a job, Ma.'

'What do you mean, job? You've got a job and the pay's not bad. What are you thinking?' Gabe started to wail and kick his chubby legs. 'Now look what you've made me do. He was just falling asleep,' Ida moaned.

'I'll explain later. I have to go. See you this evening,' Alice said. What she wanted to say was, did no one else around here want to make something of themselves? But she knew where that would lead.

A blanket of clouds was bulking up on the horizon despite it still being the height of summer. On the corner of Scottie Road, the stooped Mary Ellen – one of the street hawkers who sold fish from the market out of her cart – was sitting there as usual on her stool, her shawl wrapped tightly around her and a woollen scarf knotted under her chin. Alice felt sorry for her. She was old and bedraggled, with matted pieces of hair falling about her face like bits of rope. She had a harelip and a cleft palate, which made it difficult to understand when she spoke. Nobody knew her real name – but the one thing everyone did know about her was that she said ghosts came to her dilapidated house. That was why she stayed out on the street every hour she could.

Feeling generous and hopeful about the day, Alice thrust her hand into her pocket and dropped a copper into her tin.

'Likkle birra cod flake?' the woman asked, surprised at the gesture.

'No, ta,' Alice replied. 'That's for you to get a cuppa.'

The Mary Ellen grinned her toothless smile.

Alice took the tram down Liverpool Lane. Liverpool Lane was more than a mile long and ran in a long, straight line from the top of Scotland Road, just off the brow of Everton Hill – where, miraculously, an ancient cherry tree still blossomed every year – to the beginnings of the overhead railway at the docks. The down-at-heel court houses had disappeared at the end of the first war to make way for new terraces and flats, but when the next war came along, those plans had been put on hold. People had been too worried about what might happen next. The gaping holes separating the remaining rows of houses were marked off with chains, which had grown over with vines and brambles that twisted through the metal.

Recently, enthusiastic plans for slum clearance had started up again. On the day the war ended, it had been Hitler who was talked of most over pints of beer – more than the football, or weddings, or someone's daughter in the pudding club, or some poor demented woman who still hadn't got over losing her husband or son in the Great War. Now, though, the conversation was mostly about whose house was going to be demolished next, and who had got the letter from the Corporation saying they would get a council house. That was like winning the lottery for most people living in the leaky, barely habitable homes around Dryburgh Terrace that the Corpy had declared were slums.

Halfway down the Lane, blackberry bushes covered an entire patch of land where a blacksmith and a dairy had once stood. At the junction of Dublin Street a building was half finished, weeds growing in its empty doorways, a crabapple tree sticking out of a first-storey window-casing; a cement mixer itself had turned to concrete. Down by the road that ran off it, leading to the canal, was an old schoolhouse, empty and crumbling and boarded up.

There were signs saying 'Keep Out' and 'Construction Site', but mostly they were ignored, especially by children. The houses that remained were interspersed with small terraces of shops clumped together: grocers, tailors, bookies, the washhouse situated at the dock end. The sturdier Victorian houses were situated at the Scotland Road end, but nearer the docks, the two-up, two-downs were sootier and more down at heel.

When she got off the tram, a sudden shower was blowing in from the Mersey, rain falling horizontally and bouncing off the pavement. Head bent into the wind as it continued to sheet down, she scurried towards the imposing building down at the Pier Head where the architects' offices were located. Matty had written the address down for her on a piece of paper: the Lamp Building, Water Street. After walking through the revolving brass doors, she got into the caged lift, clanked the iron gate shut and made her way to the third floor.

She was shown into Hedley Morley's office by a woman in her forties with large thick-rimmed glasses and grey hair like a Brillo pad, who had been waiting for her at the lift and had introduced herself as Miss Maguire.

'Your nine o'clock, Mr Morley,' she said.

He was sitting at his desk, poring over a raft of papers laid chaotically out in front of him, adjusting his pince-nez glasses perched on his nose as he read. Alice's first impression was that the glasses made him look old. He didn't look up, but told her in a friendly voice to please be seated.

She did a quick inventory of the room: the two large drawing boards with expansive sheets of technical drawings on display, the ceiling-high shelves stacked with overstuffed box files, the wilting aspidistra on the windowsill beside the *Oxford Dictionary*. She had a perfect view of the steel-grey Mersey and the Pier Head through the window behind Morley's desk.

'You're Miss Lacey?' He raised his head and looked over his glasses.

'Yes, that's me. I'm Alice.'

He stood up, cracked his knuckles, and glanced out of the window. 'Oh, chucking it down now. Didn't expect that.'

He was a tall man, with dark hair; she could see

that he was good-looking, with a strong jaw and keen blue eyes, now that he had slipped the pince-nez into his top pocket. He gave her a welcoming smile. 'I'm worried about you sitting on that chair. Are you all right? You're dripping on it. And it's quite chilly.'

'Oh, it's just a bit of rain. I'm not nesh, Mr Morley.'

'Nesh? What does that mean?'

'You don't know nesh? Shivery kind of limp person who doesn't like the cold,' she said, and smiled.

'I see. You're made of stronger stuff, you mean? Here, sit on my newspaper.' She raised her bottom up, enough for him to slip the newspaper underneath her before he walked back around his desk. Despite his air of self-importance and assuredness, she noticed the top button of his shirt was undone and his tie was skew-whiff.

'Your friend Matty recommended you for the job, didn't he? He's been driving me since he finished national service, and I trust his judgement – if Matthew says I should meet a girl, then I know she will be a special kind of girl – but this is not the usual way I do things. There are agencies for secretaries, which is how we found Miss Maguire, but business is good and we're snowed under. I'm looking for someone to specifically attend to me. Matty got wind of this and asked me to see you. But Miss Lacey . . . your qualifications?'

'I don't have any formal qualifications, if that's what you mean,' she said, sitting a little more upright and thrusting out her delicate chin. 'No Pitman skills. No touch typing, either. They tried to teach us to type at school, got us typing along to music to get our speed up; but I preferred the music to the typing, which was no good, and I got in trouble for lah-lah-ing and whistling along. But I've been working since I was fourteen to bring in a wage, at the Meccano factory – bottle-washing, glove mending, Tate and Lyle's. Sugar was a demon. Got everywhere. In your hair and up your nose. Phew – that's about it.'

Mr Morley smiled. He thought about the fact that he hadn't started out with much in the way of academic success himself. 'So you're a hard worker, Miss Lacey?'

'A grafter, is how me da would put it. Not that anyone has much choice in our house. You seen the price of butter and milk these days? Some regular Dick Turpins round our way.'

'Matty said you're very organized and marvellous with figures.'

Really? She knew her times tables, but she'd been relieved, when she left school early, to finally escape the bewilderment of fractions and algebra. Morley paused and drummed the table with his fingertips, and she noticed he'd scribbled something on the back of his hand. Did he not have a notepad?

'The Meccano factory is detailed work. And our house – it's like planning the Boer War. My ma, she's fine, but she gets tired all the time, so it's left to me to remember shoes, bath night, castor oil, homework, clean socks, baby's bottle. All in the right order. Good job I've a good memory.'

He steepled his fingers under his chin. 'Tell you what. I've met you now, and I like you – you've got vim, Miss Lacey. So I'll certainly bear you in mind if we need help in the future. What do you think?'

'What do I think?'

He was taken aback, but she held his gaze. 'Sorry?' he said, clearly unsure as to where the conversation was heading.

'I think you're a bit of an untidy type, Mr Morley, if I'm honest. This office is a right mess. If you organized it, you could save yourself a lot of time. If you had someone who knew what you were like and could think ahead for you and shove you in the right direction when you needed it, you'd be fine. Not sure you need qualifications for that – it's more like instinct. Know what I mean?'

Hedley exhaled as if he'd been pummelled in a boxing match. 'Anything else?'

'Well, if you want me to be truthful, those specs on a string make you look a bit old. Be a good idea to get a smart pair of reading glasses.'

Hedley Morley fought a smile. 'And if you had to "shove me" in the right direction now, Miss Lacey, what would you have me do?'

'Tell that agency of yours you've found someone.'

Was he imagining it, or had the room instantly become brighter? He nodded, and walked slowly to his office door and opened it. He turned back to Alice. 'Miss Maguire will take you through what's what, although I'm guessing you won't need much help with all that. I'm sorry, Miss Lacey – Alice – I must go, I'm running late. Something I doubt I will ever do again. I look forward to seeing you on Monday. Five pounds a week. Agreed?'

In a flurry of papers and clumsy collecting of hat and umbrella from the coat stand, he left.

Five pounds a week! thought Alice. Nearly double her wage at the factory.

A moment later Miss Maguire swept in, carrying files. 'I'm Mr Morley's and Mr Worboys' secretary,' she said briskly, 'and I'm to fill you in. Now, as you probably know, their ambition is to rebuild the city with modern and beautiful buildings. So while Mr Morley has serious meetings with serious men, you will sit quietly and take notes. Do you think you can do that?'

'Of course. Yes.'

'Yes, *Miss Maguire*. You can call me Margaret when we're not in the building. In fact, you can call me what you want – Auntie Peggy, Mint Imperial Maguire, the old battle-axe – but always Miss Maguire when you walk through that front door. Always cast your eyes down at your notebook if you're taking notes. Filing and going through the lists will be an important part of this job. There should be no mixing with your superiors. And you've got a good pair of ankles, very distracting, so dress modestly. Don't draw attention to your curves. Even though you've not got much up top, some of these men like that, you know. Prefer it, even.'

Alice glanced down at her small breasts and wondered if Mr Morley was one of the men she was talking about.

'Now, did you notice the little green flag on his desk?'

Alice nodded.

'He has three flags in his top right-hand drawer. There's always one of them sitting on the table. Red means he cannot be spoken to. So, under no circumstances must you go in. You can see the flash of colour through the stippled glass in the door. Yellow means you can knock, go in, wait until he raises his eyes to look at you and then you can speak when he beckons you. Green means he's accepting people's thoughts and ideas and you can approach the desk without being asked. Not *your* thoughts and ideas, of course, but you could ask him if you could borrow the stapler, for example. It's my system, and Mr Morley is more than happy with it. If you stick to those rules, you and I will get on like a house on fire.'

Alice nodded again. Thoughts and ideas? She had plenty. Starting with a tin for all the paper clips scattered over his desk, and one of those ashtrays on a stand with a lid. But she wasn't going to tell Mint Imperial Maguire that.

She arrived at the Meccano factory just before eleven o'clock. From the shop floor came the familiar din of clattering machinery. As she headed for her workstation, Mr Gerson, the foreman, barked in her ear, 'What time d'you call this!'

She turned round, shrugged, and said calmly, 'I'm handing in my notice. I'm leaving.'

'Handing in your . . . What? You can't do that. *When* do you think you're leaving?'

'This afternoon.'

'No, you're not. Two weeks' notice, that's the rules.'

'Really?'

'No question, queen.'

'Funny, I remember I gave you my notice on

Monday of last week. I know it was last Monday because it was the same day you tried to put your hand on my bottom. Again.'

'You did not give me your notice!'

'I did. At least, I did in my head. I just forgot to tell you.'

The girls on the machines nearby, enjoying the scene, stopped working and fought giggles.

Mr Gerson opened his mouth and shut it again, like a fish. His cheeks flushed red.

Bernice, Alice's friend – a tall, big-boned girl with red hair, currently operating the stamping machine – whispered to the girl beside her, 'I remember too. Was definitely last Monday. It were just after he tried to do the same to me an' all.'

Alice turned and winked at her friends, then spun back on her heel. 'Ta-ra, Mr Gerson. And about the poor lamb who takes my position? This time, keep your hands to yourself, will you?'

'So you've really left the Meccano factory?' said her mother, when Alice told her the news later that day.

'Aye,' Alice replied. She had told her mother in a stream of excited sentences punctuated with 'I can't believe it!', 'Five pounds a week!' and 'I'll finally start to make something of myself!'

Her mother, holding Gabe on one hip, frowned. With the other hand she shook out a tea towel vigorously and placed it over the range.

'Ma, it's a proper job. Not just standing in line with the other girls, doing the same thing all day. It's a proper job with responsibilities.'

'Like what? Bringing them cups of tea and hanging up their raincoats?'

'Ma, don't. They're doing exciting things, architects. "Morley and Worboys. Changing the city of Liverpool. A brighter future awaits." That's their slogan. They're putting it on the side of trams. With a picture of a lovely yellow sun and a Liver Bird.'

'You'll just be fetching and carrying.'

'No. The job is more than that. He listened to me. I told him he needed new glasses. The ones he was wearing made him look ancient and he's not really. He's quite handsome.'

Ida looked shocked. 'You didn't! Why'd you do that? You'll be out of the door before you've even started!'

'He liked it that I spoke my mind.'

'Alice, that tongue of yours will get you in trouble. And Bernice won't be happy, will she? She'll miss you at the factory.'

'Bernice will be fine. She wants to get out of that place as well.'

Brian came bowling in from school, lobbing his satchel onto the armchair, followed by Gwenda with her thumb in her mouth.

'*Hitler has only got one ball!*' Brian sang gustily. Suddenly the tiny kitchen was bustling, full of noise and dust and clutter and smells, and too many people again.

'Take that thumb out, Gwen. You're too old to be sucking at it like that. I'll smear it in mustard,' said Ida. 'And Bry, stop singing that stupid song and do the coal.'

'Ah, eh, mam, not fair. It's Gwen's turn. I washed the pots yesterday.'

'Don't ah-eh-mam me.'

'Where's Da?' asked Alice. 'Wait 'til I tell him about my new job.'

'Got a meeting with a few fellas in the pub.'

'Again? What's the meeting about?'

'These bloody dock strikes. Your Morley's not the only one with his head in the clouds over a bright flaming future. Still, an excuse for a few hours' peace for me from his nonsense,' Ida said, and went back to busying herself at the range with a vegetable peeler and a turnip.

Chapter 5

Alice, taking her chance to slip out, met Bob at the end of the road.

'Am I glad to see you! Me ma and da going on at me as usual,' she said.

They set off for the Locarno, taking a tram and walking the last part of the journey, he with his arm comfortable around her waist. She told him about her new job, enthusing and gesticulating excitedly as they walked.

'You're lucky to get to work with that Morley fella,' Bob said, and kissed her on the bridge of her nose.

'He's lucky to have me, don't you mean?' she said, playfully.

He grinned and they went inside. Taking her straight onto the dance floor, he gripped her waist as they began to dance a slow foxtrot.

'You'll miss this if I go away,' he said, nuzzling her ear. Swaying together, hip to hip in the dark, to the sweet, heady sound of the band playing 'Goodnight Sweetheart', she wondered if he was subtly telling her he would expect her to stop coming here.

'Oh, no,' he said after a moment. 'Look who's here. Big-mouth Bernice. Let's go and get a drink.'

But Bernice, shining with sweat, her red hair piled

up in curls on her head, had appeared in front of them in a low-cut dress with a satin flower in her cleavage. 'Hey, you two lovebirds. Caught you. Off to the necking deck?'

Alice blushed. 'No, just need some air.'

'Right. Stop looking at my embonpoint, Bob.'

'Yer what?'

'Stop looking at my bosoms,' she laughed. 'Where's that lovely Matty? He coming down tonight?'

Bob shouted to make himself heard over the band, which had started up with a blowsy rendition of 'In the Mood'. 'Working, love.'

'Shame,' she said. 'He does things to me in that little peaked cap, turns my knees to jelly.' She exchanged a smile and a wink with Alice.

'Let's go outside,' Bob said to Alice. 'See you around, Bernice.'

The air was cooling. A tram rattled by. Bob had wanted to take her somewhere special tonight – maybe the Pier Head, St George's Hall, or somewhere romantic like the New Brighton Pleasure Gardens. But the day had run out of hours, and they had decided on the Locarno as usual. Now here they were between the gasworks and the bottle-washing factory, the smells of the chemicals rising off the scaldies.

He wanted her to stop talking, too. She had started again, firing off questions about the merchant navy as they walked towards the canal.

'I've something to tell you,' he said. 'I've signed the papers for the merchant navy. Done it already. I couldn't stop myself.'

She paused. 'Without telling me? I thought you were still thinking about it.'

He tried to take her hand, but she pulled it away. 'Will you miss me, then?' he said.

'Why would I miss you? It's not like I care about you one little bit.' She was looking straight ahead.

He took her hand firmly this time, made her meet his eye. 'Alice . . . when a fella goes away, he comes back, but he's never coming back to the place he started from. I'll be different. More experienced. Better,' he said.

She sighed. 'I suppose you're right.'

'Sometimes I won't even be going that far, maybe just to Southampton or Scotland, and back in a week or so. There'll be plenty of leave time. It's not like the war, when fellas would be gone for years.'

She lowered her head and took his other hand, gripping it firmly. 'D'you promise?'

'I promise,' he said, and with a finger tilted up her chin.

'Maybe you're right. Maybe I'm just jealous. I wish I could think of a way to get out of here. Morley and Worboys will be exciting, but I'm still stuck here in Liverpool.'

He threw his arms around her and hugged her, then kissed her hard on the mouth. 'Alice, I love you. I knew you'd see it my way. I swear, it's not for ever, maybe I'll just do it for a year or so. Then when I come back for good, maybe we should . . .' He stopped and fished in his pocket, couldn't find what he was looking for, and hurriedly checked the other one. What was he doing?

And there it was. A ring.

'I want you to marry me, Alice.'

'Bob!' Her hands flew to her mouth. She had not expected this at all. Then she frowned. 'But you're going away?'

'Exactly. I want you to marry me when I'm back. When I'm done. Got it out me system, you might say. But before I go off – next week if I want, they're looking for fellas for the *Stella Maris* ship – I want to let the whole world know you're mine. And I'm yours.'

Alice didn't know what she was feeling. Shocked that he might be leaving so soon. Happy, yes . . . and yet . . . She looked down at the ring and then back up at him. 'It's so beautiful,' she said.

'Woolies. I'm sorry I can't afford an expensive one. But is that a yes?'

'I suppose,' she answered. 'But aren't you meant to kneel? Ask me da? Have you asked me da?'

He frowned. 'No. Not yet. Alice . . .' He brushed down his trousers and got on one knee on the pavement, under the yellow glow of a street lamp. 'Is this what you want? Will you marry me?'

She didn't know what to say. '. . . Thing is, weddings are expensive.'

He frowned. 'Your da, has he got any money? For a wedding, I mean?'

'Not now. We haven't tuppence. My ma has got her Tuesday afternoons, but they aren't going to be enough – and she's threatening to leave. Bit grim at St Mary's. Just pin money.'

'Why doesn't she get a proper job? One that pays more?'

'There's no one to look after the kiddies. My auntie comes over some days. But she lives in Parbold, which might as well be Timbuktu the way she talks about the journey to Liverpool, and she can only afford to take one afternoon every few weeks. Anyway, long and short of it is, me ma and da are certainly not going to pay for a wedding.'

'I know it's a tradition for the father of the bride to pay. But if they've got nothing, that won't stop us.'

'It will embarrass them if they can't afford a slap-up wedding breakfast for me auntie and all the cousins, and my dress and flowers and whatnot, and they'll worry, and . . . Perhaps this should just remain between you and me. For now.'

He placed a finger gently on her lips.

'Shush. Stop fretting. I love you.'

'And I love you too. But this ring . . . perhaps I should give it back to you.'

His face fell. 'Why on earth would you do that? It's just a sign that I love you and you love me.'

Was that really all it meant, though? Alice wondered. She wanted to believe him more than anything. But was there something more to it? Was it that he wanted to own her?

She pushed the thought aside. That was a terrible thing to think.

Chapter 6

On Monday morning, Alice left bright and early for her first day at work with her wild hair twisted into a neat bun, her shoes polished and skirt ironed.

Once she'd gone, Albert sat at the table polishing his pipe with an old rag. Ida moved restlessly around him, straightening the antimacassars and repinning them on the battered sofa, flicking a tea towel and brushing down surfaces.

'What's the problem?' he asked eventually.

'Alice. She's skipped off to that Morley fella, but she's a dark horse. I can never tell one way or another what's going on in her head . . . Look at this.'

Ida reached into her pocket and produced a ring, placing it on a saucer in front of him. It glinted in the light. 'That's an engagement ring. It must be from Bob.'

Albert looked at it, surprised. 'Why hasn't she told us?'

'Please God she's not in the pudding club.'

'It's probably just that she knows I can't afford a wedding,' he said, wiping his hands on the rag.

'Yes, well. That's another reason for you to give up this strike business. She's worrying about it.'

'Bloody Nora, Ida. If she's getting married, she's

getting married. It's nothing to do with me and the lads . . . Something odd about her not telling folks, though. Whoever heard of getting engaged and keeping it a secret? Unless she doesn't want to marry the lad.' He flipped the rag over his shoulder.

'Doesn't want to marry Bob? They've been going together since they were fifteen. Who else would she marry?'

Alice arrived early at Morley and Worboys' offices, nervous but excited. She enjoyed the sound of her footsteps echoing along the black-and-white-tiled corridors, with their ceilings as high as her whole house.

Living in Dryburgh Terrace, in a house that was always bursting at the seams, she craved peace and quiet. Her ma had kept insisting that Alice would find this job boring – that she'd miss the chatter of the girls at the factory, the work outings. She would feel out of place in an office full of men with lofty ambitions who had no time for lowly secretaries. But Alice knew her own mind, and knew that she would thrive on the orderliness of this place and the tasks ahead of her.

Most of her first morning was taken up with getting her bearings, absorbing Miss Maguire's instructions and carrying out some basic secretarial work. Alice found that if she gave it all her attention, her typing wasn't really so bad; something of those lessons at school must have gone in after all.

Towards noon, as she was passing the half-open stippled glass door of Morley's office, she saw a little flash of red – he was using the flag system, just as Miss Maguire had said. She hurried on.

'Miss? Where do you think you're going?' he called from inside. She hesitated, turning back. 'Alice. Come in here.'

'Morning, sir,' she said, stepping into the room and approaching his desk, where there was a map opened out. She glanced at the red flag.

'Never mind that. I'll always make an exception for you, my dear. Look at this; I need a woman's eye. You've got brothers and sisters, I expect? A girl like you – Irish blood? With that hair and those freckles? Presumably a good number of you in your house.'

'Yes, we're fairly packed to the gills.'

Morley was folding the cuffs of his shirt back carefully, revealing hairy forearms. He leaned forward and spread his hands over the map.

'Come and look at this. What do you think?'

Alice moved closer, a little nervous. She was usually invisible to men like Hedley Morley – unless they were looking at her legs, or the way her hair tumbled over her shoulders, or her hazel eyes. But here he was, asking her opinion. She had typed up a letter to the Corporation just that morning about this very design – an idea in someone's head. Now it was coming to life in careful lines and squiggles across the page, the rows of houses marked out with red lines. Little coloured wooden blocks had been placed strategically across the map.

Morley grinned. 'I want to know everything, Alice – I want to know what it's like. Come and sit down.' He held a pen aloft.

'What do you mean?'

'Well, I can't just go in with my designs and rear-range the whole of Liverpool without knowing more about what it's like to live as you do. Tell me a bit about the street you live in, your family. Their jobs. It's been tricky after the war. Strikes. The dole.'

She shrugged, feeling a little defensive. 'We all work. Always have done.'

'And are the jobs secure?'

'Da gets his work from the Pen at the docks. They know him, so he has guaranteed days. Me ma worked at the Meccano factory like me, before she had our Gabe. She says putting all the Meccano bits together sharpened her brain, but when she got home she could barely remember what day it was or who was the king of England.' She smiled at the memory and Morley smiled back, warmly. '. . . And there's always been my wage. Whatever job I do, I pay keep and whatever I can spare on top.'

'What about sleeping arrangements?'

'There's a fair bit of top and tailing, and I can't even remember a time when we had rooms of our own or didn't have a baby sleeping in a drawer – but Ma makes things cosy. She can make a nifty cot out of a drawer.'

'And what about your father? Tell me about him; does he like a drink? I only ask because we wonder whether we should include a public house in our plans for new towns. Whether it will encourage immoral behaviour.'

She looked surprised, then frowned slightly. 'No more than the next fella.'

How many times had she heard Ma saying that if Da came home two sheets to the wind again, she'd be showing him the door? But she wasn't going to tell Mr Morley that. Alice certainly wasn't going to tell him about her father never recovering from the *Malakand* fire, and how it had meant work wasn't so easy; or that there were whole days when he would stay upstairs in bed lately, complaining of his headaches.

'Like I said, he's a grafter, me da. He's a good man and looks after our family.'

'And the house?'

'Bit cramped. Bit damp. No more than the next.'

He nodded. 'Can I show you something? Look – this is Kirkby. They've already made a start there with the ROF – the factory where they built munitions – you know it?' She nodded thoughtfully as he went around to the other side of the desk. She remembered one of her ma's friends from the washhouse, Mrs Rogan, working there and coming home yellow from loading the shells with explosives.

He pushed some of the small red blocks around with a kind of spatula, stood back and squinted, then pushed them again into a different position on the map. 'These are called war damage maps. The government provides them. You know, it sounds heartless, but the Blitz – in a way, it's created a wonderful opportunity. Homes for all. It's exciting.'

And then he did something strange. He took one brick and placed it on top of another. They had little interlocking grooves and slotted together perfectly. He took a third and clicked them together, then a fourth.

'Can you imagine?' he said. 'Can you imagine if you were living in a block like this, instead of in an awful slum?' He pointed at the little bricks piled on top of each other. 'And it was warm and bright, and you each had your own room, and you had a view all the way across the countryside from your new home in Kirkby? The green fields, the rolling hills. Imagine what a start that would be to your day. Or if we built our flats – high-rises, they're called – on Everton Hill, you'd be able to see the magnificent river stretched out before you, like a long silver sleeve trailing across the ground. Wouldn't that be inspiring?'

A long silver sleeve? What was he on about? Alice thought of the grimy streets and the stubby, squat little houses that were her start to the day.

'Imagine how it would be if everyone living there had hot running water coming out of their taps?' Morley shivered and rubbed his hands together. 'And look here: every parlour house would have a garden space. Front and back. The houses are designed in this beautiful symmetrical shape. And here there are swings and slides in the courtyard flats, and so much space for the kiddies to play in. Space all around them.'

'The tenements have recs. You mean like that?'

'No, better. This will be nothing like the tenements. People all crowded on top of each other. Everyone getting TB or cholera – and the scarlet fever outbreaks. Dreadfully sad. No, we will give them fresh air and real space.' He sat back and smiled at her. 'Where exactly do you live?' he asked suddenly. 'The bomb-damaged houses are coloured black on the maps, and the ones here . . . Total destruction . . .'

'Oh, me? I live down by . . .' She trailed off. She had been shocked to hear the way he talked about Everton and the docks. It was a ridiculous exaggeration, and yet somehow she was still reluctant to tell him exactly where she came from.

'Is your street on our map?'

'Let's see . . . Oh,' she said, as her eye located Dryburgh Terrace. The words 'Stage One: Managed decline. Stage Two: Demolition' had been neatly inked in black just beneath the name of the road.

'No,' she mumbled quickly. She worried that the lie would take hold – but it was even more worrying to think that if Mr Morley knew she lived in one of the streets marked for demolition, he might hold it against her.

Besides, would it be such a bad thing if they were all given clean new homes? Maybe this was something to celebrate. She knew what her mother would think about being forced to leave Dryburgh Terrace; but surely a house without creeping damp, and mould, and ivy growing through cracked windowpanes, would be better for the children?

'Now, here's the real innovation. High-rises. Homes in the sky,' he said, gesturing in a wide sweep towards the brow of Everton Valley. He nodded seriously. And then for some reason – perhaps carried away with excitement or enthusiasm, or both – he clasped her hand.

She looked down at it in surprise, and he let go. 'I'm sorry,' he said. 'I don't know what came over me. Very improper, Alice. I'm just so . . . so *excited*.' He put his thumbs under his braces, looking delightedly at his map with its arrangement of little bricks and towers. 'That, my dear Alice, is the future.'

'The brighter future,' she murmured.

By the time Alice arrived home, she was as full of excitement as Mr Morley had been – ready to tell her family that he was the cleverest man she'd ever met and was going to change everything for Liverpool, that the end of the war was a chance to make things better. Had they ever heard of high-rises . . . ?

She stepped into the kitchen, already midway through a rush of animated chatter as she took off her coat – but then her mother turned round, and the expression on her face gave Alice pause. Slowing down, she realized the atmosphere in the small, airless room was as prickly as a field of thistles.

The twins were charging around, oblivious. 'Don't do that, Brian, you're not a horse,' snapped Ida. 'Galloping around like a lunatic. And that's the potato bag. Get it off your head . . . Go outside and play.' As he went out, she caught hold of his chin and twisted his face towards the light. 'And stop licking your lips. You're making them all crusty again.'

'Eugh, Biscuit's got the mange,' teased Gwenda.

'Go and get some fresh air. Both of you.' Ida paused. 'Now, Alice. Me and your da have a question. Should we be celebrating or not?'

'What?'

'Are you getting married?' Ida demanded, folding her arms across her chest.

Alice's cheeks burned. 'Mam! It's complicated. And aye, there was a ring, but it was in my drawer. So unless you're a thought reader, like the woman at the Empire, how d'you know?'

'Bob told me,' Ida said flatly. 'I asked him.'

'So, d'you not want to be his wife?' said her father, coming in, flapping his jacket and putting it over the back of a chair.

'Of course I do, but there's a lot for me to think about. And he's joined the merchant navy, did he tell you that as well? He'll probably be leaving any day now on his first trip. If he does, I want to concentrate on seeing him off safely, not all this . . . flim-flam.' Alice's nostrils flared. She was furious with Bob for telling her mother.

'Flim-flam!' said Ida, her eyes opening wide. 'A marriage proposal!'

Turning on her heel, Alice whisked her coat back off the stand where she'd only just hung it up and swept back out the door.

Ida looked at Albert, astonished. 'I blame this new job. It's turned her head already, after one day. Changing the world, I ask you! She's only a secretary, for goodness' sake.'

Alice marched straight to Bob's house: a short, angry walk from Dryburgh Terrace, past a parade of shops and the church on the corner, and into Tooley Street. She knocked sharply.

'Why?' she said, cheeks flushed, as Bob opened the door.

'That's a nice hello.'

'Why did you tell Ma?'

'I told her because she asked. She said she found the ring. Why not? You ashamed?'

'Of course not.'

'Then stop being so hot-headed. You know it does things to me.' Smiling, he leaned forward to kiss her, pulling her through the door by her wrist and into the house.

Alice squirmed away from his roaming hands, manoeuvring herself from under his arm. 'What are you doing? Pawing me like that in here. This house is as bad as ours. Like Lime Street station – your mates with their bottles of beer, and your sister and her kids always popping by for a brew. Anyone could walk in. You don't think you'll get away with that? Besides, I'm furious with you, Bob.'

'No one here at the minute. Come on, Alice – I go tomorrow.'

'Apart from your ma upstairs . . . !'

'She's not been down those stairs for weeks. God, Alice, I like it when you're all worked up. All fiery . . . You're a regular cherry bomb, all pink in the cheeks and fizzing with that hot temper of yours.'

He lunged forward. She pushed him away, but his grip was hard around her upper arm. He put his mouth over hers.

'Stop it!'

'I can't, Cherry Bomb. You've got me all riled up. You can't leave me like this . . .'

He was handsome and kind and so funny, she thought. But this side of him? He was also selfish. Did that matter? Bernice said you should always be selfish when you're young, it's your only chance – but even so . . .

'Let me, Alice,' he moaned. He began tugging at her skirts. 'Flaming girdle,' he said.

'Bob . . .' She leaned her head back and groaned. 'We can't, not here. Not with your ma . . .'

'Come with me into the yard, then.'

'What, with the neighbours and the chickens?' she shot back.

He kissed her again, and this time his hand went up her skirt. There was the sound of snapping and she felt her stocking go loose around her thigh. She felt the shape of him through his trousers against her leg as he pressed his whole body to hers. 'You're beautiful, Alice,' he said. 'You and me, we'll make beautiful babbies.'

'Just not on this sofa,' she said, slapping his hand away. She sat up, rearranged her skirts. 'I can't.'

He laughed. 'Can't what?'

'You know. Can't do whatever it is you want me to do. How many times must I tell you – I'm not going to be like all the other girls around here, playing Russian roulette with their fellas and then getting pregnant, getting married young.'

'I'll be careful. I always am.'

'Really? I thought I was the careful one, holding you off, Bob. And now I've got this new job I want to be especially careful . . .'

'Yer what? You mean, this new job means you'll not let me do this to—'

'No!' she cried. 'I'm just not ready for any of it. Babies. Weddings. That's the real truth of why I

hid the ring from me ma.' She sat up and straightened her clothes, fastening the buttons he had
somehow managed to undo on her blouse. 'Anyway,
can I ask you something? What do you want to do
in life? I mean, when you get back from the
merchant navy.'

'Where did that come from? . . . Nothing. Apart
from make some money and marry you.'

'But then what?'

'I don't know. I don't know what you mean.'

'I mean that I want to make something of myself.
When I see girls my age who are teachers, nurses,
secretaries – that's what I want. Not scrabbling in the
sawdust – a factory girl until I die.'

He laughed. 'Don't talk daft. People like me don't
have fancy lines of work. We have jobs.'

'But there has to be something more. I want something more. Don't you?'

'More what?'

'I've got dreams. Haven't you?'

He shrugged.

'Well?' she said.

'I dunno. You could say I'm pretty happy with my
lot. As long as I have a job and you. It's money that
gives us our freedom, isn't it? Doesn't matter what
job you're doing. If you have money, you're free as
a bird.'

'I know, but . . . doesn't there have to be something
more?'

'Like what?' He helped himself to a drink from the
bottle of sherry on the table, glugging it right from
the bottle.

'I want to do things. Important things. Get away from here, now the war has ended.'

'You know what – I love you, Alice. But I can't help thinking you're living in a world of your own. That kind of life doesn't really exist, not for folks like us.' He wiped his lips.

Before she could reply, they were interrupted by a clattering sound from upstairs. Then a loud thumping on the ceiling – a broom handle, banging on the bedroom floor above them. They both glanced up and saw the fringe quivering on the lampshade.

'*Bob!*'

'Coming, Ma!' he cried. 'Flamin' 'eck. Does she never stop mithering?'

'I need to get back to bath the kiddies,' Alice sighed. 'Otherwise, the whole shebang falls apart for me ma. I'll see you tomorrow.'

'All right, love,' he said, giving her a peck on the lips.

As they stepped into the hallway there was another disturbance: hammering at the front door, loud and persistent. Bob shook his head. 'Bloody hell! What now?'

Alice came up behind him as he opened the door and, to her surprise, saw Brian on the step, his face alarmingly pale. She exchanged a worried look with Bob, who crouched down to the boy's level.

'What's the matter, son?'

Brian was breathing so hard he could barely get his words out. 'Alice . . .'

'What's the matter, love?' she said.

'Da. He's in the hospital. Come quick. He went

back to do a late shift and he's been taken ill. He's sick, Alice. Really sick, Miss Quick said.'

'Who's minding Gabe?' she said, feeling her stomach somersault.

'Gwenda.'

'Go on home, all right? If you see anyone, tell them I've gone to the hospital. Don't cry, Bry. Everything's going to be all right. You go home and look after the little 'uns. There's scouse in the pot, and make sure you change Gabe before you put him down. Don't cry, love. Nothing to cry about until we know what's what, eh?'

An hour earlier, Ida, with Gabe in a pram, had set off to the washhouse. She had enjoyed the chatter and the gossip, and when she got there Gabe spent a happy twenty minutes playing with soap suds and being passed around from one woman to the next. They all admired his cherubic cheeks and bounced him on their knees and jiggled him in his pram until he giggled and hiccupped so much he turned pink.

When she got back home, an ashen Mrs Hallett had been standing on her step.

'Ida. I came as quickly as I could. Your Albert's in the hospital.'

'Hospital?' said Ida, frozen in place. She felt the blood drain out of her.

'Barry said they sent an ambulance. I don't have much news except, he collapsed. Legs went right under him. On the warehouse roof.'

They got inside somehow but the room seemed to sway; the furniture wavered and the light cord moved like a snake. The statue of Our Lady on the dresser seemed to be squeezing her eyes shut in response to the terrible news. Ida reached out a hand to steady herself against a chair. Gabe started to cry.

'Gabe's only two. And Brian, barely out of short trousers . . . and Gwen,' she murmured. 'Poor Biscuit and Gravy.'

'I'm sorry, Ida.' Mrs Hallett reached out a calming hand.

Ida's heart thudded in her chest so strongly she thought it might burst. She ran all the way to the hospital, ignoring Mrs Hallett's suggestion to ask Mr Maloney to drive them, knowing that by the time he had cranked up his precious Austin Ten it would be slower than going on foot. She raced up the hill in a whirlwind of dust and panic and shot through the double doors of the hospital, not knowing where she was going. She could barely breathe. The bright lights swam before her eyes. She felt a sharp pain stabbing at her chest and her throat.

'You can't go in there,' said a nurse.

Panicked, in back-to-front sentences, Ida asked them where her husband was, telling them his name repeatedly.

'Ah, the fellow from the docks – Lucky, they called him? Come with me . . .' Not so lucky now, the nurse thought, and she was right.

After two flights of stairs – strip lights thrumming, rooms with their white walls tilting – they arrived at the ward and Ida was led through a curtain to Albert's bedside. He raised his head from the pillow. She gasped at how grey he looked, hair standing up in

70

tufts, eyes rimmed with red, skin sallow and blotchy.

'Lie down, Mr Lacey. Heart attack, we think, Mrs Lacey,' said a younger nurse beside his bed.

'Heart attack!' Ida's voice quavered.

'Mild. Very mild. Nothing to worry about,' said Albert weakly.

'Mild, but still a heart attack, Mr Lacey,' the older nurse said firmly, looking over the top of her thick spectacles.

'Always pretending there's nothing wrong with you . . .' Ida shook her head miserably. 'And now here you are in the hospital. I knew it. I knew it was serious. The headaches. The pains in your chest. Your arm. Not just allergic to the zinc cargoes. He's never been right since the explosion,' she said to the nurse. 'Have you told them about that, Albert?'

'Don't go on, Ida,' he murmured.

Suddenly the curtain was yanked back and Alice was standing there, breathless. 'Da! The nurse said it was a heart attack – I came straight here.'

'I'm fine, sweetheart.'

Relief flooded her face as she sat on the end of the bed and grasped his hand.

'No sitting on beds. Germs,' the older nurse said brusquely, and she and her colleague left them alone.

'That one's a dragon, the other is a poppet. Come on – climb back up here with me, Alice,' said her father, patting the covers. 'And your ma's right, I haven't been a hundred per cent. But it's just a dicky ticker. And that's exactly what it was. The zinc, most likely. A reaction. Nothing to lose sleep over.'

Alice shivered to see how pale he looked. She

71

glanced at Ida, who was twisting her handkerchief. You could see his veins. Blue threads, like twisting pulsating knotty ropes under his skin.

'I was up on the roof at the warehouse. We had just been shifting cases of bananas . . .'

'We know.'

'But it's going to be fine. I need to get back to work. Probably just indigestion. Ida, you said some of your girls at St Mary's get it so bad, it's a pain like you can't believe.'

'No, Da, it wasn't indigestion. You heard the nurse. Heart attack,' said Alice.

'Mild,' he replied.

'What will happen?' said Ida.

'Happen? You mean the rent, if I can't work? Don't fret. They can't just chuck us out on the street, if that's what you're worrying about.'

'But you look white as a sheet. And can you even stand?'

'I'm right as rain,' he said. He struggled to sit up and failed, instead letting his head loll back against the pillow. 'Tickety-boo.'

Alice glanced at her mother, who picked up her look.

'I'm just being practical. We need to be practical, Al – when you've got three small children, you have to be. What if . . .'

'She's right, Da,' said Alice.

'I am being practical.' He winced.

She saw her mother's lip quivering.

'What you need to do is go to Barry and tell him what's happened,' her father said. 'If they hadn't

pushed me to come back in and do that late shift . . .
I shouldn't have been on the roof in the first place.
The *Echo* might even do a story. I'm only forty-two
– and me lungs . . . One slip and you're on the
scrapheap.'

Ida bristled. 'Maybe if you didn't smoke so much.'

Alice squeezed her eyes shut. How could her mother
go from one minute looking as if her life would be
over if anything happened to her beloved Albert, to
berating him in the very next breath?

The older nurse reappeared, pulling back the
curtain. 'Visiting over,' she said firmly. 'He needs his
rest. Don't you, Mr Lacey?'

'That's us told,' he said, and smiled. 'Go on home
and don't make a fuss. I'll be up and about in no
time.'

But Alice heard his laboured breathing, and saw
how his hands trembled and his eyes dulled. She had
a horrible feeling this would not end well.

Chapter 7

'Alice, I don't like leaving you, with your da ill like that,' said Bob.

He'd been waiting for her at the house, pacing the linoleum. It was already worn smooth but it would soon have a hole in it if he carried on walking up and down like he was. 'Should I tell the ship's master I've changed my mind? I could be away for three months . . .'

'Don't be stupid,' she said, with more confidence than she felt. 'We'll manage. He'll be home from hospital soon and making plans with his union mates – taking on the world. It'll keep him going. What time does your boat leave?'

'Eight thirty tomorrow. Though we're supposed to board this evening.'

A cloud came over her expression. 'I'll come and wave you off,' she murmured, and kissed him on the lips. Her eyes turned glassy with tears as she lingered for a moment.

'You don't need to, Alice, love. It's not like the war. No danger of us being bombed.'

'Please come back safely.'

'Three months will go quickly. I'll be back before you know it and we'll make up for the time I've been away, eh? We can start planning the wedding. I've always fancied a wedding at St Anthony's, and me and Matty can do a pub crawl. The Liverpool Lane mile.' He kissed her again, plunging his tongue into her mouth, twisting it around her teeth. 'Be a good girl while I'm away, won't you? You can send me word with the postman if you catch him at the docks, let me know how things are. It'll get to me eventually. Look after your da and the kiddies. And your ma.'

She felt his heart beating against hers as he pulled her even closer and kissed her harder.

'Aye. Me ma. That's the tricky one,' she murmured as his hand squirmed under her blouse and squeezed her breast. 'Gerroff, Bob,' she said, slapping it away.

'You still telling me I have to wait until I'm back?' he said sulkily.

'Aye. Absence makes the heart grow fonder.'

'And it's the thought of that absence is making me Johnson—'

'Bob! Don't say it! You're terrible!' she said.

'I'm sorry, Cherry Bomb. But you turn me into a wild animal, just the touch of you, and the smell of you . . .'

'Not now, Bob. Let's just concentrate on getting you away to sea first,' she said with a weak smile. 'And in the meantime, I can get me da better.'

Ida arrived at St Mary's orphanage the following day. There was a new girl sitting at the back of the sewing class. I recognize that kind of girl, thought Ida – Liverpool is full of them. The kind that for some reason, certain people wanted to break their spirit.

Ida tried to raise a friendly smile. 'Hello,' she said.

Angela was in the centre of the room, on a rickety chair. She cradled her bump.

'The baby didn't come early after all?' asked Ida.

Angela sighed. 'No, more's the pity. I'm as big as a whale.'

Ida wanted to ask her what she would be doing once she had the baby. She looked around the room at the others. Surely some of them had an older sister, or a distant aunt or cousin – someone who would take them in after the child was born, so they wouldn't have to come back here? What must it feel like to have no one in the world who would give you a roof over your head?

'Miss – I saw a baby dress in the catalogue, Miss. It's so pretty. Will you help me make one like it?' Mildred asked. She took a crumpled piece of paper out of her pocket and opened it out to show a picture of a chubby baby, smiling on a crocheted blanket. 'Isn't he sweet? I like his matching booties, with the ribbons threaded around the tops an' all.'

Ida nodded. It was heartbreaking to think of these girls making going-away outfits for their babies, lovingly stitching and knitting and dressing them, then placing them into the arms of strangers. She wondered why the nuns made them do it but had to admit that, oddly, it did seem to give them some purpose.

'Not long until the stork comes, Miss,' said Angela. 'Month and a half, they think. I go off to the mother and baby home next week.'

Doreen giggled. 'If it'd been the swallow, you wouldn't be in this mess.'

'Such a potty mouth, Dore,' Angela snorted.

Ida was surprised and pleased to see that even June smiled at this.

'June's fine now,' said Mildred. 'Once you realize there's other poor stupid lassies like you in the same pickle it's not so bad, is it, June? We even had a laugh the other day, over your fella who says his r's like w's.'

'He's called Ricky Reardon,' Angela explained, for Ida's benefit. 'Wicky Weardon's wun off and left you high and dwy, hasn't he, love?'

'He has now.'

'Oh dear, I'm so sorry. Shall we start on our hemming?'

'She met him at the docks. He works on the ships. You were in love, weren't you, pet?'

June nodded sadly.

'Until he took a ship back to Australia,' said Angela.

One of the girls sitting at the back let out a load groan.

'What's the matter, dear?' Ida was relieved at the interruption.

'Me fingers are too big for the threading.'

'Not just her fingers. Her ankles are big an' all, Miss.'

'Oedema. The fat ankles. Read it in a medical dictionary in Sid's office,' said Angela.

'I feel like the blinking Michelin Man,' the girl said. She was trying to thread a needle and at the same time letting out short, frustrated breaths and humphs.

'Girls, girls . . .' Ida rapped a ruler on the desk. 'Can you turn around and listen to me?'

*

The rest of the lesson passed with endless interruptions and arguments, and finally tailed off when someone announced they were going out for a cigarette. Ida pretended she hadn't heard and packed up her sewing box.

When she got outside she saw an orderly crocodile of small children in brown tunics and shorts walking across the lawn in pairs, holding hands. At the front, Sister Cyril clapped her hands to keep time. '*Jesus is my Sweet Saviour . . .*' she sang in a thin, reedy voice as they walked in time, trying to sing along while she made vague conducting gestures.

Ida feared the tune would lodge in her head like a bad seed. As she turned to go, the nun moved away from the children and swept towards her.

'Ida, dear, did you have a good morning? Doreen give you her sob story, did she? And did Angela tell you her ma wants her back after she's had her baby?' She shook her head. 'The day that girl's mother takes her back is the day I'll be eating scouse with the Pope.'

'They were all grand, Sister. Good girls, all of them.'

'Good girls! They wouldn't be here if they were good girls.'

Ida looked back at the line of children. Without the nun's attention they had dispersed into little groups: a few crouched on their haunches plucking daisies, a boy threw a conker up into the air, and two girls raced round a tree.

'Turn your back for a second, it all falls apart,' said the nun with a sigh. 'I thank the Lord I'm married to Jesus – I could never have been a wife and mother.

Children are so unruly, aren't they? Why do they never do what you want?'

Ida hesitated. 'Sister, I was wondering. If I needed more days, is there anything more I could do here?'

'More sewing classes?'

'Anything. I'm ashamed to say, we're struggling a little. My Albert. He's not working. And now . . . now he's in the hospital . . .' Her voice had a slight tremor.

'I heard. You don't need to explain. Leave it with me, Ida. But we're not made of money. We rely on charity. I'll see what I can do.' She paused. 'And if it's your children you are worried about, you could always bring them here.'

'What d'you mean?' Ida said, shocked.

'We exist for people like you. Orphans of the living, remember? Admitting you have problems is half the battle. But take heart, Ida. You're not alone. You wouldn't be the first family to find themselves at St Mary's door asking for help. There's no shame in it. None at all.'

Chapter 8

The sun flashed against the glass as Alice looked out of the kitchen window. It seemed wrong somehow to have this beautiful weather, with her father struggling to even walk across the kitchen from the sink to the rocking chair now that he was back home. Each time she had padded into his bedroom in the parlour, he had sat up and smiled and promised her there was nothing to worry about. But she had heard the rattle in his breathing, and it was worse at night through the walls.

She got ready for work early, tying her hair up in its neat coil before she stepped out the door. She practised smiling on the way to the office, assessing her reflection in the windows she passed, tossing her head back. By the time she clanked open the lift doors on the third floor, you would never have known there was a knot of worry clenching her stomach. When she walked through the door and said, 'Good morning, Mr Morley,' her chin was thrust out confidently and she was smiling.

'How was your evening?' he asked.

She wasn't going to tell him that she had spent most of the night fetching water, rearranging her father's bedclothes, emptying the rancid potty, wiping his forehead with a sodden rag.

'Grand. And I've brought a tin box for all your paper clips and pennies,' she said, deftly changing the subject. 'Every day you empty your pockets on this desk and the mantelpiece, Mr Morley – and you never pick them up.'

But he was frowning, noticing that Alice's buttons were done up the wrong way, the buttons in the wrong holes. She caught his glance. 'Oh dear,' she said quickly, smiling, touching the fastenings and looking away.

He nodded gently. 'Everything all right?'

'Yes,' she said brightly.

She picked up a pen. Her neck was bent, revealing the smooth white alabaster skin where the sun didn't reach and a wild curl of hair that had escaped from her neat bun. He pulled the chair in another inch opposite her. With a quick jerk of her head, she said lightly, 'Except . . . my father, he's not well.'

'What's wrong with him?'

'Nothing serious. Just – his health has never been the same since the war, I suppose. He was tangled up in the SS *Malakand* disaster.'

'Ah, the ship. Terrible.'

'He was working at the docks that night. Nearly died. But anyway, he's had another bad turn and even though he's not well, he's insisting he's going to go back to work. He does seem to be improving, though, thank goodness. Slowly.'

Mr Worboys wandered in, wearing his bowler hat, and caught the tail end of the conversation.

'What's wrong with who?'

'No one,' said Alice. 'Just . . .'

'A fellow who's had a bit of bad luck, hey, Alice?' said Morley kindly.

'Is it the usual? Drink? This is the trouble, these types, they often don't help themselves. And with drinking so regularly. My wife sees people like this all the time. I don't mean to pry, but is that the story?'

'Kenneth, it's Alice's father we're talking about.'

'Ah, apologies, Alice, you're a good girl. I can see you're sweet and hard-working. And ambitious, Mr Morley tells me. The product of a good family. The deserving poor – although that's an unpleasant way of putting it.'

'It is, Kenneth. I've never liked that phrase,' said Morley.

Mr Worboys hung up his coat and hat and left as quickly as he had arrived. Morley opened his mouth as though he was about to say something, then shut it and tapped a pencil on his teeth, looking into the distance.

Are we Laceys the deserving poor, then? Alice wondered. Surely the fact that her father was lying with his legs hardly working in the front room through no fault of his own – it was Hitler's fault, if it was anyone's – meant they were more deserving than most. But she didn't think many would see it like that.

'This is what it's about,' Morley said, finding his voice again. 'Improvement. Bettering yourself. Which brings me to our buildings. Some of these rooms are shocking. Uninhabitable. And the rents. Are you . . . erm . . .'

'Yes, we live in a rented house.'

'Mr Worboys is a good man. He's on the board of

St Mary's. He's high-minded. His child, Dolly, was adopted from St Mary's orphanage – he and Mrs Worboys couldn't have children of their own, and she's also a bit of a do-gooder. Committees and whatnot. They're both experts on these kind of difficulties. Worboys says it's because of the slum housing that so many children end up at St Mary's of the Blessed Angels. So many with parents who can't cope. Orphans of the living, they're called.'

That sounds nearly as bad as 'the deserving poor', Alice thought.

She took a sheaf of papers from the binder and began to go through them carefully, as Mr Morley had asked her to do each morning. Miss Maguire had told her to check that each document was labelled alphabetically. As she worked, she thought about some of the people she knew. Eleven of the O'Flahertys in a two-up, two-down house; some of their neighbours with no electric; all with outside lavs and often a tin bath where they all shared the water. One family she knew even let the dog have a turn in it before the little ones. Matty had been living with his auntie and uncle and their two boys in a court house, with sanitation that was beyond repair and the washhouse the only place for a proper bath. The night watchman had soon come knocking to check for overcrowding and his auntie and uncle had headed off to Australia just after the war with their sons, leaving poor Matty to fend for himself in a small, cramped room that he rented. Children just appeared from nowhere around Liverpool Lane, as if from thin air. Billy Mercer was the baby of his family, but everyone – except him –

knew that his eldest sister was his real ma. Families subletting. Miss Quick with her withered arm from polio. And what about that couple Bernice knew – Norma someone and her new fellow? Living in sin. It sounded nasty. If everyone was to be judged by Mr Worboys' standards of the deserving poor, they would have a whole city turned down for houses or new flats.

But Mr Morley wouldn't judge. It seemed that his sunny new future – these new houses the Corpy was building, villages and towns – really would change people's lives.

'Mr Morley . . . I don't like the way Mr Worboys thinks of us. How we live.'

She pulled her little cardigan around her and pushed her hands up the sleeves.

'Go on,' he said softly.

'We're pretty proud people. If anyone comes around, me ma always lays out the tablecloth, washes and irons the antimacassars, puts out the best cutlery. We manage. The house is small and yes, we top and tail. But it's not so bad – it's cosy. If it wasn't for the damp. You can poke your finger right through some of the walls with the damp. We were promised things would be so much better after the war.'

'And are they? Have you noticed a difference?'

'Since Mr Attlee and his National Health Service? His medicines, you mean? Aye, they're free, but I'd rather not get ill in the first place. The school milk, that would be grand, except our Brian says it tastes like sick when it's left out in the sun and he refuses to drink it.'

'And will any of your brothers or sister take their matriculation?'

'Oh no, we'll need them to work. Brian is clever. He can do arithmetic but he's not bothered with writing it down. Teachers always want to see the working out. He doesn't know that stuff. But he'll know if Satterthwaite's cheat him out of a bob when he goes to buy sticky buns.'

Morley smiled. 'He'll go a long way.' He paused. 'And, erm . . . the lavatory arrangements at home? Washing. Is it a privy outside? Nothing inside?'

She thought of the potty stained green, but she wasn't going to start talking about that. She just shook her head in reply, forcing herself to smile, and then said, 'Mr Morley, I've been thinking about your plans. Where are the shops?' She came over to his desk and looked down at the map.

'Shops will be built after the houses are finished.'

'Shouldn't you be doing that first? Where will people buy their groceries? Where will they meet to have a natter if it's not at the hardware store, or the baker's, or the sweet shop?' She asked the question with sudden unexpected authority.

'Oh. It's only the houses we've thought of right now. But . . . yes . . . shops . . .'

Alice smiled. It felt good to be listened to.

He was looking at her thoughtfully. 'I have an idea. When we have our meeting at the parish hall to talk about our plans, would you come along? Perhaps speak?'

Alice blushed.

'Because you have a good instinct,' he went on. 'I

would like to give you more responsibility than just organizing me around the office. A better position. There's a future here for you, Alice. We work with architects all over the country. London. Birmingham. We could probably look at a raise, as well? And the Corporation could do with having a no-nonsense brain like yours on some of their committees.'

A raise? she thought. They needed it so much right now. 'Of course, Mr Morley.' She felt happy and excited. No one had ever asked her to do such a thing. No one had taken her seriously like this. She couldn't wait to tell her mother.

'I'm furious. Spitting feathers, I am. Your father went to work today. Can you believe it? In his state. Ridiculous,' said Ida, as Alice walked into the house peeling off her coat.

Alice wiped her brow and frowned. 'I thought he was getting better? Where is he? Still in the parlour? Ma, I have news.'

'News? He skulked off upstairs, exhausted. He can hardly move. I told him. But he wanted to meet his pals. Plotting over nonsense.'

Gwenda sighed theatrically as she sat on the rug playing with her bobbin. 'Da said Ma was mithering and Ma said he was stubborn as a pig and Da said no one understood him and he threw his boot across the table . . .' she said, eyes wide, enjoying the drama.

'Quiet, Gwen. Pigs aren't stubborn. Ma, he's just trying to do his best by us.'

Ida gritted her teeth. Frustration took hold and she banged down a dish. 'He *has* to get better. No one will help. Not even the sisters. Apart from kindly offering to take the kiddies off me. Some kind of cruel joke, that was. We need money. She's as cold as a fish sometimes, that Sister Cyril.'

'Ma, we have my wage. And guess what, Morley has offered me a better position. More money.'

'Still not enough without your da's wage, Alice. Maybe I could take in more glove-making and do more sewing. If we didn't have Gabe, I could go back to work, but I don't know, I don't know . . .'

'I'll take Da up a mug of Bovril and some dripping,' Alice said, as her mother fell silent.

'Aye, and get the nit comb and bring Brian down. I noticed him scratching again.' There was a loud thump and she glanced at the ceiling as the light swayed. 'Brian!' she yelled. 'Go and tell him to stop crashing about, Alice. Probably jumping off the wardrobe again.'

'It weren't me, Ma,' said Brian, wandering in from the back yard. He was dragging a lump of bricks cemented together, with a rusting iron rod sticking out of the mass at an odd angle. 'Look what I got from the hollas. Treasure.'

Ida tilted her head, frowning. She looked around the room. When her eyes alighted on Alice her expression changed. 'Then what was that noise, if it wasn't Bry?' she said.

For a moment, nobody moved. Then, shocked into life, Alice and Ida leapt up and ran for the stairs, barging each other out of the way, scrambling up two steps at a time.

For a moment they just stood at the bedroom door,

staring at the scene before them. Albert lay half in, half out of the bed, his body at a strange angle, thin white legs stiffly extended. And then Gwenda was squeezing between them. 'Da's not moving. He looks like one of Lewis's dummies; all stiff. Is he dead?'

'Albert!' shrieked Ida, falling to her knees at the side of the bed, grasping his lifeless hand. 'Get down to Mrs Hallett's, somebody! Or Miss Quick! Or run round to Mr Tattersall! Tell them to call for the ambulance!'

But Alice, looking at her father's head lolling to one side, his mouth open and his bloodless pallor, knew there was no point doing that now.

Chapter 9

Some weeks later, on a cold September morning, Alice was trying to feed Gabe with mashed potato and mutton. She had left the range with a fire roaring but it was still chilly. The potatoes were cubed and had been soaked in salt water overnight. Taking the big frying pan, she cut onions and tipped them in and softened them up, getting ready to make soup for everyone.

Da's funeral had been a miserable affair at first: the coffin lowered into the ground on a windy hill at St Anthony's as her mother wailed over it, and Barry Hallett nearly falling into the grave when he'd slipped on the moist earth. But somehow the day had twisted itself round and turned into a party, and everyone said it had been a grand send-off. The morning after, she had gone around picking up the debris: cans, bottles, overflowing ashtrays, someone's tie left hanging over the banister that she didn't recognize, a discarded shoe, a half-eaten pork pie . . . but at least, she'd thought to herself, they had all clearly had a good time.

Nearly everyone had brought something for the wake, and people had kept on arriving at the door over the following month. Tins of peaches, evaporated milk, tins of Spam, jars of homemade piccalilli and pickled beetroot – even a Christmas cake had appeared, baked by Miss Quick. For the first time in weeks they'd had food in the pantry, and thankfully it had lasted. They were still using up the Spam – she would fry it up today to have with the soup.

She stared out of the window down the road, through the gap where number twenty-seven had been. She could see the river, and a ship moving slowly into port. Her mother was bustling around the kitchen, pushing dirt away with the broom, ready to take the dustpan and tip it outside in the yard. Alice looked around the little house, thinking back to how she had sat with her father's body until the early hours of the morning the day he died. She was still waking most mornings wondering if it had been an awful dream. Maybe her father was outside tying the tarpaulin to the posts – he was at the Boot with his Union pals – he was fishing at Otterspool with Brian . . . But then she would open her eyes and slowly realize he was gone, and she would never see him laugh or hear his voice again. She looked out at the bit of tarpaulin hanging on a post in the yard.

The house was still noisy, but not as much, and she already missed him banging his boot on the table, putting his finger above his top lip and saluting and pretending he was Hitler, chasing Brian around the kitchen, crying, 'Aha, me hearties.' Their home life had changed in an instant, she thought – and yet, the strangeness in all of this was that it had continued. People wandered in and out of rooms;

children still needed feeding and washing; school-bags needed to be packed. More worryingly, bills needed to be paid.

An hour later, she stood waiting at the docks for the postman. The autumn mist shrouded the river in grey, and a weak sun was only just bleeding through. Steam rose from the water like smoke; the boats were perfectly reflected mirror images on a surface that was still as glass. The whole scene had a calming effect on her after the drama of the past month.

Two seagulls swooped and plunged into the river, rearranging the reflection and making ripples on the surface. Alice could see droplets hanging from the bars of the dockside's railings and beautiful, intricate cobwebs laced in dew. She could hear birdsong and the muffled clanking of a crane. The bridge was a blurred silhouette with small, hunched figures making their way across it to work. Leaves mushed under her boots. She had put a piece of cardboard inside each one but hoped the weather wouldn't get the better of them.

Three tugboats were anchored a little way away. A heron picking its way along the foreshore puffed out its chest, stretched its neck and beat its wings. 'Liverpool Marine Engines', said the sign on a boat that was grinding its way back towards the bridge. The Port of Liverpool Authority tugboat slid out from the landing stage. A man appeared on deck sipping a mug of tea.

She went under the bridge to the sound of a train above her. More bright splashes of light on the iron railings. She could smell the river, hear the creak and clank of metal. Taking the letter out of her pocket, she read it one more time.

Dear Bob,

I sent you a letter a few weeks ago but it must have missed your boat and was returned to sender. So I do hope this one arrives. I am sorry to tell you, I have some sad news. My da died. Turns out his heart was weaker than he was letting on, which made it all the worse that he had gone back to work. We only found out when one of his pals said that he was surprised he'd lasted as long as he had. Kept it from us right until the end. And emphysema was on the death certificate. Sticky lungs, Ma said.

The funeral last week was a sad affair, cart horses from the rag and bone yard with black ribbons tied on their manes and tails, and Ma happy that there were three priests on the altar, and Da's union pals with their silk banners meant that the church was so full people had to stand outside to listen. They say you can get the measure of a man by the company he keeps. Show me your friends and I'll show you where you're going, Da used to say. And they were good men, some even cried.

The kiddies are doing pretty well, it seems. Not many tears so far, more interested in trying to get a peek at the body in the front room before the undertakers took him to get ready for the funeral. Maybe growing up in the

shadow of the war has hardened them. Ma
said Brian has to be the man of the house now,
but he's only seven and it doesn't seem fair.
It's my job to look after the little ones now.
Please don't change your plans. We're all
figuring how to move forward. Money as usual
is a problem. Thank goodness for my job.
All love,
Alice

Leaning against the curved brickwork under the bridge, she blinked away the morning sunshine. It was brighter now. A small tree that had struggled up through the paving stones was gloriously backlit, each green leaf vividly picked out. A fellow rode by on a bicycle, a mailbag slung over his shoulder, swerved to miss her, then stopped. 'Letters for which ship?' he asked.

'The *Stella Maris*. Merchant navy. Bob McGurk. Probably in Italy right now.'

He nodded, took it. Another sad story in this city, he thought, judging by the look on Alice's face.

'I'm off to work,' she said, when she got back to the house.

Her mother glanced up from lifting the boiling kettle off the range and narrowed her eyes. 'Do you always wear ribbons to work? And so soon after your father has died?'

Alice touched her thick plait with its yellow ribbon. 'No, Ma. I just thought . . . ribbons. I like wearing them.'

'I don't approve. Not so soon. Don't be long. I want you to take your father's suit to the pawn shop later. Will you do that?'

Alice left the question hanging in the air. Did Ma really want her to do that? Go to the pawn shop?

Ida left the room and Alice could hear her bumping around upstairs. Deciding she would stop by the bakery on the way in and pick up a fresh bread roll, she took a few pennies from the housekeeping box; one of life's luxuries that she could still afford.

Setting off from the baker's, enjoying the warm, buttery taste in her mouth, unexpectedly she found Matty on the corner of the street leaning against his car. He told her she shouldn't go into the office if she was needed at home, that Mr Morley would understand about her ma not coping. Matty was the one person she had felt able to really cry with. He put his arms around her while, wet-cheeked and runny-nosed, she sobbed noisily into his shoulder, but she still insisted on going to work. As he drove her down Scotland Road, she made him promise not to tell Mr Morley what had happened.

'Come in here and sit down,' said Mr Morley abruptly when she arrived at the office. Alice could tell that something was wrong. She slumped in the chair opposite him and waited for him to speak.

'Why didn't you tell me?' He spoke quietly, his gaze gentle but probing. There was no doubt in her mind about his meaning. When she didn't reply, he went on, 'Miss Maguire is on friendly terms with one of the priests at your father's funeral.'

Of course she flipping was, thought Alice.

'I don't know,' she said. 'I didn't like to trouble you. If I'd asked for time off, I might have lost my job. Or you might have told me to stay at home, which is almost as bad. Coming in here every day has helped me through the worst. I'm fine now.'

'You're not. How can you be?' He leaned forward over his desk. 'I'm looking at you, Alice. You are not fine, but don't jump up and start bouncing about, trying to prove me wrong, because I am not sending you home. I should have noticed, that's all. The redness around your eyes and the struggle to smile.'

'Sorry, Mr Morley.'

'And as for firing you – that's ridiculous. In fact, I should fire you for even thinking as much.'

She couldn't help but smile at that.

'It's selfish of me not to, but we start the first stage of building in six months. That's official. You can't say anything, so mum's the word for now. And as I wouldn't know what day it was, or where I'm meant to be, or where I've put the final drawings without you here, and with these changes finally happening – good news, preliminary plans approved yesterday – you'll have to stay, I'm afraid. I need you for that meeting with Mr Higgins from the Corporation at the parish hall. If it's too much, tell me . . . But if you would say a few words? Do you think you could do a short talk on how our ideas will improve everyone's lives around here? You have such a way of reaching out to people, Alice. They smile when you walk into a room.'

'I'd like that.'

'I'm so sorry about your father. Do you need

money? You've Christmas coming up. Expensive for any family.'

'No, we'll manage. Thank you.'

'Good. Here's five pounds, anyway.' He pushed an envelope across the desk. She could see a crisp white note peeking out of it. 'Not because of what happened – it's simply a bonus, something to celebrate our success. Push it back at me and I'll have Miss Maguire throw you out in a second. Now tell me, what on earth am I doing this morning?'

Chapter 10

Ida was hammering a piece of hardboard over a part of the wall where black mould had appeared overnight. She paused and sniffed at her fingers. 'This is what's getting to Gabe's chest,' she said. 'The damp behind here. It's useless. This place. This flipping place.'

'Ma. This isn't going to go on for ever. There's things happening. Improvements. It's going to bring new houses for us all. We'll get a letter.'

'What do you mean?' Ida said, distracted, pushing the hardboard. 'Sometimes I can't understand a word you're saying.'

'This city is going to change soon. And it really is a change for the better.'

Ida looked at her daughter and snorted. 'Is it going to stop Gabe coughing tonight? I'm worried about him not getting through until morning. What's the point in thinking about what might happen in two years' time, when he might be dead before the week is out?'

'Dead? How bad is he?' Alice said, alarmed.

'He'll be fine. But you know what I mean.'

'I've seen the plans. More council houses. New Corpy flats. Ones that go all the way up to the sky. Ones with gardens, front and back.'

'And will Mr Morley be getting me a horse-drawn carriage and a gin and French to go with me new house he's giving me? Perhaps he can throw Montgomery Clift in as well. I wouldn't say no to that.'

'Just you wait, Ma. Just wait and see. Mr Morley wants me to speak about it at a meeting, talk to everyone around here about the plans.'

'You?'

Alice felt a blush rising from her throat to her cheeks. 'Yes, Ma.'

'That won't go down well. A slip of a thing like you! Anyway, what plans? Sounds like he's wanting you to do his dirty work.'

'Ma, why d'you always have to be so unkind to me? When are you going to accept me working for Hedley is a good thing? You're just suspicious of things you don't understand. Just because this job makes me different to folks round here.'

Her mother raised her eyes and shoved her hands into the coal bucket. 'How?'

'It gives me a future. And money. Money makes you free, Ma. And I want to be free.'

'Oh, Alice. You don't have a clue, love.'

Gabe appeared in his ragged pyjamas, round-eyed, barefoot and clutching his toy rabbit.

'Go back to bed, love,' said her mother. 'I'll bring you a teaspoonful of sulphur, then you can sleep off that cough and you'll feel better in the morning.'

Alice was bent over the range when there was a knock on the door and when Gwenda ran to answer it, she returned closely followed by Matty. Alice straightened up and wiped her hands. Matty was holding a rolled-up *Liverpool Echo*. He nearly always wore his uniform, thought Alice. Like a man with a job that was one up from the docks and showing the world he was proud of it. She surprised herself at how pleased she was to see him standing there.

'Mrs Lacey, let me do that,' he said, as Ida, still tapping the hammer, tapped her fingernail and yelped.

He took the hammer and with a few firm thumps hit the nails fully into the plasterboard.

'There you are.'

'You're a marvel, Matty,' she said, standing back to admire his work. 'That's Gabe yelling. I need to see to him. Alice, can you get the kids a piece of bread and marg? And get a brew on. Matty, will you have a tea?'

'No thanks, Mrs Lacey, I can't stay.'

'I'll have a cuppa, Alice.'

Alice raised her eyes as her mother left the room. 'Shall we go for a cigarette? Do you have one?'

'I didn't know you smoked?'

'I don't. Not much. But I could do with one right now.'

'So, what's going to happen next with your ma?' he said when they got outside. They rested their bottoms on the windowsill. He cupped his hands around a match and lit two cigarettes, one of which he put between her lips.

'Says she needs to get a regular job. That means she needs to find someone to look after the kids,' Alice said, sucking on the cigarette and blowing smoke out through her nose. 'I think she means me.'

'You're not going to give up Morley and Worboys'?'

'No. I can't do that. We need my wage. And anyway, I don't want to.'

'Aye,' he said thoughtfully. He paused. 'You're looking beautiful, Alice.' Beautiful and sad, he thought.

She turned her head towards him and looked at him. 'Beautiful?'

'Sorry. It just came into my head and I had to say it.'

'That's all right,' she smiled. 'As long as you mean it.'

He said nothing for a moment and Alice took another short puff of her cigarette.

He looked over at the Mersey glittering in the distance. 'You still not heard from Bob?' he said and blinked away the question.

'No.' There was an awkward pause. 'Not heard yet. I've sent a letter to the ship.'

'I expect you will soon. And work?'

'Work's fine. Hedley has asked me to speak at the parish hall about their plans. He was asking me about my family again. I think he wants to really understand how we live.'

'Hedley, is it now?' he said, raising an eyebrow. 'What d'you mean? How we live?'

'How we act and suchlike. He seemed astonished when I told him that we shared beds with brothers and sisters.'

'Did you fill him in?'

'Obviously not about the damp and the flaming mouse. Our Brian actually enjoys watching the horrible thing dart in and out of the gaps in the skirting boards. He even made a little fort out of old bits of wood, and he just giggled when it scurried up the little drawbridge.'

He laughed. 'Definitely don't tell Morley that.'

'Of course not.'

'Or about the rats as big as cats in the back yard?'

'Don't exaggerate,' she tutted.

'And your ma? How is she, really?'

'When times are hard, keep your dignity and look after the children – that was what my da used to say. But I'm not sure she's doing either at the moment. The kids wander off; Brian seems to have given up on school. She doesn't think I notice but she's reaching for that stout bottle every night. She marched up to the doors of Da's beloved *Echo* saying they should write a story about him and the *Malakand* explosion, but she was squiffy, and of course they didn't show much interest. There are men all over this city who've been damaged by the war or the back-breaking dock work. Who cares?' She sucked on the cigarette harder. 'It's easy to see how things fall apart. The Corpy sent a nurse around. Said she wanted to check the kids' heads, but I'm sure she was snooping. Ma flew into a rage and called her Nitty Nora and told her to jump into the Mersey, and said she knew where all her nosy questions led. St Mary's. You heard about orphans of the living?'

He shook his head.

'That's when they take kiddies off you if they think you can't cope. Send them into orphanages or Sally Army homes.'

'You're not saying that would happen to your family? You're a long way from that.'

'I hope not, Matty. But I need to be here to look after them. Not sure Bob would understand that. This wedding, I certainly don't want that now. It's not the right time.'

He frowned. 'When is, then? Have you changed your mind altogether?'

She tossed away the cigarette, ground it into the pavement with her toe, and paused, slightly taken aback. What was that tone in his voice? Hope? It made her think he wanted her to answer yes.

'No,' she replied. 'But he's like a dog with a bone and I never really wanted to say yes in the first place. I'm not sure I *ever* want to be married. There's so many things I want to do in my life. Marriage is pretty low down on the list.'

'Is it marriage, though, that's the problem? Or is it Bob?'

She looked at him, shocked.

'Well, there's a question,' she said. She sighed. 'Best go back in. See to the kiddies.'

When she went upstairs, she found her mother searching through the chest of drawers. 'Someone's taking stuff round here,' she mumbled. 'I'm sure of it. Where's my necklace?' Rattling the handle, she pulled the drawer right out of its casing.

'Don't be daft. No one's taking things. Ma, you're not thinking straight. *Ma*,' she said. Banging another drawer shut, Ida left the room, muttering. Alice followed her downstairs and into the back yard. She knocked on the door of the privy but there was no answer. 'What's the matter?'

'Nothing. It's fine, leave me alone. Apart from,

102

Barry Hallett just told me again your da knew he was ill. Much sicker than he ever let on. Why didn't he tell us?' she moaned. 'I would never have let him go back to work if I had known.'

'These things happen, Ma. It's no one's fault. But d'you think you could be strong for the kiddies?'

'Go and shut the back gate. I can hear it banging and it's making my head hurt,' came the reply.

For weeks Alice had moved around the place in a kind of fog, barely able to eat, not sleeping more than an hour at a time. But now, seeing her mother wandering around with her cardigan hanging off one shoulder and her usually neat hair wild and straggling, she realized that if anyone was going to keep this show on the road, it would have to be her.

Perhaps she had come back to work too soon after her father had died and needed some time off, Matty suggested gently one day. Alice shook her head; Hedley still expected her to talk at the public meeting, and she very much wanted to do it. However, it felt as if she'd just been about to move on and make something of her life at last – and now it was all in danger of crashing to a halt. She shivered as she heard a church bell and an ominous rumble of thunder in the distance.

Marje Hallett dropped in one evening and showed them a pamphlet. 'British Electric. They're taking women at the electric now, Ida.'

'To do what?' asked Alice, stirring a pan of pea soup.

'Read the meters.'

'How could I do that with Gabe?' asked Ida.

'Well, he's two now, isn't he? You'd manage it. Anyway, Barry's spoken to the foreman at the docks and there's some good news. He's heard from the docker's fund. You'll have two choices. You can either have a small widow's pension, which will keep you going – it's not much, but it's for ever – or you can have a one-off payment. They call it a lump sum.'

Ida's eyes widened.

'How much?' asked Alice.

'Not sure. About fifty pounds, I think.'

'Fifty pounds! Think what I could do with that!' Ida's gaze drifted off. 'I could open my shop.'

'Shop?' asked Alice, confused. 'What shop? You're not listening to Marje.'

'Selling baby clothes.'

Marje's eyes darted towards Alice. 'That sounds nice. And I know you like sewing and you know how to cut a pattern, but . . . is now the right time? Is it reliable?'

'I don't know. Really, I have no idea.'

Marje looked at Ida with concern. 'I think you should probably put that out of your head for now, love.'

'Why? Just imagine!' Ida shook her head and gazed into the distance, wistfully.

'Ida, concentrate.' Marje took a deep breath, thinking about what to say. 'If you take the lump sum and decide to open a shop, that will just go. To be honest, the only ones who take the money in one go are mostly sick and have no future. You're not sick, just sad. The pension payments are better for those in situations like yours – people who need a weekly income to keep the family going.'

When Marje left, Ida made herself a cup of tea and read the letter again by the light of the fire. 'Fifty pounds, Alice!' she said. 'What should I do? I could take the pension. Or I could take the lump sum. But the money each week, I'm not sure, it's not much, only ten shillings, and I would still need to work. It would barely cover the rent.'

Alice was alarmed to see her mother's eyes shining. Ida looked possessed, drunk on the thought of the fifty pounds. 'But Ma, just think. Ten shillings a week. It would be for ever.'

'It's making me giddy to think of what I could do with fifty pounds. Maybe it's the start we need. I could open my little shop. The one I've had my eye on.'

This again, thought Alice. 'What little shop are you talking about?'

'There's a shop around the corner, you know, the old chandler's. It's been empty since the beginning of the war. I could rent it. Just imagine – no more traipsing down to the orphanage, I could keep tabs on the kids, I could nip home and make them dinner, bring Gabe with me. If I needed to shut it for an hour, I could just close up and no one would tell me not to. I've dreamed of this for years. Me and your father talked about it often.'

Alice faltered. She chose her next words carefully. 'Who knows what will happen to it, though?'

'What do you mean?'

'Well, with all these plans. Who knows? They've

already started demolishing the slums in Bootle. Everton Valley. It's all bulldozed now. What if they start here next?'

'Don't be silly,' Ida said. 'No one's going to touch the houses around here. They're sturdy. Not that bad.'

'Not that bad! You're always complaining about this place falling apart!'

'Not at all. Only when the kids have bad chests. We make do. I know up by Holy Cross Church, Feather Street, the tenements – we all know people live like rats there, and they're terrible with the over-crowding. But we're different. We won't be getting council houses. Not yet. We're way down the list round here. Anyway, don't be a killjoy, let me tell you my idea.' She moved the papers from on top of the table and leaned in towards Alice, excited. 'I could put my sewing to good use. I want to sell baby clothes. And children's clothes. I'm good at stitching. I've thought hard about it. Babies never stop coming. And everyone knows me round here. There's always someone who needs a new christening outfit, or a Holy Communion dress, or something mending. God knows I practised enough with you lot.'

Alice was bewildered. The more Ida said, the more fantastical her idea sounded. She wanted to tell her it was ridiculous – people loved going to George Henry Lee's or Owen Owen for these special occasions, or any of the department stores in town. Some even went to New Brighton or Dublin, for heaven's sake. It was a big day out, a day marked on the calendar, and that wouldn't change.

'What about just doing a stall at Paddy's Market

on Saturdays at first? To see how you get on?' she said tentatively.

'Along with all the other Mary Ellens and hawkers? You're joking. I want my own shop. I want that shop round the corner. I pass it every day. I've set my heart on it.'

'No, you're not listening to me, Ma – I'm telling you that place might not even exist soon. What if the Corpy wants to demolish it, when they move everyone out? There's plans. I've seen them. Talked about them with Mr Morley.'

'Don't be daft,' Ida said.

'Me, daft?' retorted Alice.

'Oh, it comes to something when my own daughter thinks she's cleverer than me.'

'I don't know, Ma. Don't make any decisions in haste. Just . . . let's talk this through.'

'You know, I think this shop opportunity is a gift sent from your father from heaven. He's looking after us.'

'Ma, that's ridiculous. That doesn't make any sense.'

'I've got ideas. And I'm a dab hand with a needle. Oh, isn't it going to be wonderful? Isn't it, Gabe?' Ida said in a sing-song voice. She clapped her hands together, picked Gabe up off the rug where he was playing with an old rattle and pulled up his vest, blowing a raspberry on his bare stomach. He giggled and gurgled with laughter.

'Oh, Ma,' Alice said. 'Promise me you'll be sensible . . .' Her voice trailed off into silence because she was so worried, she could think of nothing else to say.

Chapter 11

Three weeks later, on a Saturday morning, Alice left the house for the pawn shop with her father's suit, frustrated after yet another disagreement with Ida. Alice thought it was odd to pawn the suit and they would probably only get pennies, but her efforts to get this across to her mother had been twisted into yet another row over money. She was glad to get out into the fresh air, at least; maybe it would clear her head. Ida had given her a list of other errands to run as well.

The Mary Ellen was on the corner, coming back from Paddy's Market, hugging her shawl and lugging a bag full of fish. The usual musty smell followed her, and Alice wrinkled her nose in spite of herself. She bent her head, feeling in her bones the bitter wind coming off the Mersey. The Mary Ellen must be cold as death with so much of her time spent out of doors. A little way ahead, someone came out of one of the houses and bashed a piece of carpet against the end-of-terrace wall; a cloud of dust rose from it and seemed to swallow the old woman up.

By the time she returned home a few hours later, Alice was weary and chilled. As soon as she stepped into the house, she sensed there was something wrong.

There was a large, unfamiliar felt hat with a peacock feather lying on the table. On the dresser was an unopened cardboard box. And her mother was balanced precariously on a chair, putting up curtains at the window. The curtains were ready-made, heavily embroidered with jaunty cherries, and Ida was hooking them onto the rail. On the floor beside her, Alice could see a pair of children's patent leather shoes gleaming in an open box.

'Oh, Ma. What's this? You took the money? You told me to take Da's suit just to get me out of the way while you went shopping!'

Her mother shrugged. 'The cheque came last week. Into the Post Office account. Just sitting there. All that money. Can you imagine? Da would have done the same. Kiddies' clothes hanging off them lately, they're all bones and sharp angles. They need feeding up. And why not with cake? Look at those beautiful little coats. Look at the velvet buttons. And I bought you a pair of shoes. Wait until you see them – where are they . . . ?'

Alice gritted her teeth.

'Don't look like that.' Ida clambered down from the chair. 'I can't describe how wonderful it felt to walk into the department store knowing that I could buy whatever I wanted. How many times have we just stood there, not even dared to go inside, our noses pressed against the window, wishing? But I could walk in with my head held high. Didn't even bother going down to Owen Owen's basement for the seconds and the scraggy bins. Took the lift to the first, second, third floor, all the way to the top.'

'Ma . . . I'm in shock,' said Alice, feeling sick.

'Oh, and didn't I just do that. It was marvellous. And when I finished buying the coats, and a little violin for Gwenda from Rushworth's – and a wonderful thing! A soda syphon to make your drinks fizzy! – I went upstairs to Cooper's on Church Street. You can't imagine. I had a Knickerbocker Glory, which is ice cream and little biscuits on top and sprinkles of nuts. And I've never tasted anything so delicious in all my life.'

'A violin? Why?'

'Bring a bit of joy into the house.'

'But Ma! She can't play the violin!'

'She can learn! A bit of the fiddle would cheer things up around here. Imagine: *Delany had a donkey* . . .' Ida trilled.

'You've lost your mind! And a soda syphon! Are you mad?'

'How dare you? It was a one-off! I won't be buying things like this every day. Just once in my life, I wanted to know what it felt like. Stop pulling that face, Alice. You could curdle milk.'

'Shouldn't you be keeping every penny for your flaming *shop*?' Alice could hardly bear to think about her mother rolling the pound notes from the bank into a fat bundle and setting out to burn through so much of it in a single morning.

'One splurge is not going to make a difference. The shop is marvellous. Mr Maloney has put me in touch with the landlord. Rubbish, by the way, that nonsense you said about demolishing the street. The landlord has heard nothing. And I have plenty of money left.

I just needed a treat. Now, pass me that bag. Here – these are for you.'

She thrust a bag towards Alice, who opened it to see a pair of shoes. They were pink satin with small Cuban heels, a strap and a satin-covered button to fasten it. Beautiful, but about as useful to Alice as a chocolate teapot. She wanted to scream at the stupidity. The rain would soak up from the bottom of them; they looked too small; they wouldn't go with anything she owned. Had her mother gone mad?

'Do you like them, dear?'

Alice turned them over in her hands. 'I'm not sure if they'll fit,' she said flatly.

'Well, in that case, give them back to me.' Ida snatched them back. 'I fancy those shoes. I'd look like Greta Garbo in them. I could buy a fur stole to match.'

'Perhaps you should take them back?'

'Don't be so ungrateful, Alice. I'm not taking them back. I'll wear them myself. Or Gwenda will. And don't you dare ask for anything from me again.'

'I didn't ask for them.'

Her mother pursed her lips. 'You've been sulking about this from the moment I mentioned it. See if I care, lady.'

Alice frowned. Had Ida been drinking? Probably. It was getting worse, her nightly tipple. Her words sounded bitter and had the sour hint of alcohol in them.

Brian appeared in the doorway, giddy with delight.

'Alice, will you look at this? Ma bought me a wristwatch, and Roy Rogers! And his horse!'

'And me a dolly!' cried Gwenda. 'It's called a Saucy Walker Doll and her legs move! Look!'

She marched the doll over the table and the range.

'It's like Christmas, but better!' cried Brian as he bashed the Roy Rogers figure against the doll.

Gabe laughed and clapped his little hands, picking up on all the excitement. He put the empty Saucy Walker box on his head as he toddled around, turning awkwardly and bumping into furniture.

'Isn't he funny!' laughed Ida. 'Look at Gabe! You're so funny! My sides are splitting,' she spluttered, slapping her thigh.

'Ma, where's this heading?' said Alice quietly.

'Oh, don't be miserable. Now where's that violin? Give us a tune, Gravy. Go on, have a go. *Delaney had a donkey* . . . Biscuit, Gabe, sit on my knee. Let's have some cake!'

What a fool her mother was, Alice thought. What an absolute fool. Sitting there eating apple cake, as if things were about to get better. She would only make herself sick; her stomach had shrivelled to the size of a walnut years ago.

Gwenda dropped the doll and took the violin out of its case. She scraped the bow across the strings. It made a screeching, ugly sound.

'Ooh, Gravy, that's dreadful! It's set me teeth on edge,' laughed Ida. 'It's so bad, it's funny.'

How could she find it funny? Alice was appalled at the whole scene. How could she find any of this mayhem funny? Gabe was starting to cry; he'd tripped over the range and banged his head. Brian looked as though he was going to be sick from eating so much cake, and announced his belly hurt. Meanwhile, the scraping of the violin grew louder, harsher, ever more discordant and jarring. It perfectly matched the feeling of dread that lay heavily on Alice's chest, making it difficult for her to breathe.

Lying on her bed fully clothed the next morning, Alice opened her eyes to a low thrumming sound, like something mechanical operating some distance away. Then someone rapped noisily on the front door. It stopped abruptly as she heard the door open and then Brian called up the stairs, 'Someone to see you, Alice.'

She came out onto the landing, bleary-eyed, to see Bob standing at the front door. He was wearing his navy-blue jumper, bell bottoms and hobnailed boots. She yelped.

'When did you get back? Aren't you supposed to be on your way to Portugal!' she cried, galloping down the stairs two at a time.

'Late last night. I've come straight from the ship, pretty much. And we're loading up and leaving tomorrow. Just couldn't not nip off to see you, Alice. Couple of the fellas are covering for me.'

He wrapped his arms around her neck and kissed her on the cheek, and she kissed him back on the mouth.

'Alice and Bob, sitting in a tree, K, I, S, S, I, N, G . . .' chanted Gwenda, sticking her head through the banisters.

'Gwen, you'll get stuck. Oh, Bob. It's been awful. Such a shock.'

'I'm just sorry I left when I did. Your da. I could've . . . If I'd known, Cherry Bomb . . .'

'None of us knew. And there's been so much going on. Look at you, brown as a berry! And your hair. It's like straw!'

He nuzzled into her and buried his head in the crook of her neck. 'I know. I'm so sorry about your da. Oh, my Alice. Looking more like Elizabeth Taylor than ever. The smell of you.' He pushed a curl away from her forehead and tucked it behind her ear.

As she stood back and smiled at him, it occurred to her that there was something different about him. He was still handsome – he was tanned and had longer hair, the beginnings of a beard. But now he also looked like a man who had seen something of the world. The way his lip curled when he smiled, maybe.

'What was it like?' she asked, pulling away from him.

'I could tell you stories that would make your hair stand on end. Some of the ports – the things that went on there! And two of our fellas got so drunk they missed the boat back. Now they're stuck there with no money. I'm only hoping the floozies whose fault it was let them stay at their lodgings. But now the lads are broke, I doubt it.'

'Floozies? What floozies?'

'Never mind. Close your eyes,' he said, stepping over the threshold and into the house.

'What?'

He shut the door, leaned his back against it. 'Now open them.'

When she opened her eyes he was holding something out in front of her. 'Do you like it?'

At first she didn't know what she was looking at, but then he held one end of it with fingertip and thumb and dangled it in front of her. 'I got it in Madeira.' He placed it in her palm.

'It's beautiful,' she said, turning it over in her hand. It was a gold bracelet studded with rubies, made of tiny chain links that fashioned it into a gold mesh band with a delicate clasp. 'I've never seen such a thing.'

'Try it on.'

She slipped it onto her wrist, then turned it to the light of the lamp so that it caught the rubies and the gold mesh glittered.

'I'm glad you like it. I got it from a little shop in the market. I'd like to take you there one day.'

She looked up at him from under her long black lashes, not knowing what to think.

'Alice . . . I know you've all had a terrible time. But don't you think the wedding might be what you all need?'

'What do you mean?'

He gazed at her, tipping his head to one side. 'Isn't it time we set a date? My mother is not getting any better – I'd like her to see me getting married. What mother wouldn't want that? I want your Gwen to be a bridesmaid – I'd like to see that tomboy in a white frock. Bernice, as well. Long as she doesn't show off her . . . bonbon whats?' He gestured at her cleavage.

'Embonpoint,' she sighed.

'That's it. Save her bonbons for the dance hall. Matty will be my best man, what d'you say to that? I'll make sure he doesn't tell the story of the girl straddling the marrow in the Dig for Victory allotment. That would make a whore blush.'

'But it's so soon. After Da . . . and my ma . . .' she stuttered. 'She's not right at the moment either. She's got this wild idea in her head about opening a shop, so I reckon in about two months' time we'll be down to nothing again, after it's shut down. She won't listen.'

'Look at my horse,' said Brian, hanging over the banister.

'He's smashing. And here, I've got you a present too,' said Bob.

He reached into his pocket and brought out two lemons. Brian came charging down the stairs two at a time. 'What's them?'

'Lemons. You can eat 'em with fish. Fella told me that was nice. With pilchards. They'd all love a taste of a lemon round here. Sharp-tasting.'

Brian leaned forward and stared hard at the lemons. 'Then I'm not gonna eat 'em. I'm gonna raffle 'em for everyone!' he said, eyes brightening.

'They put our da in the front room, Bob,' said Gwenda, skipping around him as Alice poured water into the kettle. 'I didn't like it. Ma dressed him up in a shirt and a tie and put her rouge on his cheeks and his lips and he looked like one of them scary fellas in the booth at the fair.'

'Ma insisted the priest came round, but what with the little ones shrieking and racing round the coffin . . .' said Alice.

'Bry tied a piece of string to me da's toe, and it frightened me because when he jiggled it, I thought Da was coming alive,' said Gwenda, giggling.

'Don't know what Ma was thinking of, keeping him here for nearly three days. This lot were giddy with it, weren't you? Covering mirrors and holding glasses to his face and saying he was still breathing, and Bry swearing he saw his soul float up to the ceiling.'

'We did. The room went all purple, like,' said Gwenda. 'Full of the Holy Spirit. We saw his soul wobble like jelly.'

Bob guffawed. 'Like jelly on a plate? Wibble, wobble . . .'

'No you didn't, Gwen. Come and see Ma, Bob,' said Alice, leading him into the front room.

'Bob?' said Ida, looking up from her sewing.

'Mrs Lacey. I'm so sorry. Must have been a shock.' He was alarmed to see how different she looked. Thinner, paler, hair like a bird's nest, greying at the temples.

'More of a shock to us than him. Turns out he'd been ill for a while. Kept it from us. Some say that's a kind thing he did, but I'm not so sure,' she said, sadly.

'Can I have a lemon an' all?' said Gwenda.

'You can share Brian's.'

'No, she can't,' said Brian.

'Have you brought me summat, Bob?' pestered Gwenda.

'Here.' He rummaged in his pockets. 'Snake whistle.' Delighted, she took it off him and began to blow.

He knelt down to face her. 'Eh, listen to this, Gwen.

We can play together. I can hum through me nose. Learned it in Morocco.' Pinching his nose, he began to make strange vibrating noises like a trumpet as Gwenda continued to blow the whistle.

'The kiddies seem to be enjoying themselves,' he said a few minutes later, after Ida had left to answer the door to the coalman. They were watching the twins race around, taking turns to blow into the whistle. 'They've taken it all right? Your da, I mean.'

Alice frowned. 'They get on with things. They don't have much choice. Thanks for cheering them up. They have their moments. Can't seem to get Brian to go to school, and Gwenda is always scraping away making a racket with that awful violin.'

'Violin?'

'Aye. That's me ma's fault. Don't ask.'

'And you, Alice? You managing?'

'I'm too busy to feel sorry for myself. But I miss me da like you couldn't imagine.'

'Oh, Cherry Bomb, if I could kiss away that sadness, I would. Shall I see you later, darling? At the Locarno? We'll have a dance and a drink. I love you. And it's good to be home.'

How had the months gone by so quickly? thought Bob as he walked along Rodney Street, an elegant Georgian terrace, to the Chauffeur Club. The building had a well-proportioned frontage, with deep steps leading up to its entrance and a triangular pediment above the door.

'Bob?' Matty said, standing on the steps and pushing his cap to the back of his head. 'I didn't know you were back already! When did you get in, mate?'

Bob shook his hand enthusiastically, clapping him on the back. 'Last night. I'm still on my sea legs. I need a drink, pal, let's get inside. Have I got stories to tell you.'

They settled themselves at a table by the window, with a beer and a packet of crisps each. Bob's face was weather-beaten from his weeks at sea and his hair was shorter and blonder, but still tousled on top. Matty thought he looked older and, oddly, less sure of himself. He watched him take a gulp of beer.

'Does Alice know you're here?'

'Aye. I've just been there. The house was full as usual. Not much point hanging around. Quick peck on the lips was all I got, not even a squeeze of her kahunas. I'm seeing her later. Maybe we'll manage a quick knee-trembler down the back alley.'

That's a bit off, Matty wanted to say. Bob was as crude as ever.

Bob laughed. 'I'm joking, lad. Don't look so serious. Besides, I'm here because I wanted to see you. Find out how she's been.' He seemed about to say more, but took another drink instead.

'She's been grand. Apart from her da, of course. Came as a shock to them all. Where did you end up? Greece, I heard?'

Bob put his glass down. 'All over. It's amazing, pal. Stopped off in the Med, Italy, then Cyprus. Hard work, mind you, twelve or fourteen hours on, and it took a while to stop chucking up everywhere, but when you make port, you make up for it, I can tell you.' He touched his nose with his forefinger and the corner of his eye with his little finger and smiled as if to say, *you know what I mean, don't you?*

Matty looked at him, long and hard. The comment seemed inappropriate, out of step with the moment.

Bob avoided his stare. 'Anyway, how is our Alice? Behaving herself? She still talking about me?'

''Course she talks about you. You're engaged, aren't you?'

Bob forced an uncomfortable chuckle and ripped open the packet of crisps Matty had bought him, sprinkling the blue sachet of salt over the contents.

'We are. I know that. And I love her, Matty, don't get me wrong. But you know how it is. One girl, for the rest of my life. Think about it – one girl.' He carefully selected a crisp and examined it. 'That's why fellas join the merchant navy. I realize that now. And these Italian girls, Matty, they're all over you. Especially lads like me with fair-ish hair. They love it. Think I'm Kirk Douglas. And Greek women. Just flaming beautiful.'

Matty nodded. What was it Alice had said? You go away, but you come back a better person? Or was it, you go away and come back a different person?

Chapter 12

Ida sat opposite Sister Cyril, in front of her large mahogany desk. Gabe squirmed on her knee.

'I don't think I've ever seen such a pretty boy. And I've seen a lot of children, as you can imagine. Do people think he's a girl? Come here, Gabriel.'

He leaned forward and from her drawer she produced a piece of cinder toffee. His eyes lit up and he popped it into his mouth and sucked, smiling delightedly at his mother as it prickled his tongue.

'All the time,' replied Ida. 'At least, when he's behaving himself. When he's running around with a catapult or bashing his brother over the head, maybe not so much.'

The nun looked a little overwrought, Ida thought. Her face was flushed, contrasting with the white coif and black habit she wore. Her lips were pressed together in a line, her eyebrows knitted. She seemed a little thinner as well, especially in her face, with its razor-sharp hollowed-out cheekbones.

'So you see, the reason I haven't been here lately is that I've been opening my shop,' Ida explained.

She had made the decision to tell Sister Cyril about her plans in the hope that the nun would help her – perhaps placing an order for the uniforms at St

Mary's, or for christening outfits for the babies. But seeing her expression, she felt doubt creeping in. Gabriel squirmed more energetically.

The nun's lips were pursed. 'A shop?'

Ida faltered. She had thought that if she could put forward a plan that would benefit the orphanage, they would all be happy, but she was fast losing confidence. 'Yes, a shop, Sister. Selling baby clothes. But I was thinking – I know you rely on charity – the little ones' uniforms, I could make those for you? I wondered if we could continue to work together?'

'Work together? But you're leaving us? Is that what you mean? I'm confused. I thought we had given you time off to mourn your husband, not open a shop. Pity. The sewing classes were important. It's vital that these girls make something of themselves.'

'Don't do that, Gabe,' Ida said, snatching away the sweet that he had sucked into a sharp point. 'I know that, Sister, but . . . my little shop is a way out for my family. Wouldn't you like me to continue working as a seamstress for you?'

'We liked you teaching here. It encouraged the girls to have some connection,' the nun said.

'But now that Albert has . . . passed . . . I need to provide for the children.' Ida glanced down at Gabe, now sitting cross-legged on the floor. 'And to do that, I need something more permanent. A proper line of work. The shop is around the corner from where we live. It's going to be a lovely little place. You could come and place orders for St Mary's?' She was aware she was beginning to sound a little desperate. A little more pleading. She winced inwardly.

'Orders?'

'The uniforms, and – and whatnot. If you need communion dresses or confirmation dresses, please think of me. Crowning of the May, the children will all need new dresses for those feast days. Sister, I've brought you a dress that I made to see if you like it. I could do twenty of them.' This made good sense to Ida as she scrambled in her bag and produced a pretty frock with an overskirt of embroidered satin, and a gauze veil with crucifixes and forget-me-nots stitched along the edges. It had taken hours to make them, with her eyes feeling the strain as the autumn light faded and her fingers red raw, but she was proud of the result.

But the nun sat stiffly in her chair. 'I don't think we'll need anything like that. Why can't you get your daughter to work at your shop on Tuesday afternoons, and you can come back here?'

'Oh, no, Sister, Alice is very busy with work.'

'What kind of work?'

'She has a good job, Sister. We need her wage.'

The nun looked at her. 'Really?'

There was something unsettling in the way she said it. A short silence followed as she tapped her fountain pen on the edge of the desk for a few seconds, thinking. 'Ida. We have no shortage of seamstresses here – Angela, June. They have made great strides. Sister Bernadette. We order our uniforms from T. J. Hughes.'

Gabe had now crawled over to the desk and was examining the wastepaper basket. 'Gabe, don't. He puts things on his head,' Ida said, apologetically.

'You can't rely on St Mary's to fund your shop.

Perhaps you should have considered that first. I'm not best pleased about being left high and dry.' She paused, narrowed her eyes. 'You know, if you're struggling with the baby, Ida – as I've said to you in the past, you can always bring him here. We'd be happy to have him. He's so bonny.'

Ida was confused for a moment. 'Oh, you mean if I'm working?'

'I mean that we have places for people in need like you. There are plenty of orphans of the living here. Father Donnelly could organize it. We always try to be kind, particularly to those in our community. If you need us to have your children, we can do that. I've said it before.'

Ida shuddered. It seemed like a cruel suggestion, not a kindness. 'No, Sister, I don't need that kind of help. I've Alice. It's going to take a bit of time and it will be a struggle, a risky venture on my own, but I'll manage. I'm seeing it as a way of making something for my family.'

'Yes, well – never forget where it started. It started here, Ida.'

'I won't,' she replied in a whisper, and rose quickly to go, scooping Gabe up and excusing herself.

'Wait – before you go. There is something I can do for you . . .'

Ida felt a spark of hope. Even Gabe stopped wriggling for a moment and looked at the nun quizzically. Had she changed her mind?

'I can pray for you,' she said.

When Ida got outside, having carried Gabriel along with her, she set him down and took a deep breath of the chilly air. It seemed as sweet as nectar compared to the atmosphere in that stuffy office.

What an unkind thing to say. Or did the nun actually believe that prayer would help? She pulled the little boy close again and kissed his mop of golden curls. Why was it that nuns were so terrifying? After all, underneath those habits, they were just the same as other women: made of flesh, bone and blood.

Chapter 13

'Sorry, Alice. Bob sent this,' said Matty, thrusting a slip of paper under her nose.

She was standing waiting on the doorstep, expecting Bob, not Matty, and her face said so. She opened the note and read it.

> *My Cherry Bomb,*
> *All gone to hell in a handcart. The ship loaded up by seven this evening, which means we are leaving earlier than we hoped. Some of the fellas chose to stay, but I took the extra work. I hope you understand. Say hello to your ma. Wear my bracelet and the ring, and I'll be back before you know it – drinking in the Pool and buying pale ales all round. Sorry, honey.*
> *I love you,*
> *Bob*

Another thing she hadn't expected was to see Bernice coming along the road, wearing a tea dress with a nipped-in waist and a full skirt. 'What colour do you think this dress is? Looks blue, doesn't it? But look – when I spin, it's green. Yellow in the pleats, see?'

Alice smiled. 'It's lovely. But Bob's had to leave,' she explained.

'That doesn't matter. Us three can still go dancing tonight. Can't we?'

Matty frowned and raked his hand back through his hair. 'I have to meet Morley at seven. Sorry, Alice. I just wanted to give you the letter.'

'Did I frighten him off?' said Bernice, as they watched him hurry away down the street.

'No,' Alice answered quietly.

'The dress. I'm crazy about it. You think Matty liked it? You think he might come to the Locarno later tonight? A girl can hope, can't she? Let's go.'

'But Bob . . . I'm not sure . . .'

'Don't you dare say you're not coming because he's not. All the more reason for you to go, so I can cheer you up. It's the Rockets on tonight. And you look so pretty in that poodle skirt. You've done your hair differently, too.'

Alice touched the ponytail she had coiled into the nape of her neck and tied with a ribbon. 'No, I'm not sure.'

'I am. Come on,' Bernice said, nudging her.

'But . . .'

'No buts. You need a night out and so do I. I'm gasping, and if I don't find a fella soon, I'm going to dry up like an old prune. In me prime and it's all passing me by. I'm wasted at that bloody factory. And Matty's still not taken the bait.'

Before Alice could protest Bernice had linked arms with her and dragged her out of the door, and they were trotting off in the direction of the tram.

Ten minutes later they were queuing outside the Locarno.

'You still feeling blue about your da?' Bernice asked, seeing Alice's serious expression as they waited.

Alice sighed. 'Sometimes it's like . . . like I have this empty space where my heart used to be. But I've got to get on with it. If I think about it too much, I start to . . .' She blinked away tears.

Bernice took Alice's face between her hands and pushed a tendril of her dark hair behind her ear. 'I'm sorry, love. Sod's bloody law, isn't it? The war were a devil of a time, all manner of people bombed, and your dad got through that and then dropped dead with what?'

'Oh, who knows. They said he'd always had a bad heart. And his arm. All useless.'

'And how's your ma?'

'Not good,' Alice said. 'It's the kiddies . . . And with Christmas coming up . . .' The sentence tailed off. Now was not the time to tell Bernice the full story of her mother's latest madness. 'Ma's not thinking straight. Accused me of stealing her necklace the other day. It's a horrible, gaudy glass thing. Why would I?'

'And how is it without Bob?'

'He wouldn't like me being here, that's for sure. He told me not to come dancing.'

Bernice's eyes widened. 'I hope you told him where to stick that. If we didn't have the dance hall, where would we go?'

'I know. That's what I thought.' She could smell the noxious fumes of the gasworks. 'This is where Bob proposed.'

'He never did! It stinks. So romantic, that one.'

As they went inside, the sound of jive music lifted Alice's spirits. On the dance floor there was a girl she knew, Cynthia Rogan, with her fella, Alfie, twirling like spinning tops around the hall. Alice and Bernice clicked over the polished tiles. As always, the first stop for Bernice was the ladies', and she grabbed Alice's hand and pulled her in behind her. There was a crowd of girls three deep around the mirrors standing in clouds of cheap perfume. 'Make way,' she said. 'Senior partners coming through.' A couple of them snapped their compacts shut and popped the lids back on their lipsticks. Bernice was an irresistible force and they obligingly moved out of the way.

'How do I look?' Bernice puckered her lips and patted her hair into place.

'Lovely.'

'Come on then, chin up, let's go.'

Alice was surprised to see Matty sitting at one of the small tables. He stood up when he saw them. 'I thought you were heading off to meet Morley. But look at you, as handsome as Frank Sinatra – and that uniform of yours gives me the shivers. In a nice way,' laughed Bernice.

He smiled awkwardly. 'Morley had left by the time I got there. Hoped I'd still catch you. And here you are.'

'You want a dance, Matty? Is that OK, Alice?' she said breezily, taking him by the hand and pulling him to his feet. She twirled him onto the floor.

'Is it?' asked Matty, looking back over his shoulder at Alice with a grimace.

'Go on,' she called after them, smiling. 'I'll be fine.'

*

129

When Alice arrived home, she closed the door quietly and turned on the oil lamp. In the shadowy room she could see Ida dozing in her chair.

She sat down and rubbed her feet. Her boots were too small now; she didn't know why. She had stopped growing long ago, but maybe too many times getting them wet – that puddle outside the door she always stepped in – meant the leather was shrinking. Sitting back, she let her gaze travel around the room, taking an inventory. The violin lay on the table. Roy Rogers was straddling a lampshade, and his horse lay upturned on the dresser. Only yesterday, the rag-and-bone men had knocked on the door and asked if they wanted to donate Albert's clothes, but Ida had refused. That would be a waste; she could take in the trousers, shorten the sleeves and they would make do for Brian to grow into. His boots she could stuff with newspaper, and Brian would get at least another year out of them. It was all a strange contrast with the previous week, when she'd been behaving as if they were rich as Croesus and promising to buy him a suit from Owen Owen.

Her stomach tightened when Ida stirred. 'Ma? What are you doing sleeping down here – are you all right?'

Ida didn't answer straight away but sat up, blinking, and then she too removed her shoes and began rubbing her feet. The curtains were still open and from the window you could see all the way down to the docks, the sloping roofs and the river. Ida gazed out as though suddenly distracted by the sight of the Mersey, even though she'd seen it every day of her life.

'You been to the Locarno with Bob?' she said after a moment.

'Not with Bob,' Alice said quietly. 'I was with Bernice.' She paused. 'And Matty.'

Ida raised an eyebrow. 'Matthew? How long will Bob be away this time?'

'A month or so, I think.'

'It was nice to see him. Even for a short time. It's what we all needed.'

'Yes, well, he cheered the kids up, but he's left in a whirlwind.'

'You made any more plans for the wedding?'

'Oh, that – no.'

'Why not?'

She couldn't really think of an answer.

'You miss him?'

Had she missed him? Of course. But there had been so much going on. 'Bob and I have no firm plans. He seems to be enjoying being at sea.'

For once, thankfully, Ida made no comment.

Chapter 14

Over the next few weeks, the house saw people coming and going, discussing things with Ida and delivering parcels. Meanwhile, the children seemed to be lying in bed on a school morning more often than not, food was scarce and the washing mounted up in piles around the house.

'State of this place,' murmured Alice. During one of her sudden cleaning urges, she talked to Gwenda about helping out a little more with the housework. She showed her how to blacken the range, cook some basic meals, and sweep under the dresser. But Gwenda soon grew bored, and when she demanded that Brian should do his fair share as well, an argument broke out between the twins that led to a shoe being thrown across the room, swiftly followed by a lump of coal whizzing past Gwenda's ear.

Ida was oblivious to this, out on the step taking delivery of another bundle from the postman. For now, the idea that she should make all the clothes for her shop herself had been put aside: no time for her to sew so many dresses, not the right material, still waiting for the patterns. So she had bought satin matinee jackets with bows from Paddy's Market and Owen Owen's; the woman down the road had sold her half a dozen romper suits; and she had found a bassinet and made up a baby's trousseau, which she had put in the shop window. She had laid everything out on the wooden display trays that had been left behind in a cupboard. Drawers that had once been filled with nails and screws were now lined with tissue paper and filled with blankets in baby blues and pinks. Ida had had someone put in a slotted rack to hold knitting and sewing patterns. She'd bought a baby's mobile and wondered if there was room for nursery furniture, and she had replaced the old oil lamps with fashionable light fittings and laid a new piece of linoleum on the floor. Barry Hallett had helped refresh the peeling paint of the front door with a new coat. Alice had tried to avoid the whole business, but Ida had insisted she come and take a look at it.

'How much did all this cost?!' she asked, checking the surfaces with her fingertips. 'Ma, you said you were going to budget!'

'I'm trying. But you don't want me to be like your auntie. She certainly puts the *miser* in economizer. You need to spend a bit to make a bit. And it's my dream come true – don't touch that shelf! It's wet,' Ida said, taking a slurp of tea.

At least the shop premises were now clean and Ida, delighted that all the panes of glass were still intact as she'd hoped they would be, had got to work with vinegar and a rag. There had been a fine layer of dust on all the shelves; she rubbed her finger on the countertop and it left a bright spot. 'Just needs a good dusting and sweeping. Come on, Brian. I'll give you three shillings if you help get these windows clean.'

133

His eyes widened. 'Three shillings!' he said.

'Three shillings! That's too much!' said Alice.

'Why not? No tick man any more. I can even get Da's suit out of the pawn shop.'

'Why do you need Da's suit?'

'Stop it, Alice.'

Alice thought of Morley: the way he approached life, walking in and making demands. These were people who got things done and made good decisions – not like her mother. Ida had been surprised when Miss Quick had told her she would need to go down to the Corporation and get a licence – you couldn't just set a shop up, you had to have things like insurance. But after she had done that and handed over yet more money, she'd spent the morning with Brian scrubbing down the shelves and throwing out rubbish. Mr Tattersall had come along and cast an approving eye over the shop. 'You've done a grand job. And when do you start?'

'Soon. I just need to get more stock. More baby clothes.'

'Where will you get them from?'

'I'll make most. Knit. And sew. I've started with buying a few bits like christening shawls. And I know a woman who makes kiddies' frilly knickers. I saw some lovely dirndl skirts in T. J.'s. Brian's doing a grand job. Who's for a bit of parkin I bought from Satterthwaite's?'

Alice clenched her fists and bit her tongue. She didn't want to spoil the day.

The new shop at the far end of Liverpool Lane, where the houses were clustered together, with its sign saying 'Lacey's Trousseaus', made Ida happy; at least that was a good thing in the short term, Alice supposed. Ida hummed 'White Cliffs of Dover' when she moved around the house, took time to brush the children's hair, smiled and even stopped to watch Brian's vanishing coin trick that Bob had taught him. A few people had wandered in over the week, curious to see how she was getting on: Marje Hallett, the O'Sheas from down the road, Mrs Maloney, Miss Quick. Bernice had turned up with flowers. Mr Tattersall suggested a formal opening, so, with a burst of energy, Ida ordered bottles of orange squash and made a tray of porridge oat cakes and put a sign up saying 'Grand Opening Saturday'.

There was a commotion and even a queue outside at ten o'clock. 'Free oat cakes!' someone shouted. Brian passed them around on a tray and people accepted them gratefully. The thrill of people buying some of the booties, and a small christening shawl, was like nothing Ida had ever felt before. The money seemed to go warm in her palm and as she stuffed it into the tin, she felt a strange buzzing sensation in her head.

'You've done it, Ida!' said Mrs Hallett. 'Who would have thought!'

A smiling woman at the front of the queue asked her if she could order three more of the romper suits and Ida told her of course, she would deliver them the next day. She felt herself bursting with pride. The woman left the queue, but then she realized that she needed to check the colours, so Ida trotted after her to the front of the shop, where she was standing in a small huddle with two other women just inside the door. Ida's smile remained fixed as she stood there, pen held aloft over her notepad.

'Did you get your letter? About the compulsory purchase order? They've all had them in Beckton Street and the tenements. Everyone's talking about it. Who's next?' the woman said to her friend. Ida's smile faltered. She felt her heart lurch.

So that was why some of them were looking so serious, standing together in small groups gossiping about the eviction notices, nodding and sucking their teeth as they munched on her cakes, she thought. The woman turned. Mrs Hallett nodded at Ida.

'Did you get one, Ida? Compulsory purchases? You heard from your landlord?'

'Oh, *that* letter. Probably. We've had plenty of those,' she said brightly. 'Eviction for rent arrears, night watchman for overcrowding, the Corpy rates going up. I ignore them all.'

'People are making arrangements. Some are leaving already. Mrs Cook in the next street – they've offered her a beautiful house in Norris Green. Her own front door. She can't believe it. She's delighted. And the prefabs in Bootle are luxurious, I heard. Ironing boards built into the walls.'

'Managed decline round here, what does it mean? Will you ask your Alice? Doesn't she work for them architects?' asked Miss Quick.

The room had gone quiet. Alice, standing in the back room, pressed herself against the wall and listened. The worrying thought flitted through her

136

mind that she might be blamed for whatever it was they were talking about.

'Morley and Worboys? What have they got to do with it?'

'Maisie knows the Maguire woman. Their name is on it. It means they're tearing up this area . . .' She stopped mid-sentence, tipped her head. 'What was that?'

Just as she said it, a boy came hurtling down the street. They all turned to see him skid to a halt as he gripped the lamp post to stop himself, gasping for breath.

'They're bulldozing Carlton Street! Right now. I've gorra stitch 'cos I've pegged it all the way here. They're smashing down the houses. You can feel it. The ground is vibrating. Feel that?'

'Aye, and that's probably the end of this place,' muttered Mrs Hallett to the woman next to her. 'Just don't tell Ida that. She was so hopeful five minutes ago.'

Such cruel timing, Mr Tattersall thought, twisting his cap in his hands. He saw Marje Hallett puff herself up and stare over at Miss Quick with a 'told you so' expression. The war had made some people hard around here, but that was no surprise, was it?

Chapter 15

'I got yer, I shot yer, I got yer, I shot yer . . .' cried
Brian to Gwenda, squinting back into the musty darkness of the shop. They had waited until Ida had fallen
asleep in the chair, then crept out of the house to
come back into the shop without her knowing. 'Come
on, balance on this chair and give me a leg up.'

Gwenda hesitated. 'But Ma? What will she say if
she finds out we're in here?'

'She won't know. C'mon . . . Anyway, we're not
trespassing or nothing. It's Ma's shop.'

Gwenda turned away, unconvinced. She started
opening and shutting drawers, fingering the baby
clothes, rubbing silky material between finger and
thumb curiously, pressing a pair of knickerbockers
against her cheek and breathing in the new smell of
them.

'. . . We'll still catch it if she notices we stole the
key, Bry.'

'She won't, though, will she? C'mon. We're going
upstairs and into the loft. See what's what in the Mary
Ellen's house next door.'

They went through the back of the shop and into
a small, damp-smelling stockroom. Gwenda stopped
to open a drawer that was full of cotton reels and

rags, but Brian tugged her sleeve and urged her to move on. From there they went up to the first floor, although the staircase was dilapidated with several steps missing. 'Shin up the banister,' Brian instructed. 'In case you fall through.'

Upstairs there were two empty rooms, floorboards missing in both. One had an old rocking chair in it, another a stained potty and a cracked enamel jug on a washstand; but no one had lived here for years. There were ragged grey curtains and a threadbare, moth-eaten rug. In the back room there was a stepladder which went up to a trap door in the ceiling.

'Looks like someone's had the same idea as us.'

'Aye, it were Tommy told me it was the craic.'

'Bet it's pitch black up there,' said Gwenda, following Brian as they gingerly went up the rickety ladder. 'And I bet it smells like dog breath. Why we going into the loft anyway?'

'Tommy says there's no walls between the houses, so you can crawl right along and we can spy on the Mary Ellen. She's half mad. She talks to herself and thinks she sees ghosts. Shush. She might hear.'

They pushed aside the door, hoicked themselves up and wriggled through the hole into the musty attic, which was pitch black apart from a few fingers of light through loose roof tiles. They got on their hands and knees and then lay flat and began to inch over the beams on their stomachs.

'Creepy,' said Gwenda. 'And it smells funny. Like rotten eggs. Told yer.'

'Shush.'

They pushed cobwebs out of the way. Brian sneezed,

and Gwenda spat. 'I'm choking on a cobweb!' she said. 'I might have swallowed a spider!'

'Perhaps you'll die. Like the old woman who lived in a shoe. Don't be daft. Here, I've found the Mary Ellen's trap door. Shall I open it? Do you dare me to go into her bedroom?' said Brian, with a wicked smirk.

But he had already slid it aside and before she could stop him he had lowered himself into the room below, dropping to his feet with a thump. Gwenda, with her head poking down, could see that it was sparsely furnished. It smelled strange.

'C'mon. Don't be a chicken, Gravy.'

Gwenda swung her legs and, clinging on to the sides of the loft door, dropped into the room. Giggling, giddy with knowing they might be found out at any moment, for a moment they just grinned at each other. There was a clock telling the wrong time on a mantelpiece over the fireplace. A stuffed squirrel in a glass dome sat on the floor beside the washstand. Coats were piled up on the bed. Gwenda tiptoed over and opened the wardrobe door. 'Ah eh, there's nothing in 'em. Apart from some manky long johns and pipe cleaners. Look, she's left her bloomers on the bed. And a stinking potty. Who's this?' she said, wandering back over to the bed to take a closer look at a framed picture of a boy in a soldier's uniform from the small table beside it. The boy was holding a rifle and smiling, and something made Gwenda pick up the photograph and run her finger round the edge of the gilt frame.

Brian grabbed the bloomers and waved them around his head. '*Hitler has only got one ball!*'

'Shush up!' said Gwenda.

He grinned. 'These floors are like marshmallows. All spongy,' he said, pushing his toe into a gap in the floorboards. 'And it's freezing in here. Smoke comes out of yer mouth . . .' But then he stopped and drew in his breath, tipped his head. 'I just heard something downstairs! Quick!'

Hearts hammering, they scrambled onto the rickety chair and heaved themselves back up through the trap door, Brian hauling Gwenda up behind him under her arms. In the loft, in the cavernous dark, they fought sneezes and coughed on brick dust.

'I'm scared of spiders, Bry. Why's there so many cobwebs? I might actually die. Brian! Wait!' she cried as he scrambled on ahead.

There was a loud clattering in front of her and the sound of something large and heavy – a chunk of plaster or a lump of cement – dislodging and falling with a crash, followed by a wail from Brian that chilled Gwenda's blood. For a moment she was frozen in shock.

'Brian! Brian? What's happened? Brian, where are yer? Was that you? Are you down there? Did you fall?' She stuck her head into the gaping hole that had appeared ahead of her, allowing light to flood through into the loft.

'Me leg,' he cried, from the hard floor below. He had fallen straight through the ceiling to the upstairs room below. 'Me leg's busted . . . Get someone quick. It hurts like hell,' he whimpered, wincing in pain, before unconsciousness came upon him and he fell back, exhaling loudly, into a deep and restful nothingness.

Gwenda crawled out of the loft and down the ladder, made her way back through the shop and then ran out into the street, shouting and waving her arms. A man stopped and she related what had happened in a panic. 'The ceiling of me ma's shop collapsed, and our Biscuit went right through. His leg's all twisted!' Within minutes the man had set off, wobbling on his bicycle, for the police station, while someone else was desperately knocking on doors to find a home with a telephone to call an ambulance. There weren't many with phones around here. Maybe the corner shop would help.

A few minutes later, a man ran into the station. 'Need an ambulance,' he said breathlessly. 'Need someone, need someone now. Kiddies . . . one of them fell through the ceiling. Ambulance. Come quick.' During the war you couldn't move for ambulances, he thought; there seemed to be one on every street corner, but now it was different. 'Need an ambulance,' he said again, gasping and pressing his hand on his chest.

Miss Quick had to wake Ida up by shaking her shoulders. Speaking directly into her face, she said, 'Your shop, Ida. Something's happened. Trouble.'

'My shop?' she replied, confused, rubbing her eyes.

Minutes later, she was up and out of the door after grabbing her shawl, thrusting Gabe into Marje Hallett's arms. Someone, a blurred figure, was running towards her, gesticulating. Her heart was pounding. She heard the clang of an ambulance and the sound of its engine. She ran out and threw herself in front of it, waving her arms wildly so it had to swerve to miss her. But a man grasped her arm and pulled her back. 'Queen, what do you think you're doing?' he shouted at her. Her eyes were searching up the street one way and then down the other. 'Listen to me, missus. You're not going anywhere!'

'I am!' She was resolute, her chin jutting forward, eyes full of fire. 'Someone's broken into my shop!'

'Aye, and fell right through the floor. They were next door. Little varmints, been using this place to play in for months. They go through the lofts. Should have been bricked up years ago. No dividing walls. These slums. But there was bomb damage. And the floors, they're rotten.'

'These kids are left to roam the streets. They're like wild things,' muttered a man at the door. 'I blame the parents.'

She could feel herself shaking with anger.

'The seven-year-old. The one with the hair . . . tight curly . . . wiry thing . . .'

And then she felt her blood run cold. 'What's his name? Not our Bry? Is it Brian? What's happened?'

When she burst into the house and ran upstairs, her worst fears were confirmed: Brian lying on the floor, his little leg folded right back underneath him as neatly as a camping chair, moaned. 'Brian!' she gasped. He screamed so loudly when she bent and touched him, more people came running. Someone tried to lift him and then someone else said that was the worst thing they could've done. Brian winced and then his eyelids began to flutter. Every instinct screamed at Ida to pick him up in her arms and run with him, she didn't know where. The hospital was a mile away, the doctor's was half a mile away – and everyone kept saying *don't pick him up, don't pick him up*.

'Sorry Mam, sorry Mam,' whimpered Brian, as more pain cramped his thigh.

When Alice got to the shop she found her mother pacing furiously on the pavement, sweat pouring from her forehead. Gwenda was nearby, pale and tear-stained.

'Ma. Bernice told me. The floor! Brian fell right through! Oh, Ma. Are you angry?'

'No. I'm not angry!' she said, spinning away in frustration. 'But where's the flaming ambulance? It must have gone the wrong way! Why isn't it here?'

'Was it the house next door to our shop?'

For a moment, guilt tore through Ida. 'Didn't I tell you not to play in these houses? Didn't I tell you!' she said, her face darkening. How could a mother be that angry with her own child? thought Alice. Ida seized Gwenda by the arms and shook her. She was shaking the life out of her.

'It weren't my fault!' said Gwenda. 'Does this mean you'll take the Saucy doll back?' she whined.

Alice stepped in. 'No – it was the fault of this place. It's all falling apart around us. You should have somewhere better to play than this . . . this hell-hole,' she said in a low, soothing voice, kneeling to speak to her sister, moving her away from Ida to calm her.

The sound of a clanging bell approached along the road. When the ambulance stopped outside the shop, two men brought a small stretcher.

'Gerra move on!' someone yelled. 'Boy's inside upstairs.'

Ida followed them back in and was on her haunches leaning over Brian. 'He's going to pass out again from the pain,' she said.

A woman she didn't know, a neighbour, was pressing a damp rag against his forehead. 'Kids next door on the roof,' she said. 'They've been in and out of these houses like rats since the Blitz. And no one wants to go down this bit of the road. There's a mad Mary Ellen living in the end house next door. She's crazy. She kept saying there were people in her house and no one believed her, thought she was seeing things, ghosts – her nephew even wanted to put her in the asylum. Turns out there probably were people in and out of her house, but they weren't dead. Just kids running through the attic, like this lad.'

Ten minutes later Alice stood trembling on the pavement as she watched the ambulance men put Brian, on his little stretcher, into their vehicle, helping her mother up behind him. As they pulled away, an earnest-looking young man approached her and introduced himself as Henry Cherry.

'I'm from the council,' he explained. 'Would you mind coming inside with me, Miss Lacey, so that we can have a chat about your family?' The expression on his face was grave.

Chapter 16

Alice sat with Gabe on her lap in front of the dying embers of the fire, watching the flickering coal begin to split and shards of orange float upwards. It was reflected in the glass of the frames on the mantelpiece: pictures of the Pope and the Sacred Heart, and faded wedding photographs.

This family wouldn't be able to cope with two tragedies in such a short time, she knew – no matter what she had said to that nice Mr Cherry about how everything was fine in the Lacey household. It would break them all, and she knew as much.

Gwenda came in, yawning. Alice placed a bowl of dripping in front of her and she took it gratefully, dipping bread in and biting into it greedily.

'Bed now, love,' she said, after the little girl had eaten it.

'Shall we fetch someone? Someone who can help us? Someone sensible who will know what to do?'

'We'll be fine on our own,' Alice replied. 'I know what to do.'

Half an hour later, she was still moving wearily around the kitchen after giving Gabe his mushed-up bread and dripping and putting him to bed. When the two children were asleep she went downstairs and laid everything out in a neat line for the following morning. Then she sat waiting, sitting in the parlour, watching a few people walk by; but every minute seemed to pass more slowly than the last, and still there was no more news.

At last, just as she was about to go to bed, there was a knock at the door. She opened it to find Matty standing there.

'Your ma,' he said. 'She's asked me to get word to you. Broken leg. She's staying at the hospital tonight. They've made up a little bed for her in Brian's room. She's exhausted so I expect she'll sleep.'

Alice sighed. 'He's alive. He'll live, and that's the main thing for now. Though the man from the Corpy – he was asking questions about Ma. How much she drank, that kind of thing. Did the kiddies have anywhere that they could go when I was at work, if Ma wasn't around? Any relatives. Had Bry had any accidents before? He's always bruised or with a black eye, is Brian. Tearing around and falling over things.'

'That sounds bleak.'

'Aye, it does. The Cherry fella seemed kind, but it makes you wonder. I think it'll be left to me to look after them now. And how can I do that as well as working? I'm supposed to be doing that talk tomorrow at the parish hall – it's already been postponed once. Who will look after the kiddies if Ma's not back in the morning?'

'I will. Morley's on your side. At least you know that. And I am too, Alice. You've got me. We'll get through this together, love. If there's one thing I can do, it's to make sure this turns out as best as it possibly can.'

'Thanks, Matty. I don't know what I'd do without you.'

'Me neither. What I'd do without you, I mean.'

There was a short silence before Alice smoothed down her skirt, slapped her thighs and said, 'Spuds. You'll help me peel the spuds for kiddies' tea tomorrow, then?'

'You're not too nervous, are you, about doing this talk?' said Morley, handing Alice a briefcase on the steps of the parish hall the following morning. 'Especially with everything that's been happening at home. I was very sorry to hear about your brother.'

She looked up at the red-brick building, then at the double front door with its brass knocker.

'No,' she said. 'Why should I be nervous? I've known these people all my life.' In fact, she had spent the night tossing and turning, but she hoped it wouldn't show. She'd been thankful her mother hadn't come home before she'd left the house that morning.

'Good girl,' he said, and squeezed her hand. 'I'll make myself scarce. People know me and Mr Worboys, but I'm not sure they trust us. Mr Higgins from the Corporation will be waiting for you, and his secretary.'

Inside, Alice found her way to a large, airy room that still had blackout curtains and crosses marked in tape on a couple of higher-up windows. There were chairs lined up in rows facing a simple stage at the front, where a pitcher of water and a glass had been set out on a small table. The room was already half full and there was a low murmur of people gossiping and chit-chatting.

'Our Pat says she's getting a house in Knotty Ash, but she's still had no letter. I don't believe it,' Alice heard a woman say.

She lingered near the door until she spotted Mr Higgins from the Corporation, who greeted her and led her to the front. As they passed between the rows of chairs, she exchanged a brief smile with one or two familiar faces.

Some mothers had brought along children who squirmed on their laps, and some men had clearly come straight from the docks – a few who she recognized, more that she didn't. Then there were a few teenage boys, fidgeting and twisting their heads. *Alice Lacey and the Corpy are coming to talk about changes on Dryburgh Terrace. Let's go for the craic.* Mrs Hallett was there with her arms folded across her bosom; Miss Quick with a notepad. Alice took a deep breath and lifted her chin as she made her way forward, clutching the briefcase.

As they mounted the steps at the side of the stage, Higgins patted the air with his hands for silence. Alice sat down in the chair beside his and cleared her throat, shuffling her papers.

'A few points of order,' Higgins began. 'I'll be taking notes. No speaking over one another. We will let Miss Alice Lacey give a short talk to introduce the meeting. And then, any questions, you'll have time. We are at the very beginning of this. But let's start and hear what Miss Lacey has to say.'

Surprised that she would be speaking first, Alice

rose hastily to her feet. Her chair scraped and she could feel herself trembling, but straightened her spine and took another deep breath. She would just have to hope they wouldn't notice her papers quivering in her hands. She looked out over the sea of heads, clear-eyed.

'Friends and neighbours . . .'

A figure slipped quietly in at the back of the room. It was Bernice, threading her way to an empty seat. She gave Alice an encouraging wink and smiled that smile of hers, which made Alice feel slightly more at ease. She smiled back, cleared her throat and continued.

'Since the war, it feels like things haven't changed around here quickly enough for us folks. How many more kiddies will fall through a floor, or out of a window? We all know about EWS steel drums full of water, but some of the little ones jump inside and swim about in them, dare each other to jump in. I've seen it with my own eyes. How they survive, I don't know. Even the scaldies are full of chemicals. One of the Corpy men did a test the other day. Went down with a test tube, and do you know what? It's official. It's toxic.'

'No surprise,' someone shouted. 'You come out yellow from that water.'

'But they're back again soon as the sun comes out,' said Mrs Hallett.

Alice raised her voice. 'Change is what we need. And if Mr Morley and Mr Worboys working with the council can go some way to making that change, they will. Starting by rehousing you in better, cleaner areas. Like the prefabs. Building more of them as we speak, in Bootle and Kirkby, Norris Green. They're clean with mod cons, some two storeys. Asbestos sheets on the outside walls, corrugated iron roofs, very quick to put up.'

'Rabbit hutches,' said a voice at the back.

Higgins shushed to silence them. He stood, thrusting his hands into his pockets. 'Dryburgh Terrace and Nelson's Row have been designated for demolition. We're here to advise you that if you receive a compulsory purchase order, you should take it – don't argue. Compulsory means compulsory. Refusing will only mean more delays. "Houses for all" is the government's goal.'

Mrs Hallett stood to ask a question. 'It's the landlords that are being offered cash handouts with these compulsory purchases, not the tenants.'

Alice faltered. 'You'll be offered resettlement grants, even if you're renting. It's best you take them. I'm here to say, you should trust the council. They only have your best interests at heart. The houses in Speke, they'll be lovely.'

She was surprised to see that Hedley had also slipped into the back of the hall now. He nodded to her and gave her the thumbs up. Alice repeated the answer she had given to Marje Hallett when someone asked her the same question.

'You're naive, love,' was the response. 'We'll be dead before you build 'em. There's still hundreds homeless. Five years after the bloody war! Some living in huts, caravans – one fella I know has put a thatched roof on an old tram. You're on the wrong side of the argument, you are. Telling us how to live our lives.'

'And she can't even look after her own family,' a woman on the front row added in low tones, just within earshot of Alice. 'Ma's all over the place, brother is in the hozzy. The kids are never at school.'

Alice felt her cheeks smart. It seemed this had suddenly become an even closer-knit community than it had been during the Blitz – only this time everyone was united against her, not Hitler.

'Have you ever thought that the Corpy and these toffee-nosed architects are using you, Alice?' someone shouted.

'Have you?' asked Hedley later, when they were outside.

Alice bristled. 'That's ridiculous,' she replied.

'Alice, you've not been exactly truthful, have you? I had no idea you lived in Dryburgh Terrace. In one of the houses that we are planning to demolish?'

She blushed, her cheeks stinging. 'I'm sorry, Mr Morley. I didn't want it to . . . complicate things.'

His eyes widened and he raked his hand back through his hair.

'That took some grit, Alice. For you to get up and stand and speak to those people – your community.'

'I know what's best for them, Mr Morley. I've seen the future through you. I just want them to listen.'

'Attagirl.' He smiled. 'I believe change means you have to be courageous. Change is terrifying and bewildering. But without change, we just crawl towards our graves. Isn't that so?'

'Yes, Mr Morley.'

'Alice, you are going to do great things in your life. I can feel it, my dear.'

They passed a small boy with a mud-smeared face, sitting on a step playing with a cotton reel on a string. 'Hey, Alice, you gonna get me ma one of them new flats in the sky?' he yelled. 'Will it 'ave a baff?'

'Maybe, Tommy,' she replied.

They paused as they reached the corner. 'Go home,' said Hedley. 'You were marvellous today, but you must be exhausted. Enjoy the weekend, and I'll see you Monday.'

She had planned to go back to the office to catch up on filing for the rest of the day. There was a mountain of paperwork waiting for her. But she was suddenly exhausted and, with a small smile at him, she turned and headed slowly for home.

At home, Alice went into the kitchen and saw an empty glass on the table. As she stood looking at it, her mother came into the kitchen looking sour and began clapping slowly. 'Bravo. Bravo.'

'What, Ma?'

'Miss Quick has been round. She told me about your *speech*. She's signed up to move. So what are we going to do now? Miss Alice with all the answers.'

Alice struck a match and lit the lamp. The noxious fumes of paraffin oil filled the room. 'Do? I'm going to have to concentrate on my job, Ma. I've done everything I can around here. How's our Brian?' she said, trying to defuse the tension in the room. She sat down at the table and rubbed her temples wearily, wondering where she was going to get the energy for another argument.

Ida sighed. 'He's going to be all right. But I could still kill him. His antics just mean another person like that Mr Cherry poking round and asking questions. Also, I've been thinking – you'll have to give up that job. Get something else. Go back to the factory.'

'What? No! Why?'

'People around here are turning against us. What were you doing, giving that flaming talk? Getting into bed with the enemy.'

'Ma, how can I possibly do that? Of course I'm not going to do that. I love that job. Mr Morley isn't the enemy. Ridiculous. Besides, we need my wages to pay your debts.'

Her mother snorted and sat down at the kitchen table.

'I'm not giving up my job,' said Alice firmly.

'You and your big speeches.' Ida's voice was heavy with scorn.

Alice thumped her fist on the table. 'Why don't you ever want me to do well? To make something better of myself? To lift us out of this place? And why is it all right for you to try and do something, open your shop, but not me? When it comes to me it's just, *stay at the factory, look after the kids, marry Bob*.'

'Why not marry Bob? Too good for him now?'

'What?'

'I don't trust that Morley. Looking down his snooty nose at us, wearing his stupid little glasses. Marje is right. You told me he said things were supposed to get better, Alice. But not for us.' Ida took hold of the glass in front of her and ran a finger round the rim. It made a strange squeaking noise. 'I don't know why you trust that man.'

'He's a good person. He truly wants things to improve.'

'Oh, aye? And what's in it for him? Why does he want to chuck us all out, then?' She staggered to her feet, swaying a little.

'He doesn't,' Alice replied tersely. 'What have you been drinking?'

'Lemon barley water. Now go away.'

Alice snatched the glass from her and sniffed it. 'It doesn't smell of anything, Ma. Which means it's not lemon barley water. It's that awful potato vodka again.'

'Is it?' replied Ida. Somehow, she seemed genuinely surprised.

Alice shook her head in dismay and sat back, looking around at the cluttered room. There were unopened bags, clothes with tags on, and boxes piled up on the floor.

'Ma, what's all this mess?'

'This *mess* is my life going down the Swanee. Because of your Mr Morley, ruining our lives and getting rich off us. All our lives,' Ida added bitterly. 'It's all your fault! Who's going to come to my shop now, if they're all living somewhere else?'

'My fault!' Alice wanted to slap her mother but held herself back, curling her hands into fists. 'Don't drag Hedley into it.'

'Oh, *Hedley*. Touchy about your new friend, are we?'

155

'Yes, Ma! At least someone respects me. Learning from him is how I'll get out of this place. He knows people in Manchester, Birmingham – London, even. And as soon as I can, I'm off. Away from this godforsaken grimy town where even a trip to Llandudno is as unlikely as going to the flaming moon for most folks. Pub, work, pub, work . . .'

'London! Oh, lah-di-dah. Look at you. Lady Alice.' Ida slammed her palm on the table. 'It's all your fault everyone's leaving, selling up. They're all desperate, taking the money, afraid they'll be left homeless like all the others. Been going on for years – drip drip, another house demolished, another street, another pub closed – pretending it's because of the Blitz! That was years ago now. You and your *friends*, putting ideas in their heads – ooh, move to Speke. The air is like nectar and you can swim at Oggie beach. Have you heard you can rent a lovely prefab in Bootle? Spick and span they are, no nasty mould there. Oh, Knotty Ash is on the up. Kirkby? It's all blackberry picking and buttercups. My eye, it is. And meanwhile, this place is like a ghost town. Now they say that the shop premises are dangerous after Brian's accident, and they want to close that down too.'

Alice focused her gaze on the flickering oil lamp throughout this rant, pressing her lips together in fury.

'Alice, what did you think was going to happen? They've already put demolition notices on so many of the houses round here. No wonder Miss Quick is running on her bandy legs to get out as fast as she can. Your precious Mr Worboys and Morley and his pals have made people think there's something else out there, something better than these streets and terraces. A brighter flaming future. I'm sick to death of hearing how lovely it's going to be to have their own front doors. But they're sending them all over the place. Miss Quick is going to Kirkby. Her across the road, the gypsy lot, they're all squashed into their mother's in Scottie Road tenements, waiting to get the letter. And the landlords have snatched back their houses, trading them for compulsory purchase orders. It's blood money, I tell you. Number ten, grandparents are looking after the children in Litherland while Da's gone back to sea, because he's no house so he may as well live in the boiler room of a flaming ship. He's still waiting for the government resettlement grant. They're all trading on hope.'

'What's wrong with that?' Alice burst out. 'Only you would be suspicious of it. Most folks think it's like winning the lottery to get a new council house. There *is* hope.'

'No, it's hopeless. That's what it is. And we're flaming skint.' She shrugged and looked blankly at Alice. It was as though she was looking right through her.

'Ma. I've got money. I've got five pounds.' Alice crossed the room, yanked open the drawer, reached deep inside. She felt around for a few seconds, then went pale. 'Ma – where is it? I left an envelope in here. You know I did.'

'What envelope?'

'The envelope with the five pounds in!'

'Oh, *that* envelope. Gone. Just like everything else will soon be. My shop. Gone. My house. Gone. Our

157

friends. Gone. Your da. Gone. Gone!' Ida said with a bitter laugh.

Alice was trying to make sense of each new thing she said, but every new sentence seemed more hopeless than the last.

'Ma, don't,' she said, balling her hands into fists again. She turned away and took a deep breath, trying to remain calm, then pulled open the second drawer.

'What's all this?' she asked. 'What are all these envelopes shoved in here?' She pulled them out and squinted at them. 'Ma, you've not even opened them,' she said, worriedly.

Ida shrugged. 'They've been coming for months.'

Pushing her hands deeper into the back of the drawer, Alice pulled out more unopened, scrunched-up letters.

'What is this? The bailiffs? The landlord?' she said, scanning them. Shocked, she ripped one open, skimmed it quickly, and then another. 'Ma, why didn't you tell me? This says we're being evicted! Next week! I could have done something about this if you had told me! I could get money!'

Ida rolled her eyes. 'It's not the rent he wants. He wants a repossession grant from the council. Like everyone else round here. Anyway, what does it matter? What was it you said? They're going to be giving us a palace in the sky? I can't blinking wait.'

But Alice wasn't listening. She was reading a letter, folding it open, turning it over, the words swimming before her, her heart racing. 'Dear Mrs Lacey, I am giving you three weeks' notice to vacate the property.

You are two months behind with the rent, but as a goodwill gesture I will wait for you to pay the debt when you are in further employment.' Alice's hands were shaking. She jerked up her head. 'How long have you had this? This is an eviction notice! I warned you! You didn't listen!'

'Shut up, Alice. It's all your fault.'

'Ma, we can go to the Corpy . . . ask them for a prefab . . . or a house . . .'

'Don't you think I haven't done that already? You'll be delighted to know we're on the list. Less pleasant to know is that the list is as long as the Mersey Tunnel, and we're right at the bottom. No can do, the fella said. Not this side of Christmas.'

'What about the kiddies? What about me?' Alice asked in a quiet voice.

'What about you? Perhaps you should have thought about that before you and your fancy man decided to tear up everywhere around here and chuck us all out on the street.'

Alice had to struggle to keep from striking her mother or punching the wall. 'It's not his fault you didn't pay the rent,' she said through gritted teeth. 'It's not his fault you spent what little we had on some ridiculous shop when everyone told you not to! It's not his fault Brian ended up with his leg all twisted. You're so stupid, Ma.'

Ida snorted. 'Me, stupid! You had the chance to marry Bob, but you turned him down with all your fancy notions.'

Alice felt tears of anger welling up. They spilled over onto her cheeks and splashed onto the oilcloth.

'Don't say another word, please,' she said, gripping the edges of the chair. 'I did not turn down Bob.'

'Yes, you did. I saw him in the pub the other day and I thought, what a fool my Alice is.'

'No, you didn't,' snapped Alice.

Suddenly Ida, as if shocked into motion, climbed onto a chair and started pulling down boxes from the top of the dresser, tearing them open, tipping them up.

'But at least I have this! One lovely matinee jacket . . . with pleating . . . one gorgeous christening gown . . .' she said, shaking the box empty. 'Look at the detail on the hem . . . one beautiful baby shawl . . .' She wrapped it around her neck in a ghoulish pantomime of despair. Alice could feel herself shaking. 'All useless now,' Ida said, hurling the shawl across the room.

Alice caught hold of her arm as she scrambled down from the chair, but Ida shrugged her away. 'I need a drink,' she hissed. She whirled round and seized the soda syphon from the dresser, staggered across the room, and began haphazardly squirting it into her glass. Alice tried to take her arm again and Ida spun round, spraying Alice full in the face with a stream of water. 'Sorry, love!' she cried, laughing. 'Oops-a-daisy!' She lurched and fell backwards into a chair, spraying another arc of water over the table.

Alice, wiping the water out of her eyes, stumbled forward and wrestled the syphon off her. 'Look what you've done!' she cried.

'Oh, I haven't even started!' Ida lunged for the violin with a gleam in her eye, waving it above her head.

'Ma, what are you doing? My violin!' cried Gwenda from the doorway.

Ida froze. Seeing her younger daughter's stricken expression seemed to shock her out of her madness.

'I don't know, Gravy . . .' she whimpered. And then she crumpled. 'Help me, Alice. I don't know what's happening to me.' She began to sob like a wounded animal, clutching her head.

Alice knelt beside her. How long could this go on? Always placing herself between Ida and the children for fear of what might happen next. She looked over her shoulder at her sister. 'Go on upstairs, Gwenda . . . Shush, Ma. Shush. It's going to be all right, I promise. If we need more money, I can get another job in the evenings . . . or something. We'll find a way. Just don't do anything stupid.' She wrapped her arms around Ida and attempted a reassuring smile. 'You just need some rest. Gwenda – go upstairs.'

'I want Da,' Gwenda said in a small voice. She squeezed her eyes closed, as if to shut out the drama. 'Why can't everything to go back to how it was? I want Da,' she repeated miserably. 'I want Da . . .'

'What on earth happened here?' said Ida the following morning, looking around the kitchen. Light sloped in through the gap between the curtains. It spilled over the rug, dust motes jitterbugging in the brightness.

And for a moment, as Alice watched her mother stagger around, wondering aloud why her head was thumping and why she could only find one of her shoes, she truly believed that Ida did not remember a single thing.

161

Chapter 17

Alice hadn't slept. What Ida chose to do next was her business, but she had to think of herself and the children now.

Coming back into the house after a trip to the washhouse, she was surprised to find Brian sitting in the kitchen. He wore a cast that went all the way up to his thigh and was trying to wiggle his toes, which stuck out at the end of it.

'Brian! You're back!'

'Aye. And I'm going to the hollas,' he said, heaving himself off the chair and reaching for a pair of crutches. He stumbled forward. Alice grasped him under his arms.

'No, you're not,' she said firmly. 'You're supposed to be in bed. Have you not learned a thing from your flipping excursions?'

He pulled away. It was difficult for him to get around the room without bumping into furniture and he lurched from dresser to table to chair, knocking things over – a jug, a pile of sewing – but somehow, taking advantage of her astonishment at his audacity, he made it to the front door. With the open street ahead of him, the crutches allowed him to move faster than he could run.

'Come back!' shouted Alice – but he was already far away, scooting off down the street. Frustrated, she stood on the step gazing after him, then jumped as the Mary Ellen, lugging her cart, lumbered up behind her.

'Your fella. Saw him in the pub earlier. Buying drinks for everyone.'

Alice hesitated. 'You mean Matty? He's not my fella.'

The woman chewed her lip. 'Fair hair? Bell bottoms? Oh, it were him all right.'

Bob? Did she really mean Bob? Surely not. This was a woman who talked to the dead and believed she saw ghosts. Bob was halfway round the world by now, probably in Lisbon. No, the old woman must have it wrong.

Ida came back into the room, clutching the coal pan, her presence reminding Alice of something she, too, had said about Bob being in the pub. Could he really be back? After all, he had mentioned that the rotas often changed – if there was bad weather, for instance, or an unexpected shipment.

Fifteen minutes later, she stood on the pavement below his window. All the curtains were shut at his house. Would she wake up his mother if she knocked on the door? She approached the door and bent down to peer in through the letterbox for a sign that he was in.

As she did so, it was pulled open from inside and she nearly toppled into the house.

'Cherry Bomb!' Bob cried. 'What the 'eck?' He was holding a bag of chestnuts, cracking them open with his hand and popping them into his mouth.

Alice gathered herself, recovering her dignity, and went into his arms. 'You *are* back!'

'What d'you mean?' he said.

'Well – when did you come home?'

'Got in late last night, love,' he said breezily. They went into the kitchen and he headed for the ash pan on the range, picking out another chestnut and popping it into his mouth.

'I heard you were in the pub – the Mary Ellen said so. And my ma said you were there the other night.'

'They're wrong. Since when has that old Mary Ellen crone been talking anything less than garbage? Last night. Look, my kit bag's here.'

He gestured towards his bag and a tangle of clothes strewn across the floor.

'Where's your ma?'

'Church. Can't get down the stairs most of the time, but if it's Sunday Mass or a midweek holy day of obligation like today, she's running off to St Patrick's faster than Roger Bannister.'

'Oh, Bob.' Alice sank down onto a chair, suddenly overwhelmed by how much there was to explain. 'So much has happened – I'm in a state . . .' Her voice wavered.

'Cherry Bomb, you're shaking. Calm down and tell me everything from the beginning,' he said, putting the kettle on.

She began to tell him all about her mother and the shop, and Brian and his broken leg, and then about how the landlord was about to take the house. The words spilled out, interrupted now and then by sobs. Somehow Alice's sentences were coming out back to front, and she had to rely on hand gestures when she couldn't find the words. Bob gave her his handkerchief and she dabbed at her eyes, but then she welled up again. 'Sorry about the waterworks,' she said miserably.

'Those are real tears. Tell me again. Tell me slowly. We'll make a plan, love.'

He led her over to the sofa and took her in his arms, kissing the top of her head, listening while she talked round and round in circles, trying to think of a solution. No home. And what that would mean for the children. No money. When she pulled her flimsy cardigan around her, he reached for a crocheted blanket, tucked it over her and told her he loved her. It occurred to her that he wasn't trying any of his usual pawing and grabbing, and she was grateful for that. He just listened quietly, kissing her head from time to time and tracing invisible patterns on the palm of her hand.

Eventually she said, 'I have to go to work.'

'And I have to see the man at the Pool about my wages. The Reptile, they call him – not a bad fella, despite the name. But before I do, I'm making you a fry-up. You're all skin and bone, love. Have you got time?'

'Twenty minutes. That would be nice.' She paused. 'Bob, I know this sounds a pretty forward question.' She propped herself up, sitting on the deep sofa, tucking her knees to her chest. 'If we were to marry, how would you feel about taking Ma and the kiddies in?'

*

Bob made his way to the Pool. He had told Alice it was a grand, smashing idea – of course he had – but the truth was, he had doubts.

He was surprised by his own reaction. He had wanted to marry Alice for months, years. His girl. His Cherry Bomb. And now, soon, his wife. But something about the way she talked about it had felt . . . odd. She had sounded so practical when she brought it up. Women, he thought. At times they could be so unromantic.

Still, Alice was a girl who knew how to get things done. She was realistic, and he liked that.

He sat at a table in the Pool, took his pint glass and placed it upside down – the sign he was looking for work. Before long, a man approached him.

'I'm after a kitchen crew. I know you're away to Spain on the *Stella Maris*. But when you're back, I'm offering four months in the Azores. You interested, Bob, lad?'

Immediately, his thoughts turned to Alice. How would that fit in with her plans? She was in a terrible state. Her dilemma wouldn't accommodate four months of him hopping around between Mediterranean ports.

'I'll think about it, mate,' was his reply.

Chapter 18

Ida crunched over the frozen gravel path at St Mary's. Outside in the winter sunshine, the children were taking their lessons at desks that they had carried from the classrooms onto the lawn. A nun was standing at the front with a large stick, pacing back and forth as the children recited a lilting rhyme. The nun – Sister Dorothea, Ida thought her name was – paused, squinting at her.

'Can I help you?' she asked.

'I'm here to see Sister Cyril.'

'Ah, you're Ida Lacey, aren't you?' replied the nun, nodding as though she knew something Ida didn't.

Angela, one of the girls from Ida's sewing class, came into the garden with a bucket. She was shivering, her hands blue with cold.

'Angela, take Ida to Sister Cyril,' said the nun.

'Miss, where have you been?' Angela squealed. 'We missed you. Did you do a runner? We thought Doreen had scared you off with her potty mouth.'

'Oh, Angela. No. I've not been here because my husband died,' explained Ida, following her down the path.

'I'm sorry, Miss. You don't look so peachy. You need sunshine on your cheeks, like the kiddies practising for the Christmas carol concert. Some of 'em have scurvy, scabby knees and whatnot. It helps.'

'Oh, I see. Fresh air. I know the sun's out but it's so cold.' Ida swallowed hard as she looked back over at the children, who had begun singing 'O Come, All Ye Faithful' in thin voices.

'They nearly sent Doreen to the School for Maladjusted Girls. And June climbed over the flaming wall to see Wicky Weardon. He's back in Liverpool.'

'She's not maladjusted.'

'No. She's the most sensible person I know. It's Wicky who's to blame for maladjusting his trouser flies, and now everyone thinks there's something wrong with her.' Angela's expression changed, as if a cloud had passed over the sun. 'I had my baby. A girl. She were beautiful. I called her Junie, after June. My wee one's new ma and da will change the name, but I thought it would make June happy for a few days. One good thing to come out of a bloody awful, sad story . . .' She tailed off, looking away. Her eyes brimmed with tears, but after a moment she smiled bravely and blinked away the sadness.

Ida nodded. These girls could have been forgiven for feeling bitter and sorry for themselves, she thought, after everything they had been through. But they didn't seem that way.

'Ah, Ida.' Sister Cyril was striding over, her keys and crucifix jangling on a long rope that bumped against her leg. 'I heard about your son's accident. I hope he's all right?'

'A nasty break, Sister. He's on crutches for the moment, hobbling around the kitchen and waving them about, banging on the ceiling when he wants attention. And singing "Jake the Peg" at the top of his voice.'

The nun didn't return Ida's smile. 'But that's not why you wanted to see me,' she said. 'Come with me.'

Ida nodded. Behind them, the carol singing rose in pitch and a chanted prayer floated from the building.

Alice had left Bob's house with a stomach full of fried egg and black pudding, and was at her desk in good time for the working day to begin.

But it wasn't Hedley Morley who strode into the office at the usual time. Instead it was a slim-hipped, louche young man with an aquiline nose, a weak chin and long, wavy fair hair. He wore a cravat, a pale, crumpled summer jacket with dark trousers, and a bored expression.

'Can I help you?' It had taken Alice only moments to develop a keen dislike of him, but she kept her tone polite.

He ambled over to her. 'You're the new girl?'

'Not very new – I started in June. Can I help?'

'Is my papa in? Or should I say, my step-papa – he always calls me his stepson. Apparently I don't measure up as a fully qualified fruit of his loins.' He fished in his pocket and extracted a crumpled pack of cigarettes.

'Oh, yes. You must be . . .'

'Oh, good grief, don't shock me and say he's mentioned me?' He laughed and lit a long, slim Pall Mall cigarette that matched his long, slim body.

Through puckered lips, he aimed a stream of smoke in Alice's direction.

This exhibition made her thankful for the simple, straightforward boys she knew, like Bob or Matty. She had met this type before: arrogant, snobbish.

'I'm sorry, have I been awfully rude? I'm Roddy. I should have introduced myself.'

The room was stuffy and the smoke wasn't helping. Alice turned away towards a row of shelves, discreetly loosening her collar and fanning herself. Taking down a sheaf of papers, she spread them across the desk. 'You gave me a fright, that's all,' she said. 'Sorry, I'm in the middle of something.'

'A fright? That doesn't sound like the feisty girl my father's so obsessed with.' He gave her a grin that was somewhere between friendly and suggestive.

She was embarrassed. What on earth did he want, coming here and saying these things?

'Suppose Pa has been bad-mouthing me again. But he doesn't understand this new world. *I* do – he thinks he does, with his precious high-rise flats, but he has no idea.'

'Oh, really?' Alice busied herself with the papers on her desk.

'Yes. And I've got plans.'

She raised an eyebrow. 'Like what?'

He grinned. 'I want to run a bar. But not just any bar. It'll be like that ballroom in Bold Street that was bombed in the war. The things that went on there . . . music and dancing. Girls. And poker tables. I just wondered how far in you are with Pa? I'm planning something exciting. A new venture. The city needs something fresh and daring. The Boom Boom Club, I'm calling it. You could come and work for me.'

Boom Boom Club? How ridiculous, she thought. 'Oh, no – I couldn't possibly.'

'Why not? You're young, like me.'

He wasn't that young. 'I like it here.'

'Astonishing.' He shrugged, and she blushed. 'It might be rather wonderful. You could help me organize things. I'm absolutely hopeless when it comes to figures. Though I can see under those drab clothes you've got a rather lovely one. You're a smasher, aren't you?'

She blinked away his rudeness.

'And it would be fun. Surely you need a little fun? Stuck here with my ancient pa. Come on. We wouldn't even need to tell the old man. I would pay you well, better than you get here.'

'No, thank you.'

He snorted. 'My dear, if you can afford to turn me down . . . But if you're ever in a tight spot, think again.'

He turned to the mirror, adjusting his pale blue silk cravat, which hung loosely around his neck. Alice watched him looking at his reflection, stroking down his hair and swelling out with pride. Could a person actually be in love with himself? It certainly looked that way.

'What on earth are you doing here, Roddy?' Hedley Morley had suddenly appeared in the doorway, making them jump. His voice was sterner than Alice had ever heard it. 'I haven't time for any nonsense of yours. This is an important day for us – I'm expecting the Corporation officers at any minute. Alice, come along.'

She followed him into the back room, glancing back briefly over her shoulder at the young man.

Mr Morley was holding a long roll of paper. He unrolled it on the desk, securing it with a paperweight and a book, and stepped back.

'Now look at that. What do you think that is? That's your idea. We've designed it so that at the end of each corridor there's a small communal space – people would use that, wouldn't they? When you said they congregated on the landings and at the sinks and cooking stations in the court houses, wouldn't it be like that? I've got a good feeling about this.'

'About what?' said Roddy, behind them.

Mr Morley bristled. Alice saw the muscles in his jaw clench. 'I thought you were leaving.'

'I've only just got here.' Roddy looked casually around the room and then back at Alice, scanning her from head to toe. He approached, pushed the drawing aside and rested his bottom on the desk, crossing one foot over the other and lounging with his hands in his trouser pockets. 'I had a lovely chat with your Alice.' He nodded to her. 'My father says you're a godsend. Dragging yourself up by the bootstraps from the Meccano factory. Very impressive.'

'Well, er . . . this is an impressive place,' she stuttered, confused.

'No. *You* are impressive. Isn't she, Pa? Beautiful freckles. Sweet. Natural. That's how I like my girls. No wonder Pa pinned you for this job, ducky.'

'Oh, no. Not at all, no, I just . . . I'm not . . .'

'Just go, please, Roddy,' snapped Mr Morley.

'I'd rather hoped that I could stay. And what's all this?' he said, looking at the drawing on the desk.

Alice glanced uncertainly at Mr Morley.

'He's not really interested,' Morley told her grimly. 'Roddy. Haven't you got somewhere to be? Your smoking club? Jazz music dive, whatever it is.'

He shrugged. 'There's nowhere I'd rather be than here with this lovely girl. I can see why you're so taken with her.'

'Dammit, Roddy, get out!'

'That's a nice thing for a father to say to his son. And I *am* interested. Alice, you're a bloody marvel. I bet you keep all the balls in the air round here. And I, for one, would like to show you my appreciation of how much you're cheering my father up. He positively skips off to work each morning these days. Mummy is delighted. Of course, she might not be quite so delighted if she knew why.'

'Gerrout,' Mr Morley snarled, pushing him out of the door.

Roddy laughed. He stood just outside the doorway and lit another long cigarette. 'I would have liked to stay, Pa. Miss Meccano, you're delightful.'

'*Out.*'

'Pa, you sound so cross. Such a crosspatch, isn't he, Alice!'

Mr Morley glanced at her and then back to his stepson. 'Leave us to work,' he said firmly.

Roddy slowly pivoted towards Alice and said with a thin smile, 'Toodle pip, then. Seems I'm not wanted. But I do hope to see you again, Miss Meccano.'

'Now!' Morley barked, starting towards him as if about to seize him.

Roddy shrugged and walked down the hall with studied casualness – and yet, Alice noticed, there was an awkward angularity in his body. Almost as if the whole louche thing was an act.

'I'm sorry,' said Mr Morley. 'I'm so very sorry. Now, where were we? Sinks. Yes, let's get back to sinks and lavatories.'

Thank goodness I have Bob, Alice thought, as she left the office at four that afternoon. With his thwacking laugh and his stupid jokes, Bob could be hard work, and he was undeniably selfish at times – but compared to that spoilt fool Roddy, he was all that a girl could hope for.

Chapter 19

'So, Ida? You said it was urgent?' Nelly, Ida's sister, sat at the kitchen table, smearing margarine onto a heel of bread. 'It had better be, me coming all the way from Parbold. The roads are a nightmare and the trains are all delayed. I'm sick of the war being used as an excuse when it was over five years ago.'

The conversation had started pleasantly enough, but now Ida had to ask if Nelly would have the children for a few weeks, since they were about to lose their home. Nelly frowned and said it wasn't practical. Had she thought about their aunt in Ireland – could she have the baby? Or maybe the twins could be sent off to their brother, in Canada?

'Don't be ridiculous! Things aren't that bad. All I'm asking is for you to have them for Christmas while I get back on my feet. We're being evicted.'

Nelly crumbled a piece of bread between her fingers. 'I can't have them, not in our cramped farmhouse with my two great tall boys. There must be someone nearer in Liverpool, someone in your street who would just keep an eye on them. I'm sorry, Ida. What about your Alice?'

'Alice is floating round on a cloud right now. All she thinks about is her job. She's hopeless. And there's hardly anyone else left in this street – all moving, all taken the resettlement grants. That's Alice and her new friend's fault.'

'*Alice's* fault?'

'Never mind.'

'The shop idea was silly, if you ask me,' Nelly said. 'Besides, who knows what will happen next? We never thought there would be another war, and yet there was – and so soon after the last one. One thing we can be certain of is, we've no idea what's round the corner.'

'It felt right at the time,' Ida said gloomily. 'Imagine doing a job that you liked. Then it's not work at all. It was nearly a success.'

Nelly gave her a significant look from under the brim of her hat. 'I know what else you've been doing, Ida. Teaching girls who are in the family way about knitting and whatnot, at St Mary's. But really.'

Ida hadn't told her sister about her Tuesday afternoons. She had known Nelly wouldn't approve.

'How do you know about that?' she asked, shocked. In spite of herself she lowered her voice when she said it, as if in acknowledgement that she ought to be a little embarrassed. But really, why should she be?

She thought of herself sitting with the girls in a semicircle, perched on her small stool, showing them how to quilt a christening jacket or thread a ribbon round the top of a baby's bootie. The very last thing those young, sad mothers would do for their babies was make them christening outfits. They were too ashamed to go out and buy little dresses for their babies; too poor, too afraid of the questions that might be asked. What was wrong with helping them?

Nelly didn't answer the question directly. 'Girls like that shouldn't be encouraged,' she said curtly. 'They should be punished.'

Ida leaned forward. Her eyes were earnest and she spread her hands on the table. 'Nelly, that's harsh. Not even the nuns think that.'

Nelly pursed her lips in disapproval.

'Will you have the twins?' Ida asked her again.

Her sister glanced away. 'I've told you, I can't. How could I? You'll just have to come up with an alternative, Ida.'

'Mean cow,' Ida said under her breath as she rose and turned to put the kettle on.

'Excuse me?' said Nelly sharply. 'What was that?'

'Nothing,' Ida replied. 'Nothing.'

'Where are you going, Ma?' Alice asked an hour later. Ida was dressed not in her usual drab floral shift, but in the smart navy-blue suit she had worn for her husband's funeral.

'Can't a person get on with their own business around here?' she replied.

Alice began to move around the room, setting it straight. She found the toasting fork in a shoebox and sighed. One minute it had felt as if they were a normal family, with a normal mother and father doing normal things – and the next, they were *the Laceys*, the family for whom everything was always falling apart. Lately, each new day felt more overwhelming. As she worked through the mess – cups and crumbs on the table, unfinished bundles of Ida's sewing – she tried to play happier memories over and over in her head to block out the worry of the eviction. Like taking Gwenda and Brian to the Odeon to see a Roy Rogers film, and how they had been mesmerized by the curtain magically turning from pink to purple to lilac. Or swimming in the scaldies. Or her da with the tarpaulin and a hosepipe last summer, whipping up the whole neighbourhood into a frenzy. Those simple things had brought so much more pleasure than Saucy dolls and expensive watches. She moved to the sink, switched on the tap and plunged her hands into the water.

Her mother reappeared, now wearing a hat. *You did this, ma. Ruined everything*, Alice wanted to say. *Did I?* she would only have replied.

'Has Gabe had his milk? Where's Bry and Gwen? Out on the hollas? Brian using the blinking crutch as an oversized catapult again?' Alice asked instead.

Her mother sighed and gestured vaguely in the air with one hand. 'Gone.'

'Gone where?'

Ida shrugged.

Alice frowned.

'*Gone*, gone,' said Ida flatly. She sighed and rubbed her temples.

'What d'you mean?'

'Nelly fetched them while you were at the wash-house. They've gone to Parbold. Gone for Christmas. Just until I get sorted.'

'Why didn't you tell me?' Alice said, shocked. 'I'm doing everything to keep this family together.'

'Because you would've only made a fuss.'

'I was even going to try taking another job to get us more money.'

'Bully for you, love.'

'Ma, what are *you* doing to sort this situation out?'

'You mean us being brassic and homeless? Miss Quick owes me money for some sewing I did for her. I think she felt sorry for us. But she's upped and gone, left overnight the minute she was offered a flat in Kirkby. Said she was going for the blasted fresh air. Another one. How am I supposed to deliver it to her and get my five shillings?'

Alice felt her stomach clench. 'I'll get the bus and take it. But why didn't you let me say goodbye to the kiddies?'

'Stop asking questions. My head hurts,' Ida replied as she left the room. 'I'm off to see a man about a budgerigar,' she called back over her shoulder. Alice stood looking after her, utterly bewildered.

Chapter 20

Christmas was a miserable affair, with Spam instead of a turkey and the Christmas pudding with a button instead of a sixpence. Alice did her best, hanging paper chains over the doorway and getting the old crib out, but it seemed so strange with the children at Nelly's and Bob away at sea.

'We've got through it,' said Ida, as they sat at the table looking at one another over a bowl of broth on Boxing Day. There didn't seem much to say that wouldn't lead to bickering.

'Just,' replied Alice. 'Not much point without the kids.'

Ida shrugged. 'I'm going to church to light a candle,' she said, getting up from the table.

As if that will help, thought Alice.

Ten minutes later, washing up their two bowls and spoons, she heard the rattle of the latch and sighed. It must have come undone as her mother had left. Then she realized someone was actually at the door. Shaking the water from her hands, she went to answer it, and was surprised to find a nun standing on the doorstep.

'Hello, dear. Is your mother in?'

'I'm afraid not,' Alice said warily.

'You must be Alice. I knew you when you were a little girl, from church. You've grown. I'm Sister Cyril from St Mary's – d'you remember me?'

'Oh – er, yes . . .' Alice murmured. It was hard to tell one nun from another, in their uniform black habits.

Sister Cyril thrust a brown paper package into her arms. 'Sewing for your mother. Buttonholing. I'll need it by Friday.'

Alice took the bundle, but the nun lingered on the step. 'May I ask you something, dear? Your Brian – was he an altar boy?'

'Yes, a while ago.' Brian's altar serving had come to an abrupt end when he had been caught hiding a mouse up his cassock sleeve, tucked inside a matchbox.

'Good. Your mother said he's a little unruly. Sometimes, if they serve, Father can bring him back in line. I've already caught him throwing stones into the fishpond. We keep two fish in there, so you can imagine . . .'

Alice was confused. 'You've seen Brian? . . . Have you been in Parbold?'

'Parbold?'

'Brian's in Parbold just now, with Gwen and Gabe. They're staying with our aunt.'

Sister Cyril raised her eyebrows. 'No, my dear,' she said. 'They're all at St Mary's, in the middle of Benediction, and then they'll be saying their night-time prayers, washbasin duty and off to bed. That's if your Brian isn't leading everyone all a dance as usual. Didn't your mother tell you they're living with us now?'

*

181

'What else could I do?' wailed Ida. 'Sister told me to consider it and I did.' She slumped forward and put her head in her hands. 'She offered months ago. It's not my fault. I had no choice.'

'Ma, why is it always someone else's fault?' shouted Alice. She was still reeling after pacing up and down the kitchen for the past half hour.

'It's not for long.'

'Sit up! You should have told me! You lied!'

'They came one day while you were at work. Said it was best that they took them instead of me delivering them. Just for Christmas. Sister Cyril and Sister Dorothea. Nuns always come in twos, don't they? Why is that?'

'No, Ma . . .' Alice's heart howled in her ears. What kind of a mother would do this? 'And you didn't think to ask me about this? You lied to me!'

'I knew what you would say,' Ida spat. 'And you refused to help with the kiddies. Wouldn't give up your precious Morley, would you? You told me yourself. I'll be off, you said. Dreaming of flaming London all the time. So what else was I to do?'

'Is this a joke? Are you doing it to upset me?'

Ida tossed back her head. 'I always said it. The minute you could get out of here, you'd be off.'

'You're not listening.'

'I've been talking to the sisters for some time. There's plenty of others like us with nowhere to live. Families living in the old municipal building in Seaforth, barricading themselves in and can't use their front door because they have to keep it locked in case the police come in and turf them out. You know how they get out, to get to work and take the kiddies to school? They climb out of the windows and along the ledges. Others living in tents and old railway carriages. You want that for us? I knew what you'd say about the orphanage. We have to be realistic.'

'Ma, you've never been realistic in your life!'

Furious, Alice headed for the stairs, taking them two steps at a time. Part of her still didn't quite believe it was true. She flung open the bedroom door. The drawer that normally held several threadbare blankets and a burst pillow was empty. She scoured the room, yanked open the drawer where Gabe's little shorts and vests were kept. Empty. She flung open the wardrobe door to find all Brian and Gwen's clothes were gone too.

She went back downstairs and stood in front of Ida, trembling. 'Mother. All of Gabe's clothes have gone. And the twins. If they are only going for Christmas, why are all their clothes gone? Even Gwen's First Holy Communion dress.'

'Sister said she needed it. Alice, what choice do I have? I'm not a fit mother. They told me. And you only care about yourself, with your fancy speeches. All you want to do is leave this family. Pretend we never existed. You can't get away quick enough from the twins and Gabe – God, you must hate them. So you can climb off your high horse, my lady. The only one you give a damn about is yourself.'

Alice was speechless. It was one of the cruellest things Ida had ever said to her.

'Perhaps you could get your Mr Morley to find me

a house, now we've got to leave here?' Ida continued relentlessly. 'Or some money? I hear he's rolling in it.'

'I'm worried sick about Gabe,' Alice said. 'His cough.'

Ida sighed. 'It's not for long. Just until we get back on our feet. Just until I find somewhere for us to rent. Or the blasted letter comes from the Corpy with a new house.'

Alice could feel her whole body shaking. 'Why didn't you tell me before you did this?'

'Because you were so swept up in your ridiculous notions about being *free*. That nonsense. And because I knew what you'd say . . . So they're at the orphanage,' Ida sighed. 'That Henry Cherry fellow wanted to talk about foster care, but I prefer the nuns. Strange, he wasn't so keen on the orphanage. Tried to persuade me against it.'

The room seemed to be spinning. Alice reached out and gripped the edge of the table to stop herself from collapsing.

'Why, Ma? To send them away! Why?'

Her mother's eyes darkened. 'Because they need food in their bellies. They need someone to get the nits out of their hair. Because they need clean clothes and fresh sheets and someone to get them to school on time. Because I can't give them any of those things right now. So don't come to me with your new ideas and fancy thoughts about the future. Because I can't see any way out of this now.'

'And where are you and me going to go, if there's no way out?'

'You and me? I don't know, love. But you have money.'

'No, I *don't*. Is there any room at Auntie's?'

'No. Please don't shout, it's too much for me to take in.'

Alice looked at her, aghast. 'I'm not shouting.'

'The whole point about these places is that the children are being looked after by better people than us. The nuns said, just think of it like boarding school – like your posh Hedley probably went to. Only we don't have to pay. We can't go busybodying around there.'

'What about Mr Cherry? He said he had found foster places.'

'Yes, but they would all have had to be split up. And I like the nuns. You know, some of the girls, the fallen ones I teach, give very good reports . . . It's not so bad.'

'You told me it was terrible!'

'Did I? I can't remember. But they're good girls. I know them. And they'll be helping to look after the children.'

Alice shook her head. 'I'm going to get them.' She spoke quietly but forcefully.

'What? Do you think you can just go in and take them away? I've signed for them. You're not old enough. You're still a girl yourself. And you won't have anywhere to live soon yourself. Unless, maybe . . . your Mr Morley?' Ida's words were like well-aimed darts.

'No,' said Alice. Angry tears were blurring her vision.

185

Ida sighed. 'Alice. Don't cry. They'll be happy there.'

Alice wiped a thumb under each eye. 'I'm not crying.'

'Yes, you are. You're doing that thing you've always done since you were little. Biting your lip like that. And your chin is wobbling.'

She lifted her head up and tried to shiver the tears away. 'You know what they are now? Orphans of the living. Da would turn in his grave. You said that would never happen.'

Ida looked vaguely into the distance. 'Like I say – there are good girls there, and not all of the nuns are mean. Some are kind.'

'Ma! Listen to yourself!'

'Aye, well, when your Mr Morley finds us a house, come back to me and we can have a conversation. But until then . . . where's my potato juice? I tried to tell you, but you weren't in the mood to listen.'

Alice grabbed her coat. 'Ma, I'm going to get them back. I'm going to bring them home. I can't bear it.' She could feel her fingernails digging into the flesh of her palms.

Ida shrugged. 'Please yourself. I'm going to bed,' she said. 'Shut the door on your way out.'

After Alice had stormed out of the house, grabbing her coat on the way out, the hard, bitter lines of Ida's face crumpled into soft folds. She slumped at the table and cried, her tears splashing onto the oilcloth.

She replayed the memory of walking down the corridors at St Mary's – Sister Cyril leading Gwenda and Gabriel, and Brian swinging along on his crutches

– to the dormitories. They had gone through a door, and then through a red velvet curtain. The children, about forty of them, had all been lying in neat cots and daybeds between brick pillars, just the tops of their heads visible above the plain grey blankets. There had been a nun standing at the front, murmuring through prayers with a prayer book.

'No, boys and girls are not together. Separate dormitories,' she had said when Gwenda had tried to climb into a bed and pull Gabriel with her.

'Stop coughing, Gabriel, dear,' had been the last words Ida had heard the nun say. 'Are you doing that deliberately?'

Chapter 21

Alice hurried quickly along the dock road, heading towards the tram. She had left without tying one of her laces, tucking it inside her boot to save time. When it wriggled free and she trod on it with her other foot, she tripped and almost fell.

'Careful, miss,' said the Mary Ellen, leaning on her cart, smoking. Was she laughing at her? Alice shivered away the thought.

She made it onto the tram and jumped off when she reached the end of Liverpool Lane, her heart still thumping. When she arrived at the front gates of St Mary's she could barely speak, she was so out of breath. A nun with a smiling face answered the door.

'I'm Ida Lacey's daughter,' she said, catching her breath.

'Alice? Ida has mentioned you.' The nun placed a calming hand on her arm. 'Welcome.'

She lifted the long rope around her waist with a bunch of keys dangling from it, pushed a key into the lock of a second door and twisted. The door swung open and Alice made out an arch, and through that, a large, neat garden with a manicured lawn and statues on plinths in alcoves along the high brick walls. 'St Mary of the Blessed Angels', said the words in bronze in a wrought-iron arch above the gates of the Gothic Victorian building.

So this was the place where her mother came to teach sewing. She had met some of the nuns at church, through Ida's Mothers for Injured Soldiers committee, and they had spent evenings mending socks and darning sleeves of uniforms – but Ida hadn't talked much about the orphanage.

Alice glanced at a tray on a small table in the porch, with two cups, a plate with a scone on it, and a miniature pot of jam. 'Hospitality tray,' said the nun, seeing her glance at it. 'We never know who is going to turn up. Sometimes it's the Bishop or the Monsignor. But the other day, it was a docker and his wife in a desperate state because their dog had died. Asking for an ear to listen and a prayer to comfort.'

Alice was surprised. She had expected the nuns to be cold and unfriendly. But this one wasn't distant or remote at all. Alice hadn't even thought about what she was going to do or say. Should she shout, run past her – then somehow spirit her brothers and sister away from this place?

The nun led her further into the building. Alice glanced past her, down the parquet-floored corridor with its statues of the Virgin Mary and winter flowers in vases, a crib on a table and a large Christmas tree groaning under the weight of candles and baubles and paper bells. The whole place smelled sweetly of floor polish and the musky scent of lilies.

Sister Cyril, coming down the corridor, greeted Alice with a warm pat on the hand. 'Come into my office. We've been expecting you.' She opened a door and welcomed Alice inside. 'Now, how can I help you?'

'Sister, I'm sorry, but I've come to take Brian and Gwen and Gabe back.'

'Back where?'

'Home,' Alice stammered.

'But your mother tells me you will soon have no home. Isn't that right? The landlord has plans to take back your . . . or rather *his* . . . house?' the nun corrected.

'Yes . . .' Alice stammered. 'But . . . but . . . I think she's made a mistake.'

'So that's why you're here? You're worried? There's no need to be alarmed. Your mother was out of her mind at first, but she's fine now. Shall I show you our correspondence?' She reached into a drawer and pushed a letter across the table.

Dear Sister Cyril,

I am throwing myself on your mercy and looking for your kindness to help me out of a grave situation. My daughter Alice and I are at loggerheads. We will no longer be living at home for reasons too complicated to go into here. I hope to be going to stay at my sister's. But her house is too small. Meanwhile Alice, she is like a girl possessed. All she talks about is a great future for everyone. And little Gabe. He has the croup. The house is damp. Sister, you offered before, would you take them? Just until his chest gets better and the twins calm down and we are given a new home.

Ida

'You see, dear, there's nothing sinister about your mother's intentions. And of course we would always help your family. Ida has been so good with our . . . fallen girls here at the orphanage. This is what we are here for, after all – to help families in need. I'm sorry about your mother's shop. I heard it didn't come to much. So much change in Liverpool now. All for the good, we hope, but not for some. Turbulent times,' said Sister Cyril.

Alice looked up, her hands trembling. 'Until when, Sister?'

'Sorry?'

'My mother asked you to take Gabe and the twins, but for how long?'

The nun shrugged. 'For as long as she needs. I believe she is going to Parbold,' she replied.

'Sister, if I can find them somewhere to live – my mother wants me to give up work, but that's not going to help anything. I give her nearly all of my wages. But I'm going to ask someone I know. He may be able to help.' The thoughts were crashing around in her head, spitting and jumping like fire-crackers.

The nun smiled. 'Alice. As long as your mother thinks it's in the children's best interests that they are living with us for now, no amount of money will change that. How old are you?'

'Eighteen.'

'You're still a child yourself, when it comes to the Corporation. You could come here as well if you like? We always need a spare pair of hands. You could even take over your mother's sewing classes. The girls just need to know how to mend and stitch a pattern, buttonhole and darn. Can you do that?'

'But my job?'

'You could help get the children to bed each night. Make sure they do their bedtime prayers. That's always quite a task. Take them to church on a Sunday with Sister Dorothea. As I said, you could take over the sewing classes. And we have a reputation here. The children are always beautifully dressed when the priests come, or when prospective parents come to choose a baby. Beautifully turned out, people say. We're very proud of that. So if you are good with a needle, that would be an asset.'

'Sister, I have a job,' Alice replied flatly. Her mouth felt dry, her bones hollow. Her thoughts were full of Gwenda and Brian, but most of all, Gabe. 'When can I see the children?'

The nun sighed. 'Every last Sunday of the month is visiting day for the children who have a parent or a loved one. You can come back and take them out then.'

'But that's nearly a month away! Can't I see them now, before I go?' Alice said, trying to keep the panic out of her voice.

The nun gave her a brief, tight smile. 'Of course, dear,' she said, to Alice's surprise and relief. 'Let's go and find them, shall we? They've just finished lunch. They'll be coming from the refectory.'

The sound of young voices drifted down the corridor, and a line of children came into view. There was a surge of chatter and a clattering of boots on polished floorboards. Then they heard a familiar yelp

192

as one small figure broke from the crocodile and rushed forward. It was Gwenda, with a strange bowl haircut and wearing a brown tunic. She skidded to a halt and flung her arms around Alice's waist.

'No running!' cried a nun. Behind Gwenda came Brian, on his crutches, in brown baggy shorts. He flung himself towards her.

'Alice!' they both cried, in unison.

'Oh, twinnies,' said Alice, ruffling their hair. 'They didn't waste time with that haircut, did they, Gwen! Where's Gabe?'

'He's in the nursery, napping,' said Sister Cyril. 'Isn't he a bonny boy, though? We all think so. Now go back into the line, you two. Say goodbye to your sister.'

Alice knelt down and kissed their fingers. 'Goodbye, Biscuit. Goodbye, Gravy. I love you and I'll be back to take you home soon. I'll make sure of that. And I'll be here in a few weeks to take you out.'

'Biscuit and Gravy?' said the nun, knitting her brows.

'Just family nicknames, Sister,' replied Alice.

'I'm Gravy and he's Biscuit,' said Gwenda.

The nun pursed her lips. 'I am absolutely sure that when your mother christened you, she intended for you to use God's names, not silly nonsense names. What's wrong with the name Gwenda? I have a special affection for Saint Gwendoline. And Brian, the blessed martyr who got his head chopped off for hiding priests, was a noble holy man. Biscuit and Gravy, ridiculous,' she tutted.

Brian frowned. Considering he had heard some of

the children being called by a number, he thought Biscuit and Gravy were just fine. Besides, he had been named after his favourite grandpa, Brian, who was a bookie in Dublin.

'Sister, I'm called after me grandpa – not the noble headless fella – but he was awful holy too, 'cos he's a betting man and me da said he prayed to God every day.'

'Be quiet and stop playing the fool. Every time a boy like you comes up with some silly, godless story like that to annoy me, I remind him that it's not me it hurts – it's Jesus. Isn't that right, Alice?'

Alice nodded and managed a weak smile. 'Be good, and I'll be back before you know it. And hopefully I'll bring you home soon,' she whispered, chucking them under their chins, kissing them lightly on the tops of their heads. 'Try not to worry. Be good, lovies.'

'Back you go to class, now.'

The large classroom was off the corridor. Through the open door, Alice watched the scruffy children sitting with small chalkboards in their laps, reciting by rote the numbers on the board. The windows onto the lawn outside were wide open.

'Fresh air is good for the brain. It clears the head,' said the nun, as if to answer Alice's thoughts.

'Brian was always good at maths,' said Alice.

'Just your mother found it difficult getting them to school, did she?' she said.

'Sometimes,' replied Alice. 'It wasn't easy after Da died.'

'Catechism now, class,' said the nun, standing in front of the blackboard, rapping a large wooden ruler on her desk. 'Settle down! Fingers on lips, hands on heads!'

'Routine is what these children need, Alice. We'll see you in a few weeks. Come to the front door and I'll arrange for someone to show you to the playground. That's where the children wait for their parents after Mass – at least, those orphans of the living who have someone who can take them out for the day. There are always a good deal more of them hanging about, hoping a father or mother might turn up for them. That rarely, if ever, happens. But your children will find you.'

Alice nodded. How sad, she thought – those little children waiting at the gate, and no one ever coming.

Inside the classroom, the nun tapped her long wooden ruler on the board. 'Who made me?' she said in a clear voice.

'*God made me*,' replied the chorus of little voices.

Chapter 22

Weeks passed, during which Alice moved around the house silently, went to work, cried with Matty and made him swear not to tell Hedley Morley what was going on in her family. 'It's embarrassing. I'm embarrassed,' she said.

Her mother had plans to leave for Nelly's soon – coming in one evening, Alice saw two suitcases in the hall and concluded that Ida was almost ready to go. But sitting there silently, stitching in the dwindling light, she wasn't going to share the details of her preparations with Alice.

'You can't see. Why don't you put the lights on?' said Alice, dumping her bag on the table. This place already looked bare and shabby, she thought. And it was so quiet without the children.

'Alice, we haven't got enough money for the electric. Or the oil lamp.'

The next morning at six, Alice opened the bedroom curtains and knew straight away that something was different. She looked out of the window and up and down the street at the rows of small, stubby houses, trying to figure out what it was. The washing line had gone. That was odd. But nothing could have prepared her for the shock of what she saw when she opened the curtains downstairs. The windows were marked with large crosses of tape, just as they had been during the war.

'Ma . . . the crosses,' she said, when Ida came into the parlour yawning.

Ida looked at them for a moment. 'Today,' she said flatly. 'That means they're coming today, love.'

'And you didn't think to tell me?'

Ida shrugged. 'I must have got the dates muddled.'

Half an hour later, as Alice was stuffing clothes from her wardrobe into an old carpet bag, a noise made her look out of the window. A man was on the pavement with a cart. It really was happening.

'Repossession,' he said, when she raced downstairs and found a second man hauling the dresser in the parlour.

Alice's whole body trembled. 'What are you doing? You're not supposed to be here yet.'

'Can you move out the way, queen?' said the burly man with hands like hams.

'Ma!'

Ida backed into the room, dragging the chest of drawers. 'Oh, Alice. Stop being so dramatic. Sorry, there's nothing I can do. Go and see if there's anything you want in my room. We can stay tonight. If you want to keep that precious book or your precious clock, you should pack them up now – and the children's things. Though most of those have gone,' she said, sounding so blasé that it made Alice's hackles rise. She wanted to reach out and throw something, anything, at her mother – a shoe, the clock, one of her precious books.

'Ma, what about all those things you bought? Gwenda's violin? The fur boots? And things for the shop? Can't we sell them?'

'Do you not know how bailiffs work, love? They take whatever you have towards your debt. Thank the Lord I put the kiddies somewhere safe.'

'Let me go and speak to them.' She marched outside. The man was loading up furniture, a small table, the rocking chair. 'Mister!' she cried. 'We need more time. We've nowhere to go.'

'That's what they all say, queen.'

'No, we really haven't.'

'No friends? Relatives?'

Her mind whirled. Ida would go to Auntie Nelly, but there wouldn't be room for Alice there as well. Bernice? Miss Quick, who had always helped out with errands and babysitting? She could probably go there tonight. But these were all temporary solutions. 'We've three kiddies that live here. One's a baby,' she said, desperately.

'Where are they? I can't see any. But in any case, the Corpy should help you.'

No! she wanted to scream. *No one's helping anyone.* 'They're in an orphanage,' she said, quietly.

'Then what's the problem, love?'

Alice opened her mouth, flustered. 'I don't want them there. And my ma. She's in a bad way,' she stuttered.

'You'll get somewhere soon. Have you not seen those houses they're building out in Speke? Oggie Sands? It's beautiful there. The kids'll love it. Fishing. Newts. Tadpoles.'

'Me and Ma need somewhere now. Somewhere to go tonight.'

'Sorry, love. I really am . . .'

'Tallboy coming through!' shouted the burly man.

Alice crumpled to the pavement and cried. She could think of nothing else to do. Head bent to her chest, she shivered as she sensed her mother coming up and standing behind her. She could smell Ida's rose perfume and unwashed clothes.

'I do love you. I do love all of you. I'm going to Nelly's now. She's expecting me. You'll be all right, dear? You can go to Bernice's, can't you? You told me she would have you. She lives on her own, doesn't she? Didn't her ma and da leave her that little flat they bought above the grocer's when they went back to Ireland?'

'It's tiny, Ma,' Alice said in a small voice.

'Beggars can't be choosers.' There was a pause and then Ida leaned towards her, gripping her arm. 'I'm sorry,' she said, close to Alice's ear. 'The blasted fire with your da on that ship. That's when it started to go wrong.'

Alice drew her fists to her chest. Why did her mother always accept looming defeat so easily? Where was her fight?

'Do you want this? Found it on the doormat,' said one of the men, glistening with sweat. It was a letter – addressed to Ida, but Alice opened it. Her heart plummeted as she read the note inside.

Dear Ida, the children have settled in quite well. Now they just need some time without

distractions. Try to avoid visiting if you can.
It's always better that way.
  Sister Cyril

'Over my dead body,' Alice snarled, scrunching up the paper and chucking it into the gutter where it belonged.

Just to make things worse, looking up at the dove-grey sky, she saw that snow had begun to fall.

Matty had spent the morning driving Mr Morley and Mr Worboys up to the site of the flats being built out in Speke. It seemed a brave new world compared to the crumbling and bombed-out hollas and tenements he was used to. Building had started before the war on these new estates, but now it was gathering pace: five or six blocks of modern housing, with views across the Mersey Estuary and Oglet Shore and fields.

'They even have places to park your car,' said Mr Morley.

Who has a car? thought Matty.

It was a mess of construction, with lorries everywhere and workers trudging across the mud; the tyre tracks of construction vehicles carved makeshift roadways around the buildings. Matty thought back wryly to the drawings Hedley had shown him, brightly lit in the artist's imagination, with children playing happily and parents pushing prams or walking hand in hand.

Driving back to the office, he heard the partners talking excitedly about the future and lamenting the shortage of supplies. Worboys always seemed more optimistic and upbeat than Morley.

'D'you think you and I could live in that place?' Hedley said thoughtfully.

'I could. I don't know about my wife,' Worboys replied, laughing.

When they got back, Matty followed them into the office. Coming back downstairs a little later, he found Alice outside. She was pacing back and forth on the pavement.

'Oh, Matty! Sorry – I don't know who else to talk to. Bob's away for at least another week.'

'Steady on. What's happened now?' He could see her eyes were swollen with tears.

'The children . . . losing the house. Christmas was a disaster.'

'I heard. Bernice told me you're going to be living with her now.'

As Alice began to explain, her embarrassment gave way to the relief of being able to confide in him. It shocked her, and even made her feel a little afraid, how important Matty had become to her. He was the one she turned to when she had no idea what to do – the one she believed would always have the answer, perhaps even more reliable than Bob.

'Everything is going wrong,' she said, as they leaned against the car side by side. He listened sympathetically, not interrupting. 'A year ago I had so much to look forward to . . . and now . . . It's not fair, Matty. Fifty pounds, Ma had! What a waste.'

He whistled. 'I'd take that. Buy me own Rolls-Royce.

Set up a business driving these old fellas around Liverpool.'

'She thought the neighbours would all buy things from her. She wouldn't listen to me – I told her there was a demolition order. I saw the plans. She still thinks it's all my fault somehow.'

'Is it money? Would that get the kiddies out?'

'No, it's too late for that.'

'Morley might help, though?'

'You don't understand, Matty. Ma really thinks the orphanage is the solution. She's happy they're there. I'm beginning to wonder if she doesn't even want them back.'

He reached a hand out to take hers.

'I think the war has unhinged her,' she said.

'War does that. You stop feeling things the way you normally would.'

'Or sometimes you give up altogether. Like you don't care about anything. She used to hide the bottles after she'd been drinking at night. Then she just began leaving them lying around for everyone to see. The kiddies were using them to play skittles with.'

Matty fiddled with his gloves, smoothing them out, and quickly steered the subject back to Ida. 'Don't forget, your ma is still getting to grips with your da dying. I shouldn't think she'll do anything too hasty.'

'That's the level-headed view of things. She's worried – I know she is. Would you believe, she went to the doctor's and they prescribed her five cigarettes a day? Never smoked in her life, and now she's worse than me da was. I'm not much better.'

He straightened up. 'Hop in – let's take a drive.

Morley won't need me or the car until after lunch. I did hear about your ma. She was in the snug at the Boot last week and I thought that was unusual.'

'They'll all be gossiping about us. Orphans of the living. That's about as low as you can get, when you send your children away.'

She fell silent as she slid into the passenger seat. The smell of leather, the gleam of the chrome with the low sun bouncing off it as they drove along the dock road past the tobacco warehouse, calmed her a little. Her palms prickled.

Keeping one hand on the leather-covered steering wheel, Matty reached out with the other and squeezed her hand. Alice kept her gaze on the road ahead, as if mesmerized by it.

'Is there anywhere you'd like to go?' he asked.

'I don't know. Anywhere. Away from here.'

He glanced at her, not quite sure what to make of her mood now, but he veered off the road and swept out of the city.

'Don't go too fast,' she said. She could hear the tyres on the road, the engine revving, the clunk of the gears shifting.

'These cars can go like lightning. You need to make this beauty understand that you're the one in control.'

'That's what my da used to say about my mum. He never was, though.'

'Sometimes Mr Morley lets me take her onto the sands.'

'The beach? What about the sea?'

'Not much sea where we're going. The tide goes so far out, it hardly ever comes in. Sands stretch for miles. You just have to know where to head and be careful on the sandbanks. If you go too far, the sea sneaks behind you and you turn around and see a lake.'

Five minutes later, after coasting down the dock road then picking up speed through wider tree-lined roads, the car was turning off and going through a small village and into a road fringed with pine trees.

'This place is like nowhere I've ever been,' she said, staring out of the window.

'You walk in those pine woods, and you lose yourself. You wait.'

The car purred off the road lined with huge houses and down a sandier undulating road with dunes on either side, and then more pine trees, and then finally pulled into a clearing after bumping over potholes.

'Here we are. This is the farthest tip of the coast.'

As Alice opened the door, she could feel the wind whipping her face, and when she got out it was buffeting her back. She tasted salt air on her lips.

Matty took her hand and they walked towards the pine trees. Deeper into the woods, with the soft needles underfoot, they were enveloped in an eerie, muffled quiet. They were alone and sheltered. The wind hissed through the spiked branches. As they came out the other side of the woods and met the steeper bank of dunes, it swooshed and moaned and stuck Alice's hair to her cheeks and made her eyes water. He looked at her, laughing, as they started up the ridges of gently sloping sand. She could feel her feet sinking as they began to climb a dune, the clumps of marram grass prickling her shins. On reaching the top, they stood

staring out towards the sea as a gull shrieked overhead.

'This place is beautiful,' she said.

'The view lifts the spirits, doesn't it? Look – follow
my arm – beyond the dunes. That's Liverpool . . .
and Wales. And Blackpool the other way. Come on,'
he said.

Alice ran down onto the beach with him pulling
her along by the hand. It felt as if her muscles weren't
strong enough to hold her, and she had to give in to
gravity and hurtle downwards. In the distance the sea
was thundering in waves, cresting and foaming,
tumbling onto the sand. Out towards the horizon,
the clouds were white and silver.

'Here, sit with me. It's cold.' In front of the dunes,
he took off his jacket and put it over her shoulders.
The gesture felt intimate. She blushed a little.

For a moment they sat silently, Alice letting sand
dribble through her fingers.

'Does Mr Morley mind you taking his car?'

'No. He's pretty good to me. Always has been. It's
like . . . well, I'm not sure, but he always looks out
for me. Sometimes he slips me a few extra bob on a
Friday.'

'Me an' all. Mint Imperial Maguire doesn't like it
that he lets me go in his office even when he's not
there. He asks me in even when there's a red flag up.'

He smiled. 'He let you play with them little flags?'

'He wants me to help him. In a serious way.'

He laughed again. 'I'm not surprised.'

She looked at him sternly and knitted her brows
together. 'He's an old man.'

'And they're the worst,' he said, still smiling.

'Don't be daft. What are you talking about?'

'Look at you. No man in their right mind wouldn't want you, Alice.'

Alice blushed. 'He's interested in my opinions. What the people round our way might want out of a new place to live. He wants me to help him find out. A kind of survey. What folks like about their houses and what they don't.'

He let out a little exhalation of air. 'I'm sure he does. Does he want you to do a survey on him and all?'

Alice was a little crestfallen. Was he making fun of her?

'I've got ideas. I'm bursting with ideas,' she pushed on.

He turned to her. 'I know you are. Besides, I'm only teasing. Mr Morley's lucky to have you. And he seems a good sort.'

'He is. And he has a wife,' Alice said.

'A wife! If anything, that will make him want you more. You, all optimistic and dewy-eyed, compared to her indoors nagging him to fix the stair carpet and wipe down the egg stains on his tie.'

'He just wants me to help him. He's kind. He doesn't know people like us.'

'What do you mean, people like us?'

'Don't make me say it.' She looked up at him from under her dark lashes. 'Poor people. He doesn't know poor people, not really – and he needs to know how he can help us.'

He laughed. 'Speak for yourself. Poor people! I'm not poor. I've got a job.'

'Me da had a job, but it still made us poor. And me ma, with her fifty pounds, it still made us end up with the kiddies in the orphanage. It's only supposed to be for a short time, but I'm worried sick about them right now. Fifty pounds in her pocket, but it made Ma poorer than when she started off. And stupid with it. Fifty pounds, nearly gone in a few months.'

They watched the sea for a few moments.

'One day I'd like to own a car,' Matty said. 'More than one. Maybe a whole fleet of them. I get to drive some smashing cars, but they're not mine. Even though Mr Morley lets me have it at the weekend, I still have to do things like drive his son.'

'Roddy? I met him the other day. Horrible man. And you have to drive him about?'

'Not if I can help it. Only once or twice. He's unpleasant. Lounging around, always after money from Mr Morley. One minute he's a jazz player, the next he has some scheme for selling cigars, or he's buying satin smoking jackets and wants to flog them to posh types. He has no idea where he's going in life. I'd say nowhere fast.'

'Bob doesn't really have a clue what he wants either. D'you think that's strange?'

'No, he's like every other fella I know. Getting by, day to day. Trying different things and hoping one sticks. And me owning a car? How exactly? So, keep that to yourself. I don't think I've ever told anyone that before.'

'Why not?'

'Sounds daft. Forget I said it.'

'Aye.'

'So, Alice – what next?' he asked.

Her face clouded over. 'I need to convince my ma to get the kids out of that place. I can't think about anything else.'

'Are you sure it isn't money you need? Can I help?'

She blushed. 'Matty, you're so kind. Right now, it's a roof over our heads we need. There's just nowhere to rent but I'll keep looking. In the meantime, I'm going to ask Bernice if she knows anyone who can help me find a job in the evenings. For now, I need to get us all back together somehow, and I'm saving to find somewhere while I figure that out. It isn't right that we should all be split apart so suddenly. I want the world to know.'

'That's my girl. Ever since you gave Mrs Golightly an ear-bashing over the washing line, you've stood up to people.'

'Washing Line Waterloo, my da called it. Said I was like Nelson.'

'Aye. I remember. You're proud and spirited, Alice . . .' he said, quietly placing his hand on top of hers, slotting his fingers through the gap between each one of hers.

Alice stared ahead, blinking into the distance. 'Matty, I'm sorry it's always you I come to. I know that you have the words to make it feel better.'

'And I'm sorry I made fun of you and Mr Morley. I know you and he . . . would never . . . Alice, I . . .' She turned her head towards him as his words tailed off into silence. But then he jerked his hand away. 'Look!'

He struggled to his feet and pulled her up with him. Rabbits, dozens of them, had appeared on the brow of the grassy hill between the dunes. It was a strange sight to see them hopping about, bathed in the soft winter light, with their bobbed white tails picked out by the low sun. Alice wondered why it cheered the heart so much. Life, she thought. That's what it was. A scene so alive and so vivacious, it made her smile just to look at it.

Matty put his arm around her shoulders and hugged her to him, and they listened to the icy wind passing through the trees and the waves crashing onto the shore.

Chapter 23

Alice woke on Sunday to a bright morning. She left for the orphanage early with a basket over her arm. She had slept on Bernice's small daybed after a night of endless cups of tea and toast and dripping over an open fire. It was the thought of seeing the children that pushed her on.

At the orphanage, the children had woken up to the sound of the gong being banged. The nun swept into the dormitory. Gwenda sat up and rubbed her eyes. After a cup of watery powdered milk, brought on trays by Sister Bernadette, they all pulled on the uniforms that they kept rolled up under the pillows, stood with their hands joined in prayer and started to murmur through the rosary. This place was strange and sad, and the sound of some of the children crying in the night – the thought that they had no mothers to comfort them – made those seeing their families today, on a Sunday, feel relieved and guilty at the same time.

A smiling nun was waiting on the convent steps, as Sister Cyril had promised Alice. She was also met by Angela, who had answered the bell.

'The playground is round the back, but I'll take you through the nuns' garden,' Angela said.

They walked together past the neat lawn. 'What are they doing over there – those children kneeling on the grass? With that nun standing over them?' asked Alice, puzzled. 'Are they praying?'

'No,' laughed Angela. 'They're cutting the grass.'

'Cutting the grass?' Alice squinted towards them. One of the children turned, and she saw that in his hand something glinted: a pair of scissors. 'In winter? With *scissors*?'

'Aye. That's Sister Mary Joseph for you. I'd avoid her if you can.'

'She makes the children cut the grass with scissors?'

'*Skissors*, as she calls them,' Angela said in an exaggerated Irish accent. 'But yes.'

'As a punishment?'

'No, it's just a thing the children do. Keeps the grass neat for visitors. The nuns are very keen on appearances.' She gave a wry smile.

A gaggle of children were milling about near the gate of the playground. A few were engrossed in playing a game of tag, and some kicked at the wall disinterestedly; but there was a group who hovered, eyes keenly searching anyone who approached.

'Who are you here to see?' asked a girl.

'My brothers and sister,' Alice said, smiling. 'Gabe, the little one, is only three.'

'The pretty one? You must be Ida's daughter, then? We loved Ida. Whoever would have thought her kiddies would end up here?'

Alice felt embarrassed. She was also embarrassed to be standing here in front of the other parents, but judging by their expressions, they felt the same. No one wanted to be here. No one wanted to be a parent who had put their children in an orphanage. Each was a little ashamed and with a miserable story to tell, no doubt. Everyone in this little rag-tag group seemed intent on finding their own child and leaving as quickly as they could.

And then Alice saw them: all three of them, holding hands as they came towards her. Gwenda and Gabe were skipping along, and Brian seemed to be managing well with just a single crutch now. Her heart lurched. Looking at the twins, she had to admit that even after such a short time, they appeared healthier. Their cheeks had filled out and were rosy, and their skin glowed. And they were smiling. Not only that but their hair had been washed, their clothes pressed, and their shoes weren't scuffed and muddy; they even had their socks pulled up, and mittens on elastics hung from their duffel coat sleeves.

'We was playing flinches, no free strides,' said Gwenda.

'What's that?' Alice smiled.

'Bit like grandmother's footsteps but that's what the nuns call it. Sister Dorothea plays it with us,' she explained.

'Aye, and she pokes you with her keys if you flinch.'

Alice hesitated. She couldn't quite work out what they felt about this, whether it was a good or a bad thing.

'Come on, let's get out of here,' she said brightly. 'Move it, slowcoaches. Don't want to miss the train, do we?'

She chivvied the twins along and tried to hurry

Gabe, who stopped intermittently to examine some weeds that had struggled up between two paving stones, or to clatter a stick along the railings and then chuck it randomly. They hopped behind her, skittering and weaving around her. To casual passers-by, it seemed a happy group – probably an older sister looking after the children while their mother worked, or took a much-needed rest.

At the Overhead railway station, Alice bought tickets and took them onto the platform. Looking up at the clock, she saw that the next train was due in a few minutes.

'Where are we going?'

'Wait and see.'

Soon it pulled in, and they boarded – and then they were off. Outside rushed past them, the canals and the docks on either side, until they arrived at Seaforth Sands. They made their way down the platform and through the small passage that led straight down the steps to the estuary beach. Alice felt sweet air fill her lungs. The children dashed around; despite Alice telling them to keep away from the water, they ran towards the edge of the sea, shrieking and laughing. It was as if the open spaces and the beach, with the puddled sands stretching out like wrinkled washing, soothed them and breathed life into them. It warmed her heart to see the colour in their cheeks, and she lifted her face to the sky, enjoying the winter sunshine. It was going to be a grand day out after all.

She counted the coppers in her purse. Enough for a wander through the penny arcade to see if any of the stalls were open, and later a bag of chestnuts from the

Italian man's cart. Brian plopped down with legs splayed and began making sand pies, then suddenly leapt up again, feeling the seat of his shorts and grimacing.

'Soggy bottom!' he yelled, running back towards Alice. 'I've gotta soggy bottom!'

Gwenda screeched with laughter, and Brian started grinning and laughing as well. Gabe toddled over to sit with Alice.

'This is lovely,' she said, shading her eyes against the sun, as they flopped beside her on the tattered shawl she had spread out on the sand. 'Have you made any new friends at St Mary's?'

'A few. Most have no mams and dads. One's mam and da and granny and sister all got flattened in the Blitz.'

'But there's some like us with only one ma or da who can't look after them. We've got each other, so we're OK.'

'I've gorra pet an' he is a caterpillar,' said Gabe, brightly. The sunshine gave him a halo of wobbling golden curls.

'Let's go to the arcade,' Alice said. 'I doubt many stalls will be open, but you never know.'

'Shooters is!' cried Brian, running ahead and pressing his face against the window.

'Is it safe?' asked Alice as they approached the stallholder.

'Aye. Cork guns. Harmless as long as you don't get in the way of one. Fire a cork and hit the target, you get points,' said the stallholder.

Alice wavered, then put a penny in Brian's hand. Brian, looking as though he was in heaven, handed it over and took the toy gun solemnly from the smiling stallholder.

Gwenda rested her elbows in the counter. 'Go on, Bry. Win us a teddy!'

The stallholder grinned. 'It's not easy, sonny.'

'Mister, what do I get if I hit a bullseye?'

'You can have your pick. But it's tricky, lad. The target is moving . . . And it goes pretty fast.' Brian's eyes widened. Some of the targets had pictures of Hitler and Kaiser Wilhelm stuck on them. Years of kicking the can around the hollas, knock down ginger, throwing stones at bottles on walls had prepared him well. He had been brought up roaming the bombsites and he was a good shot.

'A demon wi' a catapult, this little fella,' said Alice.

Brian took aim and squinted down the gun. The man rocked back on his heels and grinned as Brian squeezed the trigger.

'Bullseye!' he yelled. The shot had pinged right in the middle of the moving Hitler and the stallholder was so surprised he laughed and exclaimed, 'Bloody Nora!'

'Can I have the train?'

The man climbed up on a stool, reached up onto the teetering tower of boxes and handed him a train. 'Here, and for your sister – and a lolly for the babby,' he said, handing Gwenda a small doll with plaited yellow wool for hair and buttons for a nose and mouth. Gabe's eyes widened as he put the lolly in his mouth and smiled with the shock of the sugary sweetness, took it out of his mouth, stared at it in wonder, then put it back in.

'Come on, kids,' said Alice. 'That's enough excitement.'

But they weren't ready to go home yet. Gwenda ran out of the arcade and back towards the shore, Brian limping to keep up. Alice called after them to be careful. There was sinking sand here, and if they ran too far ahead, the valleys were so deep that she could easily lose sight of the tops of their heads.

It was beautiful, though. Seagulls circled. The grey of the docks seemed a world away. Along the shore, there were slabs and lumps of bricks cemented together where the Blitz had deposited leftovers: a chimney, a rusty gate, grim reminders of houses lost and lives lost. Alice picked up a brick with a piece of metal twisting through it. Behind every brick here was someone's story – someone who had lost a home, and maybe a family too, like the Laceys had.

They made their way to a cart selling chestnuts and bought two stuffed bags. After that, Alice dug in the frozen sand with her hands and made them a small boat.

'Do we have to go back?' asked Brian. 'I don't like it. I don't like the cabbage. It stinks.'

'A boy called Brendan ate a fly for a bet, and Marvin stuffed paper in my shoes and I thought me feet had grown,' said Gwenda.

'When Ma took us there, Sister took my football boots, and she still hasn't given them back to me. I hate her.'

'The sad ones fight over the food, at least the nice stuff, like oat cakes. No one fights over the tapioca and semolina. Friday, they let us have a spoonful of treacle, but it still tastes like frogspawn.'

'And when did you last taste frogspawn?' asked Alice.

'Will Ma get us soon? I don't want to turn into one of those sad kids.'

'Soon, I promise. Soon,' she said, a dart of worry piercing her heart as she gathered up their things. As they made their way from the sands up onto the pavement, she took care not to step on the cracks between the stones.

When they arrived back at St Mary's, a nun opened the door and the little group all tumbled over the step, exhausted. Alice gave the children hugs and kisses, whispering in Brian's ear to look after Gwenda and Gabe. Then she said goodbye and watched them go reluctantly down the corridor. She gazed after them until they were through the door and out of sight. She felt hollow inside, but was determined not to let it show.

On the way out, walking down the corridor alone, she heard footsteps behind her and turned to see two teenage girls, arms linked.

'You lost, love?' said one. She had cracked skin around her lips.

'No, I'm . . .'

'What you doing here?'

'I came to take my brothers and sister out.'

She could hear chanting voices from somewhere far off. 'Good for you. And how was it out there in the big wide world? We're institutionalized, aren't we, Doreen? Nice weather today.' And then recognition came across her face. 'Wait . . . you're Ida's daughter, aren't you? Your brothers and sister are here? Twins. And Gabe – the pretty one who looks like a girl?'

'Looks like an angel,' said Doreen.

'Yes.'

'How's Ida? We love your ma. We miss her.'

'She – she's fine,' stammered Alice. 'And I'll be back on the next visiting day to see the children again.'

'Don't leave it too long, love. Anything could happen.'

Alice faltered. She nodded, blinking away the image of Gabe's face as they had said goodbye, round-eyed and worried and alone.

Brian was right. This was too sad.

In the nursery at St Mary's, Sister Dorothea had appeared at Sister Cyril's side. She clapped her hands and turned to the children.

'Now, children. Before you go to your rooms, I hear you've brought back toys from your day out. Is that what you have in your hand? They go in the playroom. Brian, Gwenda, Gabriel – whatever you have there, Brian, give it to me.'

'No,' said Brian, staring up at her from under his blond fringe. 'I won it. It's mine. I won it. And you never gave me my football boots back. Sister took them when I came here, and she never gave me them.'

'You can play with the train another time. But rules are rules. They go in the toy box. It's not fair that you two should have a toy and others haven't. Jesus wouldn't like that. Jesus wants us all to be equal. He wants us to share. Share and share alike. Selfishness should not be encouraged.'

'But I won the train. It's mine,' said Brian. He started to cry. 'Jesus can go to hell!' he said, stamping his foot and twisting away, hugging the train towards him.

The nun gasped, furious, bent down and tried to wrestle it out of his hand, but he moved back again and pressed himself into an alcove.

'This is silly. Can you stop? I'm just asking you to share your toys, not sending you away to your room or giving you the slipper. Look at you, all snotty. And you've made Gabriel cry,' she said, seeing Gabriel's lip tremble. 'What if Mr and Mrs Pirbright came now and saw him like this?' she hissed.

'Who's Mr and Mrs Pirbright?' asked Gwenda.

'Never mind,' said the nun, tetchily.

'Perhaps if you just let Bry have the train, Sister,' said Gwenda. ''Cos he's given it a name. Duncan. He really loves it.'

'You don't give trains names. I told you. It's not fair. It's not fair for the other children,' snapped the nun. 'If he has something and they don't.'

'You do give trains names. Thomas the Tank Engine has a name. And his friends, Edward, Gordon. Say no, Bry,' Gwenda whispered.

'I heard that. Hand it over,' said the nun.

'No,' she said. 'Don't, Bry.'

'*Give me that train now.*'

'It's mine,' insisted Brian.

'Please, Sister. Let him have it.' Gwenda looked at her pleadingly.

'I'm trying to be fair,' said the nun. 'God is fair. When you hurt each other, you hurt God. So give me the wretched train. Now. And for goodness' sake, stop crying, Gabriel!'

Gabriel let out a wail and Brian knitted his brows together angrily. He handed the train over, shoving it into her hands. 'You can have the bloody train,' he said. 'But I want to go home. We're ready to go home now. Will you call me ma? Now I've given you me train?' he said plaintively.

Chapter 24

'I need a cigarette, Bob,' said Alice.

They were sitting in the noisy snug at the Boot with Bernice, who was shouting at someone over the bar. Bob, sunburned and flashing a bundle of green notes earned somewhere far off along the coast of Spain, grinned.

'My Cherry Bomb! So you've started smoking while I've been away? Didn't know that.'

'Yes, well. I've been driven to it.'

He laughed, taking two cigarettes and a matchbook out of his pocket. Putting both of the cigarettes in his mouth, he winked, tore off a match and lit each of them, then placed one gently in Alice's mouth. She coughed slightly and her eyes watered as she waved away the smoke.

Bernice came over. 'Where's Buttons?' she asked. 'We'd make a nice foursome.'

Bob smiled. 'Running some posh fella around in his car, no doubt. Not my thing. All that bowing and scraping. Don't know how he can stand it, hey, Alice?'

Alice blinked the comment away.

Bernice wriggled in next to them. 'I'll just have to be the goosegog with you two. These bazookas, and Matty runs a mile every time I see him. There's a heart under these magnificent bosoms and I'd give it to him.' She grinned.

Alice raised a weak smile.

'Pale ale, love? Alice?' said Bob.

'Lemonade,' she replied as he got up to go to the bar. Sucking on the cigarette, she realized it had gone out, reached for the matches lying on the table and tore another one off.

Bernice frowned. 'What's this?' she said, picking up the matchbook when Alice put it back down. 'The Crown Hotel?' She made a face and flipped it back onto the table.

'The Crown?' Alice picked it up to examine it and turned it over, seeing there was something scribbled on the back. *Wednesday 7th – Appointment with Dr Hennessey – Ten o'clock.* A doctor? This was Bob's handwriting, with its childish loops and odd slanting to the left. Her heart stopped. Was there something wrong with him?

'Bob? What's this? You've written something on the back of the matchbook,' she said lightly when he returned. He was sitting back down at the table, stuffing a pickled onion into his mouth, crunching it between his teeth. Bernice glanced away.

He snapped his head up. 'Nothing,' he said, and snatched the matchbook back from her.

'What's the matter?' Alice asked, genuinely puzzled.

His nostrils flared. He reached out and grabbed her forearm. 'Leave it.'

She yelped. His hand gripped her like a manacle. 'Ow, Bob. Is something wrong? Let go of me! You're hurting.' A chill descended in the snug, as cool as a draft under a privy door.

'Don't, Bob!' said Bernice darkly.

He let go. 'It's nothing, love – I'm sorry,' he stuttered.

Alice was bewildered. For a moment they sat staring at each other over the table, with Bernice biting her lip and looking into the distance. Something's not right, Alice thought. The pub smelled unpleasant, of sour hops and rotten sawdust, which perfectly matched the thoughts in her head.

'I'm off,' said Bob abruptly, standing up. He shoved the matchbook into his pocket. 'Got to see a man about a job.'

Alice watched him go. She turned to Bernice. 'What was that about? The Crown Hotel – you know it?'

Bernice pulled a face. 'Aye. Everyone does.'

'Is it a nice kind of place? Bob said he might take me there one day soon,' Alice lied.

Bernice's eyes widened. 'Can't he do better than that? It's a terrible place. Seedy. All sorts of things go on there . . . apparently.'

Alice's heart thudded in her chest. 'Like what?'

'I don't know. Just steer clear, Alice. Tell Bob you want to go somewhere else. The Adelphi. Or Cooper's. But the Crown – no, he'll have to do better than that, love. God knows what he's brought back from abroad. A drop in standards, that's for sure.'

'What d'you mean?'

Bernice sighed. 'It's kind of a knocking shop. And conveniently, the prophylactic clinic is upstairs. Everyone knows. Tuesday and Wednesday evenings.

It's so's the fellas don't have the embarrassment of the family doctor.'

'What are you saying?'

'Alice, love, he wouldn't be the first. But don't you go catching anything from him. That's the worst. The very worst. The itching, and the not being able to pee properly. The blisters. You're not . . . having relations with him?'

Alice blushed. She thought about all the times she had fought Bob off, all the doorways, the back yards, or up against the canal walls, when he had searched out the softest private parts of her, begging her to let him do *it* to her.

'No.'

'Don't. Not until he's sorted himself out.'

Alice felt herself go hot under the collar. Sorted himself out? What on earth did that mean?

That night, Alice thought back to Bob's behaviour recently. He had hardly kissed her, not properly – certainly no grabbing handfuls of flesh like he usually did, yanking at her skirts, pushing his tongue into her mouth whenever she walked past him. She was sure the unsettling feelings she was having had something to do with whatever it was about the matchbook and the doctor's appointment that he had been so quick to hide from her. What had made his quick temper rise and the fury blaze in his eyes when she had brought it up?

Steer clear of the Crown, Bernice had said, forgetting it was Alice she was speaking to. Nothing made her want to do something more than someone telling her not to.

The following morning, once she had rolled up the bedding she was sleeping on, she walked straight from Bernice's to Alexandra Street and slipped quietly in through the front doors of the Crown Hotel. Eyes fixed ahead, she walked past the frayed velvet sofas and wilting aspidistras, averting her eyes from the peeling paint, grubby threadbare rugs, and the bowl collecting water beneath a leak in the plaster ceiling.

The woman at the front desk looked over her thick-rimmed glasses and called, 'Can I help you?'

Alice didn't know how to reply. She had come here because she wanted to see the place for herself, because Bernice had warned her off – but now she wondered what she was doing here. There was a man sitting in one of the chairs in a brown raincoat, staring at her oddly. She backed away, stuttering that she had made a mistake.

The woman shrugged and went back to her copy of *Picture Post*. One of the wretched aspidistras tickled Alice's ear as dark thoughts churned in her head. She shivered and turned to leave. The man was smiling at her now, she was sure he was. This was all too horrible to think about. She had heard the stories. She had seen the posters during the war: *The Enemy in your Pants*. But Bob? He wouldn't have done, would he? She had laughed over that with Bernice. It had seemed ridiculous, but now it didn't feel funny at all. She felt as if she was falling even though she was still standing. What was she going to do?

A moment later she was back outside, gulping fresh air and brushing away the perspiration that trickled down her neck. She knew where she would find Matty, and all she could think of was seeking him out for advice. But she wondered why, when she was worried and frightened about what was going to happen next, it was Matty she turned to and not Bob.

There was a woman standing on the steps outside the blue front door of the Chauffeur Club, smoking, with half an inch of ash drooping off the end of her cigarette.

'I'm looking for Mr Turpin,' Alice said. The woman blew a plume of smoke and nodded.

Alice followed her eyes and saw Matty leaning against his car, one of a dozen similar vehicles lined up on the pavement. They made an arresting sight, polished and shining, as lovely to look at as their drivers, who would come here between shifts and after work in their caps and uniforms with their white gloves and long black boots.

When Matty, leaning against the Rover and smoking, saw her coming towards him, he flicked his cigarette into the gutter and screwed it into the pavement with the toe of his polished shoe.

'Alice? What are you doing here?' he said.

'Matty, I need to speak to you.'

'What's the matter?' He took her arm and led her up the steps. 'It's not often they have women in here, but we can go to the back bar. It's a men's club and the men like to keep it that way.'

'What nonsense,' she said.

On the first floor, up a creaking staircase, there was a small desk behind a moth-eaten velvet curtain. The walls were painted a rich plum colour. Alice could smell beer and cigarettes mixed with beeswax. Looking through an open door, she saw a small ballroom with a buffed and polished floor.

Matty pressed a finger to his lips. 'Through here. They're playing snooker.' There were two men bent over the green baize tables amid an atmosphere of utmost seriousness. The room was silent. Suddenly one of them twisted around and said to the barmaid sitting watching at the far end of the room, knitting, 'Nora. Put your knitting away! You're putting me off. Them needles are clacking too loud.'

Matty exchanged a smile with Alice. 'See why they don't encourage women here?'

'Ridiculous, Matty.'

'Aye, I know. Come on,' he whispered. 'Let's go and find somewhere quieter to sit.' They went up another winding staircase. The room he led her into was full of plush velvet high-backed chairs, some stacked against the wall.

'Matty, I need to talk to you about . . . male things. Things that are too horrible to say out loud.'

'Sit down. What things?'

'I don't know. Matty . . . is there anything you need to tell me?'

He paused. 'No, love. Not that I can think of.'

'I'm not as green as you think. But . . . Bob . . . is he . . . has he . . .' Her eyes filled with tears. 'You need to tell me what I should do.'

She had never needed advice like she did now. Matty was the only one who could give it. Bob was the man she was supposed to be marrying, and she wanted to know whether she was about to make the biggest mistake of her life.

'The prophylactic clinic . . . at the Crown Hotel? Bob had an appointment there.'

Matty took a moment to absorb this. 'Are you sure? He might have gone there with a pal. There could be any reason he was there.'

'Do you know about that place?'

'Aye. Everyone does. They dole out medicine. More private than the family doctor. You know, if wives are there . . .'

'It's awful. And doesn't it . . . make you go blind or something? And mad? . . . The enemy in your pants. Those posters during the war . . . Oh, Matty . . . I feel sick to think of it . . .'

'That was the old days. They give you a tablet now. But Alice – why are you telling me all this? You need to speak to Bob. Ask him what's what. But I'm sure it's not what it seems.'

'I just want him to tell me the truth.'

'And what if it's not what you want to hear?'

'Has he been with another woman? It looks that way. Is that what you're saying?'

'No. Just, maybe it should be him you're talking to, not me.'

Alice took a deep breath. He hadn't really told her anything, but in doing so he had told her everything. And she had made up her mind.

She had heard the Big Bertha gun fire twelve o'clock at the docks. Bob's mother's house was unlocked, as it often was, and she found him wearing only his trousers and vest, asleep on the sofa. Alice shook him awake. He struggled to sit up, squinting away

228

confusion. She wanted to slap him for ruining everything.

'The Crown Hotel. The clinic. Why would you want to go there?'

He sighed. 'What are you talking about?'

'Bob, I'm not stupid.'

He shook his head, rubbed his eyes and yawned. 'If you must know, I went with a pal.'

She fixed him with a look. 'So you did go? I knew you were lying. You yawn when you lie.'

'With a pal,' he said flatly.

'Who?'

'Fella from the ship.'

'Bob, I'm not sure I believe you. Can I ask you something? Why haven't you come near me lately? The first time we've been left in the house without your ma banging on the broom; you've been going on about it for months, years, what you would do if you had me on my own, how there's always too many blasted people around. And there we were, finally, with your ma out. And you didn't do anything?'

'No, don't talk daft,' he said.

'You didn't come and see me, either.'

'What?' he said, not meeting her eye again.

'You were in the pub. You didn't tell me you had come home. It was the Mary Ellen who lives round our way.'

'The one who sees ghosts? I've told you, she's a mad old witch.' But then his face changed. She could see that her words were infuriating to him and his temper was about to get the better of him. 'All right. Have it your way,' he said, slamming his fist down on the arm of the sofa. 'But Alice, you're making such a bloody fuss about nothing. What was I supposed to do? Not your bloody business!'

'It is if we're going to get married! So you *were* with another woman?'

He shrugged.

She was shocked. She hadn't expected this at all. She had wanted reassurance, for him to tell her the name of his pal and how he was helping cover for his pal's wife, and what an awful predicament he had found himself in. She felt her heart sinking.

'If this is what it's like now, while we're still engaged, what hope is there for us?'

'For pity's sake,' he growled. Muttering and raking a hand through his hair, he stormed off into the kitchen, banging the door behind him.

'Come back here!' she cried. 'Speak to me. Don't run away!' She pulled on the handle and rattled it. 'Have you put a chair against the door?'

Suddenly he slammed it wide open and stood there, cheeks flushed, eyes wild, fingers curled into white-knuckled fists. 'You want me to be honest with you? You might not like the truth.'

'Try me,' she said, her voice quivering.

He placed his hands on his hips and towered over her, breathing heavily. Suddenly she felt afraid of how tall and strong he was – stronger after these past few months on the ships, shovelling coal.

'It happened once, all right? I was just unlucky to get the flaming clap. But it didn't mean anything. What was I supposed to do? When they wanted me to go onshore to them dismal seedy bars, fellas just looked at me like I was an idiot when I said I had a girlfriend back home. And I was drunk. There's no love involved. I was just doing what other fellas do. There, I've said it. And now I've got the bloody clap. And it's your fault. Yes. And it itches like hell, if you must know. Like my skin is crawling with ants.'

She felt sick. She had feared it was coming, but the thought of him with someone else pierced her heart.

'One thing led to another, that's all. You should have left it alone instead of nagging it out of me!'

'Perhaps if *you'd* left it alone you wouldn't have the flaming clap,' she said.

'What did you want me to do? Every time I went near you, you wouldn't let me. So sodding high and mighty. You know, I always wondered if you were frigid? Cold as the Irish Sea.'

'That's not fair!'

'There are some bring it back to their wives, they don't say anything and hope for the best. I could have just . . . with you, but I didn't do that. I tried to keep away from you.'

'Am I supposed to be *grateful*?'

'I don't know. I love you, Alice,' he whined, slumping into a chair and drooping his shoulders. 'You forced me into telling you. Why did you have to do that? You women do that, don't you!' He banged his fist on the arm of the chair.

'Flaming hell, Bob! And with everything I've got going on at home!'

He scowled. 'Aye. And while we're talking about that. Very convenient, isn't it? Suddenly you want to

231

marry me because of the mess your ma has got into with the kiddies? Because you don't want to leave your precious job?'

She dropped her head and spoke in a low voice. 'I don't know, Bob. Maybe,' she said, with a long exhalation of breath, as if giving in to the truth was the only thing to do. 'I'm tired of everything. But maybe – even without me ma, putting aside what you've been up to with God knows who – was marriage ever right for us? Maybe we're just too young. If I'm honest, I've been unsure about this, you, me, us, for a long while. Maybe you do need to sow your oats.'

His face fell, the anger drained from him. 'Don't say that, Alice. I'd rather you were angry. Throw a plate at me or something, or yell at me. I don't want to do that. The woman . . . I felt sorry for her, but more for myself. It was pretty horrible. She forced me into it.'

'No. Don't say anything more. And don't blame her, whoever she was – is.'

'I just want you, Alice,' he whinged.

He lunged towards her to kiss her and she batted him aside angrily. 'No! Get off me,' she cried.

'Oh, I get it, you think I'm diseased? You can't catch it if you kiss someone. Don't be so bloody stupid,' he said, the bitter tone returning to his voice and his face darkening.

'I know that.'

He stood up bad-temperedly. 'You know, they want me on the boat that goes in the morning, and it's a long trip this time. The Azores.'

'Then that's where you should go. That's probably the best thing for both of us.'

'Alice . . . you're making too much of this.' He reached out and grabbed her arm. She twisted away.

'The truth is, Bob, the only thing I care about is the children. I'm sorry. I can't just push it aside.'

'Can't we go back and start again?' he said, with a pitiful look and that irritating whine in his voice.

'No. Besides, this is not the time to be going back. I need to make sure I have some kind of future.'

'Come on, Alice. Think how happy we were. I love you,' he said again. He cracked his knuckles. 'It was stupid, just one small mistake.'

She blinked away the hurt. 'I did love you, I really did, but we've changed. Both of us. We're not the same two kids sitting on that wall watching the planes and daft enough as to think the bombing was fireworks. Things change. People change.'

'You're the one who's changed. I haven't.'

'I've just become more confident. Is there anything wrong with that?'

'No, nothing wrong with that. But you've become . . . I don't know . . .'

'Harder to manage?'

'Mebbe.' And then he paused and swallowed. 'Who told you I came back early?'

She faltered.

'You said it was the Mary Ellen, but was it Matty?' he asked. 'It was Matty, wasn't it?'

'Doesn't matter,' she replied. Turning away, she wiped away a tear and made her way to the front door. But before she left, with an odd sense of relief, she took the ring off her finger and quietly placed it on the table in the hall.

In the bar at the Chauffeur Club, Matty stared into the bottom of his glass. Bob had found him where Alice had left him, and was now sitting opposite him.

'I'm not sure I want to know.'

Bob leaned in towards him. 'It started with the most fearsome itch the first time I got home. I was scared – I remembered how they said you used to have to put a needle up the old man. But now they have pills. And it'll clear up in a few weeks. Still, I couldn't risk letting Alice anywhere near me. If it hadn't been for that Mary Ellen snitching on me. I hadn't planned to tell Alice I was home . . . Wanted it to clear up. Anyway. I just want you to know, we've had an awful bust-up.'

'How did she find out?'

'I told her.'

'You what?'

'I know. God knows why. Women. They're canny. She forced it out of me. Now she's gone to Bernice's. The whole thing is a bloody shame, because the night she came round and me ma was away, I think she might've weakened.'

Matty bristled. 'I'm not so sure. You're a fool, Bob.'

'I know, I know . . .' He dropped his head in his hands and sighed. 'I shouldn't have said anything, you're right . . .'

'No, I mean you're a damn fool for going with another woman. You don't realize how lucky you are with Alice.'

'Do you think she'll forgive me?'

'Anyone else, you might have a chance with, but Alice is so . . . so . . . high-minded.'

'I know. I tried to tell her it was the blasted woman's fault. But she told me not to piss on me boots and tell her it was raining.'

'Alice said that?'

'She didn't exactly put it like that. Said I shouldn't blame the woman for my mistake.'

A drunk man came rushing in, waving a bin lid, banging it with a spoon and laughing. Two other fellows stumbled after him, guffawing. Matty's eyes followed them, and he shook his head.

'This city is full of fools. Not just you, Bob. There goes another idiot, no doubt with some stupid story to tell. I doubt Alice will get over this.'

Chapter 25

A tearful Alice sat with Bernice in her kitchen, sharing a pot of tea.

'Lucky escape, in one way, my lovely,' Bernice said ruefully. 'Hope he takes his diseased John Thomas to Morocco, or flaming Norway, or the North Pole where it gets frostbitten and drops off.'

Alice sighed. 'He's always been like – like a child pushing a glass of water to the edge of the table. Pushing it that little bit further, even when I warn him. It's over this time. Really.'

The wireless was playing *ITMA* and laughter bled out into the living room. It felt as though the audience was laughing at her.

'You say you want an evening job? Why?' Bernice said. 'You'll be exhausted. You already are.'

'Things are getting desperate. I've no idea how Ma is. I need to work in the night as well as at Morley's. I need to save while I think what to do, and it will take my mind off Bob. If I have more coming in, maybe I can rent us something. I'm so worried about the kiddies.'

'There is one job going I know of. The girls were talking about it at the factory. They're looking for lassies at a dance hall in town. Cloakroom girls.'

'Really?'

'But if it's money you need, why don't you ask Mr Morley? He might know someone.'

'He's helped me enough as it is. Besides, I don't want him to know everything that's happened. The truth is, I'm a little ashamed of how Ma's recklessness has sunk us into this dire situation.'

'Alice, you've your father's pride. Sometimes you should ask people for help. Here, then. The address. Stop squishing your hat like that, you'll put it all out of shape! I don't know much about what it's like, but you can say I sent you. And good luck, love. They want pretty girls, and you're certainly that, sweetie.'

Alice checked the address Bernice had scribbled down – 42 Matthew Street – as she made her way down a narrow passage. There it was, a green door at basement level, down some steep steps. She practised what she was going to say in her head: *I believe you have a position going. I'll work hard and I'm organized.*

Beyond the door, she could hear a blast of music – a single instrument, not a trumpet, but something she recognized. Saxophone? The sound was brittle, unsettling. The notes seem to split and crack. The melody was unfamiliar, harsher and more atonal than the bands in the dance halls she was used to. A voice joined in, rich and low.

A girl wearing a peacock feather in her hair let Alice in after first sliding open a small window in the door. 'Welcome to The Pink Flamingo,' she said. 'You're pretty. Shame about those drab clothes. But come in.'

Alice stuttered she had come for the job. 'Bernice sent me,' she said.

The girl nodded and looked her up and down. 'You an open-minded kind of girl? You better be . . . You've got a convent girl look about you, but often those are our best girls. Some have a devilish kind of streak, for sure, and the fellas go wild. Pay's good. People are friendly. Exceptionally friendly.'

As Alice went in, the first thing she noticed was the smoke hanging like a fog over everyone's head in the small, airless room draped with musty velvet curtains. It choked her lungs and made her eyes water. A beautiful, Latin-looking woman stood spotlit on a small stage, wearing a sequinned headdress of quivering ostrich feathers. She was singing 'Lovely Weekend', but pitched low, and the bass notes seemed to make the whole room vibrate. People were dancing on the small dance floor, but as the music reached a crescendo they seemed engrossed in their jerky movements, rolling their eyes, tossing back their heads, plenty of them without a partner. The scene had a kind of chaos about it, not the formal glide around the dance floor in a waltz or a foxtrot that Alice was used to.

The young woman escorted Alice towards the bar, behind which a man was polishing glasses with a cloth.

'Hello, ducky. How can I help you?' he said.

'Bernice sent her,' the young woman explained.

Alice nodded. 'Bernice is a friend. She said someone at the Meccano factory mentioned you're looking for girls right now.' She had to raise her voice to be heard above the music.

'We're always looking for girls. You a dancer?'

'Me? Oh no.' Alice glanced around the space, noticing that the man playing the saxophone was looking directly at her. This visit was becoming more unsettling by the moment.

Maybe from Bernice's description she had expected something different – something more professional. This place felt more like someone's front room, with chenille-covered tables and chairs and white lilies in vases. Whatever it was she had thought she was coming to, it wasn't this. A girl was moving around with a tray of drinks, wearing a dress with the top half sleeveless and diaphanous. It left barely anything to the imagination. The bottom half had fringes around her hips that swayed when she moved.

'You'll be selling cigarettes,' the man said. 'And you can help me out behind the cloakroom counter. Just take their coats, give them a ticket and a smile. Start now if you want, love. We're short staffed tonight. A shilling an hour, plus tips. We'll find you a cigarette tray in a minute. Look sharp, here's some customers now.'

A group of young men fell rowdily through the door. Alice took their hats and nervously gave them the tickets for a sixpence, under the direction of the young woman who had let her in. Then a second woman appeared. 'Ready for your ciggies? Go and get changed in the back room.'

'Changed?'

'You have to wear a little pillbox hat and a dress. Kind of like a soldier girl. Epaulettes and shiny buttons,' the woman said casually. 'The fellas love it.

Especially the ones that fought in the war. Does something strange to them.'

Alice made her way nervously through the fringed curtain as directed. Beyond was a door with a tatty gold star on it. The smell of powder and alcohol, and a strange, musky scent that she recognized, reached the back of her nose and made her gag slightly.

'Here, put this on,' said the woman, sliding hangers along a rail and selecting an outfit. Alice faltered. 'One of those shy ones, are we? Go behind the screen if you want, but trust me, I've seen it all, ducky. A skinny girl in her drawers isn't going to shock me.'

If she was going to turn on her heel and leave, Alice knew this was her chance. But as she stood behind the screen changing, fumbling with buttons and straps, pulling on the jacket with the buttons and wide cuffs edged in gold braid and then the short, white pleated skirt, all she was thinking about was the ten shillings she would be going home with later on.

'Oh, good God,' said the woman when Alice came out. 'You can't wear those awful hobnailed boots. What size are you? About a five? Here . . .' She rummaged in a suitcase and came up with a pair of silver sling-backed sandals. 'Soon as you're ready, go into the room down the corridor marked "Green Room" and get your tray.'

'You!' said Alice.

It took a few seconds for Roddy Morley to recognize her. 'Good grief!' he laughed. 'What are you doing here, Miss Meccano? And look at you! You look wonderful! *Ooh la la!*'

Alice felt panic rising. 'I don't understand,' she said, aghast. She was horrified to find him standing there, laughing at her in her ridiculous outfit. She pulled the pillbox hat off. 'This is a mistake.'

'No, stay.'

He gripped her arm. She froze. Why couldn't she move, run, shout?

'You look delightful in that little soldier boy outfit. Have you any idea how beautiful you are?'

'I want to go.'

'Why? Stay. I need to talk to you . . .'

'No.'

'Don't run away from me. This is fate.'

'No – it's a mistake,' she managed.

'Would you stay if I told you I need a favour?'

'No.'

'It's to do with Pa.'

Alice hesitated. 'What d'you mean?'

'My pa, who thinks I'm useless.'

'No, he doesn't,' she lied.

'Sadly, he does. But Alice, I'm turning over a new leaf – I promise I am. And it occurred to me the other day – you see, he thinks so highly of you, Alice. And if you threw a little of your goodness in my direction . . . this is such a strange thing. You, here, at my little club. Fate, wouldn't you say?'

'I don't believe in fate. I believe you make your own luck, and this has bad luck written all over it.'

'Wait! I'll come straight to the point. I have money and you don't. Not enough. Otherwise you wouldn't be here in that jolly little outfit, would you? We could come to an arrangement.'

241

'What kind of an arrangement?' she replied, shocked.

'I give you money. And you . . . well, you see, my father – I need to show him that I've changed. Just tell him you're sweet on me, that's all you need to do. Perhaps let me take you out once or twice. Tea at the Adelphi? The Philharmonic? *Private Lives* on at the Playhouse, next week. It's a hoot.'

Thoughts crashed through Alice's brain. Was this how life worked when you had money? Did these people believe they could buy their way out of anything?

'Why not try it? What have you got to lose?' he said.

'No.'

'Oh, come on. Be a sport. Don't you see – my life is so vapid and shallow. At least, that's what Pa thinks – and you have such passion and kindness. It would change everything for me. I'm sure he would think better of me. I promise I will make it worth your while.'

'I can't believe what you're saying . . .'

'I've been a little flippant with you. You know, you really are a beautiful girl, and I see now what my father was talking about. I know all about your family, that your mother is in a tight spot. And the children. Come on, play the game. It would work for both of us. I just need you to pretend that you and I . . . that we are in love.'

'Your father is not that stupid.' Alice shook her head firmly. 'He would see straight through that.'

'It's worth a try, though, isn't it?'

He moved towards her. She could smell alcohol on his breath, mixed with something she couldn't quite put her finger on. Sweet and sickly, and she couldn't help flinching. 'I really am leaving,' she said, pulling away.

He grasped her chin with his finger and forefinger, twisted it towards his face. 'You're not going to budge, are you? I just want to kiss you, if the truth be known. The minute I saw you, I just wanted to put my lips on yours. Come here . . .' He leaned in to her, but she squirmed away again. 'God, I'd love to take you places that you wouldn't dare imagine. That sweet, innocent face. Bet you've never known real pleasure? That's something deeper than love, my dear. Darker and delicious. And you are *dangerously* beautiful.'

'Get off me!' she cried, ducking out from under him.

'Hah! We're playing games, are we? Well—'

Suddenly a girl with a silver shawl hanging loosely around her shoulders came tumbling through the door, accompanied by a louche-looking older man. The girl was sniffing and had a pained expression on her face. Pushing past them, she slumped onto a moth-eaten velvet chair, a shoe hanging off the end of her foot. The man collapsed and sprawled across the chaise longue, his head lolling to one side. He swivelled his eyes and regarded Alice with a curious but dazed stare. The girl picked up a cigarette holder and tried unsuccessfully to shove a bent cigarette into the end of it, then gave up and slumped again.

'My eyes, honey,' she groaned, pressing her palm to her forehead. 'Shut the curtains.'

The room was already dark, shadowy and bathed in a sickly pale pink light. There wasn't even a window that Alice could see, never mind curtains.

'Don't worry, dear. She's hallucinating again,' said the man. He turned back to Roddy. 'You got some of your wake-up pills for her?'

'Ooh, yes, daddy-oh, Roddy-oh . . .' the girl said, slurring her words.

Then, seemingly for no reason, she stood unsteadily, dropped the shawl, undid the zip of her dress and calmly stepped out of it. 'That's better,' she said and shivered, standing there in her silk cami-knickers, shakily trying again to light her cigarette.

'Hard to kick the habit, isn't it, honey?' said Roddy, smirking.

Alice watched in amazement.

'Gimme . . .' said the girl, and stuck out her hand.

Alice shivered. 'Your father. Does he know about this?' she said in a low voice, as the girl with the glazed eyes put her hands loosely around her friend's neck, half grimacing, half smiling.

'It would break his heart, wouldn't it?' He laughed and rolled his bottom lip.

'Yes,' she said quietly.

'He adores me really, despite how it might look. You're not going to tell him? He would only take against you. Of course, he knows about my . . . addictions . . . Only he thinks it's the booze.'

'You should tell him. He might . . . help you.'

'Perhaps I should. He might even be impressed. It's the one thing I'm rather good at. I can take five Pervitin in one night – that's my weakness, I have to

244

say – and a bottle of whisky to wash them down, and still wake up the following morning bright as a button. Or afternoon, rather. Constitution of an ox. The Nazis invented Pervitin, so when I wake up and, surprise, I'm not dead, I like to think that's my small victory over Hitler.'

'Roddy, more,' whined the girl.

'Poor dear. She's a little jaded to it,' he whispered to Alice.

Alice glanced over at the man, who had taken a bottle from his pocket and was swigging straight from it, before shivering and wincing.

'Oh, Alice, dear,' sighed Roddy. 'Where are your manners, Quentin? Don't drink that stuff in front of the ladies. So uncouth. Absinthe. It's lethal. Put it away.'

She felt sorry for Roddy. Sad and stupid and sorry little man. But there was only one thing on her mind. How was she going to get out of here? So when she heard a banging on the other side of the door, more of a thumping hammer, she prayed it was the woman who had shown her in. Meanwhile, the man on the sofa had risen unsteadily to his feet. He rolled up a newspaper and selected a stale bread roll from a discarded tray of food.

'Cricket! Splendid!' cried Roddy in delight.

The door began to open.

'Watch out,' said the louche young man as he whacked the roll with the newspaper. It flew across the room.

'Matty!' spluttered Alice, as the roll whizzed past her and struck Matty's shoulder.

'Who's this?' Roddy sneered over his shoulder.

Matty clenched his jaw. 'Alice. Do you want to come with me? Get your coat.'

'Who are you?' said Roddy.

'Never mind.'

'Well, Mr. Never Mind, unless you tell me where you fit into the story of Alice, we're just going to carry on with our game! Howzat!' he yelled, as the giggling girl swung the newspaper bat and whacked another bread roll towards him, which he caught.

Matty bristled and stepped forward, speaking directly into Roddy's face. '*Don't ever come near Alice again.*'

Roddy smirked and took a bite out of the bread roll. 'Alice is a game girl. She can handle herself, ding-dang sure about that.'

'Come on, Alice,' Matty said.

She rushed back to the dressing room, changed into her old boots at the speed of light, and scooped up her clothes and handbag. As they stumbled out into the air, the reflections of the streetlights shimmied in the puddles. This city. So much trauma, she thought, as she fell into Matty's arms.

'Are you all right? What happened in there?'

'I'm fine,' she replied. 'Just a little humiliated, but mostly, I'm mad as hell. You wouldn't believe how dreadful a human being Roddy is. Thank goodness you turned up, Matty. Did Bernice tell you I was there?'

He nodded, as he led her to his car.

Matty listened, kindly and patiently, as they sat in the Rover with the rain wriggling down the window.

'I was only trying to earn a few more shillings to help Ma. Help the situation,' she said, sniffing. 'I'm so embarrassed.'

'You should have come to me,' he said tenderly. 'What a pathetic excuse of a man. He didn't even recognize me. Probably because I'm not in my uniform.'

'And Bernice told you I was there? But what made you come to find me?' asked Alice.

'I'd heard of the place. The clue was in the bloody awful name. The Pink Flamingo. Last week it was the Boom Boom Club. They get shut down and open again the next week, pretending to be under different management. I could have given you money, Alice.'

'No. You've been kind enough. Wake-up pills. What are they, Matty?'

'The Yanks prescribed them during the war for their soldiers. Pretty soon, dope girls were handing them out like sweets all over Liverpool. For a price. They're amphetamines. Fancy a drink to calm down?'

She shuddered. 'Yes. That poor girl,' she said, in a quiet voice.

They had parked under the docker's umbrella – or the Pneumonia Express, as her father used to call it when he had travelled to Gladstone Dock each day squashed in with every other docker, all coughing and barking and wheezing – so Alice could change her clothes.

'I won't look,' said Matty.

'I don't care,' she said, smiling. She wriggled out of the skirt, pulled off the shirt and put her shift dress on over her head. When she had arranged herself, they got out of the car and headed towards the Caradoc pub. But when they opened the door it was heaving with men, full of sailors and dockers who worked on the Blue Funnel Line. There was a man with an accordion, and everyone was singing along to 'Over There': '*Johnny, get your gun, get your gun . . .*'

Matty shouted over the racket, 'It'll be a US ship just docked. The Yanks come here because they've got two tills. One for British money, the other for dollars! That's why it's packed to the gills and they're all singing American songs. Let's go to mine for a cuppa.'

They drove to Conway Street and climbed a narrow, winding staircase to Matty's small flat above a fish-monger's. He explained that his landlady was a little erratic, her mood depending on whether her beloved Everton Football Club had won or lost that week.

'Mrs Roach?' he called. 'My friend Alice is here. She's in a tight spot. Can she come in? Just for a cup of tea.'

'One brew. As long as she leaves after that. Then I'm locking up,' the landlady replied brusquely.

'Does that mean they didn't win?' whispered Alice.

'I'm afraid that's her good mood,' he replied. 'You should see her when they lose.'

'What if that Roddy fool turns his da against me?' Alice fretted, over a cup of tea with three heaped spoonfuls of sugar.

'That will never happen. Drink up,' he said.

Alice sighed, and drank.

They chatted for another half hour, mostly going round in circles. Eventually she said, 'It's late – I should go. Bernice will be waiting up for me. Let me wash these cups.'

'Put those away. I'll do them later,' he said, as she started to rinse the cups in the small sink. 'I'll see you home.'

'I'll be fine.'

He laughed. 'Alice, you're not very good at being told what to do, are you? Put the mugs down, get your coat and let's go. I'll just have to knock and wake Mrs Roach up. It's her fault she has these stupid rules and won't give me a key.'

Their hands touched as he gently took the cup from her, and for some strange reason, panic shot through Alice. 'Thank you, Matty. You're kind.'

'We'll get you out of this nightmare, Alice, trust me. You're not the type to be defeated. Not Alice Lacey.'

Chapter 26

Alice listened to the rain sheeting against Bernice's roof the following morning. She was deciding whether to take the bus to Kirkby and drop off some sewing for Miss Quick, although really it would be an excuse to talk to her about Ida. Miss Quick might know what to do. So when the sudden downpour began to ease off she set out on the seven-mile journey, and by late morning she had reached the half-finished road where her old neighbour lived.

In years gone by, the Laceys had often visited the village of Kirkby to go blackberry picking during the summer holidays, but since the munitions factory had opened, vast swathes of new roads and drab buildings had begun to make it unrecognizable. Horses pulling ploughs had long given way to bulldozers, cottages lay derelict and orchards were hewn down. Now potholes had appeared and weeds were already struggling through the newly laid pavement slabs.

'Hot water coming out of the tap!' said Alice, after Miss Quick, carrying Pennywise, invited her in and showed her around her new second-floor flat. It was part of a block in a cul-de-sac.

'And an electric cooker. And kettle. It's lovely. How was your journey? I'm sorry I couldn't drop off the sewing, but it's such a long way. And the dust here, from all the building. Lorries every day. It gets to my chest.'

Alice sipped her tea.

'Oh dear,' Miss Quick said, 'I need some sugar. Do you take sugar? I hope not. There's no borrowing a cup of sugar from your neighbours here, like we all did in Dryburgh Terrace. I don't know my neighbours. Not well enough to be popping in for cups of sugar, any road. And I'm afraid there's no shops to nip out and buy some.'

'No shops?'

'Not yet. They say they're building a parade soon. All we want is a greengrocer's and maybe a butcher's, and a little corner shop like Connolly's – but we've been waiting for so long. It's not easy carting butter and milk from the village a mile away. It melts in the hot weather. But never mind that. How's your mother?'

Alice faltered. She was becoming so used to lying; so used to saying brightly, *She's fine*. But here she felt far enough away from Dryburgh Terrace and all the gossip, and close enough to Miss Quick, to blurt out, 'That's why I'm here, actually. We're in a terrible mess. Ma has sent the kiddies away to St Mary's.'

'The orphanage? Oh, my. Why?'

'We've lost the house. Ma thinks they're fine, but I don't think they are. One of the nuns makes the children cut the grass with scissors. Ma's . . . not good. How can she know what's going on behind those walls?'

'Your da was never the same after the *Malakand*.

I'll never forget that night. It felt as though the whole city was burning. Just one ship, and the sky was red for days. We all thought your father would never live through it. He was so badly burned. His arm . . . that scar . . .'

'Yes. You think a person has recovered but unless they somehow get it out, they never really do, do they? He never talked about it.'

Alice got up and went over to the window, looking down at the barren field criss-crossed with wheel ruts from the lorries.

'The views are wonderful,' said Miss Quick. 'I can see all the way over to the blue hills in good weather. Sometimes I'll stand here all day with Pennywise and just stare out of the window. Thank goodness for the views.' She gestured at the vast expanse of fields and then beyond, and smiled.

But what about the river? wondered Alice. Where was the long silver sleeve Mr Morley had spoken of?

'Miss Quick, now that you know about me ma, I was wondering, is there space here for her and the kiddies? We're in a tight spot.'

She looked startled. 'Oh, Alice, dear. We're not allowed. The rules are strict. Very strict indeed. No more slum overcrowding. I'm not even allowed to have Pennywise here, but I couldn't bear to leave him. I'm so sorry. That's why we're all here. To live healthily with space and fresh air. If I could, I would, but I just can't. Let's hope you find a place soon.'

It felt like a crushing blow, another roadblock, but as Bernice said to her later while they sat shoeless on the sofa, 'What did you expect, love? Miss Quick is hardly the type to be throwing open her doors to your feral brothers and sister. She wears the temperance pin as well. That's not going to go down well with your ma and her potato juice. By the way, Matty came asking for you.'

'Matty?'

'Yes, love. He's got two tickets for the Palace Ice Rink. Wants you to go with him. They've finally reopened it after the beating it got in the Blitz.'

Alice frowned. 'Oh . . . I . . .' Her eyes met Bernice's nervously.

'Is it me you're worrying about? All right, I'm jealous. Of course I am. But Alice, I just like to tease him. I'm not stupid. I terrify him. Go on. It's the Danny Adair quartet playing, and you could do with a night out. I think he's a little bit in love with you.'

'Matty and I could never be more than friends,' Alice said, blushing and drawing her knees protectively up to her chest.

'But you do adore him. And I mean in *that* way. I know you do. I've seen the way you look at him when he smiles at you, or when he does that thing when he rakes his fingers back through his hair. And when he rolls his sleeves up and sits with one foot crossing his knee and leans forward to listen to you . . .'

'Stop! Bernice, stop. We're just friends. Nothing more.'

'I don't see why not. He's gorgeous in that sweet way that he doesn't know he is . . .' Bernice stopped as if a new thought had occurred to her. 'Please God, it's not Bob you're worried about? After all he's done?'

'No . . . not Bob. But life is already so complicated.'

'Morley? You've not been up to naughty stuff with old Morley?' Bernice laughed, her eyes opening wide.

'Don't be ridiculous!'

'Or his dreadful son? Rupert?'

'Roddy. No. He's appalling.'

'Then go and meet Matty. Even if it's just as his friend. The tram goes straight there from outside here. He said he'll meet you outside at six. You'll have fun. Skating is always a hoot. There's always some poor devil sliding on their arse for you to have a good laugh at . . .'

'Probably me. I'm useless.'

'Well, there you are. I'm already laughing just at the thought of it.'

Palace Ice Rink, Alice read, as she stood outside the building on the corner of Hope Street and stared up at the bold black letters above the door. She looked both ways along the road, towards the cinema and then back towards the hostel for seamen and servicemen.

'Alice!' cried Matty, bounding out from inside. He had been waiting in the foyer. 'You came! I didn't think you would.'

'Why not?'

'I don't know . . . I . . .' Was he going to mention Bob? He didn't, and Alice was relieved.

She smiled. It made her happy to see him beaming at her.

They went in through the double doors with Matty's arm around her waist and were immediately hit with a blast of music: someone playing a trumpet, a snatch of a tune she vaguely recognized, one of Gracie Fields' songs maybe. The sudden drop in temperature made her shiver and she felt the hairs on the back of her neck stand up stiffly.

Matty rubbed his hands together. 'We'll soon warm up.'

The crowd jostled forward and they pushed one another to the front of the queue and to the turnstile, where they bought tickets at the booth. 'You all right?' he asked, sensing her nervousness.

'I'll be hopeless at the skating. I only came because I didn't want you to waste the tickets.'

'You'll be grand. I remember we once went skating on the lake at Sefton Park. You managed to stand up all right.'

'That was Bob's daft idea, wasn't it? My ma went crazy and made me stay indoors and peel spuds for a week when she heard about a couple of kids falling into the pond when the ice broke. She always went as mad as a hen with Bob. Remember when we went bomb-watching?'

'I do. I remember that an' all.'

They went inside the cavernous ballroom. Around the edges sat older-looking women on chairs, some of them knitting, and men who were leaning on the rails with bottles of beer. Plenty of people had come just to watch and listen to the music, as the band were beginning to make a name for themselves. A few couples were already on the glittering ice, moving rhythmically to the musicians, who played on a dais under ruched curtains. They were getting under way with a version of 'Chattanooga Choo Choo'.

Alice and Matt leaned against the rails to watch the skating. The boys were in brightly coloured sweaters and the girls were wearing short plaid skirts and thick tights, performing dizzying spins and jumps, shards of ice showering the air as they skidded and looped and lunged. These were the ones who knew how to do it. The competition skaters. In a short time, the ice would be opened up to everyone else.

'Your breath is like little puffs of smoke,' said Matty, smiling down at her.

'I'm not exactly sure why I'm here,' Alice confessed, 'seeing as I can't skate.'

He grinned. 'Come on. Our turn in a minute. Let's get our skates.' They each handed over their boots and took a pair of skates at the small booth. 'I wasn't much good when I first came. But don't worry. I'll teach you.'

She laughed. 'My fingers are already cold,' she said as she sat beside him on a bench, trying to fasten the hooks and eyes on the cumbersome boots.

They made their way to the gate as it opened, and Alice cautiously put one foot in front of the other as she stepped down onto the ice with Matty's help.

'You just hold on to me tight, and everything will be all right. It helps that you do it in time to the music. The main thing is to keep leaning forward.'

She carefully began taking tiny, awkward steps, scared to move away from the edge and further out onto the ice, clinging on to the handrail. But then, when he gently pushed her out in front of him, to her amazement she slid forward, wobbling a little but soon regaining her balance.

'You won't fall. I've got you – let me put my arm around your waist. Trust me.'

They went around like that for a short time. Slowly, hesitantly, but with his help and the help of the music, Alice found a rhythm, and astonishingly she remained upright. Relieved that she wasn't such an embarrassment after all, flushed and smiling, she relaxed into something near happiness, with the music and the swish of the blades on the ice and the cool rush of air pinking her cheeks.

After nearly an hour of skating, with a short break for a lemonade for Alice and a cigarette for Matty, he retrieved their boots and her coat. She put it on and they went out into the cold night air. It had been raining softly, and the street lamps threw a buttery arc of light across the wet pavement.

'That's where we watched the bombs drop,' he said, linking her arm as they climbed the steep incline towards the tram. He nodded into the distance. 'Up there . . .'

'Aye.'

He stared ahead as he spoke. 'I remember Bob took your hand and told you not to be afraid.'

'Did he?'

He paused, trying to unravel his tangled-up thoughts. 'I've always wondered – if it had been me who had done that, would things be different? I always knew it was Bob who could make you laugh, but . . . well . . .'

'What are you saying?' she replied, turning to meet his eyes.

'I just wondered. Did you ever think about that?'

'Oh, Matty,' she murmured. 'You and me. We have to be friends. Just friends. We can never be anything else. I'm sorry.'

He nodded thoughtfully. *Why?* he wanted to ask, but instead he took a deep breath, and then they continued up the hill.

'Alice. You know how I feel about you,' he said after a few moments. He was looking ahead as they walked, concentrating on the gasworks with its plume of blue smoke. 'But can you please separate me from Bob?'

'Oh, Matty . . .'

'And can you try to forget about me as the little kid always there with both of you, following you around, tagging on behind, from kick the can, to penny for the guy, swimming in the scaldies . . .'

'Why would I want to do that? I didn't see it like that. I wouldn't have been without you.' She looked at him, genuinely bewildered.

And then her mind turned to how it was Matty, not Bob, who had always listened so earnestly, watching her face when they had a conversation – just like he was doing now. How her heart fluttered when he slipped his hand in hers. How he always made her feel safe and adored. Of course, she had always wanted him there. She had *needed* him to be there.

She bit her lip. Tears were welling up in her eyes. 'Those were the happiest times of my life. And you were the most important part of that, Matty. You still are. You always make me feel so . . . so . . .' She stopped walking. She was breathing hard. 'That's why . . .'

Why what? What was the matter with her? For all these years, Matty had been at her side – from childhood to adolescence, and as a young man – and suddenly she was asking herself why she couldn't allow herself to, what . . . *love him*? Why on earth not?

In that moment, it was as though she was seeing him for the very first time. And although it was rare for Alice to do anything in her life impulsively, somehow words had become useless, and she found herself leaning forward and kissing him, gently and quickly, on the lips.

A moment later, his tongue was twisting round her teeth and she was kissing him back, tearful, but feeling something strong and overwhelming; a tidal wave of – what was it? Longing? No, surely it was love. And as they stood holding each other, a tangle of limbs and mouths, the space around them became nothing. Bob had never kissed her like this. Alice didn't want to make comparisons, but she couldn't help it.

'I love you, Alice. I've always loved you. But you've known that all this time, haven't you?' he said quietly.

She nodded. Because of course she had. And in turn, she had always loved him. She hadn't the slightest doubt she loved him now, and it had been that way right from the beginning. Everything else along the way to this moment, standing under this street lamp with the rain softly falling on her flushed cheeks, had been a distraction. It was startlingly clear.

As Matty traced his fingers over her cheek and down the bridge of her nose and then gently slid them through her hair, they both felt such love, waves of it. And as Alice tilted her face to him, she realized just how *much* he loved her, how he had been carrying this burden for years, and now, as his lips found hers again, how they were both free. His breath was sweet, and she felt desire welling up inside her. And how strange. After years of pushing away Bob's groping, pinching and grabbing, she would have allowed Matty to do anything with her. She would have allowed him to touch every part of her, opened herself to him as if it was the most natural thing in the world.

'I love you. You're just the most wonderful girl. Noble and truthful . . . and God, so flaming beautiful. Let me help you, Alice. Will you?'

Chapter 27

When Alice arrived back at the flat, Bernice was toasting a crumpet over the electric fire. The little room glowed orange.

'So come on. Post mortem. Did he teach you how to swizzle? You do a little stroking?'

Alice blinked.

'Don't look so serious – they're ice-skating moves. I'm only joking.'

'Matty . . .' Alice faltered.

Bernice quirked an eyebrow.

'Matty and me, we . . .' she began again.

'Spit it out, love. Matty and you, what?'

'Oh, Bernie . . .'

'I'll say it for you. You and Matty did a bit of swizzling and stroking, then progressed to the tonsil tennis, and you've finally admitted that you're crazy about each other.'

'Yes. Yes, yes! Bernie, I'm so sorry . . .'

'It's all right. I've known for months – I've seen the way he looks at you. Don't worry about me. I frighten the life out of him, and I would probably squash him if we ever went for a roll about in the hay.'

'Oh, Bernie. You're really not angry with me?'

'Don't be daft, Alice. If it's written in the stars, no amount of thrusting my magnificent girls in his direction will change that. You'll just have to find me a nice fella who won't be scared of me. Preferably one in a uniform. Fireman top of the list, and a proper sailor second; none of your merchant navy fellas like Bob. Shiny buttons and gold tassels. Now come on, I want to hear every last detail. Is he a good kisser? I'll bet he is.'

Alice set off on Monday morning for work, relieved that Bernice had been so generous. The day was bright, but it had been raining, which made the steps up to the office precarious. She was dressed in her coat and scarf, and had Bernice's old cloche hat with a flower on it pulled down over her ears.

When she reached the third floor, Mr Morley was striding out of Kenneth Worboys' office on his way to his own. On seeing her, he stopped abruptly and gave her a look before walking on while calling back over his shoulder, 'I'd like a word, Alice.'

She checked the wall clock. She was a good ten minutes early. Even so, she was apprehensive as she followed him in. He was settling into his chair as she closed the door.

'Now, Alice. I have news. We haven't forgotten your triumph at the parish hall. February twenty-first I'm going down to London to prepare for the Ideal Home Exhibition.' He opened a drawer and frowned into it, clearly looking for something that wasn't there.

'If it's the Festival House file you need, it's on the shelf marked "Festival House",' Alice offered.

He stopped, smiled and sat back in his chair. 'Yes, of course it is. Alice, I wondered if you'd like to come with me. There's a heck of a lot to do before preview day. What do you think?'

Alice had never in her life been further from home than Parbold, and the thought of London made her heart jump – but then she felt it fall to her boots.

'I'm sorry, but I – I can't,' she stammered apologetically.

'Whyever not? I thought you would jump at the chance.'

'I'm sorry. I appreciate you asking me. And I would want nothing more, but just now – I really can't. There's just too much going on. Family, the usual, I'm afraid . . .'

The sentence tailed off into nothing. Alice felt heat rising to her cheeks. She dreaded him asking more questions, and willed him not to as she twisted her scarf and fiddled with the button on her glove.

'Alice. This is exciting for you, isn't it?' Miss Maguire swept into the room. 'London.' Her words were laced with bitterness, like little darts.

Alice shook her head. '. . . I'm afraid I'm busy.'

Miss Maguire's eyes widened.

Alice opened her mouth to say more, but nothing came out.

'Alice has family commitments,' said Mr Morley quickly. 'And that's how it should be. Alice, you have explained it to me – you don't need to go through it again. There will be a next time, and hopefully then you will be able to come. You're an asset to this company. Isn't she, Miss Maguire?'

Miss Maguire blinked, then gave a brisk nod. 'Of course.'

'Probably a boy,' she remarked to Morley a minute later, when Alice had left the room. 'Family commitments? You didn't really believe her, did you? It's always a boy. Girls like Alice always have such plans, such ambitions. But the moment a boy comes on the scene waving an engagement ring, promising a sticky bun at Cooper's and a weekend on the dodgems in New Brighton, all those lofty dreams come crashing down around them.'

'Really?' he asked. 'And how did you manage to escape the allure of a weekend at the Tower Ballroom, Miss Maguire?'

He regretted the words as soon as he said them – they sounded unkind. But she didn't seem the least bit troubled.

'I was made of stronger stuff,' she replied. 'Character. Backbone. It's what's missing in the youth of today.'

Mr Morley half smiled. He didn't agree with her. He knew Alice had those qualities in abundance. And he had every confidence that she could be persuaded to change her mind about London.

Chapter 28

Two weeks passed. Matty took Alice to Sefton Park to see children floating boats across the pond, and they kissed under the monkey tree; there was a trip to Lyons' Corner House, where they gazed into one another's eyes over an Ovaltine, and a walk holding hands around the gardens at the back of St George's Hall. When she wasn't with him she kept going over him in her head: the spread of his hair when the wind was in his face as he walked up the hill; the feel of his hand resting on the curve of her waist; his clear blue eyes fluttering shut when he kissed her; and the way he had of making her feel she was the only thing that mattered to him. As soon as they parted she found herself longing to see him again, a feeling so different to when she had missed Bob. The need to see him, to touch him and kiss him, was so acute that it was almost physically painful.

All the time Alice was filing and writing memos at work, she was thinking about Matty – about what he was doing, where he was. She pictured him driving Hedley around, his hands on the steering wheel, his face, clothes; and she thought about how it would feel when she next saw him.

Matty had said he would come to pick her up this

morning and give her a lift to work, a little early so that they could spend some time together; then, taking a breath, he had whispered in her ear that he loved her. Remembering the sound of his voice as he said it sent a shiver down Alice's spine. It seemed absurd she hadn't noticed that he was in love with her before now.

She went downstairs and poured a jug of water from Bernice's washstand into the enamel bowl. Plunging her hands into it, she scooped up the water and splashed it over her face. It felt refreshing and she shook off the moisture, rubbed a finger under each eye and patted her cheeks dry with her flat hands. She looked at herself in the cracked mirror, ran her tongue over her teeth. Should she put lipstick on for Matty? Would he notice? She wanted him to, and yet she didn't. Tying a ribbon into her hair, she sat at the table in a spot where she would have a good view of him walking down the street.

It was the sound of his whistling that she heard first, a tune he had been humming a lot lately. Jumping out of her seat, she went to the front door and opened it. She didn't want Bernice to come out and start busybodying around them, asking questions and making pert remarks. Stepping out onto the pavement, she shut the door behind her.

'You look lovely,' Matty said, kissing her lightly on the lips. 'I'm parked round the corner.'

When they got into the car, he touched her gently on the cheek. For a second there was silence as they sat gazing at each other. He seemed a little nervous, as though she might not feel the same now that a

couple of weeks had passed; but as their fingers inter-
twined, his other hand moved up her thigh as they
kissed properly, all worries vanishing.

'Listen to this,' he said. 'The car has a radio now.
Mr Morley had it fitted in Manchester. Parlophone.'

He fiddled with the knobs on the dashboard, and
Alice gasped as a sweet, sensual song filled the car.
*'Beautiful baby . . . It was heaven that made you,
and the angels who sent you . . .'*

'Did you plan that?' she said, astonished.

'No,' he laughed, and kissed her. 'You can't do
that.'

As the music played, they couldn't stop looking at
one another, tracing patterns on each other's palms,
he delicately on her knee, she on his cheek, and kissing
as if they might slip away or spin into air if they
didn't keep touching one another to be sure this –
whatever it was – was still real.

'Come back inside with me?' Alice said breathlessly.
She had just seen Bernice leave, trotting down the
street, puffing on her cigarette. 'I've forgotten something. An envelope I need to drop off at the council
offices.'

He nodded, and they both got out and walked back
towards the house, knowing perfectly well what might
happen inside. And as they tumbled through the door,
all thoughts of envelopes were forgotten. In a world
where everything seemed so wrong, whatever was
happening now, as he was kissing her and she was
leading him over to the sofa, felt so very right. Feeling
his strong hands over her limbs and belly and breasts,
flesh against flesh as he undid his shirt, soothing the

stiffness from her aching muscles as he pressed his thumbs into the knots and bumps of pain and effortlessly moved from this blessed relief and searched out the deeper, private parts of her, taking her to a deliciously heady place where she could forget the drudgery, the poverty, the worry, she soon lost her whole self in a long, slow breath and glorious, rippling, shuddering waves of pleasure.

'Oh, Alice. My Alice. God, my life will never be real now unless you're there with me,' he said tenderly, looking down at her face.

She smiled. 'You've a beautiful way of putting things.'

He paused. 'And Bob, what will he have to say about this? You and me . . . ?'

'Bob will just have to think about a way of accepting it. If he's honest with himself, he'll know that there was never a real future for the two of us – otherwise, he wouldn't have done what he did. Anyway, he's gone – run away, again. Let's not worry about him now.'

When they went back out there was a steady drizzle falling. She clutched the large envelope that she had tucked inside her coat to protect.

'I have to drop this for Mint Imperial Mags at the council offices on the way, is that all right?'

'I'm the one in the uniform. You're the boss – I'm at your beck and call, aren't I?'

'Chop-chop, then. Make it snappy or I'll dock your wages.'

He grinned at her and started the car.

'You're going up in the world, are you? Hedley can't stop talking about you.'

Alice sighed. 'I was. Until Ma ruined it.'

'You're too young to think that way. I love you, Alice. It will be all right. There's two of us now.'

It was slow going, the drizzle making the usually carefree drivers more cautious. Matty stopped outside the council building and turned to her. 'I'll run it in. You sit tight.' He took the envelope from her and opened his door.

'Get on, then, there's a draught.' She smiled, and he grinned back as he closed the door.

The front seat of the car was a little untidy, Alice noticed as she waited. Mr Morley wouldn't like that, even though this was Matty's territory – Mr Morley always sat in the back. She bent down and gathered up rubbish: a sherbet wrapper and a flyer saying Davido Conti's trio was coming to the Locarno. Crumpling them, she put them into her pocket. As she straightened the floor mat with her foot, she noticed the edge of what looked like a letter underneath. She reached down and pulled it out. It had been opened and was muddied with dirt from the floor, but she recognized Bob's childish handwriting immediately. Staring down at it, she turned it over in her hand, ran a finger over the edges. Would she dare read it?

Suddenly there was movement at the driver's side – Matty was back, opening the door. Instinctively, Alice stuffed the letter into her bag. She felt her cheeks flush at the thought of what she had done, but there was no way of undoing it now.

Making her way into the office after saying goodbye to Matty, she felt as if the letter was burning a hole in her pocket. Sweating, she sat down in a chair by the window and took it out. She looked at it, hesitating. Why had she taken it? Bob was in her past; her future was with Matty now. And hadn't he told her he loved her? But her mind was turning. Simply seeing his handwriting had made her steal the letter, and she hadn't been able to stop herself.

She looked at the envelope. The postmark was unreadable – perhaps she was only wondering where he was now, and if he missed her. Some part of her hoped he was regretting everything. Taking a deep breath, leaning back against the door, she slipped out the letter and unfolded it.

The first thing she noticed was the date – September 1950. She felt her stomach lurch. Not long after her father had died.

Genoa, Italy

Matty pal,

I should have written before, but letter-writing is difficult for me and I hardly get a minute. I'm here sitting on the quayside looking at my ship. We're boarding in a couple of hours and I want to post this before we sail. I don't get seasick any more, and if I throw up it's because of the awful food they give you on board that we have to cook on the burners. Drinking too much in port doesn't help either. Just had 48 hours' leave and I should have rested but we were out on the town for the last two nights and I'm bleary-eyed and have a thumping headache. If you ever decide you want to sow your oats, join this lot. The girls here are always ready for a good time, especially if you're willing to part with a few bob or a bit of jewellery or a trinket, and they don't hold back like they do in Liverpool. Last night I was at a jazz dive in port and kissing one girl all night long, so hard my lips were sore, but I ended up going home with her best friend. I reckon if I'd tried harder I could have gone home with both of them! Anyway, the second one made good work of me, if you know what I mean. And with her mother in the next room.

Hope I get home soon, but for now we're off to Cairo. Christ knows what I'll get up to there. Only thing you have to watch out for, everyone tells me, is the flaming clap. The fellas have told me the doctors have made great strides – you don't have to have the old needle up the chap any more and you certainly don't go blind – a week of pills and Bob's your uncle, you're good to go. Imagine coming home and getting the old feller out with a bad dose, not a pretty sight. Imagine Alice's face.

Look after her. Thanks for keeping an eye on her for me, like I asked. Make sure she's not hanging around the dance halls with flaming Bernice. That one's trouble. Keep me up to date with her movements. Also, I don't trust Morley. It was a good wheeze you getting her the job so we could keep tabs on her, but I'm not sure I trust him. I hope she doesn't

*realize that it's not a coincidence every time
you pop up in the most unexpected places. Of
course, I don't need to say don't tell her about
my little jaunts that I can't seem to drag
myself away from. You can't imagine what one
lassie was doing with a whisky bottle and a
threepenny bit. And for a paying audience!*

*I look forward to your reports of my little
Cherry Bomb. Thinks she's changing the
world. Let her have her dreams. She'll soon
realize being a wife and ma is the thing that
will make her truly happy.*

Your best pal,
Bob

Alice was motionless, as if frozen in her seat. In
the minute it had taken to read the letter, her entire
world – any trace of the happiness that had seemed
to be within her grasp – had been destroyed.

Matty had known. He had known what Bob was
up to, known about the women, and said nothing.
Bob had never been serious about her, that was clear
now – and *wife and ma*! How patronizing!

But the worst thing was realizing that all along,
Matty's friendship and kindness to her had been built
on this horrible little arrangement, on Bob arranging
for Matty to follow her, report back and tell him
what she was up to. How dare he? And for Matty
to be part of this – it felt like such a betrayal.

Not only that, but he had used her grief to lure
her into his arms. Her heart pounded as she thought
about it. He had let her open up to him, talked about

her being noble and truthful as if it was important to him, and all the time he had known things – awful things he had been covering up for so long. She could barely breathe. What would she do now? How could she face him?

She moved around the office silently for most of the day. When she got home she undressed and got into bed, knowing she wouldn't be able to sleep. Soon she was sobbing silently into her pillow and pulling the blankets over her head, hoping Bernice wouldn't hear her great gulps of sorrow through the thin walls.

Chapter 29

'Mr Morley, is it too late for me to change my mind about London?'

Alice stood in front of Morley's desk, trying to hide her nerves. Her forehead was shining with perspiration as she suppressed a wave of anxiety. It felt as if her job, her relationship with kind Mr Morley, was all she had left, and perhaps that was in danger of falling apart too if she didn't do something to shore it up.

'Of course it's not,' he said, looking pleased.

She felt her palms sweating. Should she go? She would have to make sure that they would be back in time for her to visit the children on Sunday – the last Sunday of the month. But all she could think about was getting out of this city.

'Excellent. We'll need to organize trains and book the hotel – the Savoy. Expensive, but that's where everyone stays. Down tomorrow, back on Friday. Is that all right?'

'Yes. I'll book your room and find somewhere for myself a little closer to the exhibition.'

'For heaven's sake, no, Alice. I think this company can stretch to a couple of rooms at the Savoy. Besides, I'll need to go through plans with you in the evenings, and you'll need to shove me in the right direction. You know, the way you do.'

'Yes, sir. Thank you.' She turned to go.

'Oh, and while we're there, please call me Hedley. I know Miss Maguire would have your guts for garters if she heard you doing that. But she's not going to be down there to wield the rod of iron, so it's Hedley – I insist.'

Alice smiled weakly and nodded, turning away. She got as far as the door before he added conspiratorially, 'Perhaps you'd better not mention the Savoy to Miss Maguire either. When Kenneth took her down to London last year, he put her in a cheap dive in Earl's Court. She's got a jealous streak. You know what they call her?'

'Mint Imperial Maguire.'

He laughed. 'Yes. But of course, she's excellent at her job – and beneath all the huffing and furiously sucking on those little sweets, she likes you, Alice.'

She watched as he leapt up and strode over to the connecting door to Miss Maguire's office. 'Miss Maguire – Alice has changed her mind about London. Would you organize a ticket for her, please?'

Leaving work, Alice saw Matty on the steps of the Lamp Building, grinning. She felt a little sick.

'How did you know I was here?' she asked tetchily. 'Don't answer. Matty, I know that you've been following me like some kind of spy, on Bob's orders. Is that why you're here all the time, hanging around outside the door? Pretending you're delivering parcels and lemon bonbons to Miss Maguire's office? Is that why you pretended you wanted me? To think I fell for all that love stuff.'

'What?' His face was blank with shock.

'The least you can do is give me the courtesy of not thinking I'm as much of a fool as Bob is. I know what's been happening. I found the letter Bob wrote to you in the car. Move out of the way.'

'It — it's not how it looks,' he stuttered. 'He did ask me, and I made a promise. But Alice—'

'But what? You didn't think to tell me he'd asked you to *spy* on me?'

'It wasn't spying!' he said, reaching out a hand to clutch hers. She yanked it away. 'He didn't want you to know, and at first . . . Alice, love, that letter was from months ago.'

'Of course he didn't want me to know. The things he was doing with those . . . those . . .' She rubbed tears from her eyes angrily. 'And you were happy to be his spy.'

'Stop calling me a spy. I love you.' He reached out again, but her expression was so forbidding that he couldn't quite complete the gesture, and his arm fell back to his side.

'And yet here you are. Every day, turning up. Oh look, there's Matty. At the Locarno. Oh look, how lovely, he's waiting for me after work. Or he just happened to be at Dryburgh Terrace as I walk around the corner! Oh, thank God, Matty's saved me from Roddy. What a coincidence. And all this time, I thought you *wanted* to see me! And you . . . you . . . what I let you do to me!'

He loosened his tie as if it was strangling him. 'You've got it all wrong!'

'Now I see it. I can't bear it. I need to be on my own.'

'No, wait. Alice – you know I love you. And because I love you, I didn't want to tell you. Because I knew it would hurt your feelings!'

'You think I'm not strong enough to cope with that? Nothing would have surprised me with Bob. But you? I'm surprised and shocked you couldn't be honest with me.'

He opened his mouth to speak.

'No, stop. I don't want to hear,' she said, pushing past him and walking down the steps.

He watched her miserably, his cheeks flaming. When she reached the pavement, she whipped round and jabbed an accusing finger up at him.

'And the orphanage! Whose idea was that? Yours? Have you been yakking with me ma? Why is everyone always trying to do what's best for me? You, Bob – even Mr Morley? You're all trying to pull strings behind me back. All plotting!'

'No, Alice. That's ridiculous! With Bob . . . it was a mistake. I couldn't bear to see you upset. I want to help you now!'

'I'd rather make a mess of things on my own, thank you.'

'Alice, you don't mean that . . .'

'You could have told me about those women he was seeing. But you didn't.'

'Alice . . . I was following you around because I love you, because I hate being apart from you, not because I was spying on you! Because I wanted to be near you every moment of the day. Because without you, my life has no meaning. I love you, Alice.' He spoke desperately, urgently.

'Stop talking, Matty. Leave me alone. My life is in enough turmoil with the children and Ma, without you adding to it.'

'What will you do?'

She shrugged. 'What's it to do with you?'

Furious, eyes blazing, she turned on her heel and walked away. A tram was passing, and she leapt gratefully onto it and marched towards the back.

If she had turned around, she would have seen Matty standing motionless on the pavement, tears in his eyes, watching her go. It was perfectly clear to everyone who passed by in that moment that his heart had just been broken into a million tiny pieces, and he had no idea how to put it together again.

Chapter 30

The following morning, as she stood under the clock at Lime Street station holding Bernice's vanity suitcase, Alice still felt as if she was trying to catch her breath.

Matty had been knocking at the door and pushing pathetic notes under it every few hours, or that's what it felt like. Alice had poured out the whole sorry tale to a sympathetic Bernice, who had suggested it would probably help to get away – it might give Alice space to think. So now here she was, and she felt obscurely anxious that someone might see her. But then, she told herself, that was stupid. All these people around her, getting in and out of taxis, slamming doors, kissing their loved ones goodbye – why should they notice or care about what she did?

Mr Morley was travelling first class. 'I'm happy to pay the extra for you to sit with me,' he said, surprised and a little disappointed, as she explained she had a second-class ticket.

'No, Mr Morley. I'm your secretary. Really, I'm happy in second. I usually travel third.'

Over breakfast in the restaurant car, he told her in businesslike tones about who they would meet and the house they would be seeing – which he had designed, and which was being built inside the exhibition hall.

A whole house! Alice thought, marvelling. Their breakfast was served by smartly dressed waiters who sounded
just like her and yet called her 'madam'. Afterwards,
she slipped off and settled down in her second-class
seat, where she watched the countryside race by and
tried to put Matty out of her thoughts.

There seemed to be as many people in Euston station
as in the whole of Liverpool. As they made their way
to the Savoy, Alice was surprised to see ten times as
many cars and buses on the roads as she was used
to. She made a mental note never to step off the
pavement without looking three times.

She had never seen such an imposing hotel; maybe
the Adelphi in its day, but that was now showing its
age, and was always black with soot. The Savoy, by
contrast, with its clean art deco lines, marble pillars,
marble floors, gilt mirrors, beautiful tiles and cascading
velvet drapes, and pot plants on brass stands, exalted
in its luxury.

Stepping into her room, she gasped. Had there been
a mistake? This was a place she couldn't even have
envisioned in her dreams. She sat on the end of the
double bed, looking at herself in the ornate mirror
above the dressing table, and laughed at her reflection.
'Laydeee Alice Lacey,' she said, imitating the accent
of a woman announcer she had heard on the BBC
wireless programme. 'Air, hair, lair. The rain in
Spain . . .' She tried rolling her r's. Then she fell back
onto the quilted satin bedcover, stretched her arms
above her head and ran the palm of her hand over
the mountain of pillows stacked against the headboard.

Turning over, she pressed her face into one of them and breathed in the clean smell. This room alone could easily hold her entire family.

'How do yooo dooo, Laydeee Alice?' she asked the chandelier above her, throwing the pillow up towards it. She caught herself wishing Matty was here to see it, before shrugging the thought away in a shiver of disappointment.

Half an hour later she was in a cab with Mr Morley on her way to Olympia, where the exhibition preparations were under way. When they arrived, she had to keep her wits about her to avoid being run over by handcarts loaded with boxes, and even large vans, slowly threading between the scurrying workers on their way to the larger exhibits. There was hammering from every corner of the vast hall, the banging sound bouncing off the high ceilings.

'Shall I take notes, Mr Morley?' she asked, raising her voice above the cacophony.

'Call me Hedley! Come on. I'm going to show you the Festival House. Spectacular. Oh, Lord,' he added, as they rounded the corner. 'At least, it will be spectacular in a couple of days.'

They stood in front of the jumble of large rooms without doors, large and small packing crates everywhere and workmen nailing, painting and tightening screws. She could see how impressive the house might be in a crescent or at the end of a drive, and yet here it was dwarfed by the lofty space of Olympia. Watching Hedley tapping on shoulders and pointing to various parts of the house, barking orders at the workmen, she thought how serious he looked. A serious man doing a serious job. Every so often he hurried back over to her and dictated a list of things that had to be finished, or tasks that he needed to be reminded of; but she also had time to wander the halls, amazed at the speed with which the exhibition seemed to be coming together. In a few hours, carpets and rugs would be laid; chairs and tables, though still wrapped up, would be in place; the window frames would have glass in them, and outside plants and even small trees would appear. A display of gas-powered washing machines, large cooking ranges as big as their kitchen at home, appliances that whisked and chopped, and gas heaters with instant hot water all astonished her.

For a time she watched the work going on inside another house, much smaller than Hedley's. 'The Women's Institute House', said the sign, proudly announcing that it was based on thousands of suggestions made by Women's Institute members. Taking a tentative step through the doorway, Alice saw to her surprise that the detached house was compact but had ample space for a family, with a kitchen in the same room as a good-sized living space. There was a dining table and a separate room with a machine for washing clothes. It all seemed ingenious. There was even an ironing board that folded out from a cupboard.

She thought sadly of her mother, stomping around and declaring that the Corpy was the enemy. A future like the one Alice was looking at here would be impossible for Ida to imagine.

Half an hour later, she went to find Hedley after

his meeting to go back to the hotel as they had arranged. As she reached the main staircase on her way out, she paused. 'Wedding Gowns for the Ordinary Woman', said a sign. Four mannequins smiled haughtily, gazing into the middle distance. Alice admired them, trying to put Matty out of her mind.

'Would you like to come in, miss?' said a sales assistant, noticing her wistful stare. She shook her head, a little embarrassed. These beautiful dresses weren't for girls like her. Besides, without Matty, what was the point in even looking?

'Alice, you were hungry,' Morley noted with a smile.

'Oh, I . . .'

'No. Don't be embarrassed. I like a girl with an appetite.'

She felt herself blushing as she dabbed her lips with the linen napkin. 'It's a bit of a scrum in our house. A race to get to the table. My mother always says I'll get a hernia, I eat so quickly. I'm sorry.'

'Stop saying sorry, my dear. I haven't enjoyed myself so much in years. Watching you tuck into that steak.'

'I've never tasted anything like it. And the park fete pudding was delicious.'

'Parfait pudding. Sweet cicely parfait, it's called,' he said, smiling again.

'Sorry,' she said, with a blush.

'You have nothing to be sorry for. Now, let me tell you a little about tomorrow. I have another meeting first thing. Excruciatingly dull people, but usefully influential. Will you be able to entertain yourself?'

She looked at him and paused, her teacup halfway to her mouth. 'I'd rather come with you,' she said, lifting her chin.

He laughed. 'Really?'

'I don't say things if I don't mean them.'

'Then let me tell you what it's all about,' he said.

He described who they would be meeting – the mayor, a few dignitaries, then the architects who were partners – and went on to say that he would be very happy for her to say a few words about what was happening in Liverpool, if she wanted. Just as she had done at the parish hall.

'Of course I will,' Alice said. It occurred to her that she hadn't even thought about Matty and the wreckage back home for at least half an hour, and she decided that was probably just as well.

A little later, she stepped out of the hotel and walked along the Strand and down towards the Thames. She stood in a swirling mist under a street lamp on Westminster Bridge, looking at Big Ben and the Houses of Parliament. She had seen these places in pictures and on the Pathé News at the Forum cinema in Lime Street – but to be standing here, watching the glittering vessels going up and down the Thames with water cresting at their hulls . . .

The boats reminded her of Bob, and in turn, she thought of Matty. A shudder passed through her as her mind flashed back to the moment she had found the letter. Two lads together. How long had they been smirking behind her back? A secret they had kept from her – and when Bob was gone, Matty had made his move. It felt as if she had just been passed along from one man to another.

And yet . . . and yet, some might say that for all their faults, the two men had loved her in their different ways, and she had loved them. Other girls might have found it easy enough to turn a blind eye to what Bob had done – she couldn't ever do that – but Matty's crime might have been no more than protecting her.

This high-mindedness that she seemed to have inherited from her father – would it ever lead to happiness? In two days she would be back in Liverpool, and who knew what awaited her there? Worry and sadness. Was London her future?

She took one last look at the ink-black night sky, delicately threaded with stars, before walking back to the Savoy and the fleeting comfort of her room.

Chapter 31

At St Mary's orphanage, a gaggle of children were filing into the library, sitting cross-legged on the floor, all fidgeting and bobbing heads. Doreen slid in at the back of the room, but as some turned and saw her and pointed and smiled and waved at her, others did the same. Gwenda and Brian shuffled onto the edge of the carpet. Gabriel sat beside them.

'Well now, children, how many of you would like to go to the seaside?' said the priest sitting on a chair, smiling, with his arms folded across his chest.

'Me, Father,' cried a small boy. He could only have been about eight. A few others shot up their hands. Even younger, five or six, some of them, and he was asking them if they wanted to go to Australia.

It seemed preposterous, and yet their eyes widened and bottoms shifted with excitement. More hands went up. There were a few squeaks and squeals of delight. One girl clapped her hands together, and a boy stood and jumped up and down as if overwhelmed with excitement. Others were silent and round-eyed with worry. Gwenda and Brian were among them, both stiff-limbed with shock.

'I finally have news. Because you're the special children who are on our list, remember we talked about the boat and the sunshine and the oranges and the lovely, lovely, farm with the horsies – and because we've all been praying so hard, the Lord has answered us. And so, after a lot of conversations and to-ing and fro-ing with the Archdiocese and the Corporation, we have some excellent news. Have any of you heard of a place called Tasmania?'

'Farder, will we back in time for tea?' said a small boy.

'Is Tasmania near Blackpool?' a girl asked.

'No, not Blackpool. Not exactly.'

'I can't wait to get away from them bloody nuns,' Gwenda heard a girl beside her whisper to her friend. 'Australia. A land of hope and freedom. Grand, isn't it?'

'Father, can we come back, you know, if we don't like it?' said a younger child, nervously chewing the gloves that were threaded through the arms of her coat on pieces of elastic.

'Aye, Father. If we don't like it, can we come back?'

'Don't worry. You'll love it. No one has come back, and we have sent hundreds and hundreds of children. You wouldn't believe it. Have you ever ridden a horse, Tommy?'

Tommy shook his head. 'I've rode a pig. It was a big 'un, like. But I got clobbered for it by me ma.'

'A horse is very different to a pig, let me tell you. And don't you think riding bareback on a horse would be marvellous? And these horses are nothing like the ones pulling carts at the docks. These horses are beautiful, wonderful stallions. Imagine little Tommy Gallagher galloping across the meadows.'

'Like John Wayne? Ride 'em, cowboys!' cried another boy, and shoved his fingers in his mouth and whistled.

'I'm getting jealous myself, lads. I might ask Sister if I can come to Australia with you.'

'Pow, pow!' shouted another. 'I'm John Wayne!'

'No, you ain't – I am.'

The priest laughed. 'How about if we sing "The Leaving of Liverpool"? Do you know that one? Sister, will you lead us on the piano?'

The docile nun padded over to the piano, swished aside the skirts of her habit, and sat down to play. The priest led them in a raucous chorus, conducting enthusiastically with his long arms.

'*Goodbye to Liverpool, Land of Australia onwards we are bound . . .*'

Sister Dorothea came to the door. 'Quieten down,' she snapped. 'Father! Really! We're all getting over-excited. Fingers on lips, hands on heads and ten Hail Marys, everyone. That includes you, Father,' she added flatly.

So it was true, thought Doreen. They really were doing this. She glanced at Gwenda and Brian. Someone needed to tell their mother before it was too late.

'Brian, Gwenda, did you enjoy Father's talk?' Sister Cyril asked later, as she handed round hymn books for them to share.

Gwenda frowned. 'Do they all want to go?'

Brian glanced at her warily.

'Of course they do. You saw how happy they looked. It's an adventure.' She paused. 'You and Brian

288

might consider it yourself. You'd get away from horrid old me,' she said, and nudged Gwenda, laughing. 'That's a good enough reason, I bet.'

'I don't want to go to Tanzmailia,' whimpered Gabriel. 'I just wanted you to give Bry his train back. That's why I were cross.'

'*You're* not going to Tasmania, silly. You're going to Brighton-le-Sands. Come with me.'

Half an hour later, Gabe stood with his back to Sister Cyril's office door, scowling. He had been dressed by Sister Bernadette in clothes he had never worn before – a shirt with a tie, shorts and white socks to the knees held up by elastic with a little ribbon tag, and a pair of shiny shoes. The shoes were too small and they pinched his feet when he walked; the tie was too tight around his neck; but he knew not to complain. It was such a small thing compared to all the other tragedies in his life.

A woman in a brown pencil skirt suit and sensible shoes sat on the edge of a chair. A man in a raincoat stood by the window. 'He's beautiful. Would you mind – can you ask him to say *ahhhh*?'

The woman smiled. 'Darling child. He looks like such a good boy. An angel.'

Sister Bernadette's instinct was to put her hand over Gabe's ears. But he was gazing into the distance, frowning.

'He's a lovely little lad. Not difficult, not challenging like the ones who have medical problems,' said Sister Cyril.

'Like the girl in callipers we saw. Polio? Who takes those children?'

289

'No one. That's why they're here, Mrs Pirbright.'

The woman had brought a small blue shawl with her and she took it from her bag, walked over and wrapped it around Gabriel's shoulders. He shrugged it away.

'Stand still,' said the nun.

'We've brought this heavenly outfit,' said the woman. 'Perhaps he should put it on now.'

But when the woman took out the clothes from the carpet bag, even Sister Cyril looked surprised.

'A dress . . . ?' said Sister Bernadette.

'No, not a dress – knickerbockers and a matching smock top. When we saw those pictures the other day of Prince Charles in his little outfit, he looked so pretty, and this boy is so pretty. This one almost looks like a girl. We wanted a girl. But this little boy, with those curls – well, he could easily pass for a Gabrielle.'

'I can assure you that he's a boy – he's only three, but he certainly is all boy. And he's quite lively.'

Gabriel looked up at them sulkily from under his fringe of curls. 'Not wear dress,' he said.

'He knows what he likes, I'm afraid.'

Gabriel stood listening to all of this. He rolled the plump part of his lip between his fingers. 'I like flying saucers. And I like them lemon bonbons. An' I like football. An' Roy Rogers. And I like sherbet dip. An' I like dripping an' I like, I like scouse, an' I like gobstoppers. An' I like playing knock and run wi' our Biscuit and Gravy—'

'Be quiet, Gabriel. Shall we put this outfit on?'

Gabriel folded his arms across his chest and sucked in his cheeks.

'Sister Bernadette – get Angela to change him into these new clothes. The knickerbockers are fine.'

The man and woman exchanged a glance.

'He won't wear it, Sister,' said Angela when she came into the room. 'I'm sure he'll refuse.'

'Come through to my office, Mrs Pirbright. We shall do the paperwork. Get him changed, Angela.'

After they had all left, Angela sat for a moment on the window seat with Gabriel's hand loosely in her lap.

'Don't want to go,' said Gabriel. He nestled beside her and rested his head on her lap.

'It's not your fault,' Angela said, leaning down and snaking her arm around his quivering shoulders and stroking his hair. He sat up, and she kissed him lightly on his forehead. 'You're not being punished,' she said. 'You haven't done anything wrong, Gabriel. And you don't have to wear the stupid clothes.'

He looked up at her from under his fringe.

'Ready?' said Sister Cyril, putting her head around the door. 'Just stick your tongue out so the nice lady can have a look if she asks. Don't be stubborn.'

The Pirbrights followed Sister Cyril into the room, and Gabriel humphed and reluctantly stuck out his tongue with a scowl. It seemed more like a rude gesture than compliance. The woman took out a small torch from her pocket, told him to open wider and peered inside his mouth. 'He is a beautiful boy. His hair . . . it's so thick and curly and glossy, and the golden streaks catch the light, don't they? But why won't he put the clothes on?'

Sister Cyril smiled and replied, 'Who knows?' She

handed Gabriel a small suitcase. Gabe looked startled and frightened. He dropped the case and the contents spilled out: a Bible, a pair of battered shoes. A knitted jumper and a conker.

They all looked at him, chewing the cuff of his sleeve. He was beautiful. Just maybe a little sad looking, with those wide-apart eyes and shivering curls.

Sister Cyril waved them off with a smile that slid from her face the moment they walked out of the gates. She turned to Sister Bernadette. 'They choose the angelic ones, but some children have devilment behind their eyes. Gabriel used a swear word the other day. Several. The b-word. He's three,' she sighed.

'Did he? Poor child, though. He's a lovely little boy. Just frightened, probably,' said Sister Bernadette.

'Seduced by the boy's curls. Never does to have your head turned by beauty, does it? They're blessed with good looks, the Lacey family, but it's so temporary, isn't it? The mother is already losing her beauty. The daughter will soon. Sorrow does that.'

'I feel sorry for them, though.'

'Don't. You know, there's one thing I can't stand: pity. No one wants to be pitied. Mrs Lacey doesn't want to be pitied. She insisted that the boy should find a good home. That's all she wants for him. A future. It's turning things around that matters, and everyone deserves a new beginning, don't you agree?'

'Yes, Sister. But I thought Mrs Lacey wanted a foster home. Not . . .'

'Not what?'

'Nothing. I'll pray for the boy.'

'And at least we've finally made the Pirbrights happy. They've been coming for months trying to find a child. Father is something important in coal. Donates to us every year. They might be fostering the boy, but it won't be long before they will be formally adopting. Have you seen the mother lately?'

'I'll pray for all of them, Sister,' said the nun.

Angela, from a shadowy alcove nearby, listened to all of this. Afterwards, when she met Doreen on the stairs, she said in a low voice, 'I suppose they could have put him on one of the blasted singing ships. He could be singing all the way to Australia or Canada, like some of the babies here. At least he's still in Liverpool. So all hope's not lost yet.'

'I'm sure Mrs Lacey wouldn't want this for him. It seems unreal. Sid is probably lying about her wanting Gabe to start a new life with another family. And I know for a fact sometimes the kiddies get adopted without the parents agreeing. We've all heard the rumours about that.'

'Aye. And worse. Father's talk about Tasmania to the kiddies were grim. Frightening.'

'So we at least need to make sure. Where's the older daughter – Alice? Can anyone get word to her?'

Chapter 32

Mr Morley had asked that they meet early for breakfast the following morning. Alice came down in her usual workday clothes and ordered bacon and egg, with a pot of tea. She noticed Hedley looking at her closely, as if there was something on his mind. When the waiter took away her breakfast plate he said, 'Stand up, would you?'

'Stand up?'

'Yes. Please.' He lifted his palm as if raising her up. Alice stood, feeling self-conscious in the crowded room. 'We'll stop off on the way there to buy you a new outfit. Perhaps you can have your hair styled too.'

'Are you saying I look a mess?' said Alice, thrusting out her chin. Part of her felt a little uncomfortable at the idea of Hedley Morley buying her new clothes. It felt odd, but maybe this was just what rich men did. Threw money at a problem, whatever it was. Besides, she desperately needed a new dress. The one she was wearing with the frayed tulip collar had been stitched and restitched, darned and hemmed so many times.

Hedley stood up and took her by the shoulders, smiling encouragingly. 'You could never look a mess even if you were wearing a sack, Alice. But today I want you to be at your best. The Lord Mayor and Lady Mayoress will be there, and before our meeting I've decided you ought to be the one to show them around our exhibit.' He raised an eyebrow. 'Will you do that for me?'

'Me? The Lord Mayor?' she said, stunned.

'Why not?'

'Oh, I . . .'

'Alice, you have no idea of the power of your beauty, and you have a brain to match. And all of that is made even more charming by your modesty.'

Alice's hair was set and styled at the hotel before the taxi took them to Harvey Nichols in Knightsbridge. On the second floor, she was met by an elegantly dressed, coiffured and perfumed lady who clicked across the polished floor in teetering heels, measured her and returned with a selection of outfits for her to try on. Hedley made himself scarce, wandering up to the menswear department to buy an umbrella. When he came back down, Alice was wearing an elegant two-piece suit in dark green with white piping on the pockets and a scalloped white collar.

'This is the one,' she said.

Hedley regarded her admiringly, a faraway look in his eye, while the perfumed lady said anxiously, 'We do have a larger selection, Mr Morley.'

'I like them all,' said Alice. 'But this'll do.'

'I simply couldn't persuade her any further. I'm sorry. The new Balmain two-piece has just arrived from Paris, but she knows her mind, this one. Don't you, dear?'

'Oh, I think she's quite right. That is perfect.' He stood with his hands deep in his pockets and continued to look at Alice for several more seconds, before turning back to the perfumed lady. 'Thank you.'

'Shall I wear it now?' asked Alice.

'Of course. But we'll need a suitable pair of shoes. And then I'll settle up, please,' said Hedley.

An hour later, catching sight of her reflection in a shop window, Alice could hardly believe it was her. What would Matty say if he could see her? Arriving at Olympia, where the workers had been busy all through the night and were still adding the final touches, she felt confident as she strode through the 'magic garden', a rockery with a spectacular display of colourful roses and peonies that had no right to be showing themselves in late February. The Festival House looked immaculate, just like everything else, and above it all, huge drapes had been hung from the hall's ceiling to give the effect of the entire exhibition being inside one vast marquee.

At midday, the dignitaries arrived. Hedley took her aside and briefed her on what to say to a Lord Mayor and Lady Mayoress of some borough in the suburbs of London, as well as a few facts about the fixtures and fittings. Precisely what she had written on a memorandum to him the previous week, she thought wryly.

'Here we go. Deep breath,' Hedley murmured as they made their way into the house, where six chairs had been placed in a semicircle in the front room. 'It's a bloody nightmare. Too many people, and you have to watch patiently as they tear your dream house to pieces. Everything that isn't nailed down will be carried off in someone's pocket or up someone's jumper. Last year, a woman tried to walk off pretending two rolled-up rugs were a pair of crutches.' Alice stifled a laugh, which made him laugh too. As people started to enter, he calmed himself enough to whisper, 'Anyway, that's why the girls check every evening, and why there are ten boxes of replacement items in our storage area.'

'I like your suit, dear,' said the Lady Mayoress. 'And you seem to know everything there is to know about this exhibition,' she added, after Alice had pointed out the various features and innovations.

Alice was pleased, but she also noticed, when she took the mayor and Alderman Something-or-other on a short tour of the kitchen and upstairs, that whenever she turned to tell them an interesting fact, their gaze was directed at her ankles and lazily moved up her body.

When Mr Morley had to pose for press photos he insisted that Alice stand at his side, brochure in hand.

'You're doing a smashing job, Alice,' he whispered, leaning in to her and giving her a reassuring squeeze around the waist as they walked back into the room where they were meeting the other architects.

Three efficient but unsmiling young women arrived carrying clipboards, and Alice briefed them on their duties for the remainder of the exhibition, just as Mr Morley had requested. The next day the doors would open to the public, and Alice felt a stab of disappointment that she would not be there.

'My dear, Hedley tells me you have experience of

the . . . *living conditions*,' said the mayoress, sitting to the right side of her. She had a red-lipsticked mouth and a heavily powdered, slightly furred face. She leaned in close to Alice as everyone was settling into their chairs.

Alice paused. 'Sorry?'

'These houses will change everything, won't they? A more civilized society for your people. It all looks so beautiful. I've seen the plans. So beautifully laid out.'

Alice blushed and thrust out her chin. 'My people?' she said, with a brief, tight smile.

The woman raised an eyebrow. 'Your . . . type. I recognize that accent. Birmingham? Or is it Blackpool? You sound a little like Gracie Fields.'

Alice bit her lip. 'If you mean those of us who are hoping to be rehoused, yes, it's all very exciting. And beautiful. But years after the war, people are still waiting for homes. And by the way, I'm from Liverpool. Not Birmingham, or Blackpool.'

'Speak up. What's she saying?' said the man at the head of the table.

Alice cleared her throat and turned to the man on her other side. 'I'm saying that these houses are wonderful, and Mr Morley has a brilliant mind. And hopefully it will change everything. Nevertheless, some people are getting frustrated waiting for their new houses, and that's when they become scrappy and unreliable.'

'What are you saying? What has this to do with anything? Scrappy and unreliable? Why is she telling us this, Mr Morley?' said the mayoress.

Hedley cleared his throat. 'I believe Alice means that we shouldn't get too wrapped up in our "vision". Is that right, Alice?'

Alice paused. 'Yes, Mr Morley. I see people losing heart.'

'Tell us, miss, about a typical family. Maybe about the problems they're facing,' said the man. 'Stand up.' He leaned forward in his chair. 'Don't be nervous, dear. I'd like to hear more. I'd like to hear about what's happening in Liverpool. The challenges that a family might face.'

'You mean the houses?'

'No, we know that. I want to know about the *people* for whom we are building these houses.'

Alice pushed back her chair, rose to her feet and cleared her throat. 'I'll not use their real names. But I can tell you about . . . Mrs Smith. Her husband died after the war when his lungs and his heart finally gave out, after he had been poisoned by ash and shrapnel after an explosion on a ship. She made some stupid decisions with money, but her children needed feeding, and she had to choose between rent and putting food on the table. This Mrs Smith had a lot of pride. Too much of it.

'When the Corpy offered her landlord money for a compulsory purchase order, unsurprisingly he took it, and she was left with nowhere to live. Her resettlement grant went on debts, and because her family were scattered after the war – evacuated and not come back – they couldn't help. And she couldn't ask for help from her neighbours. Because her neighbours had gone. Some were lucky enough to get a

299

prefab in Bootle, some living on the new estates. All frightened of the demolition order. All living miles away. And so this woman, when she was waiting for one of your houses, had to send her children into the care of the Corporation. Duty of Care, they call it. They put the children in homes. And these homes are not places where any of you in this room would want your children to be. Perhaps they tried once to be institutions where children were cared for kindly, but there are just too many children – so many, you can't imagine. And there's a harshness that's crept into those corridors that seems to have become normal.'

By now you could have heard a pin drop, the room was so quiet.

'Think of Mrs Smith. Because before long, another well-meaning person like you, on another well-meaning committee, will decide that perhaps her children would be better off without her altogether. And that, I'm afraid, will be the end for Mrs Smith.'

'Really? Good grief. Is this our fault? What does this have to do with houses?'

'That's not for me to say,' Alice replied. 'The gentleman asked me about these people who are still without a front door to call their own.'

'Your people, you mean?' said the woman flatly.

'Yes. My people. And I'm not ashamed to say it.'

'Miss . . .' said the alderman. 'Your Mrs Smith – she could get a grant from the government. She could fight the compulsory purchase order.'

'No, sir. Because she's just so tired. She's so very tired.'

She glanced at Hedley, who was looking down into his lap. Had she gone too far?

The applause started slowly, and then built up, and soon the whole room was clapping. Even the mayoress managed to tap her gloved fingers into the palm of her hand.

'Thank you,' Alice answered quietly, lost in contemplation. Her mind was drifting back to Miss Quick, stroking Pennywise and standing alone on her balcony, with the dust and barren earth stretching out in front of her as far as the eye could see.

Later, she sat around the table taking notes.

'Alice is our man on the ground,' Hedley said to everyone, with a smile.

A huddle gathered around her.

'Young lady . . .'

'Miss Lacey,' she said.

'Any more thoughts?' The man was scribbling on a pad.

'The middle-class homes, those in the smarter areas – everyone sees them being repaired. Their roofs put back on. Being reglazed. As though the people who live there are worth saving. It makes the poorer people feel pretty shoddy about themselves to see that. Some of the roads near the docks aren't as bad as they seem. They could do the same there, instead of sending in the bulldozers.'

Moving the conversation gently in the direction of Dryburgh Terrace, she said, 'Ask those mothers living in the houses at the end of Liverpool Lane, who might miss the washhouse, if they would rather have their houses repaired instead of moving. Yes, you've given them hot water coming out the tap, but they've got nowhere to go and share a cuppa in places like Kirkby. The same with the dockers who walk to work from their front steps and come back at lunchtime for a sarnie. It's too hard for some to travel miles back and forth.'

'I see.'

'And one other thing, sirs.' She leaned over the map. 'Will these new buildings you've designed have their own gardens? These plans . . . the communal gardens – those that live in the flats, they're more likely to make a mess of the gardens if they don't have their own patches to take care of.'

'Go on, Alice. She has wonderful insight,' said Morley. 'This is the kind of thing I was telling you about,' he said.

'And the church? I know there's a church in Kirkby, but it's right on the edge of your map, miles away. Not many people go to church unless they're forced to, so they aren't going to walk for half an hour. You need a church near the houses. That's what brings people together.'

'It isn't our job to build churches,' replied the man. 'Besides, it's churches that have caused so much conflict.'

'We hope that if we mix up all the orange and the green together – Protestants and Catholics – there's a plan to have greens living next door to an orange neighbour, and so on. They'll all get to know each other and get on,' said the alderman.

'Good luck with that,' Alice replied. 'Where will everyone meet? If you've got no church, that means you've got no church hall either.'

'I didn't have you down as a religious person, Alice,' said Hedley.

'I'm like many people in Liverpool. Not especially religious, but you can't escape it, can you? The priests and nuns have made sure of that. No, all I'm saying is, where will you have the pram club on your brand-new estate? Or the jumble sales? Where will people get married or have their babies christened? The wedding breakfasts and communion parties? We all look forward to those days. Only time we get a new frock,' she said with a smile. 'Everyone in new hats. And the girls so done up and boys looking like proper young men, in their dicky bows and shorts.'

Flushed and happy, Alice was preparing to leave with Mr Morley half an hour later, when she felt a tug on her sleeve. It was the mayoress.

'Quite the little star. You've left the label on the dress, dear.' She reached out and tugged at the tag. Alice froze. 'And I must say, those shoes. Who bought you those shoes? Mr Morley?'

Alice shivered as she turned away. Some people could be so unkind. The mayoress had a mean twist to her mouth that reminded her of Sister Cyril.

Chapter 33

Alice was exhausted, but Hedley, sitting opposite her in the American Bar, seemed to be giddy with delight at how the day had gone. He had drunk at least a bottle of wine and three large whiskies. They had talked about the Lady Mayoress, the designs for the new housing estate, the soldiers' charities Mr Worboys and his wife were involved with – and yet he still wouldn't let her leave. He was slumped back in his chair, his tie loosened.

'I'm sorry, Mr Morley, if I spoke out too much today.'

His eyes widened and he sat straighter in the chair, raking a hand back through his hair. He looked confused. 'Alice, I was so proud of you. You were on fire. You're looking very beautiful. Do you know that?'

'Thank you, sir.' She still couldn't bring herself to call him Hedley. She was confused by his tone.

'You remind me of someone.' He tipped his head, looking at her the same way he had that morning when he'd first seen her in the new green suit. 'Can I tell you a secret? You must promise not to be shocked.' His speech was slightly slurred, but he was choosing his words deliberately.

'How can I promise if I don't know what it is?'

'Good point.' He paused to take a sip of his drink, his expression serious. 'Many years ago, I had an affair. I'm a little ashamed, but there it is.' He lapsed into silence. 'I was very young. So was she.' He took another sip. 'You remind me of her.'

Alice stood up abruptly. What did this have to do with slum clearance? She felt her palms sweating. Was he trying to manoeuvre himself into her bed? Bob, Matty, awful Roddy, and now Hedley Morley. 'I'm tired. I need to go to bed,' she said, in a clipped voice.

Hedley looked at her in dismay, reached out a hand. 'No. No, please sit down a moment. This is important.' She remained on her feet. 'Please,' he said softly.

Against her better instincts, she settled back into her chair.

'These things happen. Bad timing, really. That's life, sadly. If only one could wind the clock back twenty years. Although I'd hate to live through the bloody war again. I sometimes think, if I could wind my own clock back and I was sitting here now, aged twenty . . . And so in love. What mistakes would I make trying to prevent myself from losing . . . ?' He glanced drunkenly at her and smiled. 'It's odd. You really are so like her, Alice. And today . . .'

He extended an arm again, almost as though he was going to touch her face. Who was he talking about? It was more than Alice could bear. She rose to her feet again, her mouth set in a thin line.

'I'm not that sort of girl. I was engaged once, and he was unfaithful. I know how that feels – horrible – and I could never do that to your wife. You have been kind to me, and I'm sorry if you think I've teased you in some way, but I never intended that. I'm going to bed now. You've had too much to drink, maybe that's an excuse, but I can't . . . can't . . . I'm sorry. Please don't spoil today.'

He was staring at her, astonished. 'Alice? Alice, do you think I'm trying to seduce you?'

She looked back at him, a little astonished herself and suddenly unsure. 'Aren't you?'

His expression changed and he began to laugh, a genuine, irrepressible laugh. 'No, no, really I'm not. Alice, sit down, for heaven's sake. I may have a heart attack at any moment and it'll be up to you to save me.'

She surprised herself by doing as she was asked, and sat there waiting until he recovered himself.

'I can see how it might have looked, but as you say, I've had far too much to drink, and when I do that, I get, I don't know . . . I get confessional. Will you allow me to finish?'

'Go on,' she replied nervously.

He sighed deeply. 'The girl fell pregnant, but I'd already met the woman I was going to marry and she had a young son of her own. So I ended it and married my wife, Catherine, just as everyone expected me to. All that remains now is a lifetime of guilt, which I try to make up for with my stepson. The other day, when someone told me of a terrible mistake they had made, my heart went out to this person – knowing how he might face a lifetime of regret, like me.' He raised his brandy and took the last gulp. 'You remind me of that girl.'

'What happened to her? Did she have the baby?'

'Yes, I believe she had the baby.'

'Where are they now?'

He considered the question before answering.

'I couldn't tell you that, but I'm damned sure she would have made a better job of bringing up the child than I have done with my stepson. Too many white lies and secrets. And then it becomes one big lie. That's my problem. Alice, I know about your fiancé. And then – you and Matty.'

'How?'

'I noticed the other evening that Matty was not his usual amiable self. Downright miserable, in fact. He was tight-lipped at first, but eventually he told me that it was over between you two, and why.'

'He shouldn't have said anything.'

'Probably not, but I can be relentless when I put my mind to it, Alice. I think he did well to hold me off for as long as he did. Look, I understand why you were angry with Matty, but I don't think *you* understand the way he saw it.'

'He should have told me.'

'And what would you have said, if he'd told you that your fiancé had been unfaithful? Would you have appreciated him for it? Thanked him for ruining your happiness? Would it have cemented your friendship; perhaps have made you fall in love with him? I don't think so.'

Alice stared, unfocused, into the distance and said nothing. She wished they were talking about something else. But at the same time, she wanted to hear what he knew and what he thought about it.

'That's not the way these things go. So instead, he tried to help you fall out of love with Bob, hoping you'd not be hurt as much when the truth came out.'

'It was the truth about Matty that hurt me. The fact that he knew,' she insisted. 'Honesty matters.'

'But if you love someone, you can't bear to see them upset. He must love you, Alice. It's simple. Do you think this was about the two of them sharing a secret and smirking? No. This was one sharing and the other being appalled, but not knowing how to tell you without losing you. All I'm saying is, think this through again. Imagine a man hoping he might be the one to spend his life with you, and then ask what else Matty could have done? Maybe he was wrong, but only because you found out. Matthew is one of the good chaps. I've seen him grow from a rather splendid boy into an impressive young man. I've followed him, watched him becoming more confident, becoming the fine person he is. If you had never seen that letter, you might be here in this bar looking forward to seeing that wonderful person again.'

Alice took a moment to think this through. Then she drew a deep breath. 'And now it's my turn to tell you something, Mr Morley – about Roddy,' she said.

Chapter 34

'Festival of flamin' Britain,' said the driver the following morning, as he drove Hedley and Alice to the station. 'Hanging stuff all over the place, blocking off streets. Be all right once it's happening – I'll make a few bob this summer. It's the getting ready that's doing my head in. All this palaver is meant to cheer us up. They oughta put a few quid in our Davy Crocketts instead. Here we go.'

The taxi lurched forward and Hedley's face purpled as he made a choking noise, his eyes widening. Alice thought he might be sick, but he held his handkerchief to his mouth, glanced at her and inhaled deeply.

When they boarded the train, he insisted she sit with him in first class.

'Milk of magnesia? Are you trying to kill me?'

'I've got aspirin too, and a box of Alka-Seltzer, but I don't think you can take them all together.' She hadn't known what to buy to help a hangover, and nor had the shop assistant on the station concourse. Alice's father had sworn by the 'hair of the dog' – in other words, start drinking again as quickly as possible – but she wasn't going to suggest that.

Hedley took a swig of milk of magnesia and

groaned. 'This is my punishment for drinking too much.' He gazed out of the train window.

They were slowly carving their way through Camden, the high brick embankments and Victorian houses rising above them. They rattled along the tracks away from London, back towards the bleakness of Alice's old life. The minutes passed and she thought he'd nodded off, his head back and turned towards the window – but then suddenly he was bolt upright, nose almost pressed against the glass. 'Look, the Grand Union Canal. See? We're following it. The railways bought up the canals and built the tracks on the land. Clever. No planning problems, see?' He pressed his fists into his temples. 'I feel so rotten.'

'That will be the tanker-load of whisky you had last night, Mr Morley.'

He smiled. 'Let's stick with Hedley.'

She nodded. 'So, is that why you wanted me in first class? To teach me history and show me a canal?'

His familiar serious expression returned.

'I'm afraid I've lost all credibility with you after last night. I overdid it on the drink. And I want to apologize.'

'You haven't. And you don't need to apologize.'

'That's a relief. Thank you. And I'm grateful to you for telling me about Roddy's behaviour – not that it was a surprise. But what I said about Matty . . .'

'I'm glad you said it. And I have thought about it. But I'd rather leave it at that, if you don't mind. Can we stick to sinks and lavatories for now?'

They took a taxi from Lime Street. Matty was busy driving Mr Worboys out to the site in Speke, according

310

to Hedley. Alice wondered if that was true. Only that morning she had been dreading the thought of being in the car with Matty; now, she wasn't so sure. She still felt she had been made a fool of, but something had imperceptibly changed.

As she made her way back to Bernice's, she looked at the Mersey rippling in waves towards the banks. How different this river was to the Thames. It was muddy, silty and scrappy. And the streets; these dirty cobbles, the crumbling dockyards, the bomb sites – all had an air of dereliction about them.

But this was her home, in all its grime and dust. She felt as if a part of her was in the stones, in these walls covered in moss, in the soot under her fingernails. This place had made her, and she would bring it with her wherever she went, she was sure of that. There was something about it that anchored her. London had been exciting, and she wanted to go back some day; it had felt like a place where her ideas and ambition could flourish, where she would be listened to. But her business here was not finished yet. Right now, there was still the matter of Gabe and the twins, and of helping her mother recover somehow.

And there was Matty.

Chapter 35

Bernice was waiting for her with a cup of tea and an Eccles cake.

'I think I've made a terrible mistake,' was the first thing Alice said as she tumbled through the door.

'Why, what happened? Was it Hedley? Did he . . . ? He didn't . . . ?'

'No, no. Hedley was fine. But he made me see that I've been wrong about Matty. You were right. I shouldn't have been so hard on him. The things I said. He's a good man. Kind,' she blurted, pacing the room, twisting her hands together. Bernice shoved a piece of cake towards her on a plate. Alice tried to take a bite to be polite, but it tasted bitter in her mouth.

'I could have told you that, Alice. He's one of the best. What I wouldn't do to get my hands on his shiny buttons. But what's brought on this change of heart?'

'Mr Morley told me a story that made me see things differently. He said a life of regret is no life . . . and, and . . . oh, Bernice. I'm a fool. Matty's the one thing in my life that's good. It's Bob I should be angry with, not him.' She pushed the plate away and sat down, dropping her forehead onto the table with a groan. 'I'm so stupid.'

'No, you're not. But I did wonder why you were

so full of rage at Matty. He couldn't win. Shoot the messenger, and all that. So what are you waiting for? I last saw him at the Locarno. He told me he's been there every night since you left. He'll probably be there now, consoling himself by listening to Jan Ralfini and his band. As if he's not had enough torture . . . My ma used to go and see that lot when she was young. Pretty outdated.'

Alice smiled. 'Maybe they'll come back into style one day.'

'And maybe men will go to the moon. Go on. Skedaddle. Go and find him.'

The dance hall was crowded. It felt a little strange to be here on her own. From up on the balcony, the music was loud; people moved constantly around the floor. More than once Alice thought she recognized Matty's face in the swirling sea of bodies, but when she rushed down the stairs and onto the floor, tugging at the sleeve she thought was his, it was a stranger who turned round.

Eventually, she decided to go to his flat to find him. Bernice was obviously wrong. But when Mrs Roach opened the door, she looked at Alice coldly and shrugged. 'He's not here,' she said flatly. 'Who knows where he is? He left without a word.'

Alice's heart lurched. 'Left? Where?'

'Couldn't tell you. And I've got things to do,' the woman said, shutting the door firmly in her face.

Panic tore through her. Her hands were shaking. Did she mean left *for good*? Could he have done something stupid like leave Liverpool?

She arrived back at Bernice's a mess of worry.

'He's gone. Like everyone else in my life,' she wailed. 'I *am* stupid. I told you so. Stupid as a box of rocks.'

'Sit down, love . . .'

'No. No. I can't bear it.'

'Listen . . .' Bernice took her arms and held them stiff. 'Matty—'

'I'm such an idiot!' she said, throwing her friend off and crushing her fists into her eyes.

'Alice, will you be quiet!'

Alice looked up. 'Matty!' she gasped, feeling her legs wobble underneath her. 'You're here!'

Matty had just come out of the back room and was standing in the doorway, smiling nervously.

'I've been a fool! Will you forgive me?' said Alice tearfully.

'There's nothing to forgive.' He felt his chest open with relief, as if he had found a way to breathe again.

Bernice left the room quietly.

'Oh, Matty,' Alice said, plunging into his arms. 'I thought you'd left.'

'Left where?'

'Liverpool! Your landlady said you'd gone.'

'Oh, don't listen to her. I haven't moved out for good, I only stormed out after a silly argument about not wiping my feet and leaving my clothes around the place. I must say, I had let things slip a little. Since . . . well . . .' He trailed off, holding her tightly.

'Can we start again?' Alice blurted. 'Life's too short not to forgive.' And when she put her lips on his again, she felt she was coming home. Dropping her head onto his chest, she said quietly, 'Finding that letter was such a shock . . . Just promise me you will always be honest with me.'

'I should be the one apologizing. I swear that I will always tell you the truth, Alice, no matter how difficult it is to hear.'

'Then let's put it behind us, shall we? Let's not make what Bob did to me ruin us.'

'I'm all for that. I can't tell you how relieved I am. I'm the luckiest man in the world.' And as he kissed her mouth, her ears, her cheeks, the back of her neck, all was forgotten in an instant.

'You two finished?' Bernice looked into the room, smiling.

Alice felt herself blushing to the tips of her ears as she pulled away from Matty.

'We've a lot of catching up to do,' he said.

'As long as it doesn't involve Alice having to sit through Jan Ralfini and his band,' said Bernice. 'She had a lucky escape there.'

'What's wrong with them? They're grand. We could go this weekend.'

'Steady on. She's just agreed to take you back and you're about to ruin it,' Bernice said, laughing.

But then Matty's expression changed. He spoke gravely and directly. 'Actually, Alice, first I need to tell you – someone was asking for you. Came to the office yesterday. A girl. She knows you work for Hedley.'

'Who?' Alice was mystified.

'I have no idea, but she seemed serious. I'm driving over to Manchester in an hour to take Worboys for a meeting, staying over in a hotel, but I'll be back in two days and I'll find out then if you haven't. Your ma. Where is she? Could the girl have something to do with that?'

'She's in Parbold, at my aunt's farm.'

'Perhaps if I speak to her? About the kids. I could go by on my way back from Manchester.'

'No, that won't work.' She looked at him, tears filling her eyes.

He took her hand. 'We'll sort this out. We'll get the children out of the orphanage somehow and then see what's what. Starting by persuading your ma to change her mind. I love you, Alice. I feel like I've been given a second chance and by God, I'm going to take it.'

The following morning, Alice arrived at the Lamp Building to collect the post she needed to catch up on after her trip so she could have a fresh start on Monday. She went up the steps two at a time, and was surprised to see Miss Maguire waiting for her outside the office.

'Alice – for you,' she said, handing her an envelope. Alice ran her finger down the side of it. No doubt her expense chits for London. Miss Maguire liked everything done properly. Ripping open the letter, she scanned it quickly. What was this? Handwritten – Miss Maguire would have typed a letter. And then it dawned on her. The girl Matty had told her about.

'From a young lady. Scruffy-looking thing in a brown uniform,' Miss Maguire said, as if answering her thoughts.

Clearly, if spelling was anything to go by, the letter-writer could barely read. The words were jumbled and sloping across the page, with childish crossing-outs and capital letters in the wrong places. But as Alice began to make sense of them and unfolded the second slip of paper, her heart hammered at her chest.

'Oh, Ma. What on earth have you let happen?' she murmured when she reached the end, the words still swimming before her.

'What now?' Bernice asked as soon as she saw Alice's grim expression. Alice thrust the letter at her.

'Read it,' she said, her voice trembling. 'It's from a girl called Doreen. One of my ma's girls at the orphanage.'

'What?'

'You have no idea what's happening in St Mary's. The nuns – I think they are planning to give Gabe away. Read it.'

Bernice read aloud: 'Case three hundred and forty-two: Mr and Mrs Pirbright. Child one: Gabriel Lacey. To be fostered with a view to adoption by Elaine and Trevor Pirbright of 12 Rossett Road, Brighton-le-Sands. The child is of good health, and no mental deficiencies noted. He is a very pleasing-looking boy. Mr and Mrs Pirbright have been looking to adopt for a year. Mrs Pirbright initially requested a baby but seeing the child, feels a three-year-old is preferable. She worried about the challenges of nappies, sleeping, et cetera. The boy is lively and at times a little wilful, but overall, a suitable candidate. Mother known to the sisters. A Catholic family – the Pirbrights expressly asked for a Catholic child. Mother has been struggling to cope after her husband's recent death and is at present homeless. Mrs Lacey expressed her hope that maybe the two elder siblings who reside at the orphanage at this time will be able to return home when she has found accommodation, but she has stated that for Gabriel, she wishes for a better life, hope of a fresh start.'

Alice shook her head in disbelief. Could her mother really have said that? To separate Gabriel from Biscuit and Gravy – how could she do this? It must be a lie. Or a joke? But how could anyone joke about such a thing?

'I've got to go there – I've got to go now. But I can't just steal the children away. It's useless,' she wailed, pressing her fists to her temples. 'They once said I could live there as well. I should have said yes, instead of running around pleasing myself . . . Perhaps I am selfish, like my ma said . . . Perhaps I can tell them I've changed my mind?'

'That's a bit drastic. What about we get Matty to help? Or your Hedley?'

'Hedley? Why, because he's rich? There are some things that not even money can sort out. My mother – she's proud. The problem is, Bernice, she thinks the nuns are doing a good thing. Nothing will change that.'

Bernice took her by the shoulders. 'Let's be serious about this. You can't do anything right now. Get some rest. It's Saturday today – tomorrow is the last Sunday of the month and we can get the children from the orphanage in the morning. Then we'll think what to do about the Pirbrights. We don't even know if Gabe is there yet. Does your mother know? Have you considered that even she might not know?'

'What d'you mean?'

'Just . . . the nuns. I've heard stories. D'you really think your ma would allow this? I doubt it.'

Alice turned over the question in her mind. Why on earth might her mother have thought it was a good idea for Gabriel to be adopted? What would it feel like to be so desperate that you might think this? Was this all her fault? she asked herself, hopelessly.

Chapter 36

Alice fell asleep eventually, but it was fitful, and the pillow under her cheek was wet with tears. She cursed herself for going away to London, sitting drinking in the hotel, thinking everything was going to be all right while Gabriel was in danger. What a fool she had been!

She got out of bed as soon as she woke, remembering a dream she had had about her father, and dressed quickly. It was unseasonably warm outside, but there was a chill in her bones that she couldn't shake.

'We'll go together,' said Bernice.

Half an hour later, Alice was at the gates of the orphanage, having persuaded Bernice to wait on a bench around the corner. She had been surprised to find the gates were closed and locked, with no sign of children waiting for visitors. She remembered one of the girls taking her in through a side entrance – the doors were at the back, and she hurried round and knocked urgently.

'I need Sister Cyril – I need to see her, *now*,' she said urgently to the nun who answered the door. The nun put her arm across the entrance. 'What for? Sorry, dear. Who are you? Your hands are shaking.'

'It doesn't matter. I need to see her,' Alice repeated, pushing her way past.

'Wait. You can't go in there,' the nun said sharply, but Alice was gone. Her boots echoed down the corridor, pounding the polished parquet floors, skidding around corners.

She charged straight into Sister Cyril's office, but it was Sister Bernadette she found there. The nun was lighting a candle on the mantelpiece and turned around, startled.

'I need to see my brother,' Alice panted. 'Where is he?'

'Alice! Whatever is the matter with you?'

'My brother – Gabe – you've given him away.'

'I don't know what you're talking about, dear. I saw him this morning.'

'Is he still here, then?'

'I will find out. But it's Benediction. Sit down and stop being silly.'

Alice felt a little sick. Silly?

'I'll speak to the Mother Superior – she will help. I don't know anything about this, Alice, but I'll pray for you.' Sister Bernadette left, but not before slipping a prayer card into Alice's hand.

Alice waited, heart pounding, until her footsteps had died away, then flicked the prayer card over the desk. Was this what the nuns existed for? Was it their purpose to claim they were bringing wretched souls to God, but to destroy everything good on this earth as they did so?

'We'll see about that,' she muttered through gritted teeth, and turned back out into the corridor.

A few moments later, striding angrily along the path to the schoolrooms, she nearly collided with a teenage girl carrying a small basket of fruit.

'I remember you,' the girl said. 'You look just like your ma. Same hair, same nose, and the way you do that fluttering thing with your arms.'

Alice had been about to hurry on, but she hesitated.

'We liked your mum,' the girl went on. 'She didn't judge us. Not like the nuns. She used to teach our classes when we were having our babies. Can I ask you why you're here?'

'I wanted to . . .' Alice glanced around quickly. Could she trust this girl? 'I wanted to see the nuns, ask them if they would let me come and stay.'

'You've nowhere to live?' The girl's eyes widened in amazement. 'But – good grief. You want to come here? I've never heard of that.'

'I need to be here to look after my brothers and sister. Especially my baby brother.'

'What's his name?'

'Gabe – Gabriel.'

'The one who looks like a little girl, with the blond curls?'

She was about to reply when a second girl came hurtling through the gate. 'You got my note, then, Alice?' she said. 'I'm Doreen. Thank goodness you came. Quickly – let's go into the nuns' garden. They've said no children are allowed to see parents today,' she explained in a low voice, glancing over her shoulder.

'But it's the last Sunday of the month.'

'That doesn't make a difference. They say no, they mean no.'

They walked as they talked, round a circular path, then Doreen pulled Alice down to sit on a bench close against a clematis vine, dormant and woody apart from a few brave green leaves.

'There was a couple – we saw them walking round the schoolrooms with your brother. They looked all right. She was wearing one of those new swing coats. It was ever so nice, with white trim and velvet buttons . . . But we knew your mum. She was kind to us. And I had a feeling something was wrong. From what I remember of her, she might've asked the nuns to look after Gabe, but she would never have put him up for adoption.'

'Can they really send him away?'

'They can do that. They can do anything – like cancelling today. But there's still a chance he might come back. Often, these families, they just try the children out. One little boy last week got as far as the railway station and the new ma and da sent him back when he widdled in the geranium display. Of course, he did it deliberately. They were horrified. And the Pirbrights . . . you know, they're not monsters, some of these parents. Just sad people who are longing for a babby. They might be kind. So what d'you say? Before you do anything drastic and move in here, shall we go and find out where Gabe is?'

'Alice. What are you doing here?' Sister Cyril had appeared silently in front of the bench. She looked down at them with a fixed smile on her face.

Both girls stood up. 'Where's Gabe?' Alice stammered. 'I'm here to see him.'

'Sleeping,' said the nun, with another sweet smile. 'Come back next month. No visitors today.' Alice shuddered. She knew the nun was lying. Every bone in her body told her so.

Chapter 37

It took an hour to reach Parbold from Manchester, but Matty found the farmhouse easily. And outside, in the opposite field, there was the pigsty – just like Alice had described, with washing hanging outside, flapping on a line, and with the thatched roof on an old tram and a plume of smoke swirling from its makeshift chimney. Surely Ida couldn't be living in there? Among this collection of ramshackle sheds and decrepit outbuildings?

He was about to walk up the path when he saw her, kneeling down in a patch of weeds. She was hunched over, splitting wood with a short-handled axe.

'Mrs Lacey . . .'

'Good grief! What are you doing here?'

Her hair was unbrushed and tangled, and the two deep lines between her eyebrows were etched in dirt. She sat back on her heels, wiped her brow with her forearm and squinted up at him.

'I need to speak to you about Alice. And the children. I'm sorry if I surprised you.'

'I'm busy,' she said, standing.

Matty followed her as she carried a bucket around the muddy field, the ground sucking at his boots. A sheep had wandered in and she was distracted, waving the bucket at it and shooing it out of the way.

'Let me carry that bucket,' he said, catching up to her. 'Listen, Mrs Lacey – I want to marry Alice. I want to marry your daughter and look after the children, if you'll let me.'

She snorted. 'And where would you put them?' she said flatly, handing him the pail.

'I don't know. Yet.' He noticed that her hands were red and raw. She poked at the sheep with a stick and then turned away, walking over to warm her hands at a fire in a rusting brazier.

'I'm not sure if it's any of your business,' she said vaguely. 'My children. It's complicated.'

'But if Alice and I were married? Would that change your opinion?'

She pushed her sleeves up her arms and tipped her head to one side. 'That's your business. I'd rather you married her than live over the brush with her, but—'

'This is no place for you to be, Mrs Lacey. No place at all,' he said. 'I'd look after you as well.'

'I have a right to live in a pigsty if I want. And I like the fresh air. It's good for me. Always have. Maybe I needed a change. The people around here are friendly. We're all in the same boat.'

Matty could see her gaze moving between him and the sheep, which was now stuck against a hedgerow. A man had come out of the shack with a flapping chicken under his arm and was watching them.

'Ask me another time,' she said. 'I must finish

with that sheep. I haven't got time to think about all of this now.'

Hedley Morley had been looking forward to seeing Alice at the office on Monday, and was annoyed to find his stepson there instead. Roddy was perched on the edge of Hedley's desk smoking, sneering and smug, filling the room with the dreadful smell of his Turkish cigarettes.

'What are you doing here now? I was expecting you at five. Those blasted cigarettes – put it out, Roddy.'

Roddy grinned and blew out a plume of smoke. 'No can do – I'm addicted. Bad luck for us both. Where's Miss Meccano?'

Hedley bristled. Roddy's gold cigarette holder seemed a ridiculous affectation, and for some reason it was annoying him intensely. 'If you mean Alice, don't you dare say anything more to upset her. She's wonderful. A marvel.'

'I'm sure she is,' Roddy said, laughing. 'A marvel God made, with everything in the right place. Can't get over how pretty she is. Don't you agree?'

Hedley sucked air through his teeth. 'I've heard about how you behaved to her at your ridiculous club. I was ashamed, Roddy.'

'How could I resist? She's such a beautiful little thing. She made a marvellous cigarette girl. Too delicate, though, for nightlife.'

'She's not delicate. She's strong. She's got a great deal to offer, and being pretty is the least of it. That certainly wasn't why I employed her.'

'Come on, though, Pa. It helped.'

'Is that all you think about? Sex?'

'No, Pa. I think of horse-racing and billiards as well,' Roddy said, knowing it would throw Hedley into a rage. 'And please don't start on me. I'm recovering after a heavy night at the club. I'm shattered.'

'That girl has grown up with nothing – no privileges or handouts – but she wants to make something of herself. Whereas you . . . you . . .'

'What? I'm an idle good-for-nothing? I'm spoilt, Pa, I admit it. Your fault, though.'

'If it wasn't for your blessed mother . . .' Hedley thundered, gripping the edge of the table to hold himself back.

'Oh, that's nice, "my blessed mother". I'm sure she'd like to hear that.'

'You know what I mean.'

'Pa, I can't help it. I'm sorry – you look at me and you feel rage. But what can I do?'

Hedley stared at him, at his aquiline nose, lank blond hair, pallid skin. 'Go,' he said. 'Go.'

'Oh, come on, Pa . . .' Roddy loped over to him, put his arm around his shoulder and spoke directly into his face. 'I'm sorry I've disappointed you. But I promise I'll make you proud. I'm going to make something of myself.'

'Twenty-nine, you are,' Hedley muttered. 'Thirty soon. You never even finished school. I wanted you to go to university. It broke your mother's heart.'

Roddy wandered over and looked at the plans. 'Pipe down, Pa. I want to talk to you about my plans for the club.'

Hedley felt the vein in his forehead throbbing with tension. 'Are you jealous of Alice?'

Roddy stared at his stepfather, cold and detached. 'You look as though you're about to explode, Pa. Steady on, old man. That would be no good for any of us,' he said, with a sneer. He sat with his feet up on Hedley's desk, sucking on the cigarette.

'Take your damned feet off there.'

Roddy smirked. 'I'll go in a minute. But I wanted to see you to talk about your bulldozing. It's started in the street behind the Boom Boom Club. Do you want to know what my opinion is on the scheme? My friends and I have all been talking about it. The noise is giving me a blistering headache.'

Hedley looked at him and picked up the newspaper, opened the pages as if to read it and ignore him, but then flung it back down angrily. 'You? An opinion? Based on what? Nothing. You're so, so . . . ill-informed about everything. Why is it you think you can offer an opinion? You cannot think of the world beyond yourself and your new cravat. *I need tobacco, Pa . . . I need wine . . . fees for my club . . .* And your so-called friends? You surround yourself with people who think you're a fool. Of course they like coming to see you because you're the only one doling out the free stuff. They like to come and sit in your miserable club all night long, smoke your cigarettes and drink your drink. But when they've left you, what do you think they do? They go to work.'

'Give it a rest. What do you know?'

'I know one of them is cycling through the Mersey Tunnel every day to work at Cammell Laird's shipyards.

Another one is in accounts at Cunard, working hard for his exams. And what are you doing? You barely lift a finger!'

'How bloody dare you,' Roddy countered breezily. 'Harsh, old man.'

'Take you out of your comfort and habits – oh, not a chance. You're too afraid to make anything of yourself in case you fail, and you're sitting there smoking, talking about taking on the world, when you know nothing of it. Absolutely nothing.'

'Oh, for God's sake, Pa, where did that speech come from?' Roddy snarled. 'Now look what you've bloody made me do,' he added, brushing ash off his lapels.

'You shouldn't be smoking in here. Look at you – you hardly go out in the day because you don't get up until four in the afternoon. You look like a ghost. And you're so thin. Don't forget, your money is *my* money. I can cut you off at a minute's notice! If it wasn't for your mother – "oh, Roddy must stay here living with us, let's give him the second floor, oh, Roddy needs his own bathroom, Roddy needs a dressing room" – what a mistake that was! She wanted you to be frail so that she would still have some kind of purpose. And why is it, while we're on the subject, that you don't have a woman in your life? They come and go, but they never stay, do they? Too afraid to be a man?'

'That's it, I've had enough. I can't listen to this claptrap any more. If you want, I'll go for good . . .'

'Where?' Hedley rubbed his temples.

'What's it got to do with you?'

'You have no job. No means to go anywhere. I started off delivering newspapers. You've never done any of that . . .'

'Agreed. Shame about that silver spoon you stuffed into my mouth.'

'Shut up! Don't be so glib! If you could only see what the world thinks of you. You're a fool. You could have travelled. Studied. So many opportunities I gave you. You could have been—'

'Just when I thought you'd lost your steam, off you go again. Please God, Pa, you're not about to go on about the oboe?'

'You can't bear it, can you, if someone is better than you at something? And of course *everyone* is better than you, because you never put any work into anything. I've seen you have so many stupid arguments with your friends. They never seem to stick, those friendships, do they, any more than your women?'

'Yawn, Pa. You finished?'

Hedley slumped. 'Why do you have to do this? Enrage me. I wanted to talk to you about something serious today . . . something of the utmost gravity. But you've just got us arguing before we started.'

'What, Pa? What's so serious?'

'Sit down. It's about Matthew.'

'Who?'

'My chauffeur.'

'Your bloody *chauffeur*?' Roddy snorted.

'Yes. I wouldn't snort if I were you. But the first thing I must do is apologize. I've not been entirely honest with you, and you might be upset by what you're going to hear.'

'You're apologizing to *me*? It must be serious. Go on, stick it to me, Pa. I'm looking forward to this.'

Half an hour later, Hedley watched from the window as a shaken Roddy left the building. The young man scurried across the road, anger in every line of his body.

His stepson . . . Catherine's boy. Their relationship was completely broken. How could this have happened?

It was partly Catherine's fault. But then, was it fair to blame her? She'd lost her first son in the war, so it was no wonder she'd mollycoddled Roddy. Perhaps Hedley could have done more about it if he'd been firmer. Roddy had always had an arrogance about him; you could see it in the way he swaggered about, puffing out his chest.

Not now, though. Hedley had grown tired of Roddy's 'marvellous' ideas and ludicrous grand plans; they all came to nothing. And now, finally, Roddy knew the truth about Matthew.

Who could say what was going to happen next?

Chapter 38

Alice had the Pirbrights' address written on a piece of paper that she had looked at over and over again.

Rossett Road was a leafy street in Brighton-le-Sands, lined with neat gardens and gravelled driveways on which newly washed cars gleamed, throwing back liquid reflections of the sun. Climbing vines tangled up the walls, and the chilly air was fresh and crisp.

Alice looked at Doreen, then back at the house. This beautiful house, with its mock-Tudor beams and gables and pretty chintz curtains in the window – maybe this *was* a better life? Maybe this was what Gabriel deserved. Not nits, and damp, and blind scouse.

But then she shivered. She felt like a smashed egg, gloopy and runny and impossible to put together. She wondered what to do next. Just walk up the path? Or wait, hopefully to see some movement inside, a person?

Doreen took her hand and squeezed it.

'What will they say? Do you think they'll be furious?' Alice said.

'Who knows?'

'Look at us, Doreen. Both of us in our old coats. So scrappy and . . . and . . .'

'Poor? Who cares? One thing about scrabbling around at the bottom of the pile is you've got nothing to lose. Come on. I'll hang back, but if you need me, give me the nod. I'll wait behind that tree.'

Alice thought of the twins in the dormitories. The nuns in their bedrooms on the top floor – their cells, as they called them. Then she thought of Gabriel, probably in a white wooden cot bed in that upstairs room with the curtains closed. A quilt with teddy bears on it and matching furniture. Maybe furniture like she had seen in the window of Lee's. Maybe the living room with a green velvet sofa, a lampshade with fringes and tassels. Or a nest of tables and a rug your feet would disappear in.

They crept forward, shading their eyes, and peered in through the window. 'A rocking horse!' Alice gasped. 'It's beautiful. Like the one at Blacklers, but less scruffy.'

'Why have they got their sofa covered in plastic?' Doreen wondered.

'Keeps the furniture brand new. Save it for posh visitors.'

'Not us, then,' Doreen laughed.

'They'll have their work cut out with Gabe if they're the tidy kind.'

'Don't fancy sitting on a plastic sofa. Must make the backs of your knees all sweaty on a warm day.'

Alice raised half a smile. Her heart was pounding.

'Go on,' said Doreen. 'They might know me from St Mary's and we don't want to shock them. I'll keep my distance.'

Alice nodded and rang the bell.

Mrs Pirbright was wearing a frilled apron over a tea dress, and a pair of pink velour slippers. 'Oh, I thought you were the bread man – late again. Can I help you?' she said.

Alice just looked at her.

'What is it? Are you all right, dear?'

Alice opened her mouth to speak, but no words came out. Mrs Pirbright frowned. Something wasn't right with this girl, she thought.

'Can we come in, missus? I'm Doreen. From the orphanage? This is my friend, Alice,' said Doreen, stepping out from under the tree.

The woman's half smile slid from her face. 'What is it you want?'

'We've brought some of Gabriel's medicine. Cough mixture. It got left behind. Sister asked us to.'

'But this is very unusual. I would have thought Sister should have brought it herself, or . . . we could buy some . . .' She took the sticky bottle of linctus and turned it over in her hand. 'Trevor?' she called.

A man appeared from what might have been the kitchen, with his shirt sleeves rolled up.

'These two girls have been sent by the sisters,' Mrs Pirbright said. He looked at them and frowned, and she added uncertainly, 'They've brought some of Herbert's things.'

'Herbert!' said Alice.

'Herbert?' said Doreen, fighting a smile.

Trevor Pirbright put one hand into his trouser pocket and hooked the other thumb under his red braces. He looked at them for a moment, his eyes narrowed. Then he said, 'That's not why you're here, is it?'

Alice's bottom lip trembled. 'No. I'm here because . . .' She felt Doreen squeeze her hand, but again, no more words would come out.

'Mr and Mrs Pirbright,' said Doreen, taking a step forward. 'We're here because we think there's been a mistake. I've seen plenty like you, their worlds changed for the better because of girls like me gerrin' up the duff. And Gabe – he's a little wild, but he's a smasher of a boy . . . and I'm not saying that you should never be parents. I'm just asking you, have you made the right decision? Because I know what it feels like to make the wrong decision. And it leaves you feeling, I don't know, kind of sad, and I just think . . . that . . .'

She trailed off. The couple looked frozen in shock.

Alice took a deep breath. 'It's no good, Doreen. Mr and Mrs Pirbright – Gabriel is my little brother. And no, there hasn't been a mistake. I know that you have signed the papers. But you see, the thing is, he's part of our family. And our mother, she's in a terrible state. We have another brother and sister, and . . . I thought I'd lost everything. My ma, the twins, my fiancé, Gabe – er, Herbert – but now suddenly, unexpectedly, I have a future. I have met someone who . . . well, it means we can be a family again. Except not without Gabe. We can't. We just can't . . .'

'Did you say Gabriel's *mother*?' Elaine Pirbright said, trembling. She pressed a hand flat against her chest as if it would help her to breathe.

'You'd better come in,' sighed her husband.

'His mother?' the woman said again. 'But . . . he's an orphan.'

336

Doreen frowned. 'Is that what the sisters told you? They do that sometimes. Pretend the mothers are dead. Especially if they're – y'know, in a bad way.'

Mrs Pirbright shook her head. They followed her inside, and she sank into an armchair with its squeaky plastic cover. 'The orphans . . . I thought . . .'

'Gabe's not an orphan,' said Alice, sitting down. 'He's—'

'An orphan of the living. Like a load of us. Like me,' piped Doreen. 'I'm an orphan of the living, an' all.'

'Oh, good God.'

'Gabe was only with the nuns because their ma's in a desperate situation and she wasn't thinking straight.'

'Whatever the story of your mother, he's settled here now. You need to leave,' said Trevor Pirbright in a flat, clipped tone.

His wife turned to him. 'Did you know, Trevor? That the mother was alive? That the boy wasn't an orphan?'

'Of course not. But you heard what she said. He *is* an orphan. An orphan of the living.'

'Herbert kept saying he wanted to go back to his mother, but I thought no one had told him that she was dead. That he was too young to understand . . .'

'He's not stupid,' said Alice.

'We're trying our best. He wouldn't talk at all when we first brought him home, but he's getting better,' said Mrs Pirbright, trembling.

'Gabe? Didn't talk?'

'And he wet the bed the first night, but he hasn't

337

since.' She looked panicked, trying to make sense of everything. Her husband shot her a glance as if to tell her to stop speaking.

'Where is he?' asked Alice. 'May I see him?'

'Not a good idea,' said Trevor, in a measured tone. 'He's not here. He's with his nanny.'

'They'll be back soon, so you should leave now,' said Mr Pirbright.

Mrs Pirbright's eyes flicked over to him. She sucked her slightly protruding teeth.

'Young lady, I'm sorry for you, but this is not practical. We have signed the papers.'

'But Mr Pirbright, it doesn't mean you can't put it right. Please . . . It wouldn't be hard to send Gabe back. I know someone. Mr Worboys, he's one of the governors at St Mary's – he's adopted a child himself . . .'

'And?'

'Mr Worboys could speak to the sisters. Help you choose another baby. One without a ma. They listen to men like Mr Worboys . . .'

Mrs Pirbright's face twitched, and she plucked an invisible thread off her skirt.

There was the sound of a door crashing open.

'Alice!' Gabe yelled, hurtling into the room. He threw his little body at his sister. The Pirbrights both watched, alarmed but powerless, as he clung on to her, his arms clamped around her waist. She smothered the top of his head in kisses and ran her fingers through his curls.

'Oh, God,' murmured Elaine Pirbright, her expression pained. 'This wasn't supposed to happen.'

'Alice – I've got the itches.'

'Herbert, come here,' said Mr Pirbright. 'The itches?'

Gabriel turned to look at them, serious and sad-faced again. He was scratching at his stomach.

The nanny bustled in, flustered. 'The jam sandwiches I made. He had one in the park. One bite and he went all red in the face.'

'Strawberry jam? But he can't have strawberries, anything with strawberries in them – he comes out in hives. Didn't the nuns tell you?' said Alice, turning over Gabe's arm and rolling up his sleeve. They could all see a creeping, angry red rash.

'Jenny, take Herbert to get his milk. And find a wet flannel and some calamine lotion,' said Mr Pirbright sharply, standing up. 'Come with me, dear,' he said to his wife.

When the Pirbrights had left the room, Alice and Doreen sat rigid, not daring to move for the squeaking sound of the plastic. 'What d'you think they're saying?'

'Dunno. But this isn't right. Nothing is right about it. Sister Cyril has lied. One minute he's fostered, the next he's been adopted. It's the nuns that are at the bottom of this.'

In the kitchen, the Pirbrights were saying very little. Mrs Pirbright dropped her head onto her husband's chest and wept silently. He rested a calming hand on her head and they decided in a few exchanged stuttered sentences that with the mother alive, and his sisters and brother also, perhaps it was time to admit what they had known all along. The boy didn't want to be here.

He was difficult and unhappy. They should have adopted a baby, not a toddler. The sisters hadn't been truthful.

It was a hard thing to admit, and whatever they might do next was too difficult to think about now. They would send the girls away and decide in the morning, and tell them when they had their answer.

That night, as Mrs Pirbright tucked the coverlet around a whimpering Gabe, she looked down over his body and saw that it was still covered in hives. Whenever she touched him he yelped, shrinking away and scratching feverishly.

She paced the room. 'Shall we call a doctor, Trevor?' she asked. 'It's getting worse.'

'I don't know.'

'They didn't tell us he was a bed-wetter. And now this.'

Trevor winced. 'Herbert. Talk to us – why aren't you talking?'

Gabriel turned away, curled into himself, facing the wall.

'He's almost three, he should be able to talk.'

'He might just be wilful.'

The woman pressed a finger against her head. 'Herbert, do you feel sick?'

Gabe nodded dolefully.

'Where do you feel sick? Is it in your tummy or is it in your head? Show me, darling.'

He rolled onto his back and pressed two his fingers to his chest.

'You mean you can't breathe? Where does it hurt?'

He looked at her, round-eyed and sad, and replied, 'Heart.'

340

'Your heart is hurting?' Elaine Pirbright sank onto the end of the bed and turned to her husband. 'We took this child too soon. We should have waited for a baby. It all happened so quickly – the nuns . . . I know I didn't want to hear about Herbert's mother, but perhaps we should have asked more about her. This is a mistake, Trevor. Isn't it?'

Chapter 39

That night, when Alice returned to Bernice's, she lit the oil lamp, made a bitter-tasting cup of Bovril and sat down at the kitchen table to write.

Dear Ma,

There's been a terrible turn of events in Liverpool. If I don't hear from you, Matty and I will come to auntie's farm to talk to you. In short, Gabe is living with a couple who want to adopt him. Turns out while you're in the duty of care, the nuns can do anything. I know you meant the best, but when I found him, which I'll explain later, he seemed so unhappy. This nightmare situation has to come to an end. I love you, Ma. And I know you've always said that I have my head in the clouds, but I'm a different girl now. I have found the courage to speak out against what's wrong with the world. And if anything is wrong, this is.

It starts with us becoming a family again. Matty and I are coming to get you so you can give permission to take Gabe back from the Pirbrights and take the children out of the

orphanage. There's a risk of awful things
happening. It feels like they are in grave
danger. There's even boats that the children are
put on, all the way to Canada and America.
Imagine that horror.

    Your loving daughter,
    Alice

Mr and Mrs Pirbright waited on the sad, smooth step at the entrance of St Mary's, where so many unwanted babies had been left to start new lives.

'We expressly said that we wanted a baby,' Mrs Pirbright said, after they had been ushered inside by a nun with a pained expression etched into the lines of her face. 'We made a mistake taking the boy. Too old, you see.'

She spoke in a quavering voice, barely able to look at Gabe, who stood with his head down, kicking the skirting board. Her eyes were swollen from crying. She turned towards the leaded window that looked out over the uneven lawn of the orphanage, trying to blink more tears away. '. . . We need to speak to Sister Cyril.'

'On her way,' said the earnest nun, tipping her head to one side. 'Oh dear. What a performance.'

'*Oh dear* hardly covers it,' said Mr Pirbright, holding Gabriel's hand awkwardly.

Elaine Pirbright was beginning to sniff. 'He's . . . he's . . .'

'Feral,' said Mr Pirbright. 'Elaine, hold it together, for pity's sake. Sister, tell Sister Cyril that this was a mistake. We should have taken the baby.' He looked embarrassed. 'My wife's nerves are shredded. So are mine.'

Mrs Pirbright was wringing her hands, screwing up her gloves, and her husband in his overcoat was looking embarrassed. At the sound of the door, they both started.

'Did you want me, Sister?' said Angela, pushing her long hair away from her eyes and languidly leaning on the door jamb.

'Angela, look sharp – go and find Sister Cyril,' said Sister Bernadette.

Mrs Pirbright was scrabbling in her bag for a cigarette. She tossed aside an old tissue.

'Please, Mrs Pirbright. You can't smoke in here,' said Sister Bernadette.

Elaine Pirbright pursed her lips together in a thin line. 'Trevor, we're going.'

Sister Cyril swept in, fleshy feet pillowing out from her sensible shoes, black wooden rosary beads bumping against her leg, her habit swishing.

'Sister!' said Gabe, turning away from the wall and dashing towards her. Mr Pirbright tried to hook a finger under his jumper and pull him back, but Gabe wriggled away and flung himself at the nun, clinging on to her skirts, circling her legs.

She sighed, tilted her head. 'What have you done, Gabriel? Pick up your suitcase and go back to your room. What happened?' she asked the Pirbrights.

'We made a terrible mistake. I'm a wreck. He looked such an angelic creature, but he wouldn't speak . . . and the bedwetting . . .' said Mrs Pirbright.

Mr Pirbright cleared his throat. 'And we had no idea the mother was still alive.'

'But you were told he was an orphan of the living.'

'We didn't know what that meant,' stammered Mrs Pirbright.

'Really?' Sister Cyril glanced up and saw Angela and Doreen peering in from the corridor. 'Go back to your chores, girls,' she said, reaching out to pull the curtain across the glass door panel.

Mrs Pirbright clutched the lapels of her cardigan and said plaintively, 'Perhaps God doesn't want us to be parents.'

The nun nodded. Life was brutal and lonely, as she knew well enough herself, and she felt a pang of pity for the woman. 'Obstinate, was he? That boy knew exactly what he was doing. A boy only a mother could love,' she said. 'But if it's a baby you're after, we have one arrived here yesterday. The bonniest little girl I've seen in a while, with red hair and a curl in the middle of her forehead.'

Doreen, listening beyond the door, gasped and covered her mouth with a hand.

Later, as she lay awake, she comforted herself with the thought that at least June's child would go to a loving home. One with yellow curtains, and a warm bed with a quilted coverlet, and a rocking horse with a real mane and tail of hair and gleaming red stirrups.

Chapter 40

'You got a pair of wellies?' Alice asked Matty, when she arrived back at Bernice's flat. He had already grabbed his coat and pulled on his boots almost before she had finished the sentence.

They arrived at the farm after travelling through countryside where fields stretched all the way to the horizon, his hands gripping the wheel the whole way. As they bumped up the narrow dirt track and through the open rusty gate, hanging off its hinges, Alice realized that she could no longer remember anything she had been planning in her head to say to her mother.

Ida, sitting in front of the brazier, turned and regarded them with a curious stare before recognition flooded into her face.

'Alice?' she said.

'Did you get my letter, Ma?'

Ida stood up from the upturned pail where she had been sitting, shelling peas. She wiped her hands and forehead and nodded.

'And?' The smell of manure from the pigsty made Alice pinch her nostrils and wrinkle her nose.

'Don't pull a face. You get used to it,' said her mother.

'Does Auntie Nelly really not mind you being here?'

Ida shrugged. Alice looked at the collection of ramshackle sheds in the field. There was the old tram with the thatched roof that Matty had described, and pegged up in the far corner was what looked like an old scout tent. Her mother looked embarrassed. A child emerged from the tent, her face black with soot, closely followed by a flapping chicken.

'You see why I didn't want you coming here? . . . Your face, Alice.'

'Sorry.' It was clear in an instant, even though it would be hard to admit to. 'Can we take you home now, Ma?'

'I have no home.'

'Ma, Bernice will have us for now. It's going to be like sardines, but we need to get the kiddies out of St Mary's. Then we'll find somewhere.'

'I'm content here. We're all struggling, but we help each other. None of us have got anywhere to go, and some of them have had it a lot harder than us. Look, we've cleaned out the pigsty. We have a family in there . . .' She called out to the young girl, who was now swinging on the gate, 'Show them, Nettie.'

The girl opened the door wide next to the gate to show them a tidy room with straw on the dirt floor, a chair and a small bed. There was a baby in a cot and a man who looked surprised, but he nodded and smiled, touching his cap. You could see the exhaustion in his face.

'Don't pity me,' Ida said. 'I've made friends with these people.'

347

Alice nodded. 'All right. But you can still come home, Ma. It's time to come home.'

'Oh, Alice,' Ida said with a wave of her hand. She turned and gazed out over the fields. 'These people are good people. Mostly just families who don't want to be split up.'

'But that's exactly what you've done to us, Ma. Have you forgotten you have three young children?'

'Shush – I've told no one here. The corn has ears and the potatoes have eyes, I swear.' Ida's mouth was set in a bitter line. 'I can't give Gabriel the life he deserves – any child deserves. He still has a chance.' But then her chin trembled, her eyes closed tight, and it was as if she crumpled. Then her whole body collapsed and she gulped and gave in to a flood of tears, her shoulders heaving, sobs making even the sheep raise their heads and stare. Alice knelt beside her, taking her hands.

'Gabe needs you, Ma. And Biscuit and Gravy. They're afraid of everything. They all used to be so bold and wild, but now they're frightened of even a bump or a creak on the stairs. We all need you. I need you, Ma. We need to bring Gabe home, quickly, before it's too late. You're the only one who can do this.'

Her mother raised her head. She looked utterly miserable, but for the first time, Alice saw something of the old Ida in her expression, and it was the chink of light she needed.

'Get your things, Ma. You can come back here if you want, but now we're going to get Gabriel and the kids.'

Ida was hunched and disorientated, at a loss how to even argue. For a few seconds it felt as if they were all frozen, waiting silently to see what she would do next.

'Time to go, then,' she said, tiredly.

After she had collected a few of her belongings from the milk van, she allowed them to lead her to the car.

'Tell Nelly I've gone home. Tell her I'm not sure when I'll be back,' she said to the man leaning on the gate.

'Don't be a stranger, Ida!' he called. 'Come back and see us soon. We'll miss you. And the sheep and hens'll miss you an' all!'

Hedley Morley took his glasses off, breathed on them and rubbed them with a silk handkerchief plucked from his top pocket. He leaned back in his office chair.

Mr Worboys placed something in front of him: a scrap of paper. 'I received this note from Alice last night. She left it on my desk. She wants me to speak with the sisters at St Mary's. Apparently her siblings are there, but now her mother wants to take them out.'

Hedley looked at him in shock. 'I had no idea.' He knitted his brows together. 'Why didn't she tell me?'

'I imagine she had found herself in a bit of a hole. Pride, Hedley. Anyway, Matty just called and she's asked me to meet her there, with her mother, in half an hour.'

'So why are you standing here?'

'Just thought I should let you know, in case . . .'

'Get out of here, man!' Morley barked. But when Worboys was at the door, he said, 'Wait! I'm coming with you!'

'Here, put my coat on, Ma,' said Alice as they pulled up outside St Mary's.

'The smell? Do I smell?' Ida asked nervously.

'It doesn't matter.'

Ida buried her head into the crook of her elbow and sniffed. 'I do. The blasted pigs.'

Alice opened her handbag and squirted her mother liberally with cheap perfume. Matty sneezed.

'Come on,' said Alice. As she put the perfume bottle back into her bag, someone tapped on the car window, and she looked up. 'Mr Worboys! You came! Thank you. And Hedley!'

They all got out of the car and Alice made quick introductions.

'Pleased to meet you, Mrs Lacey. Let's get this over with, shall we? I've brought the troops,' said Hedley.

Ida hung back, watching as they passed through the gates and headed for the entrance. The men's shoes, their suits, their watches, all screamed out that they should be listened to. But she was even more amazed to see her own daughter walk ahead of them and knock on the door, chin up, head held high.

'Alice? Is that you, Ida? And Mr Worboys? How's dear Dolly?' said a smiling nun.

'Never mind that, Sister. Can we come in?' said Alice.

'All of you?'

'Sister, this is my partner, Mr Hedley Morley,' said Mr Worboys seriously.

The nun's thin face paled. Morley stuck out a hand, and she was forced to shake it. A girl up a ladder cutting back brambles, and another small group practising a dance behind the rhododendrons, stopped to watch the scene playing out in front of them.

'We're practising. Monsignor is coming to say Mass next week,' said the nun. The girls were wearing floating white dresses with veils that dazzled in the sunshine. The beauty was arresting, but it wasn't enough to distract Alice; she could only think of how cold the girls must be, and she noticed that the girl up the ladder was grimacing and sucking her scratched and bleeding knuckles.

'Sister, I'll come to the point quickly. We're taking the children out, and they won't be coming back,' said Alice.

'What?'

'Mother's circumstances have changed,' said Mr Worboys. 'And as a governor here, I know our aim is to reunite families. *Familia supra omnia.*'

'Yes. But we are *God's* family first and foremost at St Mary's.'

Alice bridled. 'Would you stop arguing and get the kiddies? Ma's not steady on her pins. You often talk about this place bursting at the seams, so I'm sure Father Donnelly will be very happy to see the young Laceys go back to a loving home with their ma. Isn't that the point? To find loving homes for the children here?'

*

351

Gwenda and Brian stood at the top of the stairs with Gabe. Brian was idly scratching his name into the banister with a pin. 'It's not a Sunday. Why did Sister tell us to wait here?' whispered Gwenda to Brian, bewildered at the scene below. 'Is it a Sunday? Who are all those people?'

Brian shook his head. 'Sunday is the day when we start with church.'

'But we start with church every day.'

'There's Alice! And Ma!' cried Brian, suddenly coming to life.

'Momma!' cried Gwenda.

Ida knew that now was not the time for tears. She tried to calm herself as her children rushed down the stairs towards her. Brian was still limping, but with his cast finally off, he was moving almost as speedily as Gabe and Gwenda. For so long she had asked herself where it had all gone so wrong. The war, the shop; what disaster had come first? Had it been Albert? Losing the house? She was a fighter, but she had just been so tired. Curling her hands into tight fists, she thought of all the nights she had spent trying to remember the smell of her children's heads, the sound of their voices; the gurgle of Gabe's snuffling sleep, or Brian's rhythmic ball bouncing against the wall, or Gwenda playing her French elastic with two chairs in the kitchen. *In, out, together, in, on* . . . It all came crashing back in an instant.

'Momma!'

It was as if she was waking from a deep sleep.

'Have you come to take us home?'

'We have, love. I promised I would. And here I am.'

The coat and the wild hair didn't seem to matter. 'Why are you crying, Ma?' Gwenda asked, touching her cheek. 'Is it 'cos Biscuit was naughty?' Ida's eyes filled with tears. 'Or Gabe? He told us about the lady's apples. He took a bite out of every single one.'

'I put 'em back, Ma.'

'With a bite in each one?' she laughed, stroking his glossy curls.

'And the nuns made him say poetry to try and get him to be a good boy. Ozzy Monday something. Or was it Ozzy Tuesday, Gabe?'

'Did they? I would have liked to see that,' Ida smiled.

'Gabe said his own poem, though.'

'There once was a fellow McSweeney, who spilled whisky and gin on his weenie . . .' Brian chimed, with a grin.

'Who taught him that?' laughed Ida. She yanked Gabriel up, wedged him onto her hip and kissed him.

And then something made Alice turn and glance over her shoulder, up towards the balcony at the top of the stairs. Doreen was there, eyes shining. Mildred had joined her at her side, smiling – and then a small group of children came into view, peering through the banisters, curious about the scene below. Mr Worboys and Hedley turned. More girls were beginning to gather on the staircase, and a few young boys. One of them began to clap. Another stuffed his fingers into his mouth and whistled.

'*Dum spiro spero* . . . there's another bit of Latin for you. While there's breath there's hope . . .' whispered

Hedley. 'And isn't that what all those children up there need to see? Hope?'

'Aye,' said Alice. 'And love, of course. Hedley, once we get out of this awful place . . . I have an idea,' she said mysteriously.

Chapter 41

Matty was still flushed with relief as he walked back towards the Port Authority office to collect his car. He had just seen Alice, her mother and the children into Bernice's, over the road – all happy, all words tumbling over each other, all blame put aside for now as they drank cups and cups of tea and toasted crumpets.

It was a busy evening. People were milling around on the pavement and spilling into the road, enjoying the thrill of dodging traffic. He crossed over to Perth Street where he'd parked the Rover. Night was falling, the light dim, just the glow from a fiery sunset over the estuary. He weaved his way through the slow-moving cars, stopped and hesitated, then called out, 'Bloody heck, hey, careful!' Squinting across the road at the Rover, he couldn't be sure at first, but as his view began to sharpen into focus, he could just make out three men surrounding his car and then moving around it, heads bent. What were they doing? Were they trying to break into it? He took off at lightning speed, shirt flapping in the wind. As he approached the car one of the men looked up, casually stuck out his foot and sent him sprawling to the ground.

'What the hell? You breaking into my car?' He got

to his feet quickly and grabbed the man at the driver's door, swung him around – but now the third man was on Matty's back, an arm around his neck. 'Stop!' he yelled. He was vaguely aware of people running across from the Slaughterhouse pub to watch the fun, jostling to get a better look.

That was when he saw him: Roddy. Standing against a lamp post, one leg crossed in front of the other, and the smoke from his cigarette drifting across his cold, blank face. The crowd were cheering the fight on, some grinning and punching the air, but it was Roddy who occupied his mind. What was he doing here? Matty's feet were moving again, his body jerking. He staggered over to Roddy.

'Help me, Roddy . . .'

'Why would I do that, chauffeur boy?' Roddy's face contorted into a lopsided snarl. 'You and your Miss Meccano . . . two money-grubbing lowlifes, that's what you both are. Taking everything from me . . . My birthright!' There were jeers from the crowd. Matty could hear a police bell ringing in the distance. Roddy lurched at him, swung a punch. Matty felt his arm bounce out of its socket, but with his other arm he somehow managed to hit Roddy square on the nose.

'Don't tell me you don't know about my father's idiocy. How long have you been poisoning him?' Roddy snarled, spitting out blood, as the sound of clanging bells grew louder and the crowd began to disperse.

The final punch that struck Matty's cheekbone meant he was bleeding profusely when he was put into the Black Maria. He had been lying flat on his back on the pavement for a good minute before someone had slapped him back to consciousness. Then policemen were everywhere, and after a passer-by pleaded in vain on Matty's behalf, the black van was driven away.

What would he tell Alice? he thought, as he began to drift off again. This wasn't the happy ending he had dreamed of only half an hour ago.

Chapter 42

The next morning, after a night where Bernice had given up her bed for the children and she and her mother had top and tailed it on the sofa covered in coats for blankets, Alice got up and examined herself in the mirror. She looked surprisingly normal, she thought, considering.

She left for work early, still with no idea that Matty had spent the night in the cells and had been taken off in a police car along with Roddy. 'Nothing serious, lad. They'll let you go in the morning,' a moustachioed policeman had assured them. 'Lads, all hoping for another war.'

At the office she went up to the third floor, hoping to find Hedley and Mr Worboys, but nobody was in yet apart from Miss Maguire.

'Mr Worboys is expected later, but I believe Mr Morley has been delayed.'

'Delayed? Do you know why?'

'I didn't ask. The phone was ringing when I arrived, and he said he would be in late. You have plenty to do, I assume?' Miss Maguire turned away without waiting for a reply.

Alice sat down and tried to turn her mind to work, but she felt uneasy for some reason.

At ten thirty, just as she got up to make herself some tea, Hedley arrived – but he went straight into Worboys' office and closed the door without seeing Alice. An hour passed before he emerged and entered his own office.

She could see the flag on his desk. Red. But also, through the crack in the slightly open door, she could see that he was sitting with his fingers steepled, as they often were when he was deep in thought. She tapped lightly on the door, but he didn't reply. She knocked a little harder, and this time he slowly looked up.

'Alice. How are you? Children sleep all right? Your mother?'

'Fine, thank you. Worn out with all the excitement.'

'Alice, I want to ask your opinion about something important. About one of our houses. I'd like you to see it. Mr Worboys' driver will meet you here at three to take you, if that suits? I have another matter to attend to.'

Alice nodded uncertainly. Hedley didn't seem quite himself. She was going to ask him another question, but something told her she should leave him to his thoughts, and she closed the door quietly behind her.

'Brought you this,' Hedley called up to a shocked Matty.

Matty had shoved up the sash window of Mrs Roach's flat and stuck his head out, thinking it was the coal man. He was astonished to see Hedley on the front step.

'An Alka-Seltzer and an ice pack – still frozen, I

hope. Mrs Morley's fancy new Frigidaire-freezer has finally found some proper use. I'm afraid Roddy has had to make do with frozen peas.'

'Mr Morley – I'm sorry,' Matty stuttered. 'Is Roddy all right?'

'He's fine. His winsome beauty is still intact, although his graceful sloping nose is slightly bent. The only thing that he really hurt was his pride. He told me he was innocently standing outside the Slaughterhouse pub in the Port Authority when you set against him. But I know my stepson well enough to see when he's putting a spin on things to suit his story. So that's the end of the matter. Now, clean yourself up and come down here – I need you to drive me somewhere. It's important.'

Half an hour later, a bruised and aching Matty – still bewildered as to why Hedley had come all the way to his flat – turned off Scotland Road towards Everton Hill, with the car thumping its way over potholes. Hedley was giving directions, clutching the strap above the taxi door as if to keep his mind and body steady. They were passing places that Matty had never been before – past the docks, with whole stretches of estuary coming into view, opening out to the glittering Irish Sea, the roads broad and lined with trees. Some of the houses had turrets, all in their own parcel of land.

Hedley directed him to pull up at a corner plot with a gravelled drive that swept up to a bank of privet. 'We'll walk from here.'

They made their way along a worn track, walking side by side without speaking. It led through a little group of oak trees, from which they emerged to see a dilapidated Victorian house.

Hedley had brought him to a house with no roof. Why?

But hidden behind the house, backing onto a tall brick wall that had clearly been the boundary of the old building, was another property. This one was a new house, modern and compact, all clean lines and newly tiled roof. Matty could see there was still work to be done on the inside, but everything on the outside was in place – even down to a crazy-paving path leading to the yellow-painted front door.

'What's this?' he said, turning to Hedley in confusion.

'A house – I would have thought that was obvious. It was intended to be a show house. Nothing to do with Morley and Worboys. I bought the plot of the old house and built it as an experiment for myself. Had to change a lot of it after Alice, as she once put it, "shoved me in the right direction", but I think we're getting there. Come and have a look.' He started up the path, stepping over a small row of paint pots.

Matty followed him into the hallway, then into the living room, where they stopped. 'Mr Morley, why have you brought me here?'

Hedley Morley pressed his lips together as if choosing his next words carefully. He settled, resting his bottom against the windowsill and crossing his legs at the ankles, one finger pressed thoughtfully to his lips.

'Matty. You are a man of character. Always punctual, a man of discretion, hardworking, never complaining. And you and Alice – it's a beautiful thing for me to see two young people so in love. Matthew, I'm proud of you.'

Matty shifted uncomfortably from foot to foot. *Proud of you*, that was an odd thing to say, he thought.

'In half an hour, Alice will be arriving here. But first I wanted to speak to you on your own.'

Matty nodded.

'Don't look so alarmed. It should be me who's worried. I hope this won't shock you.' He took a deep breath and steepled his fingers. 'First of all, I want to say I'm profoundly sorry. If you want to take a punch at me, as you did with Roddy, after you hear what I have to say, I give you my blessing. You would have every right to.'

'Mr Morley, why would I—'

Hedley raised a finger to stay him. 'Now, where to begin? Probably the morning after a night of terrible bombing during the Blitz. Liverpool Lane was hit. You must have been about nine. Someone had lost their cat.'

Frowning, Matty scrolled back through the memories, reliving the moment when he, Alice and Bob had sat on windy Everton Hill watching the Luftwaffe screaming overhead. Then his thoughts lurched forward to the following morning: the house with the collapsed roof, he and Alice picking their way through the devastation, the firemen's hoses, the lost cat.

'I believe you were given a St Christopher medal on a chain that day. I've seen you wearing it over the years. It's given me great comfort.'

Instinctively, Matty touched the medal around his neck.

'It was me who gave you that medal, and now it's time for me to tell you why.'

It was now Alice who was thumping over potholes in the back of a company car.

'Can't you tell me where we're going?' she pestered Mr Worboys' driver after he had turned away from the parts of Liverpool she recognized and began heading out of the soot and grime of the city.

'Alexandra Avenue. Those big houses on the hill,' he replied. 'You won't find many slummy kids around here.'

Alice winced. What a horrible word.

They went up the drive, tyres scattering the loose gravel, passing Hedley's car and coming to a halt beyond it. Alice got out and stood looking up at the large red-brick Victorian house. There was a magnolia tree coming into bloom, almost ready to unfurl its pink, fleshy flowers, and it felt as if clean air was filling her lungs when she breathed in.

'Alice!' called Hedley. He was standing on the step, squinting into the sunshine. He was smiling – in fact, Alice thought, she had never seen him looking so happy.

'I hope this is worth the bone-shaking we've been through in that car to get here. Some of those roads are dreadful! Why are we here?' she said.

'Always with the questions. I wanted to show you a house I've built. Come with me. It's around the back.'

'How did you manage this without me knowing?' she gasped when she saw it. 'It's just like the one we saw at the Ideal Home Exhibition – the Women's Institute house.'

'Without anyone knowing. Except the builders. I can keep a secret when I need to.' He opened the front door. 'You are indispensable, Alice, but not omnipresent.' Pushing it open, he gestured for her to go in ahead of him.

She stepped into the hall and then through to the living room, with its large windows looking out on a sunny garden.

'Your opinion would be greatly appreciated,' Hedley said.

'I think you've built a home. It'll be perfect for whoever is lucky enough to live here.'

'Alice,' he said with a smile. 'So young and so serious.'

'So what will you do with it when it's finished?' Alice wandered into the kitchen, and he followed. She could imagine a family living happily in a place like this, the sun streaming in, the garden lush and vivid green.

Hedley cleared his throat nervously.

'I've always tried to do the right thing, and for the most part I have only made things worse. I thought I could make up for not being my stepson's real father by giving him everything, and I was wrong. I see now that what he really needed was to be told *no*, not *yes* all the time – something I avoided doing for more than twenty years. Your poor Matty was in the line of fire, I'm afraid. This will be a shock to many people, but . . . I'm giving this house to my son.'

Alice felt a pang of disappointment that was almost painful. Why on earth, after everything Hedley had just said, would he give this lovely family house to Roddy? It didn't make sense. There were so many more deserving, she thought.

'Anything to say?' he prompted, as if challenging her.

'You told me once that you liked me because I spoke my mind.' She hesitated. 'The truth is, I can't bear that you are giving this house to Roddy. I don't believe any human being in the history of the world has deserved it less.'

They stood looking at one another across the unfinished kitchen. At that moment, Alice felt sure she would never enter the offices of Morley and Worboys again. Tears welled in her eyes.

But Hedley spoke softly and calmly. 'I did say it would be a shock. Let me step outside and leave you for a minute.' He turned back to the hallway and called towards the open doorway. 'Matty? You can come in now.'

As soon as Matty appeared, Hedley slipped out.

'Your face, Matty!' Alice had to steady herself against the countertop as she stared at Matty in the doorway. What had happened to leave him so battered and bruised? 'Wait – why . . . Matty, did – did Roddy do this?'

Matty hesitated. He looked unsure of himself. She ran towards him and hugged him, then lightly touched his bruised face with gentle fingers. 'I'm so sorry. That brute. I love you.' She slipped her arms around his waist and laid her head on his chest, not wanting to let him go.

'Marry me, then.'

'Oh, Matty, you can't ask me that now. What's going on? Why are you here? And what on earth happened last night?' She had an edge to her voice, but he wasn't giving up.

'Tell me you'll marry me, and I'll tell you everything.'

'I already know some of it. Hedley brought me to show me this house he's built for Roddy. But I don't understand why, after what he did to you last night . . . well, it seems cruel to taunt us like that.'

He took her hand. 'You're right, but the only way to make things better for us both is for you to say you'll marry me. To hell with Roddy. Only if you want to, of course . . . but . . .'

He dropped to one knee and produced a small box from his pocket.

'Alice . . .' He seemed nervous, and he was always such a confident person. 'I want to grow old with you. I want to have children and build a proper home and plant cherry trees in our garden . . . and help get your ma better . . . and buy you a hat with a big brim and a peacock feather, and take you to the Grand National, and . . . and . . . for heaven's sake, open it,' he said. 'Stop me blathering on . . .'

'Oh, Matty. It's beautiful!'

'Will you be my wife, Alice?'

She tugged his arm to pull him up and flung her arms around him. 'Of course I will. I love you, Matty.'

Tears rolled down her cheeks. He kissed her and led her across to the table and sat her down.

'Alice, listen. Morley took you to see this house, and you love it. And then he told you something, and you got the wrong end of the stick.'

'I didn't get the wrong end of anything. He said he was giving it to Roddy.'

'No,' he said gently. 'He said he was giving it to his son.'

'I don't understand.'

'He brought me here to show me the house, Alice. And then he told me something I can still hardly believe. You know Roddy is his stepson. But he has a son of his own. Me.'

Chapter 43

Alice could feel her whole body trembling. She felt as if she had to move, and got to her feet, but then her legs wobbled. 'I don't understand.'

'Sit back down,' Matty said gently. After a moment, she did. He took her hand. 'He's Roddy's stepfather, you know that. But before he married, he had another child. Me. My mother – well, you never met my real mother. My aunt and uncle, they brought me up like they were my ma and da. My actual ma died when I was a baby . . .'

Alice nodded slowly. 'You never talked about your da to me . . .'

He dropped his head.

'Oh, Matty . . . You didn't know who your da was. Why didn't you ever tell me? I thought he'd died as well.'

'I was a little ashamed, probably. The sad thing is, my mother passed away in a Salvation Army home. But Alice, remember when we were kids? Remember the day we ran off to watch the bombing on Everton Hill?'

She nodded, the image of the bombs and the night sky splitting open still vivid in her memory.

'The next day, there was a man rushing about

looking for a boy. He was looking for me. I don't really remember that, but later on, your ma gave me a medal that he'd said he wanted me to have. A St Christopher medal.

'So here's the thing, the job I have driving for Hedley . . . He arranged it all from the beginning – paying for me to get my driving licence. Well, this St Christopher medal . . .' He scooped the trinket out from under his collar. 'I've always worn it. It has H. C. engraved on the back. I thought it was Holy Christ or something . . .' He paused. 'It turns out it stands for Hedley Clement.'

She frowned, turned over what he was saying in her head. She didn't remember that part of it, only the sound of the bombs and the rubble and the sky that was on fire.

'He wants to give me this house. He says he's done with hiding me as though I'm some awful secret. He wants to make up for lost time and for what happened to my mother. And his wife and Roddy will just have to accept it. It's you I have to thank for this, Alice.'

'Don't be silly – it's not just me. He adores you, Matty. Always has. You've shown him exactly what I've known since we were little. That you're the very best of men. Simple as that.'

Matty blushed, tracing a pattern in the palm of her hand. 'But I haven't even told you the most exciting part of all this. There's room here for your ma and the children.'

'Oh, Matty. I love you. You've known that for ever. I just clutched the wrong hand that day when we watched the Jerry planes. I can hardly believe any of this,' she said, astonished but grateful, overwhelmed by the feeling of being loved and cherished. She sprang up and threw her arms around him again as he stood to join her.

'Who would have thought we could have an ending this happy?' she said, as she raised her face towards his.

'It's not an ending, my love. It's a beginning. And I can't wait to see what's next for us.'

And as their lips met, words became superfluous, and their futures were bound together in a kiss.

Chapter 44

Two weeks later

'Pan of scouse, Ma?' asked Bob, boots up on the kitchen table.

'Sit properly,' she said, swiping the top of his head. 'Manners of a donkey. I thought you'd come back improved, not worse.'

'That's not very nice,' he laughed.

Bob's mother rolled her eyes and ladled out the broth into a bowl.

'Fill me in, then. What's been happening?' he asked.

His mother started to speak carefully, telling him about Miss Quick leaving and the houses set to be demolished, and how the greengrocer's had shut down, and the baker's. But really she wanted to tell him the story of what everyone had been talking about these past few days – that Alice and Matty had landed on their feet, that they had a house up on the hill, that Alice's ma and the kiddies were moving in, and some said they would be . . . getting married.

'Married!' Bob exploded.

'Aye.'

For five minutes he banged around the kitchen, slamming down pots and kicking a door so hard that he winced with the pain. His mother sat and watched him, arms folded firmly over her chest.

'Are you done?' she asked when he paused for breath.

'Ma. I *loved* her. And as for that rat . . . I thought he was my friend.'

'Robert. You're not too old for me to bang you around the head with the brush. If you really loved her, you wouldn't have lost her. You've already told me you and Pamela might marry. Pam's sweet as syrup and you don't want to ruin that, just like you did with Alice.'

'But Matty . . .'

'Leave it be. I'm sick of the theatricals, son. You want to lose your only real friend? I know you think I'm stupid and talk nonsense, but mothers are not daft. Even if my poor old legs have had it, my mind hasn't, and I know you'll regret it. Take yourself around the block and think on it.'

Snarling, he picked up his jacket and left without saying goodbye.

He had an idea where he should head. It was six o'clock, and Matty's routine was to stop by the Chauffeur Club for a lemonade and pick up a copy of the *Echo* before parking the Rover in Morley's garage at the back of the Adelphi. There was a bright sun riding high in the sky, and it bounced off the gleaming bonnets of the cars lined up along the pavement outside the club: an Austin Ten, another Rover and a rather splendid Rolls-Royce. Bob felt a twinge of envy. Since his time at sea, he had wondered whether Alice was right about the merchant navy.

Was shovelling coal all he wanted in life? Would he ever get to drive a car like one of these?

Two young men in chauffeurs' uniforms were smoking cigarettes. He was almost glad that neither of them was Matty. He had been fuming when he'd stomped out of the house, but now his confidence was draining away. What was he actually going to say to Matty? He could punch him, but would that make him feel any better?

He couldn't be angry with Alice, not when he had treated her so appallingly; the fault had been all his. Nevertheless, he felt Matty had betrayed him. And yet . . . Bob had another woman in his life now. And his mother was right – Pamela would be upset if she saw him like this, hands curled into fists, marching towards the steps, face twisted and raging.

Thinking about all this, Bob was so wrapped up in his inner turmoil that it was Matty who saw him first. He was taken aback by Bob's tangle of bleached hair and his ruddy cheeks. How could someone have aged so much in the space of a few months?

'Bob?' he said, his voice shocked.

Bob squinted and stopped in his tracks. Rushing forward, he barrelled into Matty and then gripped him around his neck, putting him into a tight head-lock. Matty's face began to redden.

'Get off me, Bob!' he spluttered. As he tried to twist up to look at him, thankfully he felt Bob loosening his grip, and the next minute he was ruffling Matty's hair playfully. Matty squirmed out from under Bob's arm.

'What's this about you stealing my Cherry Bomb?

D'you want to fight me for her?' said Bob. He held up his fists and danced from foot to foot. Matty looked alarmed. And then Bob moved forward and clapped an arm around his shoulder, laughing as he mimed a punch.

'I'm teasing you, Matty. No hard feelings. I'm happy for you. My ma filled me in. Me and my new girl are getting married too. Well, perhaps.'

Later, over mugs of tea at Bernice's kitchen table, Matty told Alice about the encounter. 'Just Bob playing the joker again,' he said.

Alice looked at him, cupping her hands around her mug for warmth. 'Really?' she asked.

'Some people never change.'

'Aye. Well, he once said to me that when you go to sea you come back a different person. Maybe Bob's come back a better person. Wouldn't that be a turn-up?' she smiled, raising the mug to her lips.

Chapter 45

'Married?' said Hedley, a week later.

'Those two lovebirds can't keep their hands off each other. There'll be a wedding before Christmas, I'd lay bets on it,' said Miss Maguire.

Hedley Morley smiled. 'Wonderful. To see them walk down the aisle – that would certainly be something.'

She smiled back. 'Wait and see. First, we've such a lot of work to do! I'll send Alice in.'

Alice came in, went straight over to Hedley's desk and leaned earnestly over the map of the docks, scrutinizing every new road, every block of flats.

'Hedley, I can't thank you enough for giving Matty and me the house. It's the kindest, most unexpected thing that has ever happened to me. And these maps . . . I know what you're planning. But I can't help thinking, if you take away all the houses here, every last one of them – that's a mistake. Please, could you not find it in your heart to keep these few streets? Just the roads around Dryburgh Terrace? Some of those people who lived here, they already want to come back from the new estates. I see them demolishing houses every week, but in Liverpool Lane there's still fifty pubs the Corpy has left standing. If you can keep so many pubs, surely you can keep at least some of the streets?'

She gazed at him pleadingly and he looked thoughtfully back at her.

'I know you love your social experiments,' Alice went on. 'But the Flower Streets are still there, up by the docks. Whole communities recovering together.'

He smiled at her. So proud and spirited.

'You once said I shouldn't be afraid to ask you anything—'

'Alice, Alice . . . stop. You're making my head hurt. I don't think I've met a more impassioned girl than you. So you'll be glad to know – Mr Worboys and I, we have news. We won't be demolishing Dryburgh Terrace after all. It will be run by one of our new housing committees.'

'Oh, Mr Morley!' She threw her arms around him.

'Dear me,' he said, flustered, resisting the urge to hug her back. 'I thought we'd agreed you would call me Hedley now . . .'

'Hedley, that means I can ask you about something else, too – something that could be even more useful. The big old house that you showed us – the one in front of the new house? Don't demolish that one either. There's a girl I know from St Mary's – Doreen. She's feisty, I'll say that. And another girl, called Angela. She knows someone called Henry Cherry, and actually, I've met him before too, after Brian—'

'Slow down, Alice. Henry Cherry? Odd name. Who's he?'

'He's wonderful. Earnest kind of man. He used to have quite a lowly job working with the orphanages, but he left when he discovered what was happening with families being split up, and children being sent away – and now he and his wife, Marcia, are helping all sorts of folks in trouble. Anyway, Angela also knows someone called Ellie, who Mr Cherry has been helping after he rescued her from Australia, and . . . Well, the point is, they all need jobs and a roof over their heads. And I want to help girls like these.'

'Steady on, steady on . . .'

'Mr Morley, please – Matty and I are so very happy and grateful for our house.' With a new energy coursing through her, she added, 'But wouldn't it be perfect?'

'Wouldn't what be perfect?'

'To give the girls a home. A different kind of place to St Mary's. A place where there is no shame. Somewhere to come, for six weeks, or however long they need after they have their babies, so that they can get back on their feet. Matty and I and the children could live in the other house. Be the caretakers, if you like.'

'That's a lot you're asking for.'

'I can't help thinking about it. I can speak to Mr Cherry. You should meet his wife, Marcia, too. And her sister, Cynthia. Henry saved them. If we all pull together . . .'

'Now you're making my head hurt again. You say this Henry Cherry rescued someone from Australia? And these sisters? . . . Let me think about all of this.'

'That's the answer I wanted!' Her face lit up. 'I'll take that as a strong maybe, if not a yes!'

'And I suppose you're going to ask me to buy Matty a fleet of cars.'

'Just one,' replied Alice. 'Matty will need to drive the girls up and down the hill.'

'Alice! Stop!'

But she was up and pacing now, talking about beds and rooms, plumbing systems and boilers. And he knew he was lost.

A week later, Hedley sat at the kitchen table in Alice and Matty's house. He was nodding and listening closely, his spectacles halfway down the bridge of his nose. Alice had just introduced Henry Cherry, a serious but enthusiastic young man, and his new wife, Marcia, who was perched on a stool beside him, smiling.

'Alice has told me all about her idea,' Henry said, 'and we do have plenty of girls who would find this a great support.' He turned to Alice. 'Will you and Matty live here when you're married?'

'Yes. Or before. I don't care what people might say about us living under the brush, or any of that nonsense. We need somewhere straight away for my ma and the kiddies. For Doreen and Mildred and Angela. And this girl, Ellie, you've told us about – the girl you've brought back from Australia – she has no one, you said. Isn't it lovely, the way the light floods in through these sash windows?'

Henry Cherry cleared his throat. 'I'm sure the Corporation would consider investing in it. This house could be a very useful trial project, a chance to see if we can do things differently from the nuns at St Mary's, or the homes for maladjusted girls and the industrial schools.'

Alice shivered. 'By the way, I don't want that unkind label. No shameful names. No *errant girls*, or *maladjusted*, *fallen women*, *homes for the feeble-minded*. Just somewhere where we can look after babies and mothers, so they can find their feet.'

'A home for girls who wouldn't be judged for their misfortune. Wouldn't that be something?' murmured Hedley.

'Yes. Where they could come with their babies and have a roof over their heads while they found a job, somewhere to live. A chance to be reunited with their families. So often, families soften when faced with an actual baby. Babies have a habit of making the world a kinder place.'

'Alice, you've blindsided me again. But will the Corporation listen to me, Mr Cherry?'

Mr Cherry nodded, now looking as if the possibilities were firing up his imagination. 'Opinions expressed by prominent men like you can make a real difference,' he said earnestly.

'But it's women like me who shape those opinions – wouldn't you say, Hedley? And it's not just you,' Alice pointed out. 'There's an army. Me and Doreen, and Mildred. And Angela. Marcia here. Mrs Worboys. Even Miss Maguire, would you believe it? Turns out she went on a march for the dockers' strike the other day. Even Sister Bernadette and Sister Hilda from St Mary's are behind it. There's a lot of good people in this city, Hedley. Good people who want change.'

He smiled. She could see in his face that he understood her.

'You know, then we could also use other houses to

help people with other kinds of problems. Like . . . well, like Roddy. Where professionals could take them in, those who are struggling with the drink and . . . and other nightmares.' She paused. 'Wouldn't *that* be something?'

Hedley nodded thoughtfully. 'Like Mr Worboys' wife's soldiers traumatized by the war? Places of respite.'

'Yes.'

'Alice, you are admirable. I have never seen such strength in a person.'

She smiled. 'You never know how strong you are until being strong is the only choice you have. I learned that from the girls at St Mary's. Now, who's for a cup of tea?'

Epilogue

A year later

Doreen, wearing blue dungarees over a pink-and-white checked shirt, wobbled on a wooden ladder. It was a warm, sunny day, there was a smell of spring in the air, and they had thrown the windows wide open.

'Slap the paint on, Mildred,' said Angela, with a bright smile.

'Don't slap it on! Take a bit of care! Mr Cherry and his wife are coming here soon,' said Alice.

Doreen laughed. She had paint in her hair, a dab on her cheek, splodges all over her forearms and hands.

A child scooted through the airy room on a wooden trike, chased by another. In the kitchen, Angela was whistling as she greased a cake tin, sprinkled it with flour and poured batter into it. The whole place had an air of joyful chaos.

'Can I go out, Miss?' said Mildred. 'Me and Doreen want to take my Daisy to have a ride on Blackie.'

'Blackie?'

'Blackie the rocking horse is back at Blacklers. Now they've finally reopened after the terrible Blitz damage, all the children in Liverpool can enjoy him again.'

A memory of the rocking horse at the Pirbrights' flashed into Alice's head. 'Milly, you don't have to ask me if you want to go out. There's no doors locked here.'

Matty stood at the window and smiled as the small group left. 'Whoever would have thought living here with all these girls, and the awful hardships they've faced, would mean we'd be surrounded by such happiness? Mr Cherry asked what this place should be called – Alice House, he suggested.'

She tutted. 'No, I don't need that.'

'You know, Alice, they were so excited about our plans at the town hall. They're certain this will change everything.'

She looped her arms around his neck and kissed him gently. 'All that time, I thought I needed to get away to find whatever it was I was looking for – but it's here. With my people, my friends, family. Isn't it wonderful?'

He nodded. And then they heard a crash in the next room, and a yell.

'Doreen's knocked over a pot of paint!'

Yellow paint was spreading across the floor, growing from the size of a side plate to a dinner plate and running along the skirting boards.

'Doreen! What did you do!' cried Alice.

'What did *I* do?'

They all looked at Gabe, who was running around in happy, energetic circles with paint on his hands.

'Let's write our names on the walls, before Matty wallpapers over them. One day someone will find them.'

There was a knock at the door. Alice opened it to

see a girl looking at her, round-eyed and smiling hopefully, holding a battered suitcase covered in shipping line stickers. They were expecting this girl, and Alice had imagined that she might be ravaged by the tragic experiences they had been told about. She was a little gaunt, but pretty, with a lively expression, bright eyes and a freckled, sunburned face.

'You must be Ellie,' Alice smiled. 'Mr and Mrs Cherry have told me all about you. You've got quite a story, I believe. You arrived back in Liverpool from Tasmania last week?'

Ellie nodded. 'Aye. I'm good up ladders – I learned that in Australia. I was working on a farm.'

Alice nodded. Now was not the time to talk about the other things Ellie had learned at her homestay halfway across the world, where she had been sent by the nuns of St Mary's.

'Ma will come to get me soon – that's when I find her. Miss, I couldn't go back to St Mary's. Not when they were the ones who sent me away.'

'No. You won't have to. You have a bed here for as long as you want it. Come in, then. Good with ladders, Ellie?' Alice put her arm around the girl's birdlike shoulders. 'Just what we need. You'll fit in well here.'

The swelling in Alice's belly was just a small rise beneath the waistband of her skirt, but you could see it nevertheless.

'A baby?' Ida gasped, and then kissed her on both cheeks. 'That's what we need! A wedding! And a reason for me to knit again!'

*

'You're having a baby?' Bob said, surprised, two weeks later. He was standing at the door with a bunch of daffodils in his hand and a girl at his side.

'Yes,' said Alice. 'I know – I'll go to hell for it. But we're getting married, so, like half the girls in this city, no one will mind much. T. J. Hughes has a whole rack of wedding dresses with ruched bodices and smocked skirts. Keep it under your hat, though. Thankfully not many people round here are good with maths when it comes to babies' due dates. Or at least, that's what they all pretend. Nice to see you, Bob.'

'I'm happy for you both. I'd like to shake Matty's hand and take him for a drink to celebrate. This is Pamela, by the way. She wanted to meet you. I said you might throw something at me.' He turned to the smiling girl, who had a pleasant, round-cheeked face. 'This is Alice. The girl around here who's changing everything. You're famous, Alice.'

'Bob!' said Matty, coming up the path.

Bob turned and stood with hands on hips, legs apart. 'You naughty fella. Can't believe you beat me to it. Alice with a bun in the oven!' He winked and grinned.

'You told him, Alice?'

'We won't be able to keep it a secret much longer,' she laughed. 'I'll soon be the size of a house. Anyway, we're among friends.'

'Me and Pammy are getting married, too,' said Bob.

Pamela blushed. 'Bob! I haven't told me ma yet. What me da will say about me getting hitched to you, I don't know.'

'You're a braver girl than I am, Pamela,' said Alice. 'But then, Matty says Bob's changed.'

'Hey, do I get to put my two penn'orth in? I have changed. Just like you, Alice. I've improved. I'm a much better person than I was. I can light a match with my thumb now, and drink a whole pint standing on me head. Wait 'til I show you. Aren't I just the best, Pam?'

Matty and Alice's wedding was a day like none of them had ever known. Everyone had been excited about May Day, with bunting hanging from lamp post to lamp post, but for Alice and Matty it would always be their wedding that marked that first glorious week of May sunshine. Forget-me-knots embroidered on the hem of Alice's dress, stitched by Ida, and a posy of spring flowers, and Bernice and all the girls – Doreen, Millie, Ellie, Angela, June – fussing over her veil, and Gabe toddling up the aisle. Gwenda was a bridesmaid, scattering rose petals that Ida had put in the sun to dry; Brian was in a suit. There was apple blossom in the churchyard, and all kinds of flowers everywhere.

Ida had somehow, somewhere, found the large cream hat from Owen Owen in a box. They had all been amazed that it had survived, what with all the moving about and the bailiffs. It was a relief that she would soon be back in Liverpool Lane, though in a different house around the corner from Dryburgh Terrace, with a new roof, new windows and not a trace of damp.

There had been a funeral, too – the Mary Ellen,

whose name, it turned out, had been Mary Callaghan. It felt fitting that she was buried with everyone finally knowing who she really was: a proud woman who had lost her son and her husband in the Great War. She had always said she would have to be carried out of her dilapidated old house, and in the end she was. Even when the Corpy had tried to tell her they were coming in for repairs and offered to find somewhere else for her in the meantime, she hadn't wanted to go. She had sat on the step, refusing to leave, refusing to let anyone in.

'No one believed her when she said she heard ghosts in her house, and then it turned out it was just the kiddies moving around from loft to loft. Those houses were never built with walls in between, to save costs. But I wonder if it was the ghosts that kept her dragging the cart,' said Matty to Alice.

'Perhaps she knew something we didn't. People are still leaving for their new houses. Their children will be catching dragonflies in the fields down by Oggie Sands, instead of catching the lurgy from the scaldies. Do you think they'll be happy?' Alice wondered.

'Who knows? Some are coming back, but some are hopeful.'

'I hope, for Hedley, it will end well. It's his dream. Open spaces. Fresh air. Palaces in the sky. The long silver sleeve of the Mersey. Who knows?'

Alice went into the bathroom and opened the taps on the bath. It was still a miracle to her when warm water gushed out and steam filled the room. She unbuttoned her dress, let it fall to the floor and stepped out of it, then slipped out of her underclothes and climbed into the tub, luxuriating in the warmth as she trickled water over the rise of her stomach. Outside she could hear indistinct voices – Doreen laughing, Ellie chasing a giggling toddler around the garden. The simple joys of living were what would carry them all forward.

And what was it her mother used to say? *We survived yesterday, we'll get through today, and we'll do it all again tomorrow.*

Yes, that was it, she murmured to herself, as she closed her eyes and turned her face towards the evening sun.

Acknowledgements

Thank you to my brilliant editor, Gillian Green, and my agent, Judith Murdoch. Thank you to Liverpool Library and Museums, where I learned about the hardships facing so many families after the rebuilding of Liverpool; when children were separated from their parents and siblings, and communities were split apart. Thank you to my grandmother, widowed mother of ten, who inspired this story. Like Ida, she planned to open a shop selling baby clothes after she lost her husband, but made a different choice; the right choice, it transpired, when war broke out soon after. I wanted to imagine how different things would have been for her if she had made the wrong decision.

Thanks to my husband, Peter, for telling me about his mother's annual visits to the Ideal Home Exhibition and the small Hovis loaves she would bring home. It led me to research the Festival of Britain. Thanks to Vicky for sharing her stories about the Chauffeur Club and her memories of growing up in Hope Street. Thank you to my Alice, whose spirit shines out from the pages of this book! And thank you to Louis and Joel, who continue to bring their stories into my life and still take time to listen to mine.

I would also like to thank my father, Peter Heery,

who worked in Kirkby and Stockbridge in Knowsley with youth groups and in education, supporting families who had relocated from the city.

This book is dedicated to the 100,000 made homeless after World War Two in Liverpool, and all those who struggled to build new lives when a third of all houses were destroyed or damaged.

The People's Friend
The Home of Great Reading

If you enjoy quality fiction, you'll love
The People's Friend magazine.
Every weekly issue contains seven original short
stories and two exclusively written serial instalments.

On sale every Wednesday, the *Friend* also includes travel,
puzzles, health advice, knitting and craft projects
and recipes.

It's the magazine for women who love reading!

For great subscription offers, call 0800 318846

 @ TheFriendMag

 PeoplesFriendMagazine

thepeoplesfriend.co.uk